A September Day and Shadow Thriller

LOST AND FOUND

Book One

AMY SHOJAI

Copyright

Second Print Edition, February 2017
Furry Muse Publishing
Print ISBN 978-1-944423-17-9
eBook ISBN 978-1-944423-18-6
Hardcover ISBN 978-1-948366-35-9

First Published by Cool Gus Publishing
First Printing, September 2012
COPYRIGHT © Amy Shojai, 2012

FURRY MUSE
PUBLISHING
P.O. Box 1904
Sherman TX 75091
(903)814-4319
amy@shojai.com

**September & Shadow Pet-centric Thrillers
By Amy Shojai**

LOST AND FOUND

HIDE AND SEEK

SHOW AND TELL

FIGHT OR FLIGHT
Introducing Lia, Tee, and Karma

HIT AND RUN

WIN OR LOSE

Chapter 1

Linda Birch raced out the back door into the snow. "Help, somebody help me!" She slipped and fell, struggled to her feet and left pink handprints when she levered herself upright.

The butcher knife had left a three-inch gash in her calf. Her stomach burned and she held her left hand hard against the stab wound in her side.

The screen door banged open. Benny stumbled down the slick steps.

She sobbed, held bloody palms toward her son. "Stop! Please!" Linda ignored the cold on her bare legs. Her bright pink Snuggie dragged through the snow.

Benny didn't mean it. His expression remained as serene and blank as the snow that blanketed the lawn. He drew his right thumb along the blade and stared at the red line that appeared. He repeated the gesture with his left thumb and crimson splattered onto the snow like the petals of a wind-shattered rose.

"No, stop, honey. Don't hurt yourself." Linda stumbled toward her sixteen-year-old son, her fuzzy slippers clotted with ice and clumsy on her feet. She stopped when Benny regarded her for the briefest moment.

Linda saw that glint of recognition, a connection, before his focus evaporated. Her eyes welled. She'd had the real Benny for such a short time before the money disappeared. But she had no choice, she couldn't pay more. Insurance denied experimental trials. Savings had lasted less than a year. They were monsters to hold a child's health for ransom.

Benny sliced his other hand. Linda ignored her own injuries. "Let me have the knife, Benny." She kept her words quiet, authoritative, despite the pain that made her tremble.

Her beautiful baby boy's five-foot-ten-inch height dwarfed her dumpy body. Snow whirled overhead and made her dizzy when she looked up. She grabbed Benny's arm to keep from falling.

"No!" He screamed. The knife lashed out and just missed Linda's cheek. She fell to her knees.

He slashed the air above her head, playing target practice with individual flakes as Linda huddled before him. She prayed the tantrum would pass so she could get him back inside before they both caught pneumonia. She coughed. Spat blood onto the snow. How could that be?

Linda pulled her hand from the warm wetness on the front of her Snuggie. It had been barely a scratch, she was sure. Benny had had his share of tantrums. He'd scared her with the knife, so she ran. That made him even more scared, she reasoned, and prompted him to follow her. He'd done so well recently, and even had a job at the local Piggly Wiggly bagging groceries.

She waited until he stopped waving the knife to hold out her hand. She didn't think her legs would support her, and Linda reminded herself to start that diet soon. Maybe the New Year's resolution would stick this time. "Help Momma up, Benny."

"Momma?" Benny stared at her and at the splatters around them. He stuck one hand in his pocket before he stepped directly into the blood spill. His shoes polka-dotted the ground. He tilted his head to see better and deliberately created stamp-art with his feet. Benny held eye contact for ten seconds this time before breaking to stare at his shoes. He paddled in the blood again.

Linda held out her hand again. Spoke words devoid of emotion, matter-of-fact. "Sweetie, let's not make more of a mess. Give your Momma a little boost up, honey."

His left hand moved inside his pocket. She could hear the click of shiny pennies under his busy fingers. Repetitive motions—spinning, rocking, twirling; what the experts called stimming—offered a focus that helped relieve stress. But Benny hadn't twirled, spun or rocked for over six weeks. He made direct eye contact, even let her touch him briefly—and touched her in return without prompting. He spoke. He made sense. They communicated. The butterfly had broken free, a true miracle.

Benny knelt down in the snow next to Linda. "Sorry, Momma. Sorry," he said. And then he stabbed her until she stopped moving.

Chapter 2

September Day sloshed another half cup of coffee into the giant *#1-Bitch* mug, and glared out the frosty breakfast nook windows. North Texas didn't get snow. That's why she'd moved back home—well, one of several reasons. She shivered, relishing the warmth of the beverage, and toasted the storm with a curse. "Damn false advertising." Her cat Macy meowed agreement.

The blizzard drove icy wind through cracks in the antique windows and made the just-in-case candles on the dark countertop sputter. She pulled the fuzzy bathrobe closer around her neck. Normally the kitchen's stained glass spilled peacock-bright color into the kitchen. Not today, though. The reinforced security grills on the windows and dark clouds outside transformed the room's slate floor, bright countertops and brushed-steel appliances into a grim cell.

Overhead lights flickered on, off and back on again. They'd done that for the past hour. Crap. More stuff for the contractors to fix. One candle guttered in the draft, and September mentally added window caulk to her list. She prayed the electricity wouldn't go out, since the backup generator in the garage would take finagling to find, let alone to start.

She added a dollop of flavored cream to her cup, and replaced the lid that kept Macy's paws at bay. The longhair sable and white cat sat like a furry centerpiece on the rose-patterned glass table. He mewed in frustration when September set her covered mug next to the muffin saucer he'd already licked clean. A white paw patted the cup's lid.

September plopped into one of four wrought iron chairs, and pulled the mug out of the cat's reach. "Nope, I know where you put your feet."

Macy paced. His tail dry-painted September's cheek and wove in and out of her long wavy mane. Green slanted eyes, coffee-dark hair, hidden claws and enigmatic smile—she'd been told more than once that she and the cat matched in both personality and looks. Mom wanted her to dye the white skunk streak at her left temple, but September couldn't be bothered, not anymore. In Mom's high-falutin' social circles of perfectly coifed dowagers it served as a thumb-your-nose warning to keep strangers at bay.

She gave the cat's elevator-butt pose a final pat, and opened the DayMinder. Macy made a disgusted *mffft* sound, gathered himself and vaulted to the top the fridge. "Sure, go ahead and sulk. You're wired enough without caffeine."

Outside, gusts flailed the November blooms of the Belinda's Rose against the window beside the new steel door. At least the cold couldn't sneak through that barrier. In fact, the temperature change had shifted the door frame so much that it took an enormous effort to latch. That was fine with her. If it was hard to latch, the door offered even more security.

The weather not only derailed her schedule, the cold hurt like a bastard. September wrapped both hands around the mug. Her fingernails had already turned blue-white, and she couldn't feel her toes despite insulated ski socks and slippers. Not even flannel PJs, long underwear and a thick robe proved adequate against the weather.

She checked the thermostat for the third time—68 degrees—to save money, for crying out loud. "Screw it." Some old habits she could afford to break. She cranked the dial to 78, blessing the contractors for the gas-fueled furnace and hot water tanks.

Her DayMinder was choked with appointments, notes, and prompts. She'd entered most of them on her new phone, currently charging on the counter, but preferred the old-fangled paper version. "Busy is good. Except on snowy days."

Hell, she didn't want to risk the roads in this weather either. But she could damage control other deadlines she'd have to miss. She'd already left a message with the lawyers postponing the deposition on the dog bite case since she couldn't evaluate the dogs at the shelter until the weather settled. But fast talk and a good phone connection might allow her to keep other appointments. September dialed, sticking her free hand beneath her armpit to warm her fingers.

"WZPP, you've reached ZAP105 FM Radio, giving you the best easy-listening 24/7, how may I direct your call?"

"Hey, Anita, it's September. Could you—"

"Feels more like December."

September rolled her eyes. "Ha ha, funny lady, never heard that before. C'mon, it's cold and I'm in a pissy mood. Could you cut the jokes for once?"

"I've been here all night, still wondering how to get home, so my bad mood trumps yours, kiddo." Anita paused to blow her nose. "You want to talk to Humphrey, I guess. I'll connect."

Before she could say another word, September was plunged into the station's easy-listening hell. The thirty seconds lasted a lifetime before Humphrey's Jolly-Green-Giant voice broke in.

"ZAP, this is Humphrey Fish."

"It's me, September. I can't make it to the station. We'll have to do a phoner for the Pet Peeves program today." Before he could protest, she added a sweetener. "I'll do it for free. And there'll be a bunch of calls today with everything shut down, so the sponsors won't care." Macy chirruped, and dove off his favorite perch to wind around her ankles.

"Did you bring this sucky weather with you?" Humphrey didn't soften his sarcasm. September imagined him bouncing up and down, a human beach ball with legs. "I thought Hoosiers drove in snow nine months out of the year, and now you're afraid of a little flurry?"

"There's a reason I moved." *Let him think the move was only about the weather,* she thought, swallowing a slug of the strong coffee. "Have you snuck outside your little glass box lately? It's the freakin' ice age out there."

Humphrey snorted. "Never took you for a weenie, September."

If only he knew. "I know how to drive. It's the local amateurs that scare the crappiocca out of me. Texans hit the gas to get out of it quicker." Macy mewed his agreement and patted her leg.

Humphrey's exasperation made him sound like a weasel on steroids. "C'mon, in-studio was part of the deal. And you've only been here once. Have something against leaving home, do you?" He paused. "Can we hurry this up? There's a live promo in thirty seconds."

September bit back a retort. She could leave the house anytime she wanted. It wasn't as if she lived in fear, not at all. She'd moved home to be closer to family. But when the Chicago habit of looking over her shoulder had been broken in South Bend, look what had happened.

She mentally shook herself. Once her hands and feet adjusted, she'd better tolerate the cold, and could run over to the radio station as promised. Besides, the Reynaud's episodes never lasted for long. And she wanted the radio platform. Her breath quickened at the thought of leaving the house. She hated driving on snow, that was why—but she told herself anything worthwhile came with hurdles.

"Okay. I'll get there. Just let me get caffeinated first. Oh, and put the state police on speed dial, ready to have them thaw me out of a drift come next May." She heard him snort back a chuckle and her shoulders relaxed. She wouldn't have to leave the house.

"Okay, okay already, you win. But call in five minutes before. No, make that ten minutes before air. Use a landline. Cell phones are shit on air. We'll run with an expanded Pet Peeves, and double-up on the calls. I'll promo between now and then to get email questions to start us off. Frog-on-a-stick, gotta run."

The sudden dead air ended the conversation. The ten-minute weekly pet advice show got the word out better than paid ads, although the tiny stipend Humphrey called a paycheck barely covered the cost of caffeine. Her pet behavior consulting business included advice by phone, although in-person training was ideal, and the radio show and her regular column in the local paper drove more than enough clients to her subscription-only pet advice website.

Besides, she didn't need much, and never would again. Chris had seen to that. She took a shuddering breath. Just a random thought bushwhacked her emotions. Christopher Day was supposed to have been part of her dreams, THEIR dreams.

September chugged half of the too-sweet coffee. She cradled the oversize mug, treasured for more than the warmth. Chris had bought it for her at a dog show. They'd often exchanged crap gifts for no reason, just to make each other smile. It was his last gift.

She set the mug down with a clunk. Macy grumbled and pressed his forehead against her socks. She stooped to smooth his fur, and her tight throat relaxed. "Thanks, buddy, but I'm fine. Later we'll play laser tag, okay?" She stooped, caught up the Mickey, and made eye contact with Macy. She waved one finger at the cat. He sat up and begged. "If you want it, then speak, Macy." When he meowed on cue, she tossed the toy across the room. "Kill it, kill it!" Macy raced after it, grappled the toy, fell on his side and bunny-kicked Mickey into submission.

September gulped another slug of coffee and checked her watch. Time enough for a hot shower before the radio show. Before she'd shuffled halfway across the kitchen, the phone chirruped. September hurried to grab the phone where it charged on the countertop before Macy decided to attack it like his toy.

September glanced at the display, sighed, and answered. "Hello, Mom."

"Holy catfish, we've already got six inches and it's still dumping everywhere! What's the weather like there?"

"I live seven miles away from you. What do you think?" The overhead lights remained a bright, steady glow. "I've got a generator in the garage if it gets worse, but so far the heat and lights are good." She watched Macy grab his Mickey and stash it back into his favorite cupboard.

"But you still have drywall to do. Doesn't the weather have to be good for drywall work?" She hesitated before rushing on. "I know you wanted the housewarming on Thanksgiving, dear. Maybe next year instead."

"Not a housewarming. We've been over this. I'm having the whole family here for Thanksgiving." Macy left the cupboard and returned to paw September's leg, one claw snagging the fabric. She bent to unhook the nail. "There's two weeks to get it done, Mom."

"We could gather at your brother's, or even one of the girls'."

"Mom, stop." She bit her lip, and struggled to keep her temper in check.

"I'll make some calls, honey. Don't you worry a bit."

"I said *no*." September took a breath. "Look, Mom, let me do this. I need to do this. It'll be fine." She'd only been back in Heartland for a few months, but it didn't take long to remember why she'd left home and stayed away for ten years. "I've got everything planned. The kitchen's finished, plumbing and electrical passed inspection, and the security system works great. Remember, I told you and Dad the password when I gave you the extra keys?" She kept talking when her mother would have interrupted. "Dining room furniture will be here next week." She noticed the candles dripping wax on the new granite countertop, and blew them out. "Macy's pet gates work just as well for kids."

"Don't be stubborn and spoil the holiday for everyone."

The doorbell bonged, followed by immediate pounding that made September's pulse thrum. "Mom, someone's at the door. Don't worry, Thanksgiving will be great. For once, just trust me."

She punched off the phone to stop further argument. Pounding knocks took turns with the doorbell chimes. Nobody in their right mind would be out in this mess. She carefully stepped through and latched the pet gate before hurrying to the front entry.

Three deadbolts secured the stained glass front door. September peered through wavy glass and her heart leaped with sudden nerves. This couldn't be good.

Two uniformed cops stood on the front step, their shoulders powdered with white. September tightened the belt of her robe and smoothed unruly hair as though that would calm her racing pulse. She pressed the button beside the door to activate the speaker. "Can I help you?"

The bigger man answered. "Ma'am. I'm Officer Leonard Pike, and this is my partner, Officer Jeff Combs." Pike was almost a foot taller than her own five-feet-six-inches. His bulky long coat didn't camouflage his extra sixty pounds. A single black unibrow rose above horn-rimmed glasses, and his earflap hat sat too high to fully protect his bald head.

"Do you have identification?" Chris had taught her well. Unexpected visits never brought good news. Police don't do social calls.

Both men pressed identification against the glass. "Can we come in?"

She unlocked all three deadbolts and cracked the door as far as the chain allowed, but didn't invite them in. September shivered in the brutal wind. If she invited them in, she could close and lock the door again. But she didn't want strangers in her house. "What can I do for you?" She hoped they'd take the hint and leave quickly.

"We're on our way back from an accident." Officer Combs looked half his partner's age. Despite the youthful expression and athletic carriage, worry lines and the cleft chin relieved an otherwise too pretty face. "There's smoke pouring out the side of your house. Over there." He waved.

"Smoke? Oh crap! Come in already. But lock the door behind you." She rushed back into the kitchen. "Has to be the clothes dryer." September fumbled with the pet door into the kitchen, racing to the adjoining laundry room, one of the first rooms the contractors had finished. When she opened the door, white smoke filled the upper half of the room. "Why the hell didn't my alarm go off?" The contractor would hear about this.

Officer Combs caught her arm to stop her rush into the room. "Do you have an extinguisher? Where's your breaker box?" He turned to the older officer. "Call it in, why don't you, Lenny?" He pulled off his hat, and his light brown hair crackled and stood off his head with static electricity.

September jerked away from his touch. "We'll have it out before they get here in the snow." She hurried into the tiny room where the clothes dryer nestled against the wall and couldn't be easily unplugged. "Aw, hell." She punched buttons on the dryer until it stopped, pulled open the door of the front loader, and watched with disbelief as acrid smoke flowed out. "The machine's not even three weeks old."

Bending low, Combs viewed September's unmentionables. "No fire. Caught it in time." He straightened with a grin. "I've been curious to see the inside of the Ulrich place since I was a kid. Didn't want it to burn before I got the chance."

September kicked the dryer and winced, remembering too late she was wearing slippers. "Need to call the company. At least it's under warranty." Just want she needed, a game of telephone gotcha with the store. Nothing was easy.

"Ma'am? Do you need us to call for assistance?" Pike leaned his oversize frame against the doorway, pulling off his gloves to fish a tissue from his pocket and honked his nose into it. "That's some smell. Might want to open the window or crack the door." He nodded toward the solid door in the nearby breakfast nook. "Smoke will set off your kitchen alarm if you don't air it out." Pike looked around the room, tossing the used tissue in the trash before adjusting his cap.

"That door stays locked." It was too hard to mess with once it finally latched.

"Why?" Pike raised his eyebrow. "Any putz could pop that lock in sixty seconds."

She flinched, and eyeballed the door. "That's not what the contractor said."

He shrugged with a "whatever" gesture. "Locks are a specialty of mine."

September pulled a step stool out of a cupboard to reach and open the small window. At least there was no intruder danger by leaving it open. Nobody could wiggle through but a Munchkin with wings. She shivered, stepped off and folded the stool.

Combs stared at September. "Are you okay, Ms.—"

"Oh. I'm September Day."

Pike cocked his head. "September, like the month, and—er, Day like the—uh, day of the week?" He jabbed Combs with an elbow. "Is she kidding?"

"Yes, the name's just like the month." September sighed. Her parents, Rose and Lysle January, cleverly named their kids for their birthday months. Her sisters born in the spring got off easy and by the time baby brother came along in March, Mom and Dad settled for the more conventional Mark. Meanwhile, she'd been stuck with September January, no middle name needed. After 28 years she'd heard every joke possible. Chris teased her that she'd married him just to change her name. She'd joked back they should name their first child Happy. At the time, it didn't seem important, since she had no interest in starting a family. . .

Combs frowned. "Are you sure you're all right? You can call me Jeff." He smiled again.

She shook off the memory and forced a smile. After all, the man had saved her house. "Jeff. Thank you. I'm fine, just pissed." She shooed them out of the laundry room into the kitchen and followed with the step stool. "If you'll excuse me, I've got cleanup to do."

He had kind eyes. Brown. Like Dakota's. She caught Pike's amused expression before he coughed into another tissue and looked away. Wasn't that just dandy.

"You're one of the January girls, right?" Combs wouldn't leave it alone. "My sister Naomi went to school with one of your sisters."

She considered him more carefully. Officer Jeff Combs might be a couple inches shorter than Pike, but his lanky frame and loose gait offered a boyish contrast to his overweight partner. Still tan from the past summer's sun, he had crow's feet that advertised humor, stress, or both. Combs was at least five years older than she, maybe more. "Probably May or June?" She'd skipped a couple of grades in high school, so she was younger than most in her class.

"June, that's right." He nodded. "You were behind us, but then you took off before graduation on that music tour thing." He pulled on his hat. "What brings you back to Heartland?"

She urged them to the front door. "Thanks again. Sorry, but I don't feel real sociable at the moment." She had come home to start fresh and get away from the ghosts that stalked her—real and imagined. She had no interest in rehashed history.

Pike pulled on heavy gloves, adjusting his hat and turtling his neck down into his collar as he duck-walked to stay vertical on the slick path back to the patrol car.

Combs paused. "Listen, Ms. Day—September. Is it okay to call you September? I wondered, you being new back in town and all—"

"Officer, uhm, Jeff. I don't mean to be rude, but I've got a phone call to make. Thanks again. You saved my bacon." She started to close the door.

"Sure, I understand. Busy day. Maybe another time?" He handed her his card, and a twinkle lightened the shadow in his expression. "At least it's a good day to wear hot clothes." He turned and hurried to the car.

Despite herself, September chuckled. So Officer Combs was a wise-ass; she liked that in a person.

She shut the door, shooting the deadbolts and rattling the knob to be sure it caught. Time enough later to throw out scorched laundry. She needed to call Humphrey Fish five minutes ago, and she'd better be scintillating as hell or he'd make her pay.

September raced back to the kitchen, climbed the step stool, pried the smoke detector off the ceiling and shoved it in a drawer. She didn't need sirens interrupting the phone call. September cut Anita off before she could say a word. "Patch me through to the studio line. I'm already late."

"Your ass is so dead." Anita put her on hold for ten seconds, which forced her to listen to Humphrey's on-air introduction. She seethed at his tone.

"Why looky there, furry friends and neighbors, September just blew in. She's finally ready to offer us the best kitty and puppy advice available. Nice of you to join us, your highness. Didja overindulge in the catnip last night?"

"Greetings and salutations your own self, Mr. Fish." Uh oh, this would be rough. "Catnip's not a bad idea. It's a kitty hallucinogen and will take your cat's mind off the nasty weather." She hurried on before he could interrupt with another crack. "I hope all the pet parents listening out there have brought their animals indoors for the duration."

"Hey, they've got fur coats, so what's the big deal?" He laughed. "Not like some of us hair-challenged humans, right?"

She jerked the phone away from her head. He'd turned up the volume to punish her without the audience any the wiser. Two could play that game. "Scaly fish are cold blooded creatures after all."

"Oooh, so you're gonna be catty, are you? Pull in your claws and give us some Pet Peeves de-tails."

"You step on my tail, I'll hiss back, Mr. Fish." A breath calmed and settled her into the rhythm of the show. "Even furry cats and dogs risk frostbite or hypothermia in weather like this. See, the fur helps hold body heat next to the skin to keep them toasty. Wind can strip that warmth away, and the wet keeps the fur from insulating them. Their ears, toes, tails, even the scrotum can freeze."

"Blue balls. I love it when you talk dirty. Let's take some calls. Hello, you're on the air with Pet Peeves and September Day, what's your question?"

September braced herself. God only knew what callers she'd get after that intro.

"Uh, hi, I got a wiener dog. I left him outside overnight. Now he's a pupsicle." Maniacal laughter bubbled until Fish disconnected the call.

"That's a good one. This is Humphrey Fish with September Day's Pet Peeves. September, what do you have to say to our wiener dog fella? C'mon, I know he's obnoxious but toss him a bone."

She winced, but didn't hesitate. "All jokes aside, the smaller the pet, the greater the danger. Also, y'all may end up with some hit-or-miss potty behavior as a result of the storm, because little dogs just don't want to squat in a snowbank and get their nether regions cold."

"We've got a theme going." Fish guffawed, but it was forced.

She heard a beep-click on the line, and recognized the call-waiting signal. She checked caller ID, and rolled her eyes.

Fish broke in. "Thanks for your question. We've got to take a station break, but September will be right back with all the answers to your litter box woes. Keep those phone calls coming." The music swelled and the taped commercial played. "Got you a new attitude today, do you?"

"I've had a hellacious morning." September heard the beep-click again—same caller—and once more ignored it. "This won't happen again."

"You don't understand. The callers love the new edginess. The phone lines lit up. They love your catty comments."

September stared at the phone. "You're kidding."

"Swear to god, September. The bitchy comebacks are great. I can dish it out if you're up for it." He paused. "It's great radio. Trust me. Just keep it clean. Sorta."

"Uh, sure. Whatever you think works." She still wasn't convinced. "Let me get this straight. You're going to be snide, and I'm supposed to put you down?"

"Exactly," he said. "Now pin on your sparkly bitch pin, and turn on the wise-ass to answer that litter box question. We're going live in five."

A long pause filled the airspace before the Dr. Doolittle "Talk to the Animals" theme came on and faded out followed by Fish's introduction. "We're back with Pet Peeves. I'm Humphrey Fish trading barbs with September Day. Me-ouch."

"Don't get your tail in a twist." Better start off mild. She still didn't trust him and didn't want to get canned.

"I resemble that remark." Fish opened the door and waited for her comeback.

"I know you do. And I got to tell you, it's unattractive." The beep-click interrupted once more. September continued to ignore it.

"Oh please, September, talk dirty to me again." Fish chortled.

She smiled. This was fun.

"Enough already with the potty talk. We need to go to the next caller."

"Sure thing. For more information listeners can click on PetPeeves.com." There. She got in the plug since Fish wasn't inclined.

"Caller, you're on the air with Humphrey Fish and Pet Peeves. What's your question?"

Quick breaths filled the long pause. "Is September there? Please, I need to talk to her."

"I'm here. What's your name? And do you have a pet question?" Dang, September hoped another break came before long. She needed her own litter box after so much coffee.

"September? Oh my God, September you've got to help me. Please, oh no oh no—"

"Calm down, I can barely understand you. Stop crying and speak up. I'll try to help if I can." Forget about the bitchy delivery, this one sounded serious.

"I tried and I tried to call you but your line was busy. The babysitter fell asleep, I could just kill her." The voice broke. "I've looked and looked, but he's nowhere around the house. You've got to track him."

The call waiting. "April, is that you?" She'd blown off her sister three times. September's mouth turned to dust.

"Steven's gone," April cried. "My baby's out in the storm, him and the dog both are gone!"

Chapter 3

Shadow raced off the path and buried his face deep in the drifted snow. The mouthful stung, numbing his tongue, and finally melted. He barked with surprised delight, grinned from both ends of his body and repeated the game, grabbing and tossing doggy snowballs as fast as he could munch.

He paused, black tail still churning the air, and stared at Steven. Maybe his boy would invite him closer?

But Steven never looked back, just plodded down the tree-lined trail. His boy ignored Shadow. Like always.

Snow blurred the route, but Steven followed the twists and turns with the confidence of one who has traveled the same track hundreds of times. Almost as if he could smell-sense the right foot placement with the keen skill of Shadow's own nose.

A new game? Just the two of them to visit the happy-place with no big humans? And no itchy vest that pushed black fur the wrong way. Shadow danced his delight. He bent double to bite the snow that settled on his back like his gnawed tattered sock.

Before they had left the house, after the old woman had fallen asleep, Steven had reached for the vest. But it hung on a hook out of his boy's reach. So his boy hung something else around Shadow's neck. It bounced now against Shadow's furry chest with each paw step forward. The cord wasn't as long as the leash. Not nearly long enough for the other end to be attached to Steven's wrist the way they practiced. And without the connection, Shadow was free to explore each side of the path, range ahead or lag behind.

Such smells. Such sounds. The cold focused every sensation until the world turned shiny bright, clean and sharp. Each white flake landed with a quiet "thpp" that made his long ears twitch, and tingled his skin at each grazed hair. Warm furry smells, rich and pungent…creatures burrowed deep out of sight tickled and teased that deep smell-place under his eyes. More, he wanted more.

Shadow raced in a tight circle, leaped high in the air to snap a withered leaf from a tree, and then dug frantically for no reason with mutters of joy. He panted, offering a happy tongue-lolling grin.

He stopped, cocked his big head to one side, and willed his boy to look at him. The white stuff clogged the air, blurring Steven's distant figure. Wind shifted and scent—and his boy—disappeared. Another gust blew snow so hard Shadow couldn't see, but it also brought back the familiar comfort of Steven's signature smell.

Shadow barked, bounded ahead three leaps, and barked again. He saw Steven flinch and cover his ears with his bare hands, but continue to stomp forward. Shadow barked again, and bent low in a butt-high bow in the most blatant invitation to play he could muster.

They could chase each other. Eat the cold white stuff. Roll around on the ground until exhausted. Shadow wiggled, barely able to contain his excitement.

But his boy never turned to see. Steven stuffed his hands back into his pockets, and trudged on.

The pup's tail slowed. He understood. The silent message shouted louder than the mouth-noise humans used. So he stood up and shook himself hard in a doggy shrug of disappointment. It wasn't Steven's fault. It was a good-dog's job to teach his boy how to have fun.

Most humans didn't dog-talk very well. So Shadow learned to watch their faces for clues to what all the mouth-noise meant. But his boy rarely varied his expressions, rarely vocalized, and spoke a different sort of body language than the adults. That was okay, though. Shadow was multilingual.

He figured out what some of the adult's words meant, like "food" and "outside." But more often, the big humans confused Shadow when they said one thing with their body and another with words. He never knew which to believe.

Steven wasn't nearly so confusing.

But his boy still carried the fear-stink from earlier. Not as bad as the boy's mother, but nasty all the same. Outside the house the cold wind washed away his fear-smell. Shadow whimpered at the thought, his ears flattened, and he hurried after Steven. A good-dog protected his boy, even if—ESPECIALLY if—scary people threatened.

Fear-stink made Shadow's fur stand up and feel prickly. Prickly and ready to bite. But he wasn't supposed to bite, ever. So he hated the fear-stink.

Shadow wanted to play. At the thought, his hackles smoothed. The cold, sharp day was made for play. For jumping and running, barking and peeing and digging out nose-tickling smells.

And fetching. He liked that word. The big humans never said the fetch-word enough.

Maybe they'd play when they reached the open field, the place with the metal climb objects. The happy place. His tail wagged at the thought. They visited the happy place almost every day, sometimes with the old woman and sometimes with the boy's mother. Shadow played, and Steven made the swings move or stacked rocks. Like his boy, Shadow appreciated routine.

With renewed anticipation Shadow raced after his boy. Maybe Steven had brought the ball—that was another word he'd learned all on his own. Shadow loved his ball; it made the best fetch game ever. Almost as much fun as to grab and shake Bear-toy to kill it. Pretend kill it, anyway.

Shadow reached his boy's side and trotted as close as possible without contact. Good-dogs stayed close to their people, and Shadow wanted to be a good-dog almost more than life itself.

Steven reached down and caught up the short cord suspended from Shadow's neck, mimicking the leash walk connection they'd practiced so many times. The pup showed his teeth like the big humans did when they were happy. He'd practiced and learned to copy their smile. He was sad that they didn't have tails to show joy and sadness, to warn and welcome. Shadow wondered why they never play-bowed. So Shadow learned to show happy teeth to help humans understand dog-talk better. They liked it, too.

He liked how his breath puffed white into the air. Panted breath surrounded his head in a cereal-scented white cloud. His boy's breath did the same thing.

From the time he'd arrived at the house, Shadow had understood his world revolved around his boy. That's how his boy's mother wanted it. Shadow knew she was Steven's mother because they smelled so much alike and because she treated his boy with the same ferocious care his own protective dam had shown.

But his boy's mother was sad a lot of the time. Even when she smiled, the sorrow crept through. It confused him. Sometimes Shadow managed to make her laugh, like when he'd tripped over Bear-toy or chased his tail. Her laugh made a wonderful swell inside his chest. When she called him "good-dog-Shadow" the day Steven pushed cereal treats off the table for him to snap out of the air, that was best of all. He thought his chest would burst with happiness.

Another lady visited him every day—the treat-lady. She taught him words and special games with rules he tried to understand. Sometimes it took a long time for Shadow to figure out what she wanted. Once he did, she made him feel so smart and happy. She called him "good-dog" more than anybody. Shadow pictured her face and wagged again. Thought of the treat-smell that clung to her clothes made him drool.

The treat-lady showed him how to understand the mouth-noises people called words. Every time he guessed right, she made a "click" sound with her mouth and fed him a treat. It didn't take Shadow long to figure out if he was a good-dog, he could make that click-treat happen. People had pockets filled up with yummy stuff for good-dogs, and hands made for scratching a dog's hard-to-reach places.

Steven didn't like the click noise, though. Shadow could tell, because his boy covered his ears. Shadow wished he could cover his ears sometimes, too. The big people didn't mind the loud-hurt noises. The scary-noises today made him squat-and-pee until it stopped. Maybe only dogs and youngsters like his boy could hear those noises.

Anyway, Shadow only got to play the click-treat game when his boy stayed in the other room. Every few days the treat-lady spent a bunch of time with him, even longer than the daily visits.

He wondered why she didn't stay all the time. He'd like that. A lot.

The treat-lady taught him what to do when she said *sit* or *down* or *wait* or *come*. *Come* was the hardest. Shadow always found something that smelled or sounded so wonderful that teased him to ignore the word, so he'd only gotten *come* right a couple of times. The treat-lady had been so excited and happy and called him "good-dog" many times. More times than he had paws—that was a lot—so he knew he'd done it right. She gave him tummy rubs and played fetch until his tongue hung to the floor and his tail was too tired to wag. But he wagged anyway. He couldn't help wagging when she was near.

Maybe if he got everything right all the time, the treat-lady wouldn't ever leave him. Wouldn't that be fine?

Lately they'd practiced with his vest. He liked to race around the big room and drag the attached leash. He made it crash into the wire crate or splash into his water bowl, pretending that it chased him. But the treat-lady frowned and shook her head when he did that. She didn't give him any treats or smile or anything. She ignored him.

Shadow hated to be ignored. It made his tummy hurt. That's how he knew what not to do. He was smart that way.

The first time she picked up the end of the leash, he pulled hard and wagged his tail and woofed, sure they'd have a tug game like with Teddy, his bear-toy. Yet she didn't want him to pull, either. How confusing.

But when he stood quiet and did nothing at all as Steven clipped the leash to his vest, the treat-lady laughed and rubbed his tummy, gave him a quiet "click" and a treat, and he knew he'd done something right. Imagine that—a good-dog for doing nothing at all? For walking without pulling and standing quiet until the treat-lady said "okay" which signaled Shadow to do whatever he wanted.

He liked the "okay" word almost as much as "good-dog."

Shadow hurried along the snowy pathway, keeping pace with Steven. He didn't pull against the makeshift tether and surge ahead or drag behind. He knew how to play this game. He'd learned the rules.

Overhanging trees and bushes bore the brunt of the wind, but Shadow's nose and ear tips stung with the cold. He shook his head and licked his nose to warm it, and pulled the makeshift leash out of Steven's hand. Shadow stopped and plopped his tail into the snow and waited, just as the treat-lady had taught. His boy paused, and felt along the line of Shadow's throat and down his chest until he was able to retrieve the line. The boy's touch thrilled the pup and made his tummy leap with happiness.

Shadow didn't know why his boy never gave him tummy rubs, and didn't like to play. But he figured out it was a good-dog's job to teach his boy how to give tummy rubs and to play chase and fetch and all the other stuff that made life an adventure for human-pups and dog-pups alike.

Treat-lady hadn't said so. Shadow figured that out all by himself. He was smart that way.

The pup wagged faster when they came out from under the trees into the open playground. He nudged his boy's side with his muzzle. Was the ball in one of his pockets? He detected something hard, not a ball, with the acrid odor of the scary "POP-POP-POP" from the morning. Shadow wrinkled his nose.

Steven shuffled to the gate, fiddled with the latch, and entered. He dropped Shadow's neck cord so the heavy end nestled into black fur. Nothing new here—his boy always let go once they arrived so Shadow could play and "take-a-break." He'd learned that meant he should squat. Only after that was he allowed to play.

But either Steven's mother or the old woman had always accompanied them before. The pup's large pointed ears drooped and he whined. Being alone with his boy made him nervous.

The old woman helped take care of his boy. She smelled of dusty powder and bacon, and made him sneeze and drool at the same time. Her loud voice hurt Steven's ears sometimes, but the pup knew she meant no harm. He liked her well enough, but would like her better if she shared the bacon.

Steven made a beeline for the playground equipment and didn't shut the gate. Shadow's unease deepened. His boy always opened it and the old woman always shut it. The gaped door looked wrong. But Shadow stepped through and slowly followed his boy anyway. Change to his routine, or to his boy's routine was bad, scary. Deep vertical lines furrowed his brow. Shadow searched the empty playground for the old woman. Maybe she woke up from the sofa and would meet them here?

Steven trudged to the snow-filled canvas slings hung from chains that clanked in the breeze. He brushed one clear and twisted the long chains around and around. Once wound tight, he let go, watching without expression. The swing twirled, unwinding in the wind. He stared until it stopped, and again twisted the chains.

Shadow cocked his head for a moment and was comforted by the familiar game his boy played. Being alone with his boy was a new game, he decided. He needed to learn the rules. He shook himself and immediately felt better.

The pup trotted through the field to the farthest point inside the fence, and squatted without anyone to tell him to take-a-break. He told himself, "good-dog" but it wasn't the same.

After an hour of doggy play and swing twirling, Shadow rejoined his boy's side, like always. It was time. They always stayed just this long.

Steven held his neck cord like they always did. And they left through the street-side gate like they always did and walked two blocks to where his boy's mother or the old woman always waited to drive them home. Shadow's tail wagged at thought of the toasty warm car ride to come. The cold bit his nose, and he flinched and squinted into the wind. Steven stumbled, braced an arm against Shadow's back to catch himself—and left his hand there. Shadow adjusted his pace to his boy's.

Within minutes, the wind and snow had swept away all evidence they'd ever entered the playground at all.

Chapter 4

September's red Volvo slid into April's driveway and skidded to a stop behind the yellow PT Cruiser parked in front of the blond brick ranch. Before she could climb out, April threw herself down the front steps and body slammed into the Volvo.

"He's gone, I don't know what to do, I looked around the house, the back gate's open, and–"

"Calm down, slow down, I can't understand you." September hugged her hard to shut off the typical drama-queen babbling. April was three years older, but you'd never know it by her behavior. "Let's get back into the house so we can talk." September nervously scanned the landscape. She'd feel less vulnerable inside with the door locked.

Dark stains on both of April's knees accented her soggy yellow sweats, and her frizzed hair and smeary makeup made it clear she'd been out in the weather without a coat. April, the "pretty one" of the sisters, had inherited Mom's wavy blond hair, blue eyes and perky figure that made September feel like an awkward giraffe in comparison. September and her brother both took after their dad's side of the family.

September urged her sister through the open door, locked it once safe inside, and immediately breathed easier. "When did you notice Steven was gone? Have you called the police?"

April twisted the ruby ring on her finger. "I left Steven with Wilma and drove to work just like always." Her expression scorched the dainty red-haired woman who stood nearby.

"My son drove me here." Wilma offered a half smile, before dabbing tears with a hanky.

"Really." September turned to April, and couldn't help the sarcasm. "You went to work in this weather? Did you expect folks to show up for jazzercise in the blizzard?"

"It's not jazzercise." April bulldozed on. "I had loyal clients scheduled; they'd show up on bobsleds to get there. I just left a sign on the door and a message on the machine that we closed due to weather, and I came home right away to find Wilma asleep and Steven gone." Her voice hiccupped to silence.

Wilma hunched at the whip-hard words. Tears streaked down powdered cheeks.

"Wilma, what happened?" September stepped further into the living room. April's house always looked ready for a photo shoot, but today a slurry of grime tracked over the bare hardwood gritted beneath her shoes. September wondered what had happened to the Persian carpet knockoff that usually covered the floor. September tried to draw the woman out. "I know it was an accident. But what happened before you fell asleep? Anything different, some clue why he'd leave or where he'd go?"

"*Nothing* happened. Same routine as always." April fell into a matching chair, and then immediately bounced back to her feet. "Why are we jabbering when we could be searching? You're the dog track expert, that's why I called you. Find him. Please." She whimpered the last word.

September tugged off her gloves and flexed her fingers to jump-start circulation. Wind rattled the picture window and peppered ice against its surface, and she shivered at the image of the tiny boy lost in the storm. At least the dog was with him. "We'll run circles without some starting point." If April hadn't found Steven hunkered down near the house, there were infinite places to look. In this weather, a twenty minute detour in the wrong direction could be the difference between life and death.

"I'd change things if I could." Wilma clutched the cover like a fuzzy shield. "Anyway, when I heard the door open and close I figured Steven let the pup in. I had no idea the child would go out in this icy weather."

"He'll freeze, he's going to freeze." April hugged herself. "I should have been here, should have protected him."

"His coat's gone." Wilma sounded hopeful. "It has a hood. He had on a sweater underneath and jeans with thick socks."

"But only thin tennis shoes. They'll soak through in no time." April's fierce accusation made the older woman flinch. "You know Steven hates having his hands covered; he won't wear gloves." She stopped at the front window. "Why are we talking about this? We have to find him!" She whirled to face September. "You have to find him."

"You gave the police his description for the Amber Alert. There can't be that many blond, green eyed seven year olds in yellow coats out alone in this weather, especially not with a big, black dog." September pulled back the heavy sleeve of her coat to check her watch, grateful for the down-filled parka more appropriate to Indiana weather. "So he left sometime after eleven." Steven's jacket was little more than a windbreaker, but he'd stand out bumblebee bright against the snow. The little boy preferred anything yellow. "He's been missing at least two hours, maybe longer. We can hope he's holed up somewhere out of the wind." Stuffing gloves into her giant pockets, she turned to April. "Where did you look? No need to waste time repeating the same search."

"We turned the house upside down. He wasn't in his bedroom or under the bed or in the closet where he likes to hide. Used to hide." A fleeting look of pride lit her face. "He stopped hiding. Hasn't for a couple of weeks now. He stopped stimming, too. Until, uhm, until this morning, and he started rocking again."

"So what happened today?" The question was rhetorical. Nearly anything could turn a seven-year-old autistic child into a runaway, or more likely, a wander-away.

April crossed her arms. "When I couldn't find him, I looked in the back yard. The gate was open. I went a little crazy then and ran around the outside of the house and yelled for him. The snow was only about three inches then but starting to drift, and I couldn't see any tracks. I made a big mess around the back of the house, in and around the fence." She paused. "I was afraid I'd mess up any way to trail him, you know, the way you do with dogs. So I stopped. That's when I called you. Tried to, anyway. You wouldn't pick up." She didn't hide the fear-fueled accusation.

"I thought Mom had put you up to bugging me about Thanksgiving." Outside the picture window, the manicured lawn, pebbled walkways, clipped hedges and decorative stone-lined flowerbed had disappeared beneath drifts. No blemish of kid tracks marred the white. Pole lights at the end of the drive stood like glittery chess pieces.

"I called you because Steven already knows you. He's scared of strangers. He hates change."

September flexed achy hands. Raynaud's was a damn nuisance and would only get worse, the numbness in hands and feet making her clumsy as hell.

She couldn't imagine how little Steven and the pup must feel. "Did the police say how long before they'd send someone?"

April shook her head. "You know all about that tracking stuff. We're wasting time. Find my son!"

"I can't track without a dog." September struggled to keep her temper. "Dakota died with Chris."

"Find my son." Her chin jutted. "I helped you. You owe me. *Do* something."

September bit back a retort. She did owe her. And April must be going crazy with worry. "I know someone who has tracking dogs. Guess we could see if they're available."

Wilma mopped her eyes with the afghan. "I do make allowances, I really do. I know he's your son and all, but he's not all that lovable." Wilma's double chins quivered. "If I don't get out his puzzles at ten-thirty, feed him exactly at eleven o'clock, or—"

"Wilma, we're wasting time. He's a child. Lost. In a blizzard. We can debate shoulda-coulda-woulda later." September could see that April was near the boiling point.

But Wilma didn't stop. "He's a fanatic about routine. Always wears his coat, hooks the leash on the dog before they go out."

"That's right, Shadow's with him. Haven't you trained that dog?" April aimed the next words like darts. "You trained Dakota, why couldn't you do the same with Shadow? What good is he anyway if he can't keep Steven safe?"

To April, the dog was a magic wand without value unless she saw instant results.

"I'm his mother. And you owe me."

September ducked her head, again acknowledging the debt. "Shadow's a nine-month-old German shepherd. He's like a bright teenager distracted by shiny objects. You want to trust Steven's safety to that?"

Her sister spoke with quiet command. "*I'm his mother.* I know what's best. Either help me find my son, or get the hell out of here."

"Great. I'll call about the dog." She pulled out her phone. "September to the rescue. Again."

April crossed her arms. "You don't want to compare messes."

That hurt. "And you won't let me forget." Leave it to a big sister to always know what buttons to push. "Wait, is it Doug? Do you think he took Steven?" April and her ex-husband Doug Childress had an explosive history over their autistic son's treatment. "Have you called him?"

"No. And don't you call him, either. I don't know if he's involved." For the first time, April's momma-bear attitude faltered. "If he has Steven, then at least he's safe. If he isn't involved, Doug will use it against me. I can't deal with him on top of everything else."

Wilma levered herself off the sofa. "Will you listen to me? Praise God, I know where he'd go." She beamed like she'd won the lottery.

April sucked in a breath. "Why didn't you say so before now? Where?"

"Ten-thirty puzzles, eleven o'clock lunch, and . . ." She paused dramatically as if the words redeemed her soul. "Twelve o'clock the park. We go every day. That's the only time we leave the gate open, when we go for our playtime in the park."

April hurried to the closet and slammed open the door. She yanked a coat out so quickly that metal hangers jangled to the floor.

September grabbed April's arm to stop her. "You're wet and exhausted. It's way past time Steven comes home from the park, right?"

April shrugged on the coat. "I always pick him up. He expected the Cruiser."

"But what if he's on his way home?" September pulled on her gloves. "Or somebody finds him, and gives him a ride, and you're not here?"

Wilma shuffled an eager step toward them. "He knows the address if somebody asks. I'm happy to wait while y'all go look. My son won't pick me up until two-thirty."

April's frown cut unhappy valleys in her brow. "I'll wait here. But you hurry. Call me as soon as you find him. You *will* find him for me, September?" Her shoulders drooped until the heavy coat slid off onto the floor.

"I promise I'll find him." September swallowed hard. The last thing she wanted was to dive into the hateful cold, all alone. Unprotected. But April was right. She'd never be able to repay her sister.

"I can't lose him." April dashed tears away. "I waited so long to have my own baby. You know better than anyone. Find my son, and we'll call the debt even."

Chapter 5

Snow knifed Shadow's ears until he shook his head to kill the tickle. He had lost his balance, fallen, and now struggled to stand in the chest-high drifts. His head turned from side to side until sniffs located his boy. Steven hadn't made much headway. In two bounds Shadow rejoined Steven.

Steven raised his feet high to clear the snow. His shoes squeaked with each step. Their progress slowed to a puppy pace, and Shadow curbed the urge to leap ahead. After all, dogs with four paws traveled much faster than people with only two.

Shadow wanted to be inside the warm car. He liked the daily car rides at the end of park playtime. But Shadow's time sense jittered his hurry-up urge. It was late. Would the car wait? The old woman wasn't here, either. What other rules got changed?

Maybe the old woman would be in the car. Or his boy's mother. She'd make the car wait. The thought felt right. It was a good-dog's job to trust adult people. They knew things dogs couldn't know, even if they did miss out on all the good smells. Shadow relaxed.

Sometimes Steven's mother rolled down the window so just the tip of his nose could sift through wind-borne sniffs. Cars moved much faster than dogs. But they never left their smelly pathway, and the smells always came from distant places far from the car territory. He'd like to follow those smells to their start, and drink deep of the scent until he knew everything about them.

He and Steven traveled the same path as always. Houses—not their own but strangers' homes—stood along both sides of the road. No sound came from the houses. No smoke steamed out rooftops. No bundled figures passed by with smiles or offers to pet a good-dog's head. Today he and his boy were alone in a world of white.

On other days, cars raced back and forth next to them with strong smells and scary noises. Treat-lady made it clear that good-dogs don't trespass into car territory. Shadow didn't want to argue. He didn't think Steven could best a car, either, so Shadow always stood between his boy and the road. Cars were creatures of habit and never left their territory.

But today the empty road looked lonely. Snow erased its borders, but Shadow could smell the difference. Only a bit further, over there by the pole where other dogs left pee-smell, that's where they always met the car.

No car waited. No amount of nose-pokes hurried his boy along, so maybe the car came and left. Or maybe it got lost with all the white in the air. Cars didn't have noses to find their way. He hoped cars could see to find their way through the white stuff. If they couldn't see, would cars swerve onto the footpath where dogs and boys walked? He whined but the wind whipped the sound away. His boy couldn't leap away as fast as a dog. Shadow viewed the car territory with new suspicion. Still deserted. No danger for now.

Steven fell again. This time he disappeared. The white stuff got deeper and deeper, soft as cat fur but cold when it swarmed through the wind. Shadow woofed and watched for Steven's angry explosion of thrashed arms to swim himself upright. But this time Steven didn't scream and flail. He just lay there. Silent.

Shadow didn't like it when Steven screamed. It hurt his ears. But it hurt his heart worse. Steven screamed when adults didn't understand, and Shadow wanted to scream lots of times for the same reason. But his boy's silence made Shadow's tummy feel strange, and prickled his skin with worry.

He plowed to Steven's side. Snow fell so thick and drifted so deep Shadow had to sniff hard to locate his boy's nest. He sneezed. Nothing smelled right unless he stuck his face deep under to reach the ground. And that made his eyes smart.

The snow wasn't fun anymore.

Shadow struggled upright, pushed ahead another two feet until he could stare down at his boy. Steven's lips trembled. Shadow hesitated. But he couldn't help himself, and slurped his boy's cheek.

Icy. Salty. He licked again, but stood ready to dodge Steven's slap, or brace against being pushed away.

But his boy just sat there. Cereal breath puffed from Steven's slack mouth, and his nose ran. Steven's lips shuddered again, and his teeth clicked. Shadow cocked his head. Did Steven have treats? No, he didn't chew, he just breathed heavy. But his tongue didn't hang out the way good-dogs pant. His slight body trembled.

Steven must be awfully cold.

He wondered why Steven insisted on two-footed walks when all fours did the job so much better in the deep white stuff. How sad that Steven had no fur to keep him warm. His own black coat helped, but the cold bit into his toes, ears and nose.

His boy could grab fur and pull himself upright out of the white stuff. They'd practiced that trick before. He learned quickly, like a good-dog should. He told himself, "good-boy" because Steven wouldn't. His tail wagged at the thought.

He waited some more, but Steven didn't move. He just stared up at Shadow. His eyes half closed.

Maybe he'd decided to walk on all fours. At the thought, Shadow grinned, his ears flattened and his tail wagged. Wouldn't that be fine? He backed up to give Steven room.

Steven finally lifted an arm but his bare hand slid against Shadow's fur. The stiff fingers couldn't move very well. Shadow reached around and risked another lick but instead of gripping his coat, Steven dropped his hand. And he folded himself the way Teddy, his bear-toy turned floppy after a good shake. Steven drew up his legs, and hid his face against them, with his arms wrapped close. His body shuddered.

Shadow's worried whine went unanswered. He stretched forward to nose poke Steven, and danced sideways to dodge the slapping hand that didn't come. So he whined again. He barked. Still ignored, Shadow stuck his nose under Steven's arm and levered.

"No, no, no, no, go away, go away, no touch." Steven wailed, flinched and unwound long enough to flap hands at Shadow. Icy fingers struck his nose, and he yelped and backed away. He watched Steven curl up and cocoon himself inside the snowy hole.

Shadow shook himself, and the nose sting faded. This was wrong. He barked again and again, deep determined woofs mixed with uncertain yelps that dissolved into a bewildered howl.

Steven shrugged into a tighter ball. He covered his ears with his hands. Wind gusts dusted white over the top of his boy. But Steven didn't move.

Shadow considered his options. Houses stared back, eyeless windows without a blink of motion. He looked the other way. The car territory remained empty. He raised his muzzle, tasted the air for anything warm.

Cocked his head, but the wind teased and swirled both smells and sounds into a directionless jumble. He whimpered.

With a final sigh, Shadow turned back to his boy, and huffed warm breath against Steven's neck. He didn't nose poke this time. When Steven shifted, Shadow placed one careful paw at a time into the snow nest, and snugged his body as close to his boy as possible.

Steven didn't have fur but Shadow had lots of fur. The cold bit into tender boy-parts and dog-parts when they were by themselves. But together they'd be warm.

Until the car came. A car always came. All Shadow had to do was wait. Cars were warm. And warm was good.

His boy's body relaxed. Shadow curled closer so his tail covered both his own head and his boy's white-blue fingers. He felt a tiny thrill when his boy didn't shrink away. They breathed together.

Chapter 6

Claire O'Dell disconnected the phone and set it on the table. She wanted to scream and throw the receiver but resisted the temptation. Any sudden noise might set Tracy off again, and it had taken longer than usual for her to settle down. Nerves over the trip. Or just Tracy being Tracy.

Their big purple bag sat at the front door, ready for Mike to lug to the car. She'd stuffed a week's worth of purple and green clothes inside to keep Tracy calm and happy for the five days they'd be gone.

Home in time for Thanksgiving dinner. A real celebration this year. A rebirth for their family.

That was the plan, anyway. "Now what?"

The door squealed open and banged into the luggage. "Ready to go?" Mike stamped his shoes free of slush and stepped into the mudroom. She wished he'd wear a hat. His buzz cut offered no protection for the flushed ears that matched the freckles he hated. On Tracy, the snub nose and freckles were pixie cute, despite her nobody-home stare. The little girl also had inherited Claire's pouty lips, black hair and blue eyes, but missed out on their mischievous sparkle. She wondered if Tracy would take after Mike's lean build or her own stocky stature. It didn't matter unless they could unlock the little girl hidden within.

Mike grabbed the suitcase and bounced on his heels with impatience. "Is she ready? Calm today?" He pulled the bag to the door, grinning. "I can't believe today's finally here."

Claire wondered how to tell him so he wouldn't explode. Both of them teetered on an emotional cliff. "We need to talk."

His grin dimmed several watts. "What?" Mike peered around the neat kitchen, noticing the new stain.

"Orange juice." She answered the unspoken question, and had already cleaned up the broken glass, but the spot on the wall hadn't dried. Her own fault. Tracy had yelled for a big girl glass instead of the Sippy cup. After all, she'd just turned seven, and Claire so wanted Tracy to have what other kids her age took for granted.

The dappled wall paper hid the worst of five years of damage. Most parents only dealt with crayon scribbles. Claire had planned to paint the walls after the trip, and wipe away the bad stains for a fresh start. Stains, though, were the least of their worries. She took a breath and told him. "The flight got cancelled."

"Cancelled. Why?" Mike glanced through the storm door at the cloudless blue sky. "Overbooked? Did you get another flight?"

"Snowstorm grounded all the flights. No, not here." She sighed. "Just our luck Chicago has great weather for November, and cowboy-land gets snow." Her hand caught his. "I've been on the phone the past two hours for a way to get there. Nothing's available."

"That can't be." Mike pulled his hand away and dropped the luggage. "It's all set. I got a half day off from work to run you to the airport. We've pre-paid for Tracy. Took forever just to get on the waiting list." His fair skin flushed to match his wind-burned ears. "Maybe they'll postpone—"

"Already tried that. I called Elaine. The other parents are in the same boat. Elaine tried, too, but they won't cancel, said too many are already on their way. We get no refund, Mike, and we go back on the waiting list if we don't show." Claire tightened her jaw and resolve. She wouldn't cry, not as long as they had one option left. She just had to convince Mike.

He flexed his fist, frustrated there was nothing to hit. You couldn't beat up the weather. "Took out a second mortgage. I'm already working double shifts." Mike's soft words punched the air. "We can't stop now. Tracy has a chance, maybe her only chance. There's got to be a way." He closed the door on the beautiful Chicago winter day.

The clear skies mocked them. "Elaine says three other families from here, five from Detroit, and two from Kansas City got grounded. Well, the ones from Detroit just landed at O'Hare. Probably others we don't know about.

But that's eleven kids with their parents and none of us can afford to miss this chance."

"What do you suggest? Strap on boots and hike to Texas?" He pulled out his phone. "What's the number of the Legacy Center? Maybe I can explain—"

"Mike. Stop."

"But she's just a little girl. We did everything they asked." He coughed, trying to cover the emotion. She knew he hated to look weak. But this was a challenge he couldn't win with skinned knuckles. "You could drive. We can ask my dad to go. It's not that far. You take the car, and I can catch rides to work with one of the guys."

Claire grabbed the phone from him. "Our old car barely gets you to and from work. I already asked about car rentals. Solidly booked. Trains take too long." She grasped his hands again, smoothed the blunt nails stained with grease and rough from cold weather. "Elaine found a bus."

"A bus? What do you mean?"

She smiled, kissing his chapped fingers. "The Detroit group meets Elaine at O'Hare to board the bus. It's a church bus big enough for everyone. From there they go to Kansas City and on to the Legacy Center in Texas." He had to say yes. "We're supposed to check in tomorrow for orientation and first treatments. We can make it if we drive straight through. But we've got to leave now."

"A church bus." Mike's mouth fell open. "They're driving a friggin' bus from Chicago to Dallas? Through a snow storm? With how many autistic kids for hours and hours?" His shoulders hunched. "You know how crazy that sounds?"

"A dozen kids, a few more parents." Claire's words tumbled over themselves. "There are three more buses with kids coming from Las Vegas, Minneapolis and Atlanta. Some others will drive their own cars. You read the program, Mike. It's limited to two hundred children, and probably half that number got zapped by the storm." She toed the suitcase, packed not just with clothes but with their hopes and dreams. "We've got twenty-four hours, maybe a little more time, to get there. With luck the snow will melt before we arrive and we'll make even better time." She squeezed his hand until he met her eyes. "Tracy can be on that bus. Me and Tracy." Claire offered a faltering smile. "It's our best chance, Mike. For Tracy. You know it is."

"I can't get off work, babe. I can't lose my job." He pulled his hands away. "Three guys are ready to take my place. I had to beg to get the half day off today."

"You can still drive us to O'Hare just like we planned. Elaine fixed everything." She embraced him, and couldn't stem the eager hope. "Please. We won't be alone. We'll help each other." She laughed. "We've all got the same experience."

He hung his head. "I wish I could go, too. I need to be there for you and Tracy."

"You are, Mike. You're a great dad, and a great husband. Just get us to the bus." She hugged him again.

"God, I feel so helpless." He grabbed the suitcase.

Claire kissed his cheek. "Helpless? Not anymore."

Chapter 7

September stamped snow from her boots at the back door. She'd found no trace of either Steven or Shadow. The drifts against the Gentry Park fence measured three feet in some places, more than enough to hide a tiny child and dog. She'd searched them all. Either they'd never been there or they had already left the park.

If they were still nearby, Dakota would've sniffed them out. She rubbed away the thought with an icy glove to her forehead. It was a waste of time to wish ghosts back to life.

Her phone rang before she could reach the door. She tugged off her gloves to fumble it out of her pocket, glanced at the caller ID and almost didn't answer. "Yes, Mom. What now?"

"Did your sister call you?"

"I'm at April's now." September hugged herself and ducked her chin into the heavy scarf wound around her throat. The snow hadn't let up.

"Oh, good. She said you could use her good silver since you insist on doing the whole Thanksgiving thing yourself. But your brother wants to bring his corn chowder. Don't you dare hurt his feelings and say no. He's very proud of that recipe."

"Mom, I'm kind of busy." Mom must not know Steven was missing, thank heaven, or there'd be hell to pay. With luck, they'd find him quickly and she wouldn't have to know. "Corn chowder sounds good. I'll call him later, okay?" She disconnected and pocketed the phone.

September entered the kitchen by the back door. April never locked the door when she was home, no matter how many times September insisted. A woman's voice spoke in the front living room, so the police were here, a pretty good response time considering the weather. "I'm back," she called, pulling off her hat and gloves. She blew on her hands and hurried through the dog gate that separated Shadow's domain from the rest of the house, and nearly skidded to her knees when she stepped on a fork.

Drawer contents lay scattered across the floor; cabinet doors hung ajar, and even the refrigerator door swung open. The place looked like the victim of one of Steven's tantrums. "April? Did they find Steven?"

Mrs. Santa Claus appeared at the dog gate wearing a hideous holiday sweater covered with embroidered turkeys. "Oh my." She looked around the room, and then met September's eyes. "We made quite a mess in our hurry." Dimples bloomed in both cheeks when she tsk-tsked and smiled. "Steven's still missing, so come help strategize how to find him."

"Who are you?" The woman smelled like fresh baked cookies. "Are you with the police?" September unzipped her parka, stuffing her hat and gloves into a pocket.

"I'm Lizbeth Baumgarten, but you can call me Lizzie." She held out a plump hand to shake. "I don't think you girls know just what's at stake." She hurried into the next room.

September quickly followed, wanting answers. April sat at one end of the overstuffed sofa with Wilma beside her. Something was off. "What's going on?" Her chapped lips tasted salty, and she wished she had a tissue.

"You find him?" April eagerly sat forward. "Any sign?" September mouthed *no* and April deflated and indicated the stranger. "I called Lizzie to help."

Lizzie turned to April with a frown. "Just how many folks did you tell?"

"Is that a problem? The more people who know Steven's missing, the better." September pushed the hair out of her eyes. "You sure don't act like a cop."

"She's Steven's…um, therapist," April said. "You've got to listen to her."

"His *therapist?*" September looked the woman up and down. "This is the high dollar treatment you needed me to fund?"

"And just who are you, dear?" There was steel beneath the woman's jolly exterior.

"I'm April's sister. Steven's aunt." September examined the disheveled room, shocked to see drawers from end tables midway open and spilling contents over the floor. "The kitchen's a wreck, too. What are you looking for? What's more important than a little boy lost in a blizzard?"

Lizzie's brow furrowed as she hurried to answer. "Of course Steven is important. We must do everything we can to find him. And we will." She squeezed April's shoulders in encouragement. "We're a team, I won't let you down."

April squeezed Lizzie back. "Thank you. And I'm sorry."

The therapist patted her shoulder, took off and polished her glasses on the hem of her sweater, and squinted at September. "April misplaced something that belongs to me. And that affects not just one child, but hundreds of little ones." She replaced her glasses.

September ignored the therapist. She glanced at Wilma, but the older woman seemed clueless. "April, what did the police say? Are they on the way?"

"The weather must have delayed them." She wouldn't look at September.

Wilma stirred. "I don't understand. The police wouldn't ignore such a thing—"

"Of course they wouldn't." Lizzie hurried to the front window and gestured at the icy vista. "Perhaps you should call them again, make sure the police understand the urgency." She patted her pockets. "I left my phone in the car."

"Do you know what the wind chill is?" September joined Lizzie by the front window, and touched frosted glass with her palm. "I nearly froze running to Gentry Park and back, and Steven's coat isn't as warm as mine." She retrieved her phone out of a pocket, thankful she'd thought to charge it.

Lizzie took a step, and slipped on the bare, wet floor. She grabbed at September to regain her balance, and smacking September's cheek in the process.

Rocking backwards, September dropped the phone, catching her weight against the window before she slid on her butt to the bare hardwood.

April cried out with alarm. "September, are you okay?"

The hardwood felt cold through her pants, and she wondered again what happened to the rug. She rubbed her face, more surprised than hurt. "Should have ducked." She flexed her jaw.

Lizzie flexed her hand. "That smarts. Sorry about that." She stooped to retrieve September's phone. She pushed wire rim glasses up her pug nose. "April told you about Steven's treatment?"

"She doesn't know any details." April shifted her weight from foot to foot. "Can't we go find Steven now? You promised to help."

Lizzie gestured with the rescued phone. "Don't get up, just relax and sit a spell." She considered the phone and then stuffed it into her pocket so the embroidered turkey bulged. "I think we got off on the wrong foot." She offered a hand to help September up. "Friends? We're all here to help Steven."

September levered herself upright, ignoring the offered hand. "You're his doctor?" She had never hesitated to fund Steven's treatment when April asked. She owed her sister that, and owed Steven, too. But something smelled fishier than Macy's Kitty Kaviar treats.

"Not his doctor, no. That's Dr. Henry Pottinger, or at least that was his doctor." She looked pointedly at April, who turned away. "But I'm on Steven's team. His safety and well-being mean everything to me. Everything. We've got a twenty-four-hour window to make sure he's okay." Lizzie's eyebrows rose and fell like a pair of white caterpillars. "Right, April?"

April hesitated, and then nodded. Her lipstick was a stricken slash.

"Didn't we come through with every promise? Are you dissatisfied in some way?" Lizzie made a decidedly unladylike sound. "There's just no pleasing some folks. Now, you listen to me. Steven's made such great strides. We turned away others to make room for Steven in the program. I can't let anyone's cold feet take that child's future away."

Lizzie spoke in riddles. "What are you talking about?" Sudden suspicion heated September's face. "Is Steven really lost?" She whirled to face her sister. "You should be calling the cops every ten minutes. Is this some sick joke?"

"Oh, he's lost all right." But Lizzie looked relieved at September's confusion. "Good girl, April, looks like you kept your word after all." She abruptly crossed the room and stood over Wilma who sat with her eyes closed on the sofa. "You can just stop that right now. I said stop it."

Wilma jumped, opening her eyes and unclasping her hands. "I'm just praying for Steven to come home safe." Her chin quivered.

"Stop it. Now," Lizzie said. "We don't need that mumbo-jumbo muddying the waters. Prayers never helped me or my family. Science and taking charge of destiny, that's what makes things right."

Twisting the afghan throw in her lap, Wilma looked away, blinking hard. September could see the pulse flutter in her throat. She'd given up on prayers after Chris was killed, too, but there was no call for bashing the babysitter's faith.

Lizzie smiled and softened her words, turning to April. "This morning when you called, I sent you help to solve that, whatsit, little difficulty with Dr. Pottinger. Didn't I?"

April nodded.

"It's crunch time. Pottinger's right about the twenty-four-hour window. Steven needs his treatment on time, and if you miss that deadline, nobody can help. Just return what's lost." Lizzie's dimples had lost their charm. "Perhaps you made an error in judgment, but no harm, no foul, you can fix that. I'm reasonable, you know I am. After all, we all want what's best. For the children."

September fought the urge to clobber those dimples. "Is Steven with Dr. Pottinger? April, look at me, not at her." When her sister refused, September turned back to Lizzie. "Is this a shakedown? Where is Steven?" Her stomach fluttered with fear. What had April gotten into?

April spoke in a rush. "Dr. Pottinger showed up this morning, told me Steven needed his next treatments within twenty-four hours or—"

Lizzie shushed her, and finished for April. "—or else Steven will get sick. He might die."

September reeled. "He could die?! What sort of treatment is this?"

"It's a miracle treatment." April clasped her hands, unconsciously mimicking Wilma's prayerful posture. "Dr. Pottinger brought proof on a flash drive. He insisted I watch the video but I never got the chance, because Steven got . . . upset . . . so I got interrupted." She looked with anguish at Lizzie. "I don't know what happened to the flash drive. Something happened to it while Wilma napped." Her stony expression battered the babysitter.

Wilma mouthed something silently. She'd resumed praying.

September's frustration grew. "What's wrong with you people? So a flash drive is missing, just ask for another copy." She moved back to the window and glanced at her watch. The snow hadn't slowed in the least.

"Oh, we have backup." Lizzie dismissed September's suggestion. "I even found where the information got emailed to another party, somebody called bodaciousbody."

Bodaciousbody, September knew, was her sister's email address that she used for work. For some reason April emailed the drive's contents to herself. April shook her head, a silent plea for September to remain quiet.

Lizzie measured the two sisters' reactions and sighed. "April understands. We can't have just anyone stumble on this information. So that loose end needs to be dealt with."

Enough already. "Give me my phone." September held out her hand, but aimed her words at April. "Call the police, or don't. But Steven needs somebody to be the parent and go after him."

April flinched. "How dare you."

"Screw it." September pulled on her hat and gloves. She hurried to the front door and twisted the deadbolt. She could have canvassed half the neighbors by now. If Steven wasn't found, at least one of them could call the cops.

Lizzie followed, and gently put a hand on the handle to stop her. "Here's an idea. April and I will go find Steven. And you can find me that flash drive. You're right; you'll need your phone." She reached into the wrong pocket, though, and pulled out a gun. Her expression brooked no argument.

September froze. She slowly pulled her hand away from the door.

Lizzie's body blocked any view of the gun from the other women. The older woman nodded once, and waited until September moved away from the door before secreting the gun. She kept one hand in that pocket.

April had always been the pretty one, a smart girl who acted the ditzy bombshell with her baby-girl voice. But ever since Steven arrived, and April kicked butthead Doug out of her life, her big sis morphed into a do-or-die responsible parent. Now she'd gotten into something that involved a gun.

Wilma's chins Jello-ed a rumba. "It's all my fault because today I fell asleep, and he's out there lost in the snow, and it's my fault but I didn't mean it. I just leave everything in the Lord's hands. Would you pray with me?"

"I told you to leave God out of this." Lizzie waved September back into the room. "Sit with April. She needs some sisterly support."

September slowly walked across the room and perched on the arm of the sofa next to April.

Wilma turned to April. "You know how Steven likes to hide shiny objects. Was that computer thingy shiny? Remember that time you lost your watch? Didn't find it for two days, until you changed his sheets, and there it was under the mattress."

April got up and crossed to Lizzie, her voice urgent. "We've got to find Steven. He'll freeze. September said she'd get a tracking dog to find him."

"What a good sister she is. I'm sure she'll do anything you ask. Won't you, September?"

September nodded, her mouth dry. April hadn't a clue.

"We'll find him." Lizzie patted April's cheek, the epitome of caring grandma. "Children are my life." She held out her hand to April. "So let's go find him."

"Oh, yes! Thank you. With all of us looking we'll find him more quickly." April hugged Lizzie.

September held her breath, relieved when the gun remained out of sight.

"It's clear the flash drive isn't here, we looked everywhere. Maybe it's still with Dr. Pottinger."

"But I don't know where he is." April's expression crumpled again.

"I know you don't, dear. Let me worry about that. Put on your coat. We'll take my Hummer. It's got four-wheel drive. The little guy can't have gone far."

April gathered her coat, and hurried to open the door. Snow smacked the warmth out of the room with one fat breath.

"Go wait in the car, April, I'm right behind you." Lizzie shrugged a checkerboard woolen poncho over her head. She waited until April shut the door.

September stood up from the couch as Lizzie retrieved September's phone from the turkey pocket. She turned it on and fiddled with the display. "While we look for Steven, you retrieve the flash drive your reckless sister lost." Her tone had morphed from grandmotherly to sardonic.

"Who are you? What's really going on?" September noticed Wilma had once again started praying, even though she'd not seen the gun.

"If you care about that little boy, you'll find that flash drive and return it to me. I control access to his medicine. And in twenty-four hours if he doesn't get his medicine, Steven falls off the ugly truck."

"Then we need to find Steven, and stop bellowing about some mysterious flash drive. Screw twenty-four hours. You've got twenty-four seconds to give me answers—"

Lizzie stomped to the door, and then turned. "When you find the flash drive, call April. She went to work this morning, so you can look there for starters." She tossed the phone at September. "And don't call the cops."

Wilma flinched. She screwed her eyes shut, and redoubled the prayers.

September lunged to catch the phone before it cracked apart on the hardwood floor.

"Consider that flash drive your ever-most-special gift to all the little girls and boys. Right in time for the holidays."

Pulling herself upright off the couch, Wilma hurried to the corner phone. She still clutched the afghan in one hand and picked up the receiver in the other.

Lizzie watched her. "What are you doing? I said no cops."

Wilma dropped the woolen cover. "I'm not calling the police. I'm calling a higher power. I'm sorry you're not a believer. But like you said, we want the same thing, having him safe. I have to get Stevie on the prayer chain since I got him lost." Her face was serene as she dialed the phone.

Lizzie flushed. Her right eyelid twitched.

"If she won't call the cops, I will." September thumbed the phone to dial 911.

"That's not a request. Put down the phone, both of you." Lizzie pulled out the gun.

Chapter 8

Shadow's ears twitched. A car? He liked car rides. Cars were warm.

He burst from the nest, white as a Polar bear until he shook off the ice. Steven snugged into a tighter ball when Shadow's warmth pulled away, but he made no sound.

Fluffy snow had changed to tiny ice balls that sizzled like bacon when they hit nearby roofs. Shadow blinked. Round yellow eyes glowed. The shiny eye-lights lit up the snow in twin pathways flung far ahead of the growly car. The eye-lights were placed higher than the ones on Steven's car. This car was a giant.

Shadow liked his boy's car. It smelled like French fries. Maybe all cars, even tall ones with big yellow eyes, smelled that way. Or even had French fries for good-dogs and their boys.

At the thought, Shadow's tail moved faster. Steven needed a warm car place. So did Shadow's toes. He licked his paws and they tingled in response. He'd like a French fry, too.

Steven didn't respond to Shadow's nose poke, so he woofed under his breath, prepared to dodge a flung fist. But his boy clung tighter to himself, hugged legs with his hands while his knees pillowed his cheek.

The engine grew louder. Yellow eyes stabbed close.

Shadow barked. Nothing happened, Steven didn't even twitch.

The giant car grumbled, and made lots more noise than the small one Steven's mother drove. Shadow watched for a moment. It didn't pause, just rolled along the car path and pushed snow ahead of its nose-less face. Would it stop? Maybe not. How would his boy climb inside if it didn't stop?

Could a dog make it stop, or just people?

He pawed Steven. His boy needed to move. Steven could stand by the car path. That's how cars knew to stop and let them inside. That worked for his boy's car, anyway. Maybe it would work for the giant car, too.

He grasped Steven's sleeve and tugged. Up, get up, stop the big car and go for a ride. Cars carried dogs and their boys home. And home was warm, with bowls full of dinnertime. Home was Teddy, his bear toy. Home was treat-lady visits. Home was safe. Shadow wanted to go home.

Steven must get up, up, up!

"No-no-no-no, leave Steven alone." His boy barely lifted his head, the words so soft only good-dogs with big ears could hear.

Shadow turned away and bounded toward the growly car. He stopped near the pole that jutted out of the drift. It carried a faint smell of dog pee where others before him had marked. So the pole must be important, maybe the big car paid attention to dog signposts, too. Shadow barked as loud as he could, and danced back and forth from the curb to the sign. He kicked up flurries, and bowed low and stuck his butt high to wave his tail in the air. That way the big car could see his black shape and know he meant no harm. Would it understand and stop to play with him?

But it didn't even slow down. Shadow stared at his boy's huddled form and wondered if the big yellow eyes could see Steven. He figured not. They didn't move from the car path. It would soon pass them by and Shadow would be alone with his boy again. They'd have to wait for another car to come. Wait in the cold.

Shadow dove into the path of the car. He wasn't supposed to. Treat-lady taught him only bad dogs moved into the car path. But he didn't care. He didn't know what else to do.

Shadow stood his ground. Barks mixed with excited yelps. The giant yellow eyes bore down on him until he could see nothing else.

Chapter 9

September froze, terrified. Once the front door latched behind Lizzie, she scrambled to her feet, stumbled to the door and threw the deadbolt. The back door was still unlocked. Didn't matter, though, too late for do-overs.

Bits of bone, blood and brain created a Pollock pattern on the wall behind Wilma's shattered head. September gagged. Chris had died from a head shot, too.

If she had just played along, Wilma would still be alive.

Her tears wouldn't stop. She hazarded a peek through the frosted glass. April waved cheerily from the black Hummer's passenger window. The sound of the gunshot must have been muffled by the house, distance and being cocooned inside the car.

Lizzie climbed into the driver's seat, scowled at September and cocked a finger-mime gun at April—implication clear. She'd kill April unless September followed directions. The car left with a flash of taillights. Snow packed over the rear by accident or design obscured the license plate.

The cell phone clutched in September's hand rang, and she nearly dropped it. Mom. Again. She cancelled the call, and stared at the phone for a long hungry moment yearning for the police.

Wilma's body slumped next to the ruined sofa. September looked away. She buried the phone deep in her pocket. If she called the cops, April would die.

She looked at her watch, considering the impossible 24-hour deadline. Not nearly enough time to find a needle in a snowstorm—two needles, counting Steven.

Wilma's dead, open eyes stared, and a bloody tear rolled down one cheek as if in sympathy.

No choice, she had to do something.

Start at the beginning. That was Dr. Pottinger. The flash drive belonged to him; he'd been here to show April. Lizzie searched the house and didn't find it, maybe because April took it with her to work. September dropped her head in her hands. Think. She had to think.

April trusted Lizzie. She hadn't seen the gun or Wilma's murder, and hadn't a clue her life was in danger. The deadline had something to do with Steven's medication. But that made no sense either.

Ice peppered the window. She felt a draft. The back door, she had to make sure it was locked. She couldn't think clearly, not if someone could sneak up on her, they'd never caught her stalker. Wait, no—that was in Chicago before she'd moved to South Bend. Now she'd moved to Texas to get away from him and the memory of Chris's murder.

Lizzie could come back. April paid no attention to locks. Without Dakota or Chris around for protection, September had to be extra careful. But Wilma was already dead. Locking doors now wouldn't protect April. Locks wouldn't save Steven from the blizzard.

September flinched, and checked the time again. Wilma had said her son would pick her up at 2:30. She wouldn't have to call for help, but she didn't want to be here and face him finding his mother. Once the cops came they'd ask questions for hours. And Steven would freeze. She had no choice. And she had to make the minutes count because once she left, she couldn't get back into the house.

She skirted the bloodstains and hurried down the hall to Steven's room. The yellow tulip quilt made by September's mom jumbled at the foot of the twin bed. Buttercup sheets stripped from the mattress tangled in a mess on the floor. Dresser drawers had been dumped across the carpet. The shelf over his bed hadn't been touched. Steven's collection of small polished stones sat with military precision in a double row.

A mobile with gold foil dragonflies floated above the bed. Three bright yellow toy trucks rested on their sides to make the wheels easier to spin. His cache of treasures, contained in a yellow plastic soap dish on the bedside table, included a shiny gold wristwatch with a broken plastic strap, several copper-bright pennies, and three yellow M&Ms. No flash drive.

She'd have to check with Doug Childress. Maybe Steven was safe and sound with his father. If not, she'd get help to find Steven in the snow. Screw Lizzie's threats.

No dust bunnies nested under the bed. April inherited their mother's clean gene, while September got their dad's haphazard style. She reached under the bed and pulled out a small, dark stuffed bear, a surprise since Steven didn't like soft toys. The ears had been chewed off. Huh. *So Shadow spends time in the bedroom with Steven—good deal,* she thought. She'd worried Steven kept the dog at arm's length. A bond better predicted the pup would protect the boy.

The bear's lopsided head showed evidence of sucking. After all, the pup wasn't much more than a baby himself. Shadow's breeder said all the littermates used toys as pacifiers.

September tucked the teddy beneath one arm, and rushed to the bathroom's dirty laundry hamper to pull out a pair of Steven's socks and stuff them into her pocket. She hurried back to the kitchen, located a fresh plastic bag in the mess on the floor, and filled it with the soft dog treats. Next to Shadow's "Service Dog In Training" vest and leash hung April's keys. September grabbed them all.

Her foot hit a hard object that spun off her boot and hit the wall. The pill bottle came to rest beneath the table. Steven's medication. He needed his evening dose, and according to Lizzie, he needed it within that 24-hour deadline. "Please, I'm due some better luck." The whispered plea was the closest she ever came to a prayer anymore. If Steven was still out in the cold, it might be too late for him anyway, but she had to try. Steven had to be her priority. "Forgive me, April." Her sister would agree. "Once he's safe, it's your turn. I promise."

She hurried to the front door. If the bad luck fairies spread it around, Wilma's son would be delayed by the weather long enough for her to get a head start. She dashed out the front door and left it unlocked. Security no longer mattered. She plowed through the snow to reach her car.

It started on the first try. "God bless Volvo." September shoved it into drive, resisting the urge to speed away. The roads doubled as ice rinks. She lifted her foot off the gas and coasted toward the four-way stop at the corner, and let the car's momentum carry her into the turn. She caught her breath at the view in the car's mirror when a police cruiser slowed to a stop outside April's house.

Adrenalin jerked September's hands on the wheel. Her foot stomped the accelerator before she managed to regain some semblance of control. Years of Indiana winter travel prompted the instinctive twist of the wheel into the skid, and she managed to keep the Volvo on the pavement. She white-knuckled the wheel and the car slid to a stop.

"Chris, what do I do?" God, she missed him. Mom would say go back, talk to the police. She wanted to. She had seconds to decide. But it would take time to explain the bizarre story, and Steven had little time to spare. She caught a flash of her reflection and grimaced. The police would never believe her. *She* wouldn't even believe her.

Decision made, September babied the gas and the tires spun, the rear end crabbed sideways a foot and finally caught. She cranked the heater as high as it would go and flexed her hands to warm them. At a steady 25 miles per hour, she rolled through deserted streets without a problem. Sane folks stayed home and off the roads today. That spoke to her own state of mind.

Once she reached a main thoroughfare into town, her speed crept up to 45. September watched for potential pursuit. She needed to check April's office before the police beat her to the punch. After that she would see Doug Childress.

No stone unturned, Chris used to say. She just didn't want anyone she loved to get buried when she started to dig. Not again, not ever again. Not like what happened with Chris. He'd wanted to protect her, and instead she had gotten him killed.

Chapter 10

The big car slid from side to side like a tug toy. Shadow barked and danced forward and away, excited by the motion as much as the notion of a game. It traveled on all fours but didn't act surefooted like a dog. He wondered if it would fall over in the snow the way Steven did.

The car beeped like his bear-toy when he bit it. Then it slid sideways but stayed on the car path.

Shadow held his ground. He would make it stop. He was good at this game. He played dare-you-tag with dogs at the park and they always turned away first. Besides, the car had to stop so Steven could get inside the warm place.

It slid faster. And it beep-beeped and flashed eyes at him, though he didn't see them blink. Maybe it didn't understand? How else to tell it to stop? The twin yellow eye beams caught him full in their glare.

He didn't like the stare. Shadow's hackles rose. His alarm barks turned to snarled warnings to keep away.

It didn't slow. It would hit him—and then who would help his boy? At the last moment he leaped away and yelped when the car clipped his tail.

It didn't stop. It chased Shadow off the car-path.

He tucked his bruised tail and hop-scotched through the snow to stand guard over Steven. He bared his teeth, howled and barked. Spittle flew from his jaws.

The beep-beep hurt a good-dog's ears, like a hurting scream that wouldn't stop. The giant car shoved snow before its flat face, bumped up against the hidden curb, and shivered to a stop.

The door wheezed open and a short bundled figure clambered down the steps. Shadow lowered his head and growled at the stranger.

The woman stepped closer, and called to someone on the bus. "That dog nearly killed himself to get me to stop. In my book, that earns him a ride."

Chapter 11

April glanced sideways at Lizzie. The older woman gripped the steering wheel with fuzzy mittens as she squinted past the thwack-thwack of the windshield wipers.

"Buckle your seatbelt, April. Safety first."

She obediently secured the restraint. The irony wasn't lost on her. Steven wasn't safe. Not by a long shot.

"Tell me where to turn. We'll start at the park and go door to door." Lizzie's sympathetic smile crinkled the corners of her eyes behind her granny glasses. "We'll find Steven, don't you worry. And we'll get him over to the Legacy Center with time to spare, just like Dr. Pottinger explained. He'll be fine."

"Turn here." She prayed Lizzie was right. The car swerved around the corner, the tires spinning before they caught traction. April grabbed the door to steady herself, admitting that more than the car was out of control.

The day had gone south so quickly. Dr. Pottinger's horrible revelation. The blood. Steven lost. At least he'd eaten before he left the house. After she had poured orange juice into the dog's bowl—the silly dog loved the stuff—Steven sipped his own juice. He rocked, shared dry cereal with the dog, and she called Lizzie to clean up the mess.

Oh God, what a mess.

She watched Lizzie, comforted by her confidence and care. Not like her own mother, for whom appearance ranked highest of all. September had not been able to handle the pressure, and fled to Chicago to escape Mom's unrealistic expectations. But April had stayed and not only met them, but exceeded them. The divorce from Doug had been a setback, but she'd make it up to Mom—and it would be worth the heartache—once Steven was cured.

"Thanks for sending help. I didn't know who else to call this morning." April rubbed her bare hands against her coat. They still felt sticky from the blood, although she'd scrubbed for what seemed like hours.

Lizzie shifted the car into a lower gear. "Tragic, just a tragic loss, but there's no going back." She smiled. "The children come first, right? Can't let such an unfortunate accident derail our plans."

Yes, it was an accident. "I can't lose Steven now. He's come so far. Did I tell you, this morning he called me 'Mommy?'" Her heart swelled at that first-ever experience.

Lizzie beamed. "Honey, that's marvelous." Her mittened hand squeezed April's with encouragement. "See, didn't I tell you? Steven will be the child he was born to be. Just trust me, stay on track." She polished fog from the window that the defroster hadn't yet cleared.

April shivered, remembering the morning's heated revelations. "That wasn't true, was it? What Dr. Pottinger said? Steven will be okay if his medicine is a little late. He was exaggerating for effect." Steven had already been off his meds for nearly a day, but Lizzie didn't need to know that. It could have been the argument, not the missed medicine that triggered his stimming.

But Lizzie's tone was stern. "Dear, there's no fudge factor in the twenty-four hours."

"Nobody told me it mattered that much." April couldn't hide her resentment. She should have been told. Now they just had to find Steven. He couldn't have gone far. She rubbed clear a spot on her own window, and watched for the splash of yellow of his coat.

Lizzie shifted the car as they climbed a gentle but slick incline. "Dr. Pottinger cared deeply about you and Steven. He didn't want any back-sliding. That can get ugly, as you discovered." She sighed. "But Pottinger got ahead of himself. The Rebirth Gathering is the right time and place for explanations and persuasions and a careful glimpse into consequences. We've revised the program, so such things won't happen again. But he took matters into his own hands sharing the flash drive. And you can see what it got him."

April stared out the window. It wasn't fair. September didn't need the money. She didn't have a child that needed special care. She ran away from her mistakes. September had only come home to Heartland to hide from her past.

Not like April, who dealt with problems head-on; dealt with September's troubles, too, and transformed what could have been a tragedy into joy. By God, she'd do the same with Steven's treatment. But this time it was September's turn to be the grown up. Funding Steven's treatment was only a start.

Lizzie adjusted the heater. "Any further thoughts on the whereabouts of the flash drive?"

"Maybe it's in Dr. Pottinger's car?"

"Gerald looked. He's very thorough, you know." Lizzie turned on her headlights and set the low beams to help see through the thick snow. "Didn't you say Steven was with his babysitter when he got lost? Where were you?"

"My office." April rubbed her face when she caught a glimpse of her reflection. She needed a total do-over. "I had to change clothes. I couldn't leave those dirty ones in my house, and I keep fresh clothes at work." Burn them, yes, that's what she'd do. Once they found Steven she'd clean up the loose ends. "I told September I had to change the answering machine, and leave a note for clients."

"Well now, that's good to know. I'm sure September will check your office, just in case the flash drive found its way there. Besides, there's still the issue of that email, am I right?"

"Sorry." She emailed everything to herself at work, where she kept all important records. "I can delete it once the Internet server comes back up. Or September can, from my laptop at work. I can call her—"

"The information on that flash drive is proprietary. Only other parents understand. Critics will say what happened today was Steven's fault." She focused on the road "We know different, don't we?"

She'd only been out of the room for thirty seconds. "It's my fault. I'm his mother. But it was an accident." He was a little boy. Steven had no notion of consequences.

Lizzie smiled. "Outsiders could shut down the program. September is still an outsider. Do you really think she'd understand?" She took off her glasses and polished them with a mitten. "It's vital we recover that information."

"Don't worry. September doesn't have to understand." She smiled grimly. "She owes me."

"That's a relief, because the price for Steven's Rebirth Gathering just went up."

"What?" April's stomach flip-flopped. "I said that I'll get my sister to pay—"

"Money doesn't matter. The whole program goes away if that flash drive falls into unsympathetic hands. So Steven's treatment only happens if September returns the flash drive—without looking at what's on it." Lizzie adjusted the glasses back onto her button nose. "It's not just about your son. All those other children need the treatment, too."

Her mouth suddenly dry, April understood that if Steven's cure went away she'd lose her little boy all over again. It was all in September's hands, a woman who had spent her fortune on a fairytale fortress against a boogeyman left behind in Chicago.

"For now, just worry about Steven." Lizzie's tone became soothing. "You've done a good job with him, April. A mother's love is a beautiful thing."

April squared her shoulders. She *was* a good mother. The best. She'd fought Doug's notions, and when he'd balked, she had enlisted Mom and even persuaded September to help Steven become all he was meant to be.

Yes, she'd let September worry about the flash drive. She'd take care of Steven, the way she'd always taken care of him. "There." April pointed up ahead. "That's Gentry Park. We can start with the houses on the same side of the street." Maybe Steven's safe and warm in somebody's house. Her knuckles whitened on the car door handle, eager to begin the search.

"Great, you run up to the door and check. I've got to make a call." Lizzie pulled the car next to the curb in front of the first house, and April unbuckled her seatbelt.

Two blocks away, the yellow HART-line bus backed off the curb, and drove away.

Chapter 12

Officer Jeff Combs stood outside April Childress's house, isolated from the whirlwind of quiet activity. Three patrol cars, an ambulance, and two plainclothes vehicles crowded the drive. The victim had already been pronounced dead, and the evidence team was inside. He'd already seen enough to know nothing he could do would help.

When the stretcher emerged he looked away, wanting to blank out the sight of the shrouded victim. Frozen tears broke loose, dusting sparkles onto his dark coat.

Officer Leonard Pike followed the body down the steps but veered away from the ambulance and headed to him. "I'm off shift, heading out. Sorry about your mom, Combs. We'll get the bastard who did this. The putz has no chance." He clapped the younger man on the back.

Combs gritted his teeth to curb curses. He felt gut punched, and wanted to hit back. He'd seen drug killings, overdoses, child battery, spousal abuse, accidental homicides and planned ones including suicides. The worst of the worst. But nothing compared.

This was his mother.

Mom, who never turned away a stray dog or kid. A woman dedicated to the church prayer chain. Who prayed for absolution for saying "drat" out loud. So proud he'd made detective, yet never spoke of his shame when it was taken away. When Cassie filed for divorce over a disturbed adolescent's fantasies, his mom had never wavered. She convinced her brother Stan to go to bat for him, or he'd not have his badge today.

"You know what's right," she'd always told him, "God won't make you wait too long. Trust yourself, honey."

Mom. Her beautiful red hair matted and stained, her blood splattered against a stranger's living room wall.

Rage shook him like a seizure. Pike reached to steady him, and Combs reflexively swung before he could stop himself. His partner dodged, grabbed and pinned his arms. "Get off. Son-of-a-bitch, let me go." Pike moved well for being so overweight.

"Hey kid, take it easy. Hang on." Pike tightened his hug for a long moment until Combs's struggles stopped. "Okay?" He released his grip and stepped away with a quick gesture toward the still-open front door. "They want to talk to you."

He'd never realized seeing red was literal. Combs took a half-step toward where his mother's body waited in the ambulance.

"Leave her be. For now." It was the first time in six months Pike had showed compassion. He wasn't known to take it easy on himself or anyone else. Pike had troubles in his own life, including a doted on disabled grandson, but he mostly kept such things to himself.

Combs knuckled his eyes. "Sorry, man. And thanks." He'd been an albatross dumped in the old timer's lap. Pike didn't have the clout to object, and didn't want to rock the boat his last year before retirement.

Combs managed to rock everybody's boat without trying. Last year, he and his old partner had built a case against a Cheese factory by getting close to one of the young kids who'd been sucked into the drug life. "Cheese" was slang for a mix of black tar heroin and cold medicine that looked like grated parmesan, and had accounted for countless teen deaths in Dallas since it was first identified in 2005. The thirteen-year-old informant ended up dead, and shortly thereafter, Combs's own career was DOA. He'd become a political hot potato, and Pike made no bones about his opinion of "babysitting duty" as he called it. Now he acted almost human.

"Doty needs you inside. Go talk to the detectives."

Combs straightened, scoured his face with gloved hands, and marched into the house.

The medical examiner hurried out. "Terrible thing, Combs, terrible thing. It was quick, though. The boys will fill you in on my prelim, and we'll find out anything else ASAP. This tops my priority list, Combs. The very top."

Combs nodded, grateful the man hurried away so he didn't need to think of a reply. He wasn't sure how his voice would sound or how long it would hold up. He looked away from the bloodstained sofa that commanded the living room.

"In here, Detec...I mean Officer Combs." Detective Kimberlane Doty, a forty-something blond Amazon with close-cropped hair whispered to her partner, Detective Winston Gonzales, a bantam rooster of a man half her age. They waited in the nearby kitchen.

Great. *The bitch who destroyed my career and her whiz kid protégé get assigned to Mom's murder.* His anger ratcheted up another notch, and he cautioned himself not to let them push his buttons.

Gonzales checked his notepad. "Victim is sixty-three-year-old white female." He looked up. "I understand you found her. Pike called it in at two fifty-seven." He paused, and acknowledged Combs with a chin jerk. "Wilma Combs was your mother. Sorry, man."

Doty broke in. "Why didn't you call it in yourself? And why'd you wait so long to tell Pike?" She ignored her partner's surprise.

Gonzales recovered, his tone apologetic. "We have to ask." Doty's lips tightened but she didn't comment.

Combs gave a slight nod to Gonzales. He appreciated the gesture even if the man had replaced him in the detective lineup. "When nobody answered the door, I looked in the window but couldn't see anything. Too much frost. Tried the door and it wasn't locked, so I came in."

Doty peeled another stick of gum and added it to the wad she chewed. The whole department knew she'd quit smoking a month before. The smell of clove gum combined with blood stench was too much to bear, but she didn't seem to notice or care. "Did you have reason to believe there was a problem?"

"Hell no. She's my mother, babysits here five days a week, and I give her a ride when the weather's bad." He couldn't stand still. He paced from the sink to the small kitchen table and back again. His shoes crunched. He looked down. Dog food and Cheerios. "Today I was late. Twenty-freaking-minutes-late." His foot bopped a one-shoe jig until he consciously planted both feet. Calm down. Be a cop. For Mom. He looked away, unwilling to share his grief, and tried to speak without expression. "The wounds..." He swallowed hard and continued with effort. "Injuries were fresh. No pulse. But she was still warm." Better. He sounded like a professional even if he wanted to scream. Twenty minutes would have made all the difference. Damn the weather, damn the traffic, and damn Pike and his turtle-slow driving!

"What time did you arrive, Officer?" Gonzales maintained a neutral expression and matched Combs's professional tone.

By the book. Doty must have reformed. Combs cracked his knuckles at the sardonic thought, and cautioned himself not to pick further at the scab not yet healed. Screw the past. Only his mom mattered today. He recited the facts, drily, with no inflection. "I looked at my watch when we pulled up. It was two-fifty. I banged on the door for maybe two minutes. No answer. Tried the door and it was open. There was blood everywhere and the place was ransacked. I thought the perp might still be in the house. So I yelled at Pike to secure the outside while I did the inside." He puffed his cheeks and blew out breath, but the tension remained wound tight. "Mom was already gone, so there was no hurry to get her help. Once we cleared the area Pike called it in at two fifty-seven."

"You sure you didn't want to get a head start on the evidence hunt, Officer?" Her tone was mild.

But Combs bristled. "Give me a break, I was a good detective. You know that better than anyone." He'd smack that feral mouth if she said one more word. Why not? His career was over anyway.

"Cool your jets, Combs. Just saying I wouldn't blame you." She shrugged. "Rules are rules, but all bets off if something like that happened to my grandma. She raised me. Nobody messes with my family." Clearly her feelings included relatives of cops.

Combs took a long, shuddery breath. He hadn't expected that. But he'd take it. Just the facts, he told himself. Feed the team. "Pike didn't even come inside. He steered clear of trace. I didn't touch anything—except to check Mom for vitals."

Doty cocked her head and gnawed the end of the pencil, her brown eyes narrowed in thought. "You sure this doesn't have something to do with last year? Coming back to bite you on the butt through your mom?"

Combs winced. "That dog won't hunt, Laney." He wouldn't give her the satisfaction, but he'd had the same thought.

They'd caught two of the three brothers who operated the lab. One was in prison, the other dead. The third had a long memory, if Spider could be believed. Despite the tiny girl's venomous tattoos of her nickname, she'd been terrified of the brothers. "If Ghoul Patrol had something to do with this, they'd want me to know."

Ghoul Patrol. The code name fit the Goth kids. Spider had had a serious case of hero-worship toward him, and Doty had pushed Combs to encourage her. "Young girls always want to feel special," she told him, "so you give her what she wants, and she'll feed us what we need." But Spider didn't tell all her secrets, after all. She reserved her most intimate fantasies—about him—for her diary. *Water under the bridge*, he thought.

Gonzales tapped his pencil on the pad. "Pike found lots of footprints out there, boot prints and tennis shoes, small, maybe a size six." He waited a beat. "A child or a woman. We found similar prints in the front room in the blood."

Combs nodded. "April Childress lives here with her son Steven. Probably their prints. The kid's a little guy, maybe five or six years old I think. Maybe that's why they're both MIA."

"Yeah, the yellow PT Cruiser out front is registered to April Childress." Gonzales made a note. "Funny she left the car if she ran with her kid. Did she call a cab, or get a ride, or what? There's at least three other tire treads out there, besides your patrol car. But I can't see a soccer mom doing the deed, unless it was an accident."

"Naw, the ME said it was up close and personal. Takes a special kind of badass to shoot someone in the face." Doty jerked her chin at Combs. "Assuming your mom was an innocent bystander, my money's on a third party. Single mom, a kid—where's the dad? Custody issue and the victim is collateral damage?"

Gonzales flipped a page on his pad. "Trace found another single muddy print on the hardwood of a man's dress shoe, size ten or eleven. Nothing outside." He looked at Doty. "Maybe it iced up by the time he left."

"Good, that makes more sense." Combs noticed his leg once more jounced to its own rhythm, and he walked a few steps to stop the urge. "Besides, the whole house got trashed. Somebody tossed it and got mad when they couldn't find whatever they were looking for." *Good, good,* he thought, turn thoughts away from that final picture of Mom.

At least Dad wasn't alive to see this. But he'd have to call Uncle Stanley. And his sister, Naomi. Aw shit—between the two of them he'd be pressed hard for constant updates. He couldn't sit on the sidelines, had to be part of it, had to find Mom's killer. He couldn't let his family down again. This was bigger than a ruined reputation. Whatever it took, even suck up to Doty, it'd be worth it to get first crack at the bastard who did this.

He braced himself to eat shit and like it. "Doty, we worked together for what, five years? I won't pretend not to want in on this. Make room on the team." Before she could shoot him down he added, "It's my mother, for Christ's sake."

"Good reason to keep your distance. You know the brass won't authorize that. Hell, they'll put you on administrative leave as soon as they find out." She stared at him, and a slight smile twitched her normal icy expression, and for a moment he thought she might relent. "Even if I wanted to, that's not my call. And after last year you used up any benefit of the doubt."

"You're just covering your ass. Again."

"Bite me." She popped her gum. "Look, Combs, go ahead and hate my guts if it helps. It's my case whether either one of us likes it or not. I want the bastard who did this as much as you. Okay, not as much, but dammit, this is personal for me, too." She looked away, nostrils flared.

She was right. Using Doty as a verbal punching bag wouldn't help find Mom's killer. But he'd be damned if he'd let Doty freeze him out. Whether officially or not, he'd find the killer. He'd nail his balls to the wall.

The phone on the kitchen wall rang. The three looked at each other. Before either detective could react, Combs scooped up the receiver. "Who's speaking please?"

"Hey, there. Just checking in, I was worried about the little guy." The deep male voice boomed so loud, Doty and Gonzales easily heard. "Is September there? This is Humphrey Fish over at the radio station."

Chapter 13

September dropped the keys twice before her numb fingers managed to fit the correct one into the lock. She opened the door and a doorbell beeee-boooped. A hand-lettered CLOSED FOR SNOW taped to the glass corroborated April's morning visit. Shouldn't be too difficult to find her laptop and business files, and learn more about Pottinger. Five minutes, tops, and she'd head over to Doug Childress's place. He lived a few blocks away. She left the keys in the door.

Body Works contained more than a dozen exercise machines in the front mirror-paneled room, with cushioned jog-in-place boards situated in between. It was designed so that members moved from machine to machine, first working upper arms for thirty seconds, shifted to a jog-board for the next thirty seconds, and on to a thigh-master machine, and so on to complete the circuit. It provided a low-impact aerobic workout favored by middle aged and older women, and April had developed a dedicated clientele in the three years since she'd opened. It made sense that she would change the message machine to prevent any wasted trips.

The mirror was not her friend. Unlike April, September rarely wore makeup, but she admitted she looked like eight miles of bad road. She had a case of terminal hat-hair that could use a good brushing.

She found two smaller rooms at the end of the short hallway. One contained a pair of saunas, two showers, and a makeup area and sink, complete with courtesy towels and toiletries. She ached for the sensation of warmth. A sauna would be heaven, but the sink would have to do.

September pulled off her hat and gloves, ran warm water in the sink, added a dollop of coconut-scented wash and submerged her hands in the steamy liquid. Invisible spiders tingled over the blue-tinged flesh. Sensation returned and her fingertips became rosy. She cupped her hands and bent over the sink to splash her face. More soap increased the gentle lather and the pooled water turned pink as the soap stung and felt good at the same time.

Blood stained the white towel when she patted her hands dry. Nose bleed. Great. She held the towel to her nose until it stopped. God, she'd love to spend more time to get warm. She looked with longing at the sauna, gritted her teeth, tossed the towel in the laundry bin and moved on.

A file cabinet, phone and printer crowded the next room, with a laptop on the small desk. Two hand dumbbells served as bookends. An emergency fire exit with an alarm centered the back wall.

She turned on the laptop, tapping her foot as it pinged and sang to itself. She rifled April's file cabinet but found nothing other than client folders filled with contracts, workout plans and contact information. "Damn." She searched the desk calendar for any clue to appointments outside of the store—for a name or a "P" that might indicate the mysterious Dr. Pottinger. The desk was clear, and no flash drive hid within the single drawer. Crap.

April's biweekly hair or nail appointments crowded between infrequent lunch dates with girlfriends or family, mostly with their mom. To be fair, April's social life slowed with Steven's arrival. But compared to September's self-imposed lockdown, April's dance card overflowed.

Most notes had to do with Steven. School stuff, meetings after class three times weekly with a "therapist" she guessed must be Lizzie, and the weekend horseback riding lessons—equine-assisted-therapy. September recalled April's rant about the Texas school systems pressed into mainstreaming special needs kids, and how inadequately trained teachers were stretched too thin to be effective. Funding Steven's therapy helped September feel better about—well, things.

That's how the whole Shadow issue arose. God knew *she* wasn't ready for another dog. Love 'em and they leave you. Dakota was Chris's idea, and she and the big dog had quickly bonded.

It had taken much longer to trust Chris. He had worked for two years to break through her resistance to marriage, but they had six years together before her stalker tracked them down. The boogeyman was still out there, waiting for her. So when April called, she ran home like a cat diving under the bed, hiding from one threat only to run smack into another.

She wondered how April had connected with Lizzie and Pottinger. Maybe there was a computer file or an email.

April subscribed to dozens of e-lists about weight training, weight loss, aerobics, business markets, autism, camera techniques, knitting, and on and on. When not working out or dealing with Steven, her sister sent and received dozens of messages daily. An email filter dumped emails into separate folders. September first tried a search for "Pottinger," and when that didn't work, she input both "Lizzie" and "Lizbeth Baumgarten," and still came up empty. She scanned the most recent subject lines in the filtered list headed "Steven" and found nothing.

She checked the clock on the wall. Time to get out of Dodge.

"Beeee-booop."

September froze. She'd left the keys in the door. She *always* locked doors. Why hadn't she locked the damn door? Please let it be one of April's diehard gym clients ignoring the "closed" sign.

No cheery 'hello' sounded. After a lifetime of silence, September inched forward, heart galloping in rhythm with quickened breath. The police couldn't be here, not so soon.

She closed the laptop and tucked it beneath one arm. As she tiptoed to the doorway, September hugged the wall before peeking around the corner.

There. In the mirror. A man so tall he had to duck to miss the ceiling fan. He wore a bat-black cowboy duster that turned pale skin and silver hair ghostly. Hunching forward, he peered around in a cobra's dance, poised to strike. He drew a pistol. Pulled back the slide to chamber a bullet. Screwed on an attachment to the overlong barrel.

Shit-shit-shit.

September pulled back from her vantage point. She didn't recognize Ghost-Man, and he sure as hell didn't belong in a woman's gym. That wasn't a cop gun. It looked like a .45 semi-automatic. She'd lived with a cop long enough to know, and the silencer was definitely not police issue.

Lizzie must have sent this reject from a spaghetti western. All the killer cared about was the flash drive when Steven had to be September's priority. If Ghost Man killed her now, Steven was good as dead, and so was April.

September frantically scanned the small space. The emergency exit wouldn't work. The alarm painted a target on her back, and the snow hobbled any ability to outrace him. Besides, she had parked right in front of the entrance and left the door unlocked for a quick getaway. Dumb. She should have realized Lizzie wouldn't trust her, and would send one of her goons to finish the job.

She stole another glimpse and jerked back—he was halfway to her hiding place. Her breath quickened. Another three steps and he'd enter the sauna. She could run past the doorway and out the front.

He'll hear. Shoot you in the back.

Damn call-waiting, she should never have answered April's call. Poor Steven, some days it didn't pay to get out of bed, and now it was up to her. If she could get out of here alive. September froze, only her eyes searching for something, anything, a way to distract or slow the Ghost Man so she had a chance to run.

There—the dumbbell bookends.

She dared another peek when he disappeared into the sauna room. *No time, no time* . . . September grabbed a dumbbell, and scurried down the short hall. She plastered her back against the wall beside the sauna doorway. Her breath jittered. She waited, the hand with the dumbbell cocked and ready.

The first door slammed open. "Come out." The next door crashed, echoed its twin. "I know you're here." This room was next. His pistol poked through the door, sniffed for her.

September swung and the dumbbell smacked the heel of his gloved hand. The handgun spiraled away. Shattered the nearest mirror. She dodged and squinted. Mirrored slivers showered a bee sting swarm against her cheek. September stumbled in the slick glass. She fell to one knee. As she struggled to get up, she palmed away tears and blood.

The gun. There, by her foot.

The Ghost Man. He dove for the gun.

September screamed. He grabbed the pistol. She kicked his hand and the gun spun away. His hand wrenched her ankle instead. He twisted and rolled, pulling her with him.

"No!" She belly flopped, and was punched breathless. But by-god she still clutched the dumbbell.

Scrambling, he scooped up the gun.

She flailed, sobbing in fear. Crabbed backwards over crunchy glass and sliced open her palms.

He strangled the throat of her coat. She twisted, flipped onto her back and he was there. He straddled her waist. She stared at the greenish barrel held level with her face. September looked up.

He had a beautiful smile. "Give me the flash drive." His knees pressed against her sides.

She struggled to suck in air.

"Where is it?" He smiled his perfect smile again, and pressed harder.

He patted the outside of her parka, searching the lumpy contents of her pockets. Bloody droplets and mirror shrapnel glittered his hair pink. He leaned close, relaxing the pressure enough for her to suck in a frantic breath. She could smell spicy aftershave. His eyes glowed like white marbles.

"You'd like to breathe again? So we're going into the next room where you'll empty those kangaroo-size pockets—"

September whip-lashed the dumbbell. It hit his temple like a ball bat thwacking a ripe pumpkin.

He dropped. Onto her.

She still couldn't breathe. Black sparkles danced behind her closed eyelids. The hard cold pistol pressed against her throat, snugged between their bodies as intimate as lovers.

She pushed him off and the gun slid to the floor. The dumbbell dripped red.

She filled her lungs at last, and noticed the bloody goose egg that marred his head. September released the dumbbell and it rolled away, crinkling through broken glass. She waited until his chest inflated, and breathed relief mixed with guilty disappointment that he still lived. She picked up the gun, hating the greasy weight. The weapon looked the same as Lizzie's weapon, only with the bonus silencer. He'd meant to kill her. She had to move, get out of here. He could wake at any moment.

She scrambled to her feet, and gasped when pain clawed her side. He'd done something to her side. She set the gun on the desk, grasped the chair with her right hand, and braced her left elbow on her thigh to pull herself erect.

The Ghost Man lay in full view of the glass entry. Best to get him out of sight, maybe confine him somehow, because once he came-to he'd be pissed and come after her with or without the gun. At that thought, she tried to pocket the gun but had to unscrew the silencer to make it fit. Then she grabbed the hem of his long coat and tugged his dead weight the short distance to the nearest sauna. She rolled him beneath the wooden bench, and dashed from the sauna. She slammed the door, jiggled it to be sure it latched, and jammed a flimsy laundry container beneath the handle. It wouldn't hold long, but it was better than nothing.

The movement jostled towels in the laundry basket, revealing a flash of yellow stained with red. Steven always wore yellow. She pulled the terrycloth aside. Beneath the white towels, she found one of April's signature size 4 workout outfits. It was covered with blood.

Chapter 14

Shadow whined and shifted on the floor between his boy's feet. He didn't like the stranger-danger smells in the big car, or the jerky motion when it moved. And his tummy told him dinnertime had come and gone.

He nudged Steven with his nose and whined again. But his boy didn't move. Steven stared out the window at the scenery, silent as when they'd entered.

The old man across the aisle stared. It made Shadow so nervous he yawned, licked his nose and turned away. Even then the man didn't have the good-dog manners to do the same. He reeked of scary-smoke scent, and he whistled when he breathed.

Not like Steven, who breathed quietly and smelled like soap and dog treats and boy-smell.

"Where you headed?" The old man sounded kind even if he did smell like smoke. "I like your dog. Used to have a German shepherd a long time ago. What's his name? My name's Teddy."

Shadow's head jerked up and he stared at the man. But despite the words, he didn't see anything that resembled his teddy bear toy. He yawned again, and averted his eyes in deference to the human, like a polite puppy should.

"Can't you tell me your dog's name? Or your name? I told you mine." The old man plucked some paper from his pocket, folded it, and wiped his nose. "Good dog you got there."

Shadow stopped listening. The stranger hadn't said "treat" or "food" or "play ball" or any other important words that signaled fun stuff. Steven ignored the man, too, and just stared out the window like he always did.

The grown-up's gap-toothed grin showed stained teeth and his breath smelled like onions when he spoke. "Good for you, son. Your momma taught you not to talk to strangers, right? That's good, real good." Teddy scratched the gray stubble peppering his jaw, and it made a gritty noise like a potato chip bag made. Shadow loved salty chips. His tummy growled.

"You're awful young to be on your own out in a snowstorm, even with a great guard dog. Right, pooch? Or are you a service dog? Where's your vest? You're just a pup yourself." His crooning tone reminded Shadow of treat-lady.

Unable to help himself, Shadow offered a tentative wag, signaling an uneasy truce, especially if Teddy offered chips or treats. It wouldn't be polite to refuse treats. Shadow licked his lips.

The big car stopped with a jerk. Shadow scrambled to keep his balance.

The old man sighed and stood up. Shadow's ears twitched at the pop noise in Teddy's knees when he shuffled down the aisle toward the front of the big car. The old man stopped by the tall door to chat with the driver.

Shadow's mouth relaxed into a gentle pant once Teddy moved away. Four other passengers sat near the front of the bus. He and Steven huddled in the last seat. His boy didn't like to be close to other people even if he knew them.

Shadow had never met any of these strangers. They stared, too, but from a distance, so his fur wasn't all prickly.

He watched the people exit one by one down the steps and out the car's funny doorway. Shadow liked that just fine. Car rides should be for dogs and their boys to relax with people they knew. Not for strangers to stare.

Shadow cocked his head when the odd-smelling man didn't get off with the others. Maybe his clicky knees made it hard for him to climb down steps? Their regular car, driven by Steven's mother, only had two seats. Shadow always sat in the back seat behind Steven's mom, and his boy rode next to him. Sometimes treat-lady sat next to Steven's mom in the front, too. All of them just hopped in or out, they didn't have to climb. Shadow watched the old man and the woman driver. Maybe if his own family had as many people in it as hers did, they'd drive a funny big car with steps, too.

"Freda, do you know the boy with the dog?" Teddy's glance brushed them, and Shadow thumped his tail again.

She shrugged. Shadow watched with interest when she pulled a fuzzy hat out of one pocket and tugged it over her short hair. He wondered what else might be in the pockets. Maybe a ball? Or treats?

She turned in her seat, and Shadow heard the cushions squeak. She looked at him.

He stared back for a moment. Fur rose on his back but smoothed down again when she looked away. The door whooshed open, and the old man's knees popped when he got off.

Always before at stops, people got off and new ones got on. Shadow's mouth closed with expectation. He knew they got off at Steven's house. That's how car rides always ended. Shadow's bowl should be filled with food by now. He wished they'd get there soon. His toes ached from the cold.

But this time the lady closed the front door before any new people appeared. Shadow stood up when she waddled down the aisle, turning sideways to fit. She stopped in front of them. "Kid, you've been riding the bus for—" She looked at her wrist. "Close to two hours now. Did you miss your stop or what?"

Shadow wagged and dropped his ears. She smelled good, like French fries and flowers. No smoky smell, and her voice wasn't rough. She didn't sound mad, but you could never be too careful with strangers, so he wriggled his butt. She smiled at him and cut her eyes away. He relaxed at once.

Maybe she'd pet him and call him "good-dog." Right now he'd like that. A good-dog was brave no matter what, so he stood between his boy and the stranger and pretended to be brave just like with the smoky man. When she leaned toward his boy, he woof-whined concern and wagged faster and higher.

She sighed, backed away and sat in a more distant seat. Shadow relaxed, but watched carefully. "I'm not supposed to let dogs on the bus. But I couldn't leave you both out in the cold." She smiled again. "Besides, I like dogs better than most people."

Shadow thumped his tail—she'd said "dog" so she must be speaking about him. Steven stared out the window.

"My shift's over. I wouldn't even be out in this mess, except I started the route before it got bad. I figured you knew where you was going, but maybe not, huh? Teddy's worried."

His head whipped toward her. But she didn't have his bear toy, either.

She waited. Steven didn't answer. "Just tell me where you live, son. Or a phone number so I can call your folks." She'd pulled a palm-sized object out of her pocket and waited expectantly.

Shadow stretched forward and sniffed her pant leg. She had at least two dogs of her own. He wondered if she ever called them good-dogs and rubbed their tummies. Or maybe fed them French fries?

"Steven Childress, thirty-three Bois D'Arc, Heartland Texas 903-555-6824." His boy sing-songed the words so quickly, the woman gasped with surprise.

"Well now, Steven, is it?" She smiled, and stood up. "Thanks for telling me, son. I'll call the number, okay?"

Shadow cocked his head when her body stiffened. Caution colored her words. Big-humans often changed the way they treated his boy after being with him. He wondered why.

***

"Am I speaking to Mrs. Childress?"

"You've dialed April Childress's cell phone. Who's this, please?"

"Freda Tybalt. I'm a bus driver for HART-Line services, and well, I've got your son and dog with me. Steven's been riding for the last couple hours."

"Thank God. We've looked everywhere for that little dickens. He's autistic, you know, wandered away in the storm. Where are you?"

"Here's the deal, Mrs. Childress. I'm at the Star Mall, my shift is over, and the next driver takes the bus on from here. But I'm late because of the ice. Dispatch says they're shutting down the runs for the rest of the day."

"I'll come to you. Be there in two shakes. Could you wait in your car if the bus has to leave? I'll pay you for your trouble, Ms. Tybalt—er, Freda."

"Naw, don't need no reward. I should have realized he was joy-riding earlier. But I had my hands full with the roads today, if you get my drift. Pun intended." She chuckled.

"Don't want to put you out, but I'd sure be obliged."

"It's no trouble to wait. I get something for dinner or snack before I head home. But my VW won't accommodate the dog, boy and big ol' me." She paused. "Probably some of the stores are closed but they'd keep the mall open. My friend Teddy is inside."

"You tell me. I'll meet you wherever."

"Okay, meet us at the mall. We'll wait at the north entrance, in the food court. I'll even treat the boy and his dog to French fries. How's that?"

"Perfect. Thanks again, Freda. I'll be there quick as I can. Sending my, uh, the boy's father. We'll insist on rewarding you appropriately."

Lizzie sat back in the car and hung up April's cell phone. She dimpled with relief. Outside the car, April plodded through the snow to knock on the front door of the next house. They'd already covered two blocks up from Gentry Park.

But April didn't need to know just yet that Steven had been found. The continued search kept April occupied until they could retrieve Steven and get him the treatment he deserved. She'd threatened to withhold the medication, sure—that's the way the game was played. But Steven was an innocent, and she couldn't punish him for the stupidity of his mother. Or his aunt. No matter what, the children's well-being came first. That was her mission, her life's calling. Nothing would stop that mission of mercy.

But Gerald was at April's Body Works to get her laptop. She needed to send someone trustworthy to collect Steven.

Who to send? Someone who wouldn't question. Someone who needed money—no, better than money. A parent who couldn't otherwise afford a miracle for a child. The answer came immediately, she knew just who to call. Lizzie smiled, and dialed the phone number.

Chapter 15

September downshifted, tires spinning as she sped away from Body Works. She wanted to curl up and hibernate for oh, about thirty years, and never think about snow or killers or guns—or little boys lost in the snow—ever again. But her hand's sense memory relived the dull "thwack" made by the dumbbell against Ghost Man's head. She clenched the steering wheel to still the tremors that rendered her already numb fingers even less effective.

"Think, get your brain in gear, and think." Blood seeped from the peppered shards of glass down one cheek. Luckily they'd missed her eyes. She drew close to the mirror to pluck a bright splinter from her brow and a hot wet thread tickled down. She palmed it away.

"Find Steven." Saying it aloud helped focus her blurry thoughts. "Then search the laptop for something, anything that can help." The computer sat in the passenger's seat next to Shadow's stuffed bear toy. She'd wadded April's bloody clothes and dropped them on the floor of the car. The clothes had to be the reason April hadn't called the police. September couldn't risk Ghost Man or anyone else finding the incriminating clothes until Steven was safe. What if the blood was Steven's? A sinking feeling made her clutch the steering wheel to keep her balance. No, she couldn't, she *wouldn't* think that way.

September pulled out her cell phone, scrolled through the programmed numbers until she found Pam, and dialed. "Please be there, please please please."

"Hullo, what's shakin', September?" The woman laughed. "Lordy, I love this new caller ID thing. How's the wonder-pup?" September could hear barking in the background.

"Afraid you were in Houston."

"Naw, the tracking trial isn't until the end of the month." The background barks increased. "Heike, Uschi, hush girls. I can't hear myself think." The barks calmed and finally stopped. "Sorry about that. I had to bring 'em inside. I've got Bruno in the garage with the two young ones, Uschi's in the kitchen with her babies, and Heike's due to whelp in another week. She's ready to pop, may go at any time."

Then it would have to be the old-timer, Bruno. The two bitches tracked better, but Pam wouldn't take them out when they had pups. And the young dogs, littermates of Shadow, barely had their noses wet in tracking. She took a breath. "I've got a huge favor to ask, Pam."

"Sure, what's up? Eugene's stuck at that veterinary conference. He finished his lectures yesterday but they grounded all flights so I'm twiddling my thumbs." She laughed again, a contagious bellow that was surprising from the slight woman. "He's going to miss our thirtieth anniversary dinner tonight, so I'm treating myself to lobster without him. I imagine he's hanging out with the other internists debating how to resolve the latest controversy over hot rum toddies."

September began to see a car here and there on the streets. "I've got a tracking challenge for you."

"Oooh, sounds fun! But in this weather?" Pam made a raspberry with her lips. "The girls won't like that. You know I can't risk Heike. And Freda's pups are two weeks old; I don't want her away from them."

"What about Bruno?" *Please, please, please*, September thought, she had to help. "I wouldn't ask but it's a matter of—well, life-and-death sounds dramatic, doesn't it?" She tried to laugh but it sounded as pathetic as she felt. She was no actress, but the less Pam knew, the safer she'd be, especially with crazies like Ghost Man lurking. "Shadow got out. I tracked him as far as Gentry Park before the snow erased sign." That, at least, was the truth.

"What? Did that dingbat sister of yours—"

"No, it's not April's fault." September cut off Pam's angry words. There wasn't time to explain.

"Bruno's retired. Besides, he's certified in human tracking. I've never trained a dog to track another dog, have you?"

"He's got a ninety-four percent find rank. It's the best shot we've got. I collected Shadow's stuffed toy and a couple of Steven's dirty socks." She slowed as a car passed. "A dog can generalize to the target scent. Bruno's savvy enough to make that leap."

Pam sighed. "I keep waiting for the punch line. You're not telling me everything."

September remained quiet.

"You've not spouted a single pun or wise-ass comment. What's really going on?" She gasped with understanding. "It's Steven, isn't it? That's what this is about if you have his socks. Am I right?"

"Pam, will you please bring out Bruno, give it a try? Please."

"I get it, say no more. You want to try before going Amber Alert. Maybe you don't want CPS involved, or you think April's ex snatched him or something. I don't need to know, long as you've got something for Bruno's old nose to snort."

September nearly cried with relief. "Thank you. I owe you big time."

"Yes, you do." Pam's good humor was colored by concern, but she still tried to lighten the mood. "Spring for a bottle of Merlot and we'll call it even. I'll expect you to give me all the dirty details when we guzzle that bottle together later tonight. Deal?"

"Deal." September coasted into the intersection. Traffic lights flashed a yellow caution so she didn't risk the brake. She could see Doug's townhouse halfway up the next block.

"I'll meet you at Gentry Park. It'll take me at least twenty or thirty minutes to get Bruno ready and slip and slide over to the park. Hopefully we can make it before the light goes. The dark won't matter to Bruno, but I sort of like to see where I'm going."

"Pam, you're a life saver." Please God, let that be true.

A half hour gave her time to check with Steven's father. April's ex sometimes acted like a jerk, but he loved Steven. And if he didn't have the little boy with him, he deserved to know about Steven's disappearance.

She drove past Doug's building. Parking spots were full except for one. The cops would want to talk to Childress if they hadn't already, and she didn't want her car to be seen when they showed up. She rounded the block, and parked in the rear next to the dumpster, right below the fire escape in the only available space. By the look of the mounded snow, the other cars hadn't moved in hours. Only the one next to hers had a semi-clean windshield. She recognized Doug's white corvette in one of the coveted covered parking spots. Good, he must be home.

Hell, maybe Pottinger was with him. He and April argued about Steven's treatment, and that's why she'd ended up helping out with the funding. That'd be luck unchained, to find the boy and the mysterious Pottinger at the same time. Folks said she was born under a lucky star—yeah, right—but this was different than a damn scratch-off game. Or the insurance policy she'd never wanted, or known about, until Chris was killed.

She checked the mirror again. Her swollen face looked lopsided. Blood crusted her forehead. September tugged her hat down, and poked coffee-colored hair beneath out of sight. Careful not to ding the car next to hers, she opened the door to scoop a handful of clean snow and scrubbed away the blood. She gritted her teeth but the numbness relieved the ache. She checked the side mirror and noted the improvement. Her flushed face just looked like a casualty of the weather.

September slogged to the rear entrance of the apartment building, jerked open the common entry, and found the elevator. Doug lived on the top floor five flights up. Thank God the building still allowed unannounced visitors. The mailboxes at the front weren't marked, so she had a fifty-fifty shot to guess which of the two top apartments he'd chosen.

A wide hallway split the floor in half. The large window at each end of the hall overlooked the dumpster and her car at the back, and office buildings and street at the front side. Doug would stroke out over the dumpster view, so she chose the front apartment, rang the bell and waited.

"Hold on, I'm on the phone."

September's jaw tightened. If he eyeballed her through the peephole he might turn her away.

"Doug, it's me, September." She buzzed the bell again. "I have to talk to you. Only take a minute."

The door swung wide, Doug Childress blocking the doorway, cell phone in one hand. Bright blue eyes nailed her from beneath groomed sandy brows. He was a perfect Ken doll to April's Barbie. "What do you want?"

She peered past him, hoping to see good news, but the living room was empty. No sign of Steven anywhere, even though she knew he got visitation each week.

"I heard you moved back. Sorry for your loss. But hey, at least you're set for life with the money, eh? Silver lining and all that."

Her nostrils flared. Yep, he was still an asshole. "Let me in."

He grudgingly moved aside, and waited for her to enter. "Not much warmer in here. The cold caught everyone by surprise, and it takes time to heat these rooms."

The living area boasted ten-foot ceilings, decorative columns and floor-to-ceiling windows facing the street. One corner held a desk and laptop, and another a big screen television opposite a hunter green leather sofa and chair group. The marble entry spilled into the kitchen side of the room, divided from the living area by a walnut counter. Hardwood floors covered by sumptuous oriental carpets—real ones, not fake like April's missing one— gave the room the air of a showroom.

September wasn't at all surprised. The man had always been as polished as his home, from cashmere sweater to alligator shoes. A decorator's dream, straight out of a magazine spread and just as real, with no room for sticky hands or imperfect kids. The glamor had dazzled April until Baby Steven's diagnosis spoiled Doug's ideal family portrait. April had been trying to retouch the picture ever since, until she finally gave up and cropped him out of the frame.

"What do you want?" He stood at the open door, inference clear.

"Have you heard from April?" September noted the small hallway. Steven might be there.

"Wipe your feet, would you?" Doug closed the front door with an exaggerated sigh. "No, I haven't heard from April. What's she done now?" He motioned with the cell phone toward his desk. "Hurry up. I've got work to do."

"When was the last time you saw Steven?"

"Last weekend for my regular visitation. Why?" He switched off the news channel on the widescreen. "What's this about?"

Maybe Steven was hidden away in a back bedroom. She strode toward the hallway.

Doug blocked her. "Why are you here? What's with the questions about Steven?" His puzzlement changed to aggravation and she stopped, realizing the boy wasn't there.

She noticed the laptop on the nearby desk, and took a closer look. No flash drive was in use, but there were several fliers that had to do with autism. She picked up one. "Meeting Dr. Pottinger? Any promotional flash drive to review?"

He stiffened. "Who? What the hell are you talking about?"

He knew the name. His body language told a different story even if he denied it. But what could she gain by challenging him, since Pottinger wasn't here? Short of knocking him down and searching the premises there was no way to find the flash drive even if it was here.

"Isn't Steven with April?" At her expression, Doug uncrossed his arms and stepped close. "Isn't he?"

It had been a wasted trip, ten minutes lost that she could have been searching for Steven at the park. Childress knew nothing about Steven's disappearance. September crossed to the windows to hide her worry and figure out what to say without further endangering April.

Childress crossed to September in three quick strides, agitation clear. "Answer me. Where is my son?"

The quiet street five floors below suddenly bustled with activity. Two cars, one a black and white, double-parked out front. A uniformed officer got out of the patrol car, and a short man and tall woman in plainclothes emerged from the other.

September whirled and dashed toward the door.

Childress stared out the window. "Why are the police here? It's about Steven, isn't it? What's happened to my boy?"

She rushed back, grabbed his arms, and shook him. "Steven's fine. I promise." She looked away, praying he didn't hear the lie in her voice. "But April's in danger. You have to help me." The police would be here any minute.

"Help you do what?" He shook her off. "Where is my son?"

"Stall the police, just long enough that I can get away and reach April." She squeezed his arm. "Helping April is helping Steven, do you understand? Will you help me?"

She didn't wait for his assent. He'd either help or he wouldn't. She dodged out the door and turned toward the elevator and noticed the indicator light showed its slow climb from the first floor. The police were already on their way up. She looked left and right for a way out. There, at the end of the short hall the EXIT sign flashed over the doorway. She bolted. Snatched open the stairwell door. Took two seconds to look back.

Doug watched, his cell phone clutched tight, his face white.

She held the door and tried one last time. "You've always been a button-down jerk. For once in your life, don't worry about how it affects you. Do something for somebody else. Not for me. But if you ever loved April, if you love your son now, trust me."

"What have you done?" He didn't bother to hide his dislike.

"Stall the police." She paused. "Please, Doug. Help me help Steven and my sister." She didn't hide her desperation.

He hesitated, and then made up his mind. "Get out of here. Before I change my mind."

She nodded and dodged through the doorway, loping down the steps three at a time. She banged out the stairwell door into the common area, and skidded to a stop. With studied restraint she strolled out the rear exit when she wanted to race for the car. The snow had slowed but the wind picked up, driving icy needles into her exposed skin. September looked up, fully expecting to see Childress or one of Heartland's finest watching through the fire escape window.

The snow had crusted the passenger door of her Volvo and sealed it shut. September tugged hard before it sprang open, banging into the adjacent car and jarring snow off the passenger window. Less than a minute had passed since her mad dash down the stairwell. She climbed into the car, hands shaking as she started the engine, backed out, and drove away as fast as the slick roads would allow.

Her phone rang. She took the call without checking the screen. "What?"

"Mark's jazzed about the corn chowder." Mom, again. "But he doesn't have a big enough bowl to serve from. Do you still have that ceramic tureen? Remember, that monstrous thing he made in college throwing clay around, or whatever it's called, before he got into the glass artsy stuff?" She waited. "September, are you there?" Her voice sharpened. "What's the matter? Where are you?"

"Just leaving Doug's place." Too much information. She immediately wished she could take back the words.

Mom tongue-clucked. "You didn't invite him to Thanksgiving, did you? April won't be happy."

"Forget Thanksgiving for a minute, will you?" She wanted to cry. Mom didn't have a clue. And she couldn't tell her.

"Oh honey, I knew it would be too much for you. I'll bring the oysters, Mark has his corn chowder and April can do the turkey. We'll do carry-in, it'll be fun." The told-you-so remained unspoken but obvious. Mom thrived on being right.

"Stop it. I don't have time for this. I'll explain later." September disconnected, and knew she'd pay for it later. But now it didn't matter.

Doug didn't have Steven. He wouldn't speak about Dr. Pottinger. But for sure he'd talk to the police, now that she'd stirred up his suspicions. "Crap, crap, crap." She pounded the steering wheel. He wouldn't be able to stall the cops for long once he realized Steven was gone. She should have listened to April and never gone to him.

April didn't want the police involved because something bad had happened this morning. Her clothes didn't get bloody by themselves. Tears spilled down September's cheeks in two scalding paths. It was the only warmth she'd felt all day.

September wished she knew how to fix this mess. Maybe she should have asked Mom. Rose January always had the right answers, and she'd tell you so herself. She just had to suck it up.

Just meet Pam at Gentry Park, and hope Bruno could lead them to Steven before he froze.

Chapter 16

Claire O'Dell braced herself when the church bus bumped through the intersection. They'd made good time until the past hour when the promised snow appeared. Even though Illinois highway crews kept the roads plowed, sanded and salted all along I-88, whiteout conditions created by wind gusts slowed progress to a crawl once they reached Des Moines. They'd been lucky I-35 South remained open.

For this leg of the journey Elaine drove the bus while her husband kept tabs on their son Lenny. The old vehicle wheezed and rattled when it idled, and the driver's side window refused to seal. Elaine's tattered coat snugged close to fend off the bitter draft and her faded muffler, matching fuzzy hat and gloves turned her into a pudgy, gray Michelin Man.

Claire sat two seats behind the driver's seat across the aisle from Elaine's husband Dwayne and their son Lenny. She wondered how they could afford the fee on a clergyman's salary. Elaine couldn't work outside the home, not when Lenny was Elaine's full-time job.

Caring for Tracy also kept Claire homebound, and she didn't begrudge giving up her career. It's what parents do for their kids, after all. After this trip, once the treatment took effect, all of that would change. It wasn't only a new life for Tracy. It would be a new life of exciting opportunities for them all. Maybe she could go back to teaching, at least part-time . . .

Tracy sat next to the window, both palms flat against the fogged glass. Every few minutes she puffed out her breath to melt the frost and then drew concentric circles on the smooth surface until it froze once more. Puff-puff-puff, draw. Puff-puff-puff, draw. Her eyes flickered now and then but otherwise ignored anything or anyone around her. A bump rocked the vehicle and Tracy swayed and her head thumped the glass. She blinked. Then, puff-puff-puff, draw . . .

Claire breathed again; relieved Tracy hadn't crumbled into a screaming mess. She'd been surprisingly calm thus far on the trip. But Claire's own nerves remained raw, and not just from the anticipation of the unknown that lay ahead.

The roads had become treacherous. At each pit stop—and there were many bathroom rests needed with the nine children on board—Claire held her breath, hoping the hamster-wheel tire spin would keep the bus on the road. They couldn't afford delays, car damage or Triple-A.

As if on cue, a childish voice at the back of the bus sing-songed a demand. "Potty-potty-potty. Potty-potty-potty."

Tracy stirred beside Claire.

The chant was taken up by two more voices, followed by an adult's calm attempt to diffuse the growing clamor.

"Do you need the toilet?" Claire didn't touch Tracy, but offered the question as a means for her daughter to focus on something other than the disturbance at the back of the vehicle. Tracy's puff-puff, finger-swirl tempo increased, her agitation clear. "Tracy, you draw so well. Draw me another circle, honey." Claire kept her tone deliberate, just-the-facts to encourage her daughter to focus.

"Potty-potty-potty! Potty-potty-potty!" The volume grew. Across the aisle, Lenny added his adolescent voice to the chant, while Pastor Dwayne spoke with quiet intensity into his son's ear.

"We'll pull over at the next exit. Two or three minutes tops, hang on, kids." Elaine's conciliatory words did little to calm the growing unrest. Claire knew the comment was more for the parents than the children, and she heard murmured encouragement from the adults.

Tracy's breathing quickened. She began to rock.

"Oh, no . . ." Claire quickly pulled out the lumpy dinosaur toy from the carryall she'd stuffed beneath the seat. "Grooby needs you. Do you want me to sing a song to Grooby?"

Tracy rocked.

Claire rummaged further inside the carryall for the purple crocheted throw. Maybe if she could get Tracy swaddled quickly, she could head off the episode.

The bus swerved to the right, bearing down the off-ramp so quickly that Claire caught herself and had to brace against the seat ahead. Tracy's forehead made contact with the window again. She began to rock faster, each forward motion thumping her head against the glass while her keening protest grew in volume. The frosted surface shivered with each impact. Claire fought to regain her balance. It was too late to stop the tantrum. The purple throw could contain Tracy, though, and protect her daughter's head if she could get it around her.

"Potty-potty-potty!"

"Eeeiiiiiii . . ." Tracy's nails-on-chalkboard cry traveled two octaves, punctuated by the head-thumping percussion Claire feared would crack the window, her daughter's skin, or both. As the bus shuddered to a stop outside the service station, Claire dropped a double layer of the purple fabric over Tracy's shoulders and arms, holding extra as padding against the window. Immediately Tracy's screams redoubled, but the rocking transformed to side-to-side head flails, eliminating the battering. Claire pulled the fabric into a makeshift hood, and the dark color muffled both sight and sound as the other chanting children were escorted off the bus.

Pastor Dwayne urged Lenny down the steps and paused to speak to his wife before he got off. "Can I get you anything, honey?" He leaned to give a brief kiss to Elaine.

"Coffee with cream, no sugar." Elaine turned in her seat. "Want anything, Claire? Something for Tracy?"

Claire nodded and spoke loudly over the keening. "Apple juice, thanks. And black coffee for me." She smiled weakly; still careful to dodge Tracy's thrashing head.

Once gone, Tracy's cries slowly lost their edge, and finally trailed off into silence. Her stimming continued while Claire braced the movement and prevented further self-battering.

A cell phone tweedled, and Claire flinched before she realized it belonged to Elaine.

Elaine looked at the display and her eyes widened with surprise. "It's the Legacy Center." She thumbed the device, and answered with caution.

Claire held her breath as she rocked with Tracy in the purple comforter, her emotions mixed. She hated the tantrums. But the brief spells after blow ups offered the only time she could touch Tracy with impunity. Rocking Tracy felt like a normal mother-child relationship, even though Claire suspected she gained more comfort from the situation than did Tracy.

"They haven't canceled the Rebirth Gathering, have they?" She'd be devastated if that happened after going to such lengths to arrive on time.

Elaine shook her head, and a smile covered her face. "Thank you so much. Yes, I'll have Dwayne call his dad immediately. It's a miracle!" She hung up the phone.

"What?" Claire felt Tracy slump against her, and fought the urge to hug the child. "A miracle? What happened? Is it postponed? Delayed? Do we have more time to get there?"

"They're deferring payment for Lenny's Rebirth Gathering. It's an answer to our prayers." Elaine wiped happy tears from her face. She glanced out the window and waved at Dwayne as he duck-walked on the icy pavement to escort their son back to the bus. The other children and parents straggled behind.

Claire squelched sudden jealousy. "I didn't know they did that. How lucky for you."

Dwayne climbed back onto the bus and traded places with his wife in the driver's seat. Elaine handed him the phone. "The Legacy Center called. They've got a security job in exchange for Lenny's treatment. Know anyone who could handle that?" She beamed.

"Really?" He crossed himself. "Thanks be to God. I'll call Dad."

Chapter 17

Officer Jeff Combs stood in the back of the elevator, Detectives Doty and Gonzales poised to rush ahead. They hadn't wanted to include Combs in this go-see with Doug Childress.

Doty changed her mind once he shared the phone call information from radio host Humphrey Fish. She had known if she shut him out completely, he'd do his own investigation, and admitted she'd do the same thing in his place. But Doty couldn't risk muddy waters, so he had to walk a fine line. Until they got word from upstairs, he'd keep sniffing around. And if the brass tried to sideline him, he'd take a leave of absence or quit to stay in the game.

"We do all the talking." She popped her gum. "Don't take advantage. You're not yet officially on a leave of absence, and not a part of the investigation. This is a one-time favor out of respect for your loss. Don't make me sorry I cut you some slack."

Combs nodded. "You're generous to a fault."

Gonzales smiled and quickly covered it with a cough.

The elevator opened before Doty could retort. She checked both directions, and marched to the man standing in the open apartment door. "I'm looking for Doug Childress. That you?"

Childress pocketed his cell phone. "What can I do for you?"

"I'm Detective Kimberlane Doty. This is my partner, Detective Winston Gonzales." She didn't bother to introduce Combs, but the slight didn't matter to him. He was here, that was enough.

Doty showed her badge when Gonzales approached and presented his own credentials. "We're investigating a homicide. Let's go inside, we have some questions for you." She didn't wait for permission, simply elbowed past Childress to the center of his living room, and Gonzales followed.

Childress didn't object. But he grabbed the door as if to counter the verbal punch. The word "homicide" had that effect on most people.

Doty counted on that reaction. She hadn't changed her brash approach; she still bulldozed her way through the job. Combs preferred a more subtle approach, and wondered how Gonzales liked the partnership. Combs waited for Childress to go ahead, following him silently into the room and shutting the door.

Doty took the lead. "We're looking for your wife, April Childress."

"Ex-wife." Childress approached the desk, tapped the keyboard of the open laptop, and closed the cover.

Doty bared her teeth in what passed for a smile. "Ex-wife, right. Do you happen to know where we can find her?"

Childress folded his arms. "April should be home. Or at work. What's she got to do with a homicide?"

"Have a seat, Mr. Childress." Doty waited until the man perched on the edge of an overstuffed leather chair. She sat opposite him on a matched settee.

Childress leaned back and crossed his legs in a calculated effort to appear calm. But his foot bounced until he grabbed his ankle to stop it.

Gonzales ran a finger across the spotless glass top table in front of Childress as though checking for dust. "Nice furniture. You have maid service? My wife would kill for something like this."

Combs smiled his approval. Childress was a detail man. The furniture gleamed, the pricy rugs shone jewel-bright. Even the desk's clutter looked organized. Childress was careful, and that would color his answers.

Doty aimed a "give me a break" look at Gonzales that would have wounded a lesser man, and then shined a high-wattage smile at Childress. "Where can we find your *ex*-wife?" She emphasized the "ex." "Do you have her cell number?"

Typical Doty. She rabbited through work with little regard for careful reflection. She concentrated on the big picture and missed details that mattered. For instance, why had Childress shut down his computer? Perhaps he had something to hide.

"She changed her cell number, it's unlisted now. She didn't want me to have it." Childress wrinkled his nose as though to a bad smell. "What's all this about? I have real work to do, as I'm sure you do as well, so if we can speed this up . . ."

Her smile slipped. "Steven's babysitter got shot in April's house. We want to talk to April. So we're asking."

"Oh my god, the babysitter?" Childress bounded to his feet. "What about my son? Is Steven all right?"

"We have no reason to believe Steven's in any danger. Do you think he'd be with your wife?" Doty's expression conveyed skepticism despite the earnest tone.

"What happened?" His hands clenched as he went toe-to-toe with Doty, but she didn't flinch.

Gonzales urged him back to the chair. "Sit down, Mr. Childress, you're understandably upset. But we're doing everything we can to find your son and ex-wife. We need your help."

Childress fell into the seat, stiff and unyielding. "I don't know where April is. How could she let something like this happen? She's changed." He paused. "Do you have kids? It changes things."

"Yep, I've got an eight-year-old boy and twin girls, who are four," said Gonzales.

Combs stepped forward. "You're right. Kids change everything." Find common ground with the man to build empathy and they'd make headway more quickly.

"I lost my wife the day Steven was born." His mournful tone seemed out of character with the earlier bluster. "You think I'm a monster, but that's the truth."

"Why is that?" Gonzales leaned forward, sympathetic. Damn, he was good.

"I love my son. I really do. I wanted that little boy more than life itself. But April and I argued all the time about the way he is damaged, and how to deal with his . . . issues. I still take care of him, I'm still his father." He took a shuddering breath. "You've got to find him."

"The way he is? You mean autistic?" Combs fell silent when Doty raised her eyebrows, reminding him of their deal. But he couldn't help thinking of his own kids, and his throat tightened. Melinda at twelve was a chubby miniature of her redheaded mother with a temper to match. Sensitive William, so much like his murdered grandmother, acted like he was nine going on forty. If either of his kids had been "damaged" like Steven, he couldn't imagine loving them any less.

Doty made a note, and looked over at Gonzales. "Pike's grandson is autistic. That's tough to deal with."

Childress picked a spot of lint off his trousers, adjusted his tie and squared his shoulders, the actions clearly designed to regain control. "Nothing like that in my family. It's her family's crazy DNA or something that scrambled Steven's brains." He stopped. "That's not what I mean…that sounds harsh. I don't know what I'm saying. April's a good mother. She'd do anything for Steven. Hell, so would I." He hunched forward in the chair. "Is that how the babysitter got killed? Did she step over the line with my son? April turns into a barracuda about Steven. As long as he's with his mother, he'll be fine." The last sentence served to convince him as much as them.

Dotty gave a slight head shake in Combs's direction. He gritted his teeth instead of smacking Childress, and waited for her answer for the team. "We aren't sure what happened. April's car is still at the house."

"The PT Cruiser? I got that for Steven. He loves yellow." He rubbed his temples. "She didn't take her car?"

Doty pressed for answers. "Mr. Childress, is there somebody April would call, somewhere she'd go for help? She may not have even been home at the time."

Childress started, and leaned forward. "You mean Steven might not be with her?" He blanched, suddenly matching the tapioca color of his sweater.

Gonzales held out his hands palms up in a "who knows?" gesture.

"I need a drink." Childress jumped to his feet again, and hurried to the kitchen, opened a cabinet, grabbed a bottle of scotch, and poured. He emptied the glass in two swallows. Without pause, he poured again and this time cradled the glass like a toddler with a binky. "Want some? It's early, but what the hell."

Doty's sour expression declined for all of them.

"You think someone kidnapped Steven? Was there a ransom note or something? Is that what this is about?" He drank again, and topped off the glass. "I mean, I do okay and I've got some investments. Maybe a hundred thousand liquid, but the rest is tied up. What are you doing to find my son?" Childress returned to the living area and settled on the arm of the chair.

"What about April? Does she have the finances?"

Childress laughed a high pitched nervous sound. "Hardly. I pay child support, and she got the house in the settlement. She has her own business, an exercise place. Can you believe it?" He rolled his eyes. "Just what I want my wife doing, dressing up in spandex and prancing in front of a bunch of fat old women. She opened the place after we split." He sipped again and some of the drink sloshed onto his knee, though he didn't seem to notice or care. "I'd never have allowed it."

So he's a control freak, wants a perfect wife and kid, and gets pissy when real life throws curves. "What's the name and address of the business?" To hell with hanging back, they needed to get moving on this. Doty said nothing, giving tacit approval.

"Body Works. Don't know the address, but it's somewhere near here. I never visited even though I'm told it's a nice location, I'll give her that. I've got the phone saved, that one's listed." He pulled out his cell phone, played with the buttons, and gave them the number.

Gonzales's mustache twitched as he jotted down the information. "We need to contact the phone company, get the records of calls to and from her number. If April's on the run, she may contact family or friends."

"September. That's what she meant." Childress whirled to confront the detectives. "April's sister September, they're tight."

"You think they might be together?" Doty made another note. "Where do I find September? What's her last name?"

Combs answered for Childress. "September Day. I saw her this morning. She's renovated the old Ulrich place, that historic brick monstrosity at the top of the hill on Rabbit Run Road. The renovations had to set her back a bundle."

Gonzales frowned. "You know her?"

He shook his head. "We'd just handled a fender bender this morning, and Pike noticed smoke at her house. Turned out to be nothing. But September got rid of us fast, said she had a busy day."

"You got to be kidding me." Doty gnawed her pencil, sighed and made the note. "September and April. Last name January?"

"You don't understand. She was just here looking for April." Childress rolled the cold glass against his forehead. "She promised me Steven was okay."

"Wait. She was here?" Doty's face turned red.

Ice clinked in the glass when he nodded. "She saw you out the front window and begged me to stay quiet, that it would help April. Crazy stuff."

Combs stalked toward the man. "She asked you to stall the police? And you agreed to obstruct a police investigation?"

Childress flinched. "I didn't know there was any investigation. She promised me Steven was okay, but said April was in trouble. She looked like she'd been in fight."

Doty hurried to the door. "Officer Combs, stay here with Detective Gonzales. Finish up with anything we've not covered." Her jaw tightened. "Which way did September…Day, is it? Which way did she go?"

Childress scooted to sit on the edge of the chair when Combs backed away. "You were coming up the elevator so she took the stairwell down. Leads to the back exit." He stood, wobbling before he caught his balance with a hand on the chair. "She must be parked back there if you didn't see her out front."

Glaring at him, Doty rushed out the door.

"You'll find Steven, right?" Childress finally noticed the stain on his trousers. "I need to change." He started toward the hallway and paused to check the time again.

Gonzales followed and reached up to pat Childress on the back. "Have a seat. We're not finished."

"What? I told you everything. You should be out finding Steven." Childress returned to the armchair and this time sank into it like a deflated balloon. "What am I going to do?"

"You're going to relax, take a breath, and tell us everything September said." Gonzales didn't say a word when Combs joined him.

Childress pulled at his tie as he gathered his thoughts. "She was looking for somebody, some weird name. And wanted to know if I had Steven." He focused on Combs. "Do you think that was just to throw me off, to confuse things?"

"Steven wasn't with her?" Combs watched as Gonzales took notes.

"Of course not." His tone was clipped, angry at the notion. "Like I already told you. She wanted a head start, didn't want to get caught up with your questions. Said it would help April and maybe Steven, too."

Doty burst into the room. "There's another body. I called for backup."

Childress sucked in a breath. "Steven?"

"There's a car by the dumpster, a body inside." She advanced on Childress, and he shrank backwards into the chair until it nearly swallowed him. "What the hell is your family involved in? That makes two in one day."

"Where's my son?" Childress's jaw worked as his fingers clawed the soft arms of the chair.

Doty took pity. "Victim's an adult male."

A relieved sob hiccupped in his throat.

"I didn't want to disturb things until we got the CSIs here. Boot prints in the snow all around, small ones, like at April's house." Doty whistled through the gap in her front teeth. "Gonzales, go downstairs and secure the scene until the coroner gets here." She turned to Combs, clearly pissed. "Okay, you're part of the team at least until the brass says otherwise. Plenty for everyone to do."

He nodded, and turned to Childress. "What car does September drive?"

"How should I know? Call the DMV."

Doty narrowed her eyes but kept her temper for once. "We need your help, Mr. Childress. To find Steven. Work with us. Can you tell us what September was wearing? What kind of shoes, for instance?"

Childress sniffed, cocked his head to one side and smoothed the soft fabric of his sweater. "That's something I still love about April. She always dresses like a model. September is a frump. I notice fashion."

"So?" Combs gave props to Doty for her patience. His own was at an end.

"September wore sweat pants, a stocking cap, and some shapeless overstuffed coat. Oh, and dingy little snow boots, no heels, just flat rubber treads." He pointed to the entry. "She tracked in snow, so I noticed."

Doty smiled. "That's a match. Betcha the prints around the body are September's."

Chapter 18

Shadow sprinted down the long corridor, scrabbled for purchase on the floor and skidded into the tiled wall. He gathered himself, dove for the glove, grabbed and shook it just like his bear-toy. It tickled his nose. He sneezed and dropped it so he could paw the fabric. It smelled like bacon and peppermint gum.

He'd decided he liked Freda when she suggested fetch. Shadow grinned around the fuzzy glove. He trotted back to where she waited at the glass doors, and pushed the glove into her hands so she could throw it again.

"Nice dog." A man on his way out stopped to button his coat, but kept his distance from Shadow.

Shadow paused, and cocked his head at the man's tone. The man was scared of him. Shadow had met a few adults who didn't like dogs or acted nervous. He didn't know why. So he dropped the glove and wagged his tail low to the ground to show he meant no harm.

Freda shrugged. "He's with the little boy over in the food court." She viewed the deserted place. "The mall's closing down early."

"Yes, everyone's leaving. I think the food court is the only place still open." He smiled, but backed away and hurried from the building.

He ducked his head against the gust that snaked inside when the man left. He was glad to be out of the cold. At the thought, Shadow sat down and licked one of his sore paws.

"You're just a good doggy, aren't you?" She crooned until Shadow lowered his ears and wiggled his butt. "Wanna fetch?" Freda called. "Bring me the glove."

Grabbing it, he pushed it into her hand and gently released it when she asked.

"Ew, you've got it all wet. You're as bad as my dogs." She stuffed the soggy glove into her pocket despite his dance to convince her otherwise.

Following Freda, Shadow leaped away when a chainlike wall rattled from the ceiling to close a nearby doorway. "It's okay, boy." She waited for him to draw close and sniff the metal.

Shadow returned to Freda's side. He'd visited buildings like this before with treat-lady, sometimes with Steven but often just the two of them. Those times he'd worn a special vest. Today he didn't even have his collar or a leash, and treat-lady wasn't here. Freda was okay, but she wasn't treat-lady.

He weaved between small tables and chairs set in the middle of the large open space to reach Steven. Smells of cooked food made his tummy rumble but he was polite and didn't beg. Shadow settled on the floor beside Steven, and laid his head against his boy's wet shoe. Familiar was good. He'd had too much newness for even a good-dog to manage.

Steven pulled his foot away. Shadow sighed. He wished his boy might—just this once—touch his head. A small touch, not even a full pet. He scooted closer and leaned against Steven's chair, comforted when his boy didn't move it away.

"Your lady friend didn't show, Teddy?" Freda pulled out a chair and sat next to the older man.

"The ice was too risky." Teddy coughed and slurped something from a cup. "You wore him out. Playing fetch?"

At the "fetch" word, Shadow raised his head and wagged. The old man laughed. "Can't get enough, can you, boy?"

"Any headway with Steven?" Freda unzipped her coat and pulled off her hat.

"Not a word." He swiveled, looked around the area. "They're shutting down the food court. I had to argue to get the French fries."

Shadow barked. In case they didn't understand—sometimes people missed the obvious—he stood up, whined and wagged. And licked his lips.

"French fries?" He barked again. "Hey, he knows what French fries mean." Teddy patted Shadow's head.

"Don't tease him. I tell my dogs French fries are bad for them." She grinned. "They don't believe me either."

"Noisy noisy, no, no, no." Steven spoke, and covered his ears when Shadow barked again. Freda's jaw dropped. "Steven's hungry. Steven's thirsty." He rocked, holding both hands over his ears.

"Drink your milk, Steven." Teddy pushed the cup closer. "I'll get you some French fries once they're ready."

Shadow barked again, and Steven's hand slashed the air and hit him. He flinched. He wasn't supposed to bark. His boy didn't like loud noises. Shadow's ears fell in apology but Steven didn't see.

Freda held out her hand to Shadow. "Shush, boy. Come over here."

After a quick glance at his boy, Shadow obeyed. "Sit." He did and placed his chin on her knee, and closed his eyes when she stroked his brow. "Steven, that wasn't nice. Never hit animals." Her words were angry but not at him.

Steven stopped rocking to grab the cup with both hands. He drank it dry. "Steven's hungry." He found the metal tag on his coat and zipped it up and down.

"He can't help it," Teddy said.

"I know. The boy's mother said he's autistic." She scratched Shadow's head. "I bet the dog's trained to help him." She massaged his ears and Shadow groaned. "But you don't know what the hell you're doing out here, do you?"

He whined and his tummy growled again.

Freda laughed. She patted him once more and stood up. "The French fries are ready. And I think this good dog deserves a couple for himself, don't you?"

Shadow wagged and woofed agreement. But he woofed softly, the way a good-dog should.

Chapter 19

September navigated the sharp turn toward Gentry Park, watching for Pam's Jeep. Her cell phone rang in her pocket, and she swerved to a stop. If it was April, she could always ask about the bloody clothes. Yeah, right, like that will happen. More likely it was Lizzie with more threats, but while she was wishing, why not hope they'd found Steven.

She dug for the phone without shedding her gloves. September fumbled Steven's empty prescription bottles before she found the phone. Caller ID said Humphrey Fish.

"Give me a freakin' break." She didn't need his crap, so she answered the call before it could go to voicemail and immediately disconnected. September tossed the phone next to the pills and laptop in the seat, pulling back onto the street.

The phone rang. Fish again. "Sheesh, can't you take a hint?" This time she let it go to voicemail. She'd delete it later.

The phone rang a third time. She needed a clear line for important calls. She punched the Phone, waited for the connection and yelled, "It's not a good time. Quit calling." September hung up before he could say a word.

The phone rang again immediately.

"Am I speaking Norwegian? What does *a bad time* mean to you?"

"Don't hang up."

"You're tying up the phone.

"Did you find Steven?"

She paused. "No." She didn't have time to explain, didn't want him involved. There was no time to waste, especially with a headlines-grabber like Fish. "I need to keep this line clear."

"I called your sister's house, and a cop answered, somebody named Officer Combs. So cut the bull. If you're in trouble, let me help. I've only got another minute or so, I put on a long-play record and told the engineer I needed a potty break."

She watched the rear view mirror for police cars, but the roads remained deserted. "What do you want, Fish? How can you help from the radio station?"

"The cops want you, September. They didn't know about you before. My bad."

"What do you mean, they didn't know about me?" So Doug Childress would come late to that party, if Fish had already outed her. Combs. . . why was that name familiar? "What did you tell them?"

"Just that you got a call during the radio show from your sister about the lost kid." He couldn't mask the delight in his next words. "The phones rang off the hook after that. I could use more on-air drama like that." He hesitated. "That's not to say I'm not genuinely worried about the little fella."

What a bozo. "Nice chatting but I'm seriously busy." She started to cut the connection.

"September, don't hang up. You need me. Let me help."

She held the phone up to her ear. "You just want the scoop, Fish. And that's low even for you."

"You got me all wrong. Sure, it wouldn't hurt my feelings to bump my image. Heartland isn't exactly a primetime market. Radio's dead anyway. It's a starter-job, or you land here at the end of a career. I need a facelift, a ticket out."

"And Steven's story would be your ticket."

"Shit, don't be that way. I care about kids, too. And small, furry Disney-esque creatures."

She didn't have time for this crap.

"Who went to bat for you for your little animal show? Sure wasn't the big muckity-mucks. We needed some warm and fuzzy and you were just the ticket."

"You? No way." She pulled back onto the road.

"Way. Listen, you need help, don't deny it. I'm sitting here toasty while you play slip-n-slide with the cops."

Her tires skidded as if to confirm his taunt. Fish had a point. And he wasn't the police. Sure, the man always had an angle, but if their different goals had a mutual benefit, what could it hurt?

"Okay, Humphrey. I'll give you the story if you give me a hand. But you have to promise not to take this public. Or go to the police."

"You're killing me." He sounded like a child threatening a tantrum. "What if they come to me? You already opened that door bailing in the middle of the show. Listeners already heard that."

"What's done is done. But not another word unless I give you the okay. You could get someone killed."

"Killed? Really? Don't tease." He sounded delighted, and then the teasing lilt disappeared. "Wait, you're not joking? Jesus-frog, September, what the hell is going on?"

September inhaled sharply. "What did the police say?"

"Nothing much. I've listened to the scanner, though. They found a woman dead at your sister's house." He hesitated, his concern real. "Tell me it's not your sister."

"No, not April." She squeezed the steering wheel and pressed harder on the gas. "The babysitter. Wilma." She glanced at the car clock, and guestimated she was still five minutes away from the park. Time stopped for nobody. "No more questions. You'll get all the details later, I promise."

"Sure. I've heard that one before." He sniffed. "Where are you, anyway?"

"Why? So you can broadcast my location?" She glanced at the seat at April's laptop and Steven's pills. "If you want to help, do a search for me on your computer." She caught up one of the pill bottles.

"Is that all?" She heard his footsteps echo, shoe lifts clip-clopping like Old Bessie. "Okay, I'm set. Google's raring to go, what d'ya got?"

"Type in Henry F. Pottinger, Ph.D." She spelled the last name.

Fish said nothing for several moments, making her antsy. "Well? Did you find anything?"

"Too much. He's affiliated with something called NeuroRealm. It's the research arm of a pharmaceutical company. They focus on neurological stuff, brain disorders, chemical brain imbalances affecting behavior, that sort of thing."

"Research? Drugs?" That made sense if he was Steven's doctor. "What do they treat? Does it say?"

"Let's see. Whole section on cancer. Something on Parkinson's, another on Alzheimer's. Then there's schizophrenia, ADD, OCD, they got all the popular initials. There's links to journal articles, you could get lost in all this frog-icity. Lots of money behind this group."

"What about autism?" September's pulse quickened. That had to be it. April hadn't been able to contain her excitement about Steven's recent improvements.

"Uh…don't see it here."

Damn, it had to be there. With an effort September refrained from urging him to look harder. The park was just ahead, and time for fishing had run out. "Is there any contact information, a phone number or name? Search the news or media page."

"Here you go. The public relations person, Martha Freemantle, has an email." He read the address quickly. "Got that? The NeuroRealm general number is 817-555-3421."

"Wait. Let me get something to write on." She coasted to a stop in front of the park and grabbed a pencil from the dash. When she couldn't find anything to write on, she grabbed the pill bottle again, and found a number was already printed on the bottle. "817-555-3421. Is that it?"

Gotcha. Lizzie spoke in riddles. So she'd bypass Mrs. Claus and go to the top.

"So—what's the deal? What does NeuroRealm have to do with you being in trouble?"

NeuroRealm had some by-damn explaining to do, and once they found out about gun-totin' grandma and her ghostly-goon, they'd pull Lizzie's fangs. She'd see to it. "Thanks for your help, Humphrey. I'll be in touch."

"Hey, I did my part. You can't leave me hanging."

"Have to run. I do appreciate it." September cut him off mid-whine. She knew her luck had truly changed for the better when she saw Pam's Jeep on the other side of the park. She took a deep breath. Time to find Steven.

Chapter 20

Combs leaned through the glass window to push his identification closer to the receptionist. "I spoke with Mr. Fish earlier. He expects me. I appreciate your cooperation. Anita, is it?" The nameplate spelled her name in tiny rhinestones that matched the accents on her glasses.

Anita sneezed and dabbed her nose with a soiled tissue. "Sweet talk all you want." Her voice was a Lauren Bacall baritone. "I already told you Humphrey's on-air." She punched a button on the phone, careful not to mess up the fresh magenta nail polish that perfumed the air. "I got a cold, got a headache, probably got strep throat, and got the crankies over a double shift. I got the don't-care-and-cain't-hep-it, so don't push me."

"The bluebird of happiness shit all over my day, too, lady." God, he didn't need attitude.

She batted red-rimmed eyes behind blue cat-eye glasses. "Quite the charmer, aren't ya?" She shuffled paper and ignored him.

He wished for a breath mint, or a cigarette. Hell, a shot of rum wouldn't be bad either. It might shave the fuzz off his tongue. He spoke in a conspiratorial tone. "Anita, I'll take responsibility. You won't get into trouble.

But I need to talk to Fish. *Now.*" He underlined the word. Controlling access into the studio, Anita had to push the button to open the glass door. "Please." He'd kiss receptionist butt if it helped. Couldn't be worse than puckering up to Doty.

She covered her mouth, coughed, and grimaced. "Me and Humphrey and the engineer are the only ones still here. Others got out before all this weather. Should have hitched a ride with them."

"You're stranded?"

"For the night, looks like." She shrugged. "I can be sick here as easy as at home. The kitchenette has instant soup. I'll survive without my flannel jammies." Anita resumed busy work.

Combs paced the tiny reception area. He dreaded Uncle Stanley's call. His sister Naomi had already used him as a verbal punching bag when he told her. After her sobs quieted, his sister agreed to inform the rest of the family. He couldn't be distracted, had to step up the search to find Mom's killer or he'd shoot somebody. Maybe even a receptionist.

"I'm grateful for the company." Anita sniffled. "Humphrey's a one-man show 'til somebody else shows up. That's a lot of fish stories." She lifted an eyebrow, expecting him to chuckle. At his stony glare, she adjusted her glasses. "He'll need a potty break before long, 'cuz he's been drinking coffee for hours." She laughed. "But he'd rather hear himself than take a break— heck, wouldn't surprise me if he just whizzed in a cup."

Whizzed in a cup, sheesh. And she called him less than charming? No matter how satisfying, it would do no good to piss off the gate keeper. "I need a few minutes. Just tell him I'm here. If he needs a break, it won't get in the way of his program."

Anita held up one finger and turned away to sneeze into a wad of tissue, honking and wiping her Rudolph-bright appendage. She winced, reaching for the half roll of toilet paper stashed in the inbox on her desk when the first wad of tissue didn't suffice. "This storm, it's a dream come true for Humphrey. He's wanted to break into the prime radio time for years. Humphrey's making points keeping the station on air."

A headache gathered behind Combs's ears. Anita's voice irritated like new shoes on a blister.

"He's taking lots of call-ins." Arm wave. "Everyone's stuck at home, nothing to do but listen to the radio and jabber on the phone." Finger fling. "This could make things happen for Humphrey." She sighed and her hands settled in her ample lap, two fluttery birds grounded. "The man just doesn't take care of himself, though. That falls to me. Not that he ever notices," she said softly.

Aha. So Anita had designs on the radio king. And Fish didn't know she was alive. "He just doesn't appreciate what you do for him. That's a shame." Combs hoped she'd come around quicker if he showed a bit of empathy.

"Oh, I don't mind. He's got a lot to offer, such an undiscovered talent. And besides, I need the overtime."

"He's taking call-ins? I don't hear the phone ringing."

As if on cue, Anita's phone jangled. "It's a different number. He's got half a dozen phone lines in there." Her phone rang again, followed by a second line. Her shoulders clenched. "I can't get away from morons calling for school and church and who-cares closings. Humphrey's been making those announcements every fifteen minutes." She wiped her nose. "Why don't they freaking listen, huh?"

Everyone in radio must be nuts.

She punched a button, speaking into her headset, and transformed into a syrup-voiced sex kitten. "WZPP, you've reached ZAP105 FM Radio, giving you the best easy-listening 24/7, how may I direct your call?"

He reached through the window, and disconnected the phone.

"Hey!" She batted his hand.

"I'm not asking. This is a murder investigation. I'll run your ass down to the station, too, Anita, because I don't have time to wait until Fish's piss-cup runneth over."

"Murder? Lord, why didn't you say so, I thought it was another unpaid traffic ticket." She pulled off her glasses, and continued in her crow-rasp voice. "He doesn't pay me enough to run interference for murder. I'll page him, but he still probably won't reply till there's a pre-recorded station break."

"When's that?" Combs checked the time.

"Quarter hours usually, but today all bets are off. Knowing him, he got all the breaks in at one time to give himself more running-at-the-mouth room."

That could be another fifteen minutes. Maybe he should have gone with Gonzales to the Januarys' house to interview September's parents. Doty didn't want him there, though, and figured his follow up with the radio guy wouldn't get back to the brass. Hell, if this Fish character had just answered his questions when he called April's house, he wouldn't be here.

"So who got murdered?" Anita winced, and reached for a lozenge. Cellophane wrappers littered the floor next to the wastebasket that overflowed with used tissues.

"You don't know the victim." Victim. Not a victim, it was his mom. He coughed and turned away.

"Careful, honey." Anita tore off several squares from a roll of toilet paper and offered them through the window. "This weather, you could catch what I got." When he waved the tissue away, she folded it and honked. "Damn, it would just be easier to unscrew my nose for the duration." She tossed the used clump toward the wastebasket as the phone rang again.

This time he reached through the window and yanked the headset off her head. "I'm sorry you feel like shit. I'm sorry he treats you like dirt. But if you don't get Fish out here in the next thirty seconds, I promise you'll feel even worse." He didn't smile, didn't yell, and didn't need to.

Anita started to say something and hesitated. "Screw it," she murmured, pressing the buzzer to release the door lock.

Chapter 21

Gentry Park hadn't changed other than a bit more snow since September's earlier visit. She twisted in her seat to reach Shadow's stuffed bear in the back seat and winced. It's only bruised ribs. It could have been worse.

To keep her hands free she stuffed the bear inside her parka and zipped up the coat. She found Steven's dirty socks, still inside a baggy, deep in one massive pocket. The smelly bear and scented socks were the best bet to find Steven.

She braced herself for the temperature change. Lordy, she hated the cold. She unlocked the door, hyper-vigilant to any suspicious movement. Her blood drummed in her ears when she stepped outside into the open, unprotected, but at least the street, the park—hell, the whole world—was deserted. The street lights reflected in the snow shined like moonlight, so bright she'd see any interlopers in plenty of time to retreat to the car.

Snow fell thick as fog. No trace remained of her earlier search of the park. September entered the fenced area and waved at Pam.

The rail-thin woman emerged from her Jeep. She wore high black Wellingtons, leather gloves, a tan, down-filled jacket, watch cap, and hood drawn over the top of her head. A fuzzy scarf, blue as a bruise, peeked out from the collar. Warm, sensible, a fieldwork outfit Pam wore like a second skin.

September motioned to the gated entrance on the wooded side of the field closest to April's house. That's where they should begin. Pam saluted her understanding, and unloaded the sable shepherd from the back of her vehicle.

The old dog jigged for a moment at the sight of the harness, and stood patiently until hooked up. Old dog senses faded with years, just like people senses, but nobody knew how much scent discrimination diminished with age. Even a fraction of Bruno's youthful abilities could bring Steven home. Tracking dogs didn't need the light.

They had to find Steven, just had to. Once he was safe, September could concentrate on freeing April from Lizzie's control.

She trudged around the perimeter of the fence to meet Pam. September didn't want to confuse Bruno with more of her own tracks. She'd already muddied the trail.

"I owe you big time." September smiled at Pam, offering Bruno a gloved hand to sniff. The dog waved his amber tail.

Pam scowled when she saw September's face. "You run into a brick wall? C'mon, honey. Has something to do with all the cop cars around your sister's house, I bet. Surely they didn't call out the troops to find a lost kid. So spill."

September wavered. It would be such a relief to share the burden with somebody else, especially a disaster-savvy individual like Pam. Lizzie hadn't said anything about telling other people, only the police. And she'd already enlisted Fish. But Pam might call the police, and get sideways of Lizzie. September shook her head. Couldn't risk it, not when she'd already got Wilma shot by misjudging Lizzie.

"I heard your radio show today, September. Was that really your sister or was it Fish's idea of a publicity stunt. Or is it something else?"

September flinched. Breathing hurt, her face stung, and she couldn't feel her hands or feet despite the extra-thick socks and insulated gloves. But her heart hurt worst of all. "Yes, it's more involved than I let on."

"I knew it." Pam punched one gloved hand into the palm of the other, clearly upset. Bruno woofed, gazing with concern back and forth between the pair. "It's Steven, right?" She cocked her head and sucked in her breath. "Something more? Is April in trouble?"

"Here's the deal, Pam." September remained leery of saying too much. "Steven's missing, and we think Shadow is with him. Other stuff happened after they disappeared, and the police are sorting that out." She weighed her words. "We don't need to distract the police from their job, especially when you and Bruno have a better chance of finding Steven. Finding him, that's the most important thing."

"No wonder you're frazzled." Pam pulled her into a warm hug. "April must be going crazy. You're a good sister."

September froze for a moment, and then fiercely returned the embrace. She fought tears, the unexpected sympathy making her want to unburden herself completely. It would be such a relief to share her fear, ask for advice, and get some encouragement that she'd made the right choices. She pulled away, and opened her mouth—

"You'll tell me the whole story at some point?" The older woman absently stroked Bruno's gray muzzle.

The moment passed. She had to keep it light. "Sure, Pam. I promise. I'll give you a blow-by-blow over steaks the size of toilet seats. And a good bottle of merlot." Pam would be safer, and even April would be protected by keeping Pam in the dark. September checked her watch. It had been less than five minutes since she'd arrived, but every second that ticked by brought her nearer the 24-hour deadline.

"Make it prime rib." Pam turned to the dog. "*Sitz. Bleib.*" The dog planted his furry rear and waited. His tail scythed a half-moon in the snow that was already halfway to his chest.

September pulled out the baggy with Steven's socks. "I've got Shadow's toy bear, too."

She wrinkled her nose. "Bruno finds people, not animals. Keep it simple or we'll confuse him. He hasn't done this in a while." She seized the baggy from September, opened it, and presented it to the dog.

Bruno stuck his snout inside. He snuffled repeatedly, inhaling the telltale scent signature that spelled "Steven" in his canine brain. Pam looked up. "You stay here, and give me a twenty-foot lead before you follow."

September nodded. "I think Steven entered there." She pointed. "He played on the swings like always and went out the other side exit." She swung her arm toward her car parked in the middle of the street. She hadn't wanted to risk getting stuck by parking where the drifts grew deepest. And she wanted the car to have easy access to a quick getaway. Just in case.

Pam concentrated on her dog. Bruno sniffed and finally pulled away from the baggy and huffed, signaling his readiness. "Bruno, *such.*"

The "find" command triggered the dog into a low slouching posture. He shoveled snow from time to time to get a better scent. Bruno trotted through the open gate for five or six feet, nose skimming the snow, and paced first to the left and back toward the right. He cast a semicircle ahead of Pam to match the scent to the socks.

September held her breath, and let it out when Bruno made a beeline toward the swing set near the middle of the park. Steam puffed from his mouth. Pam's blue scarf covered the lower half of her face as she allowed the big dog to pull her in his wake by the long line attached to his harness.

Bruno spent several minutes around the playground equipment, paying particular attention to an area beneath one swing. September heard Pam repeat the "*such*-find" command, and the German shepherd cast back and forth on the far side of the jungle gym. Once he moved in a purposeful stride toward the far gate, September followed.

Bruno's nose assured them Steven had left the park. He drove through the open gate, trotting without hesitation, and September hoped he would lead them to a nearby house, where they'd find Steven sipping hot chocolate with kind neighbors.

But less than five minutes later, the dog stopped at a street corner. Hesitating, he returned to an indentation in the snow a short distance away, pacing a tight circle and then a larger one. Bruno whined. He shuffled into the intersection, poked and sniffed deep into the snow, and finally returned to the sign to lie down.

Pam waited until September caught up. "End of the line, September." She pulled a ball looped with rope out of her pocket, praised the dog, and tossed him the toy. He caught it with ease, and teased for a game of fetch, his reward for a job well done.

"You're sure?" September couldn't hide her disappointment.

Pam played tug with the eager shepherd. "Bruno's nose doesn't lie, does it, boy?" Her expression of pleasure at the old dog's success faded when she recognized September's desperation. "Sorry. Maybe somebody picked him up?" Bruno mock-growled, tail wagging happily as he pulled against the rope toy.

"Maybe a ride, sure. But who? Steven wouldn't climb into just any car. April has to jump through hoops to get him places. That's why she bought that atrocious banana-yellow Cruiser." September noticed the sign, cocked her head a moment, and stood on tiptoe to brush the white away, revealing hidden letters. She winced when her bruised muscles protested, but the effort paid off.

HART-Line Bus Stop.

"He got on the bus?" Pam wiped snow off the bridge of Bruno's muzzle.

"They're yellow. Or sort of a mustard color anyway, that could be close enough for Steven." That was better than Steven stuck in a snow drift.

"Makes sense." Pam tugged the dog toy, and then let Bruno keep it. "*Fuss,*" she said, and he trotted in a heel position by her side back to the park. "Steven must have hunkered down in the snow for a while. Maybe he waited for the bus there."

September followed Pam. "I came within sight of that spot, I should have kept going a little further." Instead, she'd returned to April's house to be bushwhacked by crazy Lizzie. "I didn't know those dumpy HART-Line buses came this far into the suburbs. Steven loves routine. A yellow bus is the next best thing to his mom's yellow car."

"So call the dispatcher, and have them contact the drivers. They'd remember a little boy."

"Maybe not if he was alone. But Shadow with him makes him memorable." Excited, September unzipped her coat and pulled out the toy bear. "Before we go back, you've got to check and see if they're still together."

Pam considered the toy dubiously. "I told you, Bruno's not trained for—"

"Let him try. At this point any info could be helpful."

With a sigh, Pam stopped. "Okay, okay, but it could also confuse things." She turned to Bruno. "*Platz. Aus.*" The dog belly flopped into the white, dropped the ball into her open palm, and Pam stuffed the toy back into her pocket. September handed her the bear.

Bruno sniffed the toy and tried to take it. Pam pulled it out of reach, moved away, and came back. She said, "*Such,*" and offered it to him once more. He reached out tentatively, sniffed, and leaped to his feet, grabbing the bear to shake it. Bruno danced away with the toy.

Pam turned up her palms in a helpless gesture. "He thinks we're playing. I'm sorry, September, he's not any help."

"Crap. Thanks anyway." September yawned.

Pam offered the ball-tug toy once more. "*Bring.*" After one final spine-shattering shake that certainly killed the stuffed bear, Bruno dropped the soggy toy at Pam's feet and eagerly reclaimed his rope-ball.

"Call the bus company." Pam returned the bear and jogged back toward the park as September struggled to keep up. "If the driver doesn't remember Steven or a dog, find out the locations of different stops on this route. We can take Bruno around to each one."

"Great idea." September thought her ribs might poke through her flesh with every bone-jarring jog, but she grit her teeth and kept pace with Pam. "I don't know if Steven would get off at a strange stop. But that's a good next step to check." She dug her phone out of her pocket and frowned. "It's nearly dead."

"My cell's in the Jeep. You can use that. Charger's there, too." Pam handed September her keys. "Phone's in the center caddy between the front seats and the charger's hooked into the front console. You can take that with you if you like. I've another at home."

September struggled for a response. "I don't know what to say."

"Go. I've seen you checking your watch, and I know time's wasting." The woman smiled gently. "I haven't known you long, but I recognize you. You're the one who pulls strangers out of fires." She paused. "It's what you do, it's who you are. It's *who we are.*" She held her palm up to stop any protest. "You'd do it for me, and don't dare deny it. Like recognizes like."

September palmed tears away before they froze. "Thank you," she whispered.

"Go on. I'll be along in a minute. I owe Bruno at least a ten-minute playtime for his good work."

The dog trembled with anticipation but stood steady as Pam removed his halter and unhooked the long-line leash. His tail lashed at the mention of "playtime." When she lobbed the toy high in the air, Bruno launched himself like a furry rocket. Pam's expression glowed when the fetch-game turned back the clock for the old dog.

September wished she could turn back the clock, too, to a more innocent time. Before stalkers, before lost dreams and lost loves, and little boys lost. She hurried to Pam's Jeep, climbed inside, and made sure the doors were locked. With the engine rumbling, she switched the blower to high, eager for warmth and breathed with relief for the first time after hours of stress. She was safe. She finally had a plan. Steven would be found.

She didn't notice the black Hummer that approached from the far side of Gentry Park and stopped in the middle of the road directly beside her Volvo.

Chapter 22

Combs shoved through the radio studio's glass door so hard it rebounded off the wall, and he felt vague disappointment when it didn't break. He jogged down the hall and stopped below the red "on air" light above another door. The organ-rich tones of Humphrey Fish recited a litany of area work and event closings, as the live broadcast was piped through office speakers.

The studio walls—glass—formed a soundproof enclosure where a pale, skinny kid with headphones sat before a computer bank of dials and switches. When Combs opened the door, the kid rose halfway out of his seat, and made frantic shushing motions. Combs ignored him. "Where's Fish?"

The recitation abruptly stopped. "Well, well, well, look what the storm blew in." Humphrey sat on the far side of the room on a padded rolling bar stool. A football-size fuzzy mic hung above his head. "We'll be right back with a surprise guest, right after a word from our sponsors." He made a hand motion to the engineer.

The engineer twiddled dials, sat back and chugged Red Bull. "You got ninety seconds," he told Humphrey. He pulled off his headphones and stuck out his jaw at Combs. It didn't improve his weak chin.

"You're Fish?"

"In the flesh. Who're you?" Humphrey hopped off the chair.

A poor man's Leprechaun, Fish stood just over five feet, and was nearly as wide as he was tall. "Officer Jeffery Combs." He shook the man's hand, and tried to mask his surprise.

"Yeah, I know, I know, you're shocked. I'm even more handsome than you expected, right? I got a face for radio, what can I say?" He scratched his bright red poof of chin whiskers.

"We spoke before."

Humphrey smoothed the freckles on his billiard-smooth head, and pushed the microphone away. "What the hell are you doing, breaking into a broadcast? Didn't your momma teach you any manners?" But his hazel eyes twinkled. "Makes for good radio, though."

Combs clenched and unclenched his fists. "My mom is dead and I'm here to find out who killed her." He'd like to grab the man by his silly chin whiskers, or some equally short hairs, and see how he liked that joke.

"Frog on a stick." Fish produced a green paisley kerchief from his pocket and mopped his brow. "Sorry, Officer, thought this was about traffic tickets." His innocent expression failed to hide the calculation. "It's about September? I already told you everything I know."

"You've told me diddly."

Fish hoisted himself back onto the booster chair. "Maybe I do know more than I think." He eyeballed the clock. "We've got some wiggle room before we go back on air, right, Craig?" Fish waggled his fingers at the boy-engineer's puzzlement until the kid's scowl cleared and he nodded sudden understanding. Fish swiveled in the chair to face Combs. "The power of radio could get us some leads from the citizenry out in listener land. Am I right?"

Combs shook his head. "I ask you the questions, Fish. This isn't quid pro quo or some reality media circus. Real people are involved. A woman is dead, a child is missing." He wouldn't be able to stop the DJ from flapping his jaws once he left the radio station, but while he was here, he'd stay in control.

"Fine, you ask the questions." Fish folded his hands over his tummy and smiled benignly. "What's your name again? Have a seat."

"Officer Jeffrey Combs, Heartland Police Department." He settled into the indicated chair, and bumped his head into another overhead microphone. He pushed it away. "What time was September—"

Fish grinned and interrupted. "We're back, friends and neighbors, and I've got a treat to warm the cockles of your heart." He paused, and pushed his own mic away momentarily. "Play along, it'll be painless. And you might learn something."

Combs's ears felt hot. He looked around and caught the knowing grin of the boy-engineer.

Back in carnival barker mode, Fish cleared his throat and continued. "On this bitter cold November day, we're gonna play "Clue" in a real-live murder investigation with our in-studio guest, Officer Jeffrey Combs, of the Heartland Police Department." His mocking tone set Combs's teeth on edge.

Combs stood abruptly.

"Sit down, sit down, Officer Combs." Fish shook his finger at Combs like a garden gnome chastising a Doberman. "I'm afraid I've taken the good policeman by surprise, since he planned to ask me some questions first. Or maybe he's been stricken with stage fright." He was in his element. "You can sit there like a lump, answer my questions or ask your own, officer. Since you're already here, why not make the best of it?"

Combs glared, but took his seat. He crossed his arms, lips tight.

Fish reacted like a car intent on beating a red light. "When I called earlier to check up on WZPP's very own Pet Peeves guru, you answered the phone. It appears, gentle listeners, that September Day got her tail caught in mayhem." He pushed the mic to one side. "Say something already." he whispered, "They can't see your gloomy face."

Combs glared but said nothing. He'd not agreed to be part of this orchestrated fiasco. Let Fish find his own way out of the maze.

"Speak into the microphone, Officer, so our listeners can hear." Fish beamed when phone lines lit up. "There's been a death, right? And it happened at September's house? Wait no, she'd gone to her sister April's house to hunt for the missing kid. Am I on track so far?"

Combs shifted in the chair, glanced at the door and debated leaving Fish to swing in the wind. But the show would go on whether he remained silent, left, or sang a solo and if he could get control of the conversation, perhaps he'd salvage something. "We are speaking with family, friends and neighbors to locate the whereabouts of Ms. Childress and her son."

"Steven, his name's Steven," prompted Fish. "What about September?"

"Certainly we'd like to speak with Ms. Day about her sister and nephew."

"So d'ya think April is the killer or what?"

Combs recoiled from the mic. "You damn prick."

"Okay, hold your britches there, champ. I was out of line. Sorry," Fish said, clearly anything but remorseful. "As a journalist I have to ask. You don't have to answer."

More phone lines winked. Combs stood to leave.

The little man rode his chair like a jockey. "Everyone out there in radio-land, I must confess that I ambushed Officer Combs into a live interview with the promise of some answers. So fire away, Mr. Policeman, ask me anything." He waggled his fingers at the boy-engineer. "And in a bit we'll take some calls."

Combs breathed deeply, gathering his thoughts, and eyed the mic as if it was a snake. "Turn it off." He might already be dead but he'd be damned if he'd let Fish shovel more dirt on his grave. "Shut off the show, go to commercial and I'll talk. Or I'll walk."

Fish sighed. "Fair enough. Listeners, we'll be right back after these messages."

Combs waited until Fish nodded at the engineer. He stared over his shoulder at the "on air" light over the door, and once it went dark, he breathed more easily. Combs swiveled his chair to face Fish. "You said that September, uh, Ms. Day rushed out of the station after her sister called."

"Oh, she wasn't here. She called in from a land-line." He wiggled his eyebrows, enjoying the gossip. "Takes a lot to get her out of the house even without a blizzard. She called in late and left early, but we heated up the airwaves while she was here."

"What exactly did April Childress say?" Combs couldn't imagine either sister as the shooter. But they could have both called from April's house to alibi each other since neither was at the station during the show.

"She said—wait, I've got a better idea." He waved at the engineer. "We've got the show recorded. Craig, cue that up for us, will ya?" The engineer held up two fingers. "Okay, in two minutes we'll have a re-run of that gripping call."

Sweat tickled the back of Combs's neck, and he loosened his jacket. Fish kept the station shirtsleeve warm. "Can you tell where September called from? Her house, or somewhere else, a cell phone maybe?"

"Don't know. Don't care. Long as she phoned in on time, we ran with it. Not a cell phone, though. Reception sucks with those things." He swigged brown, vile liquid from a puce-colored coffee mug that must have been purchased from a yard sale and washed last during the great flood. "By the way, April mentioned a dog, too."

"Dog? What about it?" They'd found kibble all over the kitchen floor, but no sign of the pet. "Must have taken the dog with them."

"Taken? You think April and September are on the run with Steven? And the pooch? And you're dogging their trail, eh?" The round man forced a laugh.

What a piece of work. Combs finally sat in the chair beneath the guest microphone, trying to keep a civil tone. "What car does Ms. Day drive?"

"Volvo." Fish didn't hesitate. "It's a running joke between us but—um—not appropriate on-air." The engineer snickered. "Hey Craig, how you doing on that recording?"

The engineer gave a thumb's up and flipped a switch. Combs listened with interest. Fish's voice began the recording.

Caller, you're on the air with Humphrey Fish and Pet Peeves. What's your question?

Long pause. *Is September there? Please, I need to talk to September.*

Must be April, Combs thought, and leaned forward.

I'm here. What's your name? And do you have a pet question?

September? Oh my God, September you've got to help me. Please, oh no oh no—

Calm down, I can barely understand you. Stop crying and speak clearly. I'll try to help if I can. September sounded cool as a cucumber. She was either a great actress or she wasn't part of the setup.

I tried and tried to call you, but your line was busy. April spoke so fast she was hard to understand. *The babysitter fell asleep, I could just kill her, and Steven went out like he does and I've looked and looked, but he's nowhere around the house. You've got to track him.*

April, is that you? September sounded guilty, and Combs wondered why.

Steven's gone. My baby's out in the storm, him and the dog both are gone!

I'm on my way, I'll . . . September paused. *Fish? Are we still live? Shut the damn radio off, for God's sake, shut it down.* She softened. *April, sweetie, I'm on my way. We'll find Steven. I'll see about tracking, if we need to. But you need to call the police.* Another pause. *Fish, will you freakin' shut it down?* A click and a dial tone ended the segment.

Combs didn't say anything for a long moment. It didn't seem staged. April sounded frantic, and September no less concerned. So if the boy and dog—
"What kind of dog?"

"German Shepherd." Fish spoke with a bad German accent, and then reverted to Midwest twang. "Puppy was a gift from September to the kid, and I think she was training it to help the kid out." He mopped his brow with the kerchief again. "Steven's disabled or something. I never got the details. Hell, I've only known September for a few months, so it's not like I can quote chapter and verse on her life. She's sorta private for a radio personality."

The show aired before the shooting, but April never called the police about Steven. Neither had September. Partnered with April's threats, it was enough to raise the hairs on the back of Combs's neck.

Fish pulled his mic close. "This is ZAPP 105 Radio, with Humphrey Fish tap-dancing as fast as he can on this icy, blustery day. For those just tuned in, we're making history. My special surprise guest, Officer Jeffrey Combs of the Heartland PD, has been giving us an insider's view of a murder investigation. You hear it first, you hear it best, you hear it LIVE on WZPP Easy Listening." He slurped coffee, and sludge painted a nasty shine on his upper lip. He grinned and nodded at Combs.

With a muffled curse, Combs glanced over his shoulder to see the "on air" sign brightly lit once again. Sonofabitch! How long had they been broadcasting?

"To recap for you listeners-come-lately, our own Pet Peeves maven, September Day, bailed on the broadcast when her sister April Childress sent out a howl for help over the airwaves. That's the recording you just heard. We'll replay that again in the next half hour."

Shit. Must have gone live when the engineer cued up the recording. No going back now, dammit. "I need a copy of that." It wasn't a request.

"Sure, Officer, whatever you want." Fish's sarcasm was clear. "That's Officer Jeff being detective-like and official. The poor man's intimately involved because, you see, his mom—what's her name, Officer?"

Combs smoldered as he stood. He'd got what he came for. Time to get the hell out of Dodge.

Undaunted, Fish blustered on. "This defender of the public safety discovered his mother had been killed—in fact, murdered—at April's house." He faked a sympathetic tone. "And I am assisting the good officer any way that I can to help bring the perpetrator to justice."

Grabbing the microphone, Combs interrupted. "We would very much like to speak with September Day and April Childress. Anyone with information on the whereabouts of these individuals should call—"

Fish's bass voice rode roughshod over Combs. "Call the studio line here at the station, that's 800-555-ZAPP. Speaking of that, our phone lines have lit up. Sorry to keep y'all waiting, let's take some calls." Without waiting for Combs's approval, Fish pushed a button. "You're on the air with Humphrey Fish. Do you have a question or comment for Officer Combs?"

"Sounds to me like that April woman did it. Mark my words, when you find her, you'll see she done something to your mother. Maybe even to her kid."

"Thanks for calling." Fish stabbed another button, cutting off the call. "Folks, this is a trying time for Officer Combs. He's lost his mother, the murderer is out there, and two women and a child are missing, possibly accompanied by a German Shepherd, or the child may be alone with the dog. This ain't a good day to be out for man or beast so if you've got tips for us call 800-555-ZAPP."

He'd had enough. Combs strode to the door, and put his hand on the knob as Fish pushed another button. "Caller, you're on the air with Humphrey Fish—covering the biggest Fish-story of them all. What do you have for me?"

"Mr. Fish? Uh, this is Lucy, and I listen to that Pet Peeves show all the time. You really make me laugh." She hesitated. "Am I on the radio?"

"Lucy? Lucy, dear, I'm delighted you're such a fan. What do you want to tell Officer Jeff?"

Combs pulled open the door and took three steps down the hall back to the front waiting area. If he hurried, he could rendezvous with Gonzales. He could hear the broadcast continue over the hallway speakers as he neared Anita's desk.

"Oh. Well, I live over by Gentry Park, and I see a young boy out there every day, him and a big black doggy. They was here today, too."

Combs stopped. He half turned, attention focused on the overhead speaker. He willed Lucy to say more, anything that would make the radio station visit more than a waste of hot air.

"You think you saw Steven and his dog today? What time?" Fish gestured with one urgent hand toward Combs, beckoning him through the glass wall to return to the studio.

"I had to let my own Cleo inside, she was barking so loud. Cleo's a French Poodle, and she just hates this icy weather. Anyways, I seen the little boy with his yellow coat leave the park with his doggy. That was a little after one o'clock."

That's about the right timeline, Combs thought. He bounded back down the hall to the studio and banged open the door, ignoring the engineer's winced reaction to the noise. Combs grabbed the fuzzy mic as if throttling a snake, and drew it close to speak. "Lucy, was the child with an adult? Or did you see a car anywhere around?"

"He was all by his lonesome. That's not all, though. The real reason I called was there's somebody over in the park right now, with another dog."

Combs inhaled sharply. "Another dog? But people go to the dog park all the time."

The caller snort-laughed. "Not in this weather, they don't, and not at night in the middle of a blizzard. And besides, this is different. It's one of them tracker-type dogs."

Despite his excitement, Fish sounded calm. "A tracking dog. Maybe it's September trying to find Steven?"

"That's what I thought, after hearing y'all." Lucy's voice grew more agitated. "I looked out the back window again, and September—or whoever it is—fell down in the snow. I called 911 but they're taking forever to get here. I've been watching since you had me on hold. She ain't got up, and the dog's started to holler. You have to send somebody, make the 911 people speed up. The noise is making my Cleo awful nervous."

Chapter 23

Once September cranked the engine in Pam's Jeep, the blower quickly grew toasty. She loved the sports car look of her Volvo, but appreciated the utility of the Jeep. September pulled off her gloves with her teeth, and held her hands in the warm blast from the dashboard vents. The familiar prickly-painful sensation announced the return of circulation.

She located the charger, unplugged Pam's phone and connected her own. Bruno's happy bark made her smile despite herself. The fenced-in park was a perfect doggy playground. This side of the park's trees offered shade on hot days, and a windbreak against today's snow, while the other side where she'd left her Volvo had no protection.

But dogs don't care about such things. Bruno leaped and danced through drifts to retrieve his toy, ranging back and forth from the Volvo side of the park to where September sheltered in Pam's Jeep. Pretty good for an old doggy. His genes stood the Shadow-pup and Steven in good stead. She could see Pam bending to scoop and toss soft snowballs at the dog.

Using Pam's phone, September called information. "I need the number for the HART-Line Public Transportation, in Heartland, Texas." She punched in the number dictated by the recording. "Please let somebody be there." Chances were the office had closed early like everything else.

"HART-Line, how may I help you?"

"I'm at the Gentry Park stop, and need to know the route the bus travels from here. And if any drivers reported picking up a young boy and a dog."

"Dogs aren't allowed on HART-Line."

"I thought maybe with the snow—"

"It's not allowed." She was as cold as the weather.

September wanted to scream, but tempered her tone. "A little boy and his dog are lost in this mess and I think—hope anyway—they boarded the bus." She concentrated to keep her voice steady. "Could you at least check for me?"

"Lost in this blizzard? Seriously?" The dispatcher's attitude took an about face. "We've not had any reports from drivers. Hold on, let me check something."

September heard the keyboard clatter, and hoped her luck held after all.

On the far side of the field, Pam and Bruno raced around like kids on holiday. Dakota used to do that. He'd scoop up snow with his long muzzle until a little mountain of white capped his nose. She called him "shovel face." Last winter she and Chris made a snow-dog that Dakota promptly baptized yellow. Chris and the dog were so proud.

The dispatcher brought September back to the present. "All buses are accounted for, most en route to our terminal. We're shutting down early. My driver for that route didn't answer, but Freda's final stop is Star Mall, and the return route driver called in sick. So the bus will stay at the mall overnight."

"Star Mall?" Sheesh, that was clear on the other side of the city. "What stops should I check along the way?"

"Only made two stops for anybody to get on. Several got off. Do you want all the stops?"

"Yes, all of them. Thanks a bunch." Steven wouldn't get off unless he recognized his mom's car or house, but a Good Samaritan might have taken him off. Her heart hiccupped at the notion, knowing that too often, bad guys outnumbered good guys.

September jotted down the five stops on a notepad Pam kept on the dashboard. She reached for the Jeep's door latch and only then noticed the Hummer across the field parked near her Volvo. A tall man in a long dark duster clambered out, strode to her Volvo and tried the door. Ghost Man?

She scrunched down out of sight and risked a peek out the window. Pam and Bruno continued to play, oblivious to the threat.

Maybe she was mistaken. Other men wore long coats, and had white hair. It was too far to see features. Ghost Man and Lizzie didn't drive the only Hummer in town.

He eliminated any question when he hit and shattered the front passenger window of the Volvo.

September screamed, wishing she'd thwacked him harder. The Volvo's car alarm whooped but gave him no pause. He reached through the window and pulled out April's laptop.

Bruno barked at the commotion and started toward the vandalized car. Pam yelled. "Get away from there! What're you doing?" She trotted after the dog. "Drop that and get away from there!"

September scrambled to open the door, and finally managed to scroll open a window an inch or two. If it was Ghost Man, Pam had no chance. She yelled a warning.

He shot the front and rear tires on the near side of September's Volvo.

Pam cried out. Called over her shoulder to September. "Phone the police." She confronted the man, a fearless gamecock defending territory. "Bruno, *fass.*"

September preferred the rabbit-hole safety of the semi-hidden Jeep to facing danger. But Pam's bravery shamed her. She bungled open the door, and promptly fell out into the snow, and her stomach clenched as another shot popped.

A thunk-twang hit the Jeep. So much for being hidden. No silencer this time—the distance didn't allow for that—Ghost Man had braced his gun arm on the top of the open SUV door to help his aim. The snow added inches to his height, giving him a giant's proportions.

"Pam, get away!" September scrambled and managed to climb back into the Jeep's open door.

"Bruno, *hier. Hier.*" Pam screamed the recall a second time, fear for her dog overriding any notion of her own safety.

September slammed the door. She flinched when another bullet struck the side of Pam's Jeep, and she quickly started the engine. Bruno's teeth were no match for bullets. He couldn't protect Pam. September jammed the car into gear. Wheels spun, dug deep and found traction. Up over the curb, across the sidewalk. She aimed for the open gate. "Didn't like the dumbbell? Let's see how you like two tons of car upside your head." The Jeep banged through a fence post, fishtailed, and steadied.

Bruno finally obeyed and raced back toward Pam.

Ghost-Man pointed his gun. At Pam. He shouted to her, something that September couldn't hear over the engine's roar. The gun popped, popped again.

Pam fell.

"No!" September slammed the brakes. The Jeep carved doughnut tracks in the field and then shuddered to a stop.

Bruno howled. He threw himself at Pam.

September stumbled from the car. Too late, she was too late. She wanted to run to Pam but instead stood frozen. Stared at Ghost Man. She'd rejoin Chris after all, and it was what she deserved.

Pam's moans broke her daze. September dove for cover as if the snow offered protection. She crawled toward her friend.

The pale man lowered his gun. "Find the flash drive. You won't get another warning." He climbed into the SUV and drove away.

September swam through the mounds of white until she could push Bruno aside and huddle next to Pam. "Honey, talk to me." Her bare fingers were nerveless sticks that smoothed Pam's scarf aside. Bruno continued to cry.

A woman from the closest house stuck her head out the door. "Is she okay? Is the dog hurt? He's making an awful racket. My Cleo's fit to bust over it."

"Call an ambulance!" Pam's skin paled to match the snow. Breaths shallow, slow. Bubbling. "Bruno, move." September again pushed the big shepherd. He slunk to Pam's other side. Bruno licked and nibbled the fabric of Pam's sleeve, nudged her arm.

"I done called for help. Even called that radio show with the policeman already. Should I call 'em again?"

"For God's sake, call nine-one-one!" September turned back to Pam. "Can you hear me? Where do you hurt?" She couldn't see the wound. Pam's bundled coat cocooned her, hiding the injury.

Tears spilled from Pam's brown-sugar eyes. "How's my dog? He shot us. How's Bruno?" At the sound of his name, the dog howled and tried to climb into her lap.

"Bruno *platz*. Down. Good dog." September tasted blood. She'd bitten her cheek. "He's fine, Pam. He's right here. What about you?" September held tight to Pam's hand.

"Hard to breathe." Pam coughed. "You're in deep do-do." It wasn't a question.

The guilt hurt worse than any physical injury. "I never meant for you or anyone to get hurt."

Pam's eyelids fluttered as if to clear fading vision. She breathed and gasped with the effort. Distant sirens wailed. "You go. Find Steven."

Another siren joined the first. EMTs must have been in the neighborhood. September tried to gauge how soon they'd arrive.

The neighbor lady stood nearby, jaw agape. "Bring a blanket," September shouted, turning back to Pam. "Help's on the way."

"Tell my husband—"

"Tell him yourself. This is just another SAR adventure. You'll have a great story to share over that merlot." She said the words out loud to convince herself as much as Pam.

The sirens grew louder. She could stay with Pam, should stay with her, but that meant giving up on Steven. And April.

The neighbor trudged through two-foot drifts to toss a green and red afghan to September. "I don't want to get close to that dog." She sniffed, nodded at the whimpering Bruno. "He looks like a biter." She stood several feet away, watching.

Bruno's focus never wavered from Pam as September tucked the blanket around her friend, propping her head out of the snow.

"September?"

"I'm here, right here." She squeezed Pam's hand.

"Get the hell out of here." Froth stained Pam's teeth red. "Police won't let you leave. Steven needs you." Her eyelids fluttered. "My dogs, the puppies. Eugene. He isn't home. Who'll take care of my dogs?" A single tear escaped down her cheek. Bruno licked it off.

"I'm so sorry." That bastard. She'd track down Ghost Man; he wouldn't get away with this. "Concentrate on yourself, Pam. Stay with me, Eugene needs you. The dogs are counting on you." That wasn't what Pam wanted to hear, so September gave her what she wanted. It was the only thing she had to offer. "I'll take care of the dogs, no worries. I promise."

Pam relaxed. Her lips moved, but nothing came out.

"What is it? Hang on, help's almost here." September bent close, ribs protesting, her ear next to Pam's mouth. "I can't hear you, say again?"

"Hurry, go after Steven." Pam gasped with the effort to be heard. "That man. He said they found Steven."

Chapter 24

Shadow sat patiently beside his boy's chair and drooled. He watched Steven pick up a French fry, dip it in dark sauce and munch. The treat-lady gave Shadow French fries when he was a good-dog and stayed quiet during rides. "French fries" was one of his favorite words. Shadow whined. He knew the next one was for him.

The bacon-smelling Freda and old man chatted. Shadow listened for familiar words, but he remained focused on his boy when he dipped another fry. He stood, wagged and stretched to gently take the greasy tidbit. Shadow chewed once, swallowed, and sat again. He licked his lips.

The smooth, shiny floor soothed Shadow's sore footpads. Clanky cook-noises from the nearby fast food counter echoed in the empty space. The sounds made Shadow nervous, and the smells painted the air with temptation, but Shadow stayed next to his boy, the way a good-dog should. Once the French fries appeared, it became a happy place, and Shadow became a fan of both strangers.

The old man sipped his drink, a burned-smell concoction Shadow recognized. Steven's mother drank the same hot liquid every morning. Teddy coughed and wiped his mouth with a tissue before sipping again. The old man sounded growly when he talked, but without the threat. It was just the way he sounded, like a big dog that meant no harm.

Freda sipped her own drink. It smelled sweet and when some sloshed on the floor, Shadow tasted it. He pawed her, hoping she'd spill some more.

"Steven, don't you want a sandwich? A kid needs more than fries for dinner." Shadow pawed her again, and she smiled and rubbed his ears and he leaned hard against her hand.

Steven shook his head. "Steven likes French fries. Steven likes ketchup. Steven feeds good-dog French fries and sauce." He dipped another fry, sucked off the sauce, and chewed the morsel. Shadow pulled away from Freda and cocked his head in anticipation.

The old man gestured at the basket of fries, now nearly empty. "Want some more ketchup?"

His boy ignored the question. He dipped fries. Offered one to Shadow. Shadow considered the gesture as nice as a tummy rub.

Teddy looked around. "Everyone's gone already, except us chickens."

"My relief driver never showed. The office said they're done for the night. Maybe for the rest of the week. That's a cut in hours right before the holidays I don't need."

Shadow's ears flattened at her tone. Big humans who worried meant problems for dogs. What would happen when the French fries were gone? What would he do…what would his boy do, if the two adults left? Shadow looked around. The clank from the kitchen had stopped. The open room with shiny-slick floors and food smells was big, empty, and nothing like home.

Adventure and new things were fun. Good-dogs liked to sniff new places. But Shadow wanted to go home. He yawned again and yearned for his soft bed in the kitchen, a kitchen that didn't clank. His bed smelled like him, a good-dog smell. Not like wet floor and old grease. Shadow watched Freda's wide, kind face and turned to the stubble-cheeked Teddy. He whined.

"Do you want a refill?" Teddy hooked his thumb to indicate the man at the food counter. "The manager knows me, and gives me freebies on refills."

Freda smiled. "I'm done. Besides, once Steven's on his way, we hit the road. Happy to give you a ride home, it's on the way."

Shadow checked his boy before he rose and padded after the old man to the counter. It smelled of chicken, fries and a touch . . . yes, it was bacon grease. Maybe if he asked his new friend in just the right way, he'd get some.

He sat down. He cocked his head and gently pawed Teddy's pant leg. Greasy, salty French fries tasted good, but nothing compared to bacon. He whined and pawed again.

"I don't think you like coffee, fella." Teddy showed his stained teeth in a grin. "Thanks, Carl."

"You're welcome, Mr. Williams. Everyone in the mall has already left. I'm out of here, too."

Teddy laughed. "Drive home safe." Carl rolled down a noisy cover, and exited out a back hallway.

Shadow sighed. That metal curtain cut off any hope of bacon. He heard a distant door open and close when the French fry cook left the building.

Teddy limped back to Freda and Steven, and set his cup on the table. "Have to take a potty break, be back in a flash."

At the table, Shadow sniffed carefully. Most of his boy's French fries were gone. Maybe the smoky-smelling Teddy knew about another food place? At the happy thought, Shadow shook himself hard. Freda would stay with Steven, so surely a good-dog could explore? Just a little? Shadow turned and trotted after his new friend. His claws ticked on the slick floor.

He followed Teddy to a nearby room without a door. The place smelled like pee. Not clean dog pee with all kinds of exciting messages, but human pee from many different people. Shadow sneezed, and sat down to wait for the old man to come out. He couldn't smell anything that resembled food. His ears drooped and he sighed.

A cold draft ruffled his fur. He looked back to where his boy waited. A big man approached.

Freda stood up and they grabbed hands the way humans sometimes did.

The stranger pulled a tissue from his overcoat and honked. He wore a short overcoat that fluttered open like crows' wings, and a hat with flaps like floppy dog ears.

Shadow's hackles rose, he didn't know why. Behind him in the cold, hard room, water hit water and he smelled fresh old-man-pee. Shadow whined but didn't move.

Something was bad wrong. The stranger's posture threatened despite his mild tone. Shadow didn't know what to do. The prickly sensation made him want to stand between Steven and the stranger. Instead, he shivered. Shadow fought the urge to roll on his back.

He wished the Teddy would hurry. He could be brave with a trusted friend by his side. People knew things, and could tell dogs what to do.

The stranger smelled of anger and something scarier. A sharp, pungent scent that rang alarms. Alarms that told Shadow to *do something*. Shadow's tail tucked tight, and he showed attack-ready fangs. He crept closer, his body low to the ground. He padded with care to keep his claws quiet.

They didn't notice him. People missed lots of important things. That frustrated Shadow sometimes. But this time being overlooked was a good thing. Mounting courage lifted his tail into a stiff bristle that matched the fierce concern of his silent snarl.

The big man pointed something at Steven, looked at it and then held it against his head and talked into it like it was a person.

Shadow crept closer and stopped directly behind Freda. They still hadn't noticed. He heard a faint but familiar voice come from the ear-object the man held still against his head. Shadow growled, and Freda started at his voice. She finally looked at him, worried brow wrinkles asking questions. He huddled behind her and dared himself to be brave. Be a good-dog. But he couldn't move.

The stranger reached out a hand toward Steven.

He growled again, and pressed against Freda's leg. He felt her tremble. She was scared, too. Shadow needed to be brave. He took another step forward.

Freda licked her lips, and Shadow smelled her sudden fear, and the slight tremor in her voice increased his agitation. "Mr. Childress, what about Steven's dog?"

Shadow flicked his ears toward her but didn't move his attention from the stranger.

"Dog?" The man frowned, finally noticing Shadow. He reached for Steven's arm.

"Steven, run!" Freda yelled, and backpedaled so fast she knocked over a chair.

Steven screamed. And Shadow leaped to his boy's rescue.

The man grabbed Steven and pulled him before him like a shield.

His claws clattered for purchase. Shadow's bark-demands escalated when Steven screamed louder, and he skidded into a nearby table, and yelped. He scrambled to his feet, and stalked within two dog-lengths. He snarled a demand for the man to let Steven go. Would he take Steven away?

Freda kept screaming. "Leave him alone!"

Shadow knew what "leave it" meant, but the strange man wouldn't let Steven go. He placed himself protectively between Freda and the threatening stranger. He lunged and feinted away from his boy's kicks, not wanting to injure Steven.

The man blocked Steven's pinwheeling arms and held his boy hard against his body. "It's just a tantrum." He had to shout over Steven's cries, but his worried eyes slid to Shadow.

Screams hurt Shadow's ears. The man's fear-smell spilled in waves but his steady stare threatened. For the first time, Shadow wanted to bite. Bite hard. He straightened his posture, arched his neck, and flagged his tail with just the tip jerking. He stared back. Ready.

Freda fumbled in her pocket. She held something to her ear.

So much fear-stink made it hard for good-dogs to think.

"Hang up the phone." The big man held the squirmy boy by the collar the way Shadow picked up his stuffed bear toy. He backed away with Steven in his arms.

Shadow danced closer. Aimed a bite. He dodged the man's kick, and feinted again. His ears pinned back. His tail wagged, stiff and frantic. He'd never attacked anything except his toy bear, but the bad man didn't know. He could bluff. Sometimes a loud growl was enough.

"Call off the dog." He pulled something out of his pocket and pointed it at Shadow. "I don't want to shoot anyone, not even a dog." The boy-thief's glasses glinted as he looked around the big room.

Steven's screams spiraled higher and higher. He turned red, and his eyes screwed shut. Shadow gathered his haunches. Good-dogs protect their boys.

Shadow danced closer and away again. Good-dogs don't use their teeth on people. He knew that. But what if the people were bad? He wanted to bite hard, hold on, and shake him. Grab and hurt, so his boy would stop yelling. Shadow leaped, and his jaws snapped.

The stranger yelled, flinching back. Steven wriggled and screamed, making the man's pointing hand jerk.

Freda howled and tackled the man. Something popped.

A gag-making stink burst into the air. Freda crumpled. Her head thudded on the shiny floor, and the ear-object cracked open and skidded across the slick floor.

Why'd she fall down? Shadow nose-poked her but she didn't stir.

The man pointed at Shadow, still struggling to contain his boy by the collar. "Look what you made me do."

He paw-danced around Freda's form and dodged in. Shadow's teeth snapped empty air before he bounded away. The gun continued to pop.

Steven slumped, finally silent. He hung in the stranger's grip, eyes closed like when he slept. But he wasn't asleep. He'd just gone to his quiet place. He did that sometimes, and hid for hours.

Teddy hid, too, out of sight in the entrance to the pee-smelly room. Shadow heard Teddy panting as though winded from a game of fetch. He whimpered, too. Shadow whined, wanting to join Teddy and hide his face against the man. But not while his boy was in the stranger's grip.

The whole world smelled like fear. And blood. It bubbled out of Freda. That made Shadow even more determined to bite. Despite the terror. Because of fear. He glared at the man who dared take his boy. He'd make the bad man go away. It was his job to protect Steven.

The stranger stared back. He threw Steven over his shoulder, turned and lurched away.

Shadow's paws bicycled for purchase. He lunged. His teeth clacked, snapped, and sought contact. He leaped, silent in pursuit. His fangs tore through cloth, sliced flesh. Salty skin, broken flesh, blood-taste and smell. He leaped high, grabbed again. Hung on.

The man screamed, he shrieked louder than Steven. He kicked, and a shiny shoe connected with furry ribs. Shadow yelped and rolled away. In the same motion, the man hit the mall door and pushed through.

The door slammed against Shadow's muzzle. He yelped and leaped against the glass. Flecks of saliva salted the glass when he grabbed the metal crossbar. How to get through? Go after them. He could see him, the bad man. The boy-thief. Close. Untouchable. *Taking his boy.*

A good-dog would know what to do. But Shadow hadn't a clue. He'd failed.

Bad dog. Shadow howled.

Chapter 25

September pulled into the Star Mall parking lot, and slowed Pam's Jeep to a crawl. One lonely VW squatted near the bus stop next to an empty HART-Line vehicle. Score.

Guilt flogged her for leaving Pam behind, even if EMTs were on the way. She'd left a message at the shelter about Bruno and the rest of Pam's dogs. She'd done all she could, at least while she was on the run.

Steven was priority number one. The flash drive was a lost cause. After Steven was safe, she'd concentrate on April. "Let him be here," she said, as if speaking the hope aloud would make it happen. It wasn't a prayer. Hell no. God never answered. Even Wilma would agree with her now.

Snow had changed to ice that chittered against the windshield. Wiper blades on the warm glass painted the mess into a frozen sheet except for the twin spots the defroster melted.

Light spilled from the mall's glass entry, but the stores inside looked dark. The place must have shut down early for the storm, but September didn't check her watch, didn't want to know the time. Each minute ticked closer to failure. And failure meant death.

September braced herself for the slap of cold and levered open the car door. By the time she'd shuffle-skated to the entrance, sleet sugared her hair.

Her phone rang. She looked. Mom again. She didn't answer. It was close to nine o'clock. Only 17 hours until the deadline.

The smeary doors gave her pause. How odd. Janitorial services kept entrances pristine, sensitive to shoppers' first impressions. Smudges covered the glass from floor to chest height on the two center doors, and muddy paw prints slurried the tile entrance. Her shoulders unclenched with sudden relief. They were here.

She pulled open the glass door and hurried into the mall. "Steven?" September's voice echoed. Metal accordion gates shuttered store fronts on both sides of the entrance, leaving only the massive hallways passable. If the individual stores had closed, that narrowed the search. She listened but heard nothing but the ambient buzz of florescent lights. The mall was empty. Maybe she missed them. Maybe they were safe with kindly strangers. "Where are you?" Steven might not answer, but if they were here, the dog would respond. "Shadow. Baby-dog, where are you?"

A yelp sounded, and September's heart leaped. "Shadow, good-dog. Shadow, *come*. Steven, it's Aunt September, don't be scared." She raced toward the yelps. Where the dog was, Steven couldn't be far.

The pup skidded around the corner, yodeling with emotion. His big paws slid out from under him. He regained his feet and launched himself, aiming slurps at her face as he wailed and arooed happy sounds mixed with something else. Her stomach fluttered with dread.

"Baby-dog, settle down." The jumping-jack behavior said he wanted her on his level, so she knelt to hug his shaking form. "Hush, it's okay." She eagerly scanned for Steven as she dodged the pup's frantic licks, stroking his throat until he rolled onto his back. He'd wet himself. What the hell? Her throat tightened. Something was off. "Where's Steven? Shadow, calm down. Settle. Where's Steven?" She steadied herself and spoke with command. "Find Steven."

"Steven's gone! You've got to help. Call for help, my phone's dead—"

September scrambled to her feet. Shadow rolled upright but continued to wriggle and cry.

"Who are you? Where's Steven?" She backed away.

The old man shuffled closer in a frantic jig that favored a bum leg. His faded blue eyes swam with tears. His overcoat swallowed a frail body bent with arthritis, defeat, or both. He held stained bare hands before him. And shuddered.

"Call the cops. Freda's cell phone is smashed. I don't have one." He stared at his dirty hands, wiped them against the front of his dark coat, and folded them together as though in prayer. "That's a good dog, he tried to protect

Steven." His lower lip trembled. "That poor little boy." He looked at her, anguished. "Nobody's here! I've banged on every damn gate for somebody to call for help. But they closed early, nobody's here. Thank God you came."

"Is that blood?" She glanced at Shadow for his reaction, but his hackles remained smooth. "Where is Steven? He's not hurt, is he?"

The man stumbled toward her, his voice desperate. "My friend, Freda. I think she's dead." He braced himself against the wall to keep himself upright. "Call an ambulance." He whirled and nearly fell as he scrambled back toward the food court.

"Wait. Somebody's dead?" The room spun, steadied, and she dashed after him. "Where's Steven? And who the hell are you?"

"Are you deaf? Call the ever-lovin' police!" His stiff old-man gait moved more quickly than she could have imagined. "If it matters, I'm Theodore Williams. They call me Teddy."

The dog's ears twitched. He whined as he kept pace with her, insisting on contact as they moved.

"Who's dead, Teddy?"

He stopped abruptly and pointed, and September surged past. Shadow pressed so hard against her leg, she tripped.

Teddy pulled off his glasses and swiped his tears with a sleeve. "We only wanted to help the boy and he shot her!" He found a napkin on a nearby table and scrubbed his hands, then shredded the paper into confetti. "I tried to give her CPR. You've got to call nine-one-one. Help Freda." He gulped. "Stop that man who took Steven. God, the poor little kid was screaming, he was so scared." He balled his fists, white knuckled with anger and fear. "I couldn't stop him. He would have killed me, too."

They turned the corner into the food court that held a dozen or more café tables with flimsy chairs. Near a large central planter, spilled fries and ketchup mixed with brown liquid from a crushed cup. The HART-Line driver was sprawled next to an overturned chair like she'd attempted to sit and missed.

September rushed to the woman, brushing her lank hair aside. A neat hole just left of center marred Freda's smooth throat, blood pooling beneath Freda's head. She was still warm, but without a pulse or respiration. Nothing she could do.

She slowly got back up. Her bruised ribs had stiffened. Teddy stood with his head bowed, hands clasped before him, mumbling in prayer. He wobbled, and she caught his arm, noticing Teddy smelled like wet wool and tobacco when his smoker's cough rattled his lungs. Afraid to ask, she forced the words out anyway. "Tell me, Teddy. Who took Steven?"

He crossed himself, and took a steadying breath. "I bought them French fries." He stuck his free hand in his pocket, still wary of bloodstains on the canary yellow sweater he wore under his coat.

Steven would have been drawn to that color, just as he'd been willing to board the yellow bus when April's car failed to show up. She frowned when Shadow padded close to the dead woman and sniffed her leg.

"Shadow, let's go." She waited until the pup made eye contact, and then led Teddy and the dog toward the exit. "It was kind of you and your friend to help. Steven and Shadow love French fries, it's their special treat." She was talking about snack food with a woman dead on the floor, and wanted to shake him, but there was no rushing Teddy. His frantic pleas for action had morphed into dazed confusion. He looked ready to collapse. Shock did that to people. "What happened?"

"Steven told us his name, address and phone number."

She nodded encouragement. April taught him to parrot the information in case he wandered away, something autistic children often did. German shepherds helped prevent wandering like a moveable fence, and were trained to corral their charges and alert them to unusual situations.

When she looked at him, Shadow cut his eyes away and whined. His tail beat a low-held fast wag. It wasn't the dog's fault. Training took time. Shadow was little more than a baby himself. She was responsible. For all of it.

"Freda called the number." Teddy's lips trembled so much he was hard to understand. "Steven's dad was coming to get him. I was in the men's room when he got here. I heard them yelling, Steven screaming, and I should have helped. I should have done something. He shot Freda. Why'd he do that? He would have shot me!" Teddy turned and vomited.

September supported the old man, her mind awhirl. April hated Doug, she'd never send him. And if Doug did show up, it made no sense he'd shoot somebody for rescuing Steven.

Then she understood. Steven repeated April's cell phone number. Since Lizzie had April, she must have answered her phone and sent Ghost Man, although it didn't seem possible he could have beat her here from the park. "What did he look like?"

"I only saw the back of him as he left. Tall, overweight, wore a hat with earflaps. Is it a custody battle? I know those things can get nasty."

She sucked in a breath, feeling sucker-punched. So it wasn't Ghost Man. Lizzie must have an army of henchmen and sent someone else.

Teddy pulled a linen handkerchief from one pocket, and dabbed his mouth. "I should have gone after him, I should have stopped him. Steven screamed. He didn't want to go."

He could have saved Steven. She wanted to smack him, but she deserved punishment even more. She'd frozen at the park, and hadn't saved Pam. She'd as good as led a killer to butcher Chris and Dakota. She was nobody's hero. How could she blame Teddy when he'd at least tried to help?

"He didn't even know I was there. He was busy watching Freda and dodging the dog. You call him Shadow?"

The pup's head swiveled toward Teddy at mention of his name, and back at September when she couldn't catch her breath. Shadow sniffed her gloved hand and shoved his brow beneath her palm for the comfort of a pet.

But she pulled her hand away. He'd failed Steven. But she'd trained him. He wasn't Dakota. Dakota would have saved Steven or died trying, just as Dakota sacrificed himself for Chris. And left her alone.

Bile flooded her mouth. September bent, hands on knees, and retched. Her empty stomach twisted repeatedly in a painful, unproductive knot.

Now Teddy supported her. "I'm not a fighter, I'm a teacher." She wanted to tell him to shut up, but couldn't get past the dry heaves. "Taught computer science, writing programs, what do I know about guns?" His bushy eyebrows rose and fell above the rim of his glasses. "Where's your phone?"

"It's dead." She had to give him a plausible reason for not calling. Had to get away from him. Now that Lizzie had Steven, she'd won and had all the cards.

"But you have a car. I couldn't find Freda's car keys. I didn't want to move her." He sobbed, and forced himself to continue. "You can get us to a phone; my house isn't far from here. The police will know what to do, right?" He wanted answers, wanted forgiveness, and she had nothing to give. "I'm so sorry about your son."

September didn't bother to correct him. It didn't matter. Nothing mattered.

"I want to make it up to you and your little boy. Make it up to Freda." Teddy straightened to his full height, assumed a professorial dignity with the small posture change.

She'd bungled everything. Blew off April's call, missed Steven at the park, taunted Lizzie into shooting Wilma, let April be taken, and involved Pam. This poor woman's murder and Steven's kidnapping, it was all her fault, too. Everything she touched turned to crap. She didn't have the flash drive, hadn't a chance in hell to find it, and without that as ransom, April and Steven would die.

September's knees turned to rubber, and she sat down hard on the floor. Her ribs throbbed. She had no tears left. Yes, call the police. That's what Mom would want. It's what by-the-book Chris would do, too. She couldn't stop Lizzie, couldn't save anyone. Hell, she couldn't even protect herself without triple-locked doors and window bars.

Shadow pushed his front half into her lap, and she stiffened and pushed him away. "I taught you better than that." But he wouldn't be denied. Shadow buried his muzzle in her armpit and cried.

She couldn't help herself and gave in, her arms clutching and then cradling him. September held him tighter and tighter. She buried her face in the soft black fur of Shadow's ruff. And it felt good, oh God it felt so good, it had been so long . . .

"That's a great dog. I think he bit the guy."

"Good-dog," September whispered fiercely, "You marked the sonofabitch." Her words spit venom but her hands remained gentle as they stroked his fur, and then hesitated when she felt something strung around his neck.

September parted the dog's coat. She followed the fine chain down both sides of his throat to where a pendant hung hidden in the fur of his chest. "Shadow, move. Move, baby-dog. Wait." He didn't want to, but finally pulled himself away from her body. She pulled the lanyard over his head to examine the 16-GB flash drive suspended on the chain.

"Good-dog, Shadow. You're such a good boy, good-dog." She quickly slipped the lanyard over her head, and dropped the flash drive beneath the front of her coat.

Shadow wriggled with delight, ears flat to his head. He banged his tail against the floor. He'd stopped shivering.

Teddy offered his hand and helped her struggle to her feet. "What's that?"

She pressed one hand over the flash drive where it nestled between her breasts. "A miracle, Teddy. It's life itself."

Chapter 26

Combs lifted the brass knocker on September's front door and fought déjà vu. He glanced at his watch. It had been less than nine hours since he and Pike had noticed the smoke. He banged four times and rang the bell and backed down the steps with one hand on his gun.

"She's not here." Gonzales joined him.

"You check the garage?" Combs kept his hand on his gun.

"Empty. I did a walk around." He paused. "Last word we got, she's driving Pam's Jeep, but so far no sighting."

Combs craned to see the brick carriage house September used as a garage. The old wood gates remained true to the historical design but must be a bitch to open and shut in bad weather. She'd been in a hurry when she left, and hadn't bothered to close them. One door moved in the wind to carve an icy wedge in the drift. A covered walkway didn't fit the architecture but connected a brick path from the outbuilding to a side door. He guessed it opened into her kitchen.

The two men climbed the steps together. Gonzales stomped his feet on the brick entry to knock off clots of ice. "There's a lot of snow blown into the garage. She's been gone for hours."

"Not enough for a warrant. We'll have to tread lightly."

Gonzales pulled a keychain from his pocket with several keys. "Her folks gave me the keys and alarm code. They want her found." He grinned. "I explained there's probable cause she's either kidnapped or on the run from killers."

Combs smiled back. That would have to do.

The security was over the top. It took several minutes for Gonzales to find the right key to open each of the three locks in the fancy brass key plate. "Her folks were surprised September even left the house. She's convinced some stalker from Chicago followed her to Indiana and killed her husband. No proof, though, they never arrested anyone."

Combs struggled to concentrate. Uncle Stanley and Aunt Ethel expected him half an hour ago. He was the oldest. He should host the gathering. But they'd want answers he didn't have, details he couldn't bring himself to revisit, that no victim's family ever needed to know. Mom's murder had Stan panting to join the investigation, to hell with retirement. Uncle Stan was even more outside official boundaries than Combs.

At least with Gonzales, he'd make headway on the investigation. So far he'd not gotten any grief about the Fish radio incident, either, since it led to the park victim. September Day was the best lead they had.

Gonzales opened the final lock and pushed open the door. He stepped one foot inside, gun drawn. "Haloooo." He listened for a beat, and holstered his weapon when the security system beeped a warning. "Feels empty. Play heads up, but I don't think anyone's here." He located the alarm keypad beside the door and punched in the code September's parents had provided.

The old two-story house, complete with a turret on one side, originally contained a warren of tiny rooms connected by narrow halls. From the outside, the gingerbread structure was the witch's castle Combs and his friends whispered about when they were kids. But September's contractors had gutted the house, leaving the massive vertical beams in place. The work-in-progress created an open airy floor plan of casual elegance. It must have taken a boatload of money. Combs followed the detective inside, and wiped his boots on the sisal "Cats Rule, Dogs Drool" welcome mat. "What else did the parents say?"

"Not a lot. Couldn't say where the sisters might go. The mother talked to September this morning, and said she had seemed distracted and evasive. Also said there's been recent friction between the sisters over the Thanksgiving meal. Both want to host it." He shrugged as if it was no consequence. "Sounds familiar. My wife and her sister go round and round about that every year. But otherwise, they get along okay. September's even helped with Steven's treatment."

"The dog, right?"

"Yeah, the dog. But also some pricy new treatment Childress refused to fund." Gonzales looked around the house. "Nice place."

"Money to burn, like Childress said."

Gonzales shrugged. "He only had part of it right. The lottery paid out fifty grand or so after taxes. The big money came from life insurance on September's husband, at least that's what the parents say." He smoothed his mustache. "Doty thinks the sisters cooked up the lost boy story."

"Why?" Combs shook his head. "Does she think Steven got hurt or killed so they need a reason to disappear him?" Evil thought, but it did make sense.

"Maybe. Still no clue why either of them would shoot your mother." Gonzales refused to look at Combs. "Some people go off their nut when they lose a spouse. September could have lots of guilt over that, and maybe the sisters fought, and April ended up dead so September ran with the little boy."

Too complicated. Simple cause and effect was more likely. "We're turning a couple of hoof prints into a zebra stampede. We're too close to see the big picture."

"So what do you call the bloody workout clothes in September's car? With that Body Works logo, they belong to April and she's missing. Why else would your girlfriend stash them?"

"Don't call her my girlfriend." His wet shoes squeaked. He knew about the evidence of a fight at April's business, and acknowledged family feuds could lead to murder, but it just didn't feel right. "Blood on the workout clothes looked more like it came from the outside, not that the person wearing them was injured. Next."

Gonzales consulted his notes. "September's husband worked special victims in Chicago before they moved to Indiana. He was off duty when he got killed."

"Makes no sense for September to run with the kid. On the radio play-back, April said Steven disappeared from the house. She called September for help. They both get Academy Awards if that was an act."

"Don't discount the possibility of a set up. Bet it's a custody thing to get Steven away from his dad. More ex-husbands kill their wives than sisters, and Childress was hiding something." He checked his watch. "Wonder if Doty's still at the hospital. If the dog lady from the park pulls through, maybe she has a clue where they went."

Combs shifted his weight. If anyone should feel resentful of moms getting custody over dads, it was him. He had to make an appointment to see his kids. "September's Volvo was at the park. She wouldn't shoot up her own car. Somebody wanted her stranded. The witness didn't see a child. Didn't see much." He opened his coat.

"So why'd September run if she has nothing to hide? Hell, she insisted the neighbor call nine-one-one, but didn't stick around to make sure her friend got help."

That part bothered Combs. A lot.

"She grabbed the Jeep and beat it out of there before the EMTs could arrive." Gonzales stepped further into the room. "She could have set up that rendezvous at the park just to get another car, trashing her own to make herself into a victim."

"That's a stretch." Too many unanswered questions. "What makes a woman, the widow of a cop for God's sake, go nuts? Kidnap a kid and kill anyone who gets in her way?" Combs hated the guesswork, and was eager for answers and hoped the latest vic would pull through and have some clues to share. "What's the word on the dog lady's status?"

"Last I heard, still in surgery. And it's not looking good. Doty will call with any news." Gonzales peered up the impressive front staircase, and his nose wrinkled like a silk shirt on a hot day. "Damn, smells like smoke. I'll take the back, you take the front—"

"—and I'll get to Scotland afore ye." Combs looked around.

Gonzales suppressed a smile as he took the stairs two at a time.

Combs looked around the ground floor. Sheet-covered furniture leaned against walls. The room smelled of fresh paint and new carpet. Cherry crown molding contrasted with the cream walls and the carved stone mantel above a massive fireplace. He flicked up a dust sheet that covered a burgundy leather sofa and a matching overstuffed chair. Nothing here.

Combs passed through an arched doorway into a smaller room next to the kitchen meant to be the dining area. Instead, September used it for an office and music room. The rest of the house remained a work-in-progress, but this space was lived in. The cobalt carpet and matching blue ceiling contrasted with yellow walls. A small studio piano on the rear wall perched next to a large stringed instrument—cello? Bass?—that stood upright in a carved stand in the corner. Books and sheets of music overflowed the bench and a basket on the floor.

The opposite wall held a large bay window. September's desk and chair, cherry wood again, took advantage of the view. The work space held a computer, phone, and a Tiffany-style rose lamp. Combs remembered how countless rose bushes used to turn the old house into a perfume factory each spring, and wondered if they'd survived years of neglect. The adjacent file cabinet also held a printer, and a wedding picture of a beaming man about Combs's age with his arm around September. Her expression looked guarded, not that of a radiant bride.

"Talk to me, September." Combs pulled off his gloves and sifted through papers on the desk. "Tell me why."

Three gunshot victims in less than twelve hours, and September was the common denominator. Maybe she hadn't killed his mom, but she'd been directly involved, he was sure of it, but no judge would issue a warrant based on a gut feeling. He and Gonzales were here because September, April and Steven were missing, and potential victims of foul play. That was the official version, anyway, and Doty signed off on it. She was as frustrated as the rest of them.

Combs flipped through September's DayMinder, and checked the haphazard Post-It notes stuck to every surface of the desk top. He heard Gonzales clomping overhead. The hardwood floors, high ceilings and empty rooms made for great acoustics. You couldn't sneak around in this house, unless barefoot.

People carry DayMinders with them. September must have rushed out the door to have left it behind. Today's appointments, highlighted in a variety of colors, included the Pet Peeves radio show, and something called a temperament test. Each of the appointments had a checkmark, and the middle appointment included a phone number.

He dialed and got the city shelter with a prompt to leave a message. He didn't. Combs flipped the pages. An appointment marked "deposition" also had a checkmark, so presumably it had been resolved. "Deposition" meant trial. That could be about child custody. Combs dialed. Gonzales's footsteps thumped overhead.

"McIntyre, Devries, Ellis and Freeman, office hours are nine to five, please leave a message and someone will return your call," said a bored-sounding woman.

Combs recognized the firm, one of the largest in Heartland. "This is Officer Jeffrey Combs. I'm investigating a homicide and need to speak with whoever had a deposition scheduled in two days with September Day." He left his number and hung up. It had been a long shot anyone would answer at this hour.

Gonzales clattered down the distant stairs and hurried into the room, cell phone pressed to his ear. "I got Doty on the line. There's news." He listened, and hung up. "The victim from the park just died. Never made a statement."

"Shit." Combs stretched and cracked his knuckles but it didn't relieve the tension. "September made several calls today, probably to cancel appointments because of the snow. Her DayMinder has the number next to a note about a deposition. "

"Her folks said she's been an expert witness on dog bite cases." Gonzales gestured with the phone. "Maybe some good news, though. Ran a search on gun registrations, and Childress owns guns. He's a collector."

"Gee, isn't it funny he didn't mention that. What's Childress say?"

"He lawyered up."

Oh goody, now there's a surprise. "That's convenient. Something to hide, after all. What about the park victim?" Gonzales had a rep in the department as a ballistics expert. He'd gone through FBI training and had an uncanny knack and passion for all things guns.

"Snow made it hard to recover any shell casings, but I'll get to eyeball them as soon as I get back. That's prelim until the hard science guys confirm, but the best we got under the circumstances. But we got an ID on the vic at

Childress's place. Dr. Henry Pottinger, divorced, no local family. Works out of Plano."

"Plano? That's an hour away. Visiting a patient?"

"Don't think he's that kind of doctor. Doty's following up on that." Gonzales tapped his foot with nervous energy. "Like everything else, the weather's shut down most businesses. It may be tomorrow or later before Doty can find out about Pottinger. Hell, he got shot, wrapped in a knockoff Oriental rug, and left for us to find at April's ex-husband's house. Is she that dumb?" He tsk-tsked with his tongue. "Even amateurs do a better job of it."

"Yeah, I can't see either of the sisters manhandling the body into the car." His eyes itched, maybe from the smoke still in the house. Combs noted the screensaver on the desktop computer—a gorgeous, brown German shepherd—and tapped the mouse. The password prompt came up. Shit.

Gonzales pocketed his cell phone. "Another tidbit. Animal Control showed up at the park after we left to take possession of the victim's dog."

"So?" That was standard.

"We didn't call. September did." He scanned the room, glanced at the musical instruments, the cluttered desk, and the baby gate entry into the kitchen. "Animal Control already knew the victim's name, her address, that her veterinarian husband's out of town and other animals in the home need attention. September clued 'em in." He shrugged at Combs's scowl. "She doesn't act like any killer I've ever seen."

"So maybe she feels remorse?" He didn't want to hear it. "She can be sorry all she wants in prison." Combs played with the keyboard, typed in a few common passwords. No luck. "Find anything upstairs?"

"Upstairs is mostly bare, in various stages of reconstruction. There's a finished bathroom and bedroom." He hooked a thumb toward the kitchen. "Been in there yet?"

He nodded. "This morning with Pike. Laundry room connects to the kitchen. There's another staircase to the second story, and an outside door to the covered walkway that connects the garage." Combs gestured to the computer. "Want to take a crack at it? Maybe you'll find something that points where the sisters might go." Computers were not his strong suit.

"Sure." Gonzales pulled out the chair and sat down. "Give me the DayMinder. People keep lists of passwords where anyone can find 'em."

"Sure, and maybe there's secret message in the coffee canister." Combs headed for the kitchen.

He'd seen the baby gate in the doorway, and walked through it that morning, but it hadn't registered. It looked similar to one at April's house, except this one stood taller—nearly four feet—and included a small inset latched gate in the bottom. It wasn't for infants, it was for pets.

Combs scanned the room before he open the metal barrier. No dog sounds, but that didn't mean a surprise wasn't waiting. He liked animals, but he had a healthy respect for dogs, especially big ones. So far, the only sign of a dog was the screensaver.

Black ceramic stovetop. Empty bowl on the counter beside the double sink. Brushed steel dishwasher, oven, microwave and refrigerator. A magnetic wipe-off board on the fridge. Swirly gray and black marble countertops matched the mantel in the living room. Dark blue-green slate floor. Floor to ceiling stained glass windows with a view of snow-covered roses. Wall phone, the long cord looped up and caught on a hook. Stained-glass tabletop and four chairs, a coffee mug and saucer on the table. Sterilite storage box on the floor.

No dog.

Combs opened the gate and moved to the table. He picked up the oversize covered mug and it sloshed. Nearly full. He checked the cupboards, opened and shut drawers and cabinets. Moved to the refrigerator, noted the magnetic notepad filled with a grocery list.

Something tapped him on the head.

"Shit." Combs ducked and leaped away. He leveled his gun in one smooth motion.

"What? Something wrong?" Gonzales was at the open gate in two long strides, hand on his own weapon.

Combs choked back a laugh and holstered his gun. Pointed at the top of the fridge.

A chocolate brown cat lounged on the perch, one paw still trailing down the front of the refrigerator. Green eyes shined. Yawning, the cat paused to lick his white front.

"Cat grabbed my hair. Scared the shit out of me." Combs realized the storage box in the corner, about a third full of sandy material, was the biggest damn litter box he'd ever seen.

Gonzales smirked. "My sister has cats. Go in her house and the smell grabs you by the throat." He sniffed elaborately. "All I smell is smoke. No wonder the big bad putty tat scared you." He returned to the computer.

"I thought September trained dogs. Weird she's got a cat, but no dog." The cat stood on tiptoes, stretched, and jumped down to the countertop. Nosing the bowl beside the sink for one last kibble, the cat sat down and regarded Combs. And meowed.

"Nice cat. That's a good girl. Boy. Whatever," he said. "Close the gate, Gonzales. If this guy sleeps on the refrigerator, he must be some jumper." His mom had a cat, big old Simba. She'd rescued the cat from the local shelter eight years ago and said Simba gave her someone to cuddle since her kids were grown and the grandkids on the go. Combs caught his breath. He'd have to do something about Simba, now that Mom was gone.

The cat mewed again, and cheek-rubbed the empty bowl. It scooted close to the edge and teetered.

"Any luck with the computer?" Combs caught the bowl before the cat's gravity experiments sent it to the floor. He opened and closed several cupboards and checked the refrigerator, finding the cat's food.

"We'll have to get the experts in here." Gonzales frowned. "What you doing?"

Combs shrugged. "Feeding the cat. With September on the run, it might be days before he gets fed." He jostled a cup of dry stars into the bowl, shoved the bag back inside the fridge, and stroked the cat. The creature purred and began to eat. "Whatever's going on with September, she didn't plan it." He hated to admit she wasn't to blame. He massaged the cat's shoulders, and his own loosened.

"So what changed your mind?" Gonzales stepped inside and latched the gate.

"Coffee cup's still full. She rushed out without finishing. No notes on the fridge, and she's a list maker, they're all over the desk. And the biggie—if she's an animal nut, why didn't she leave food for the cat? Or at least make arrangements for it?" To him, that was most telling of all. "She called Animal Control for the park victim's dog, but didn't leave a few days' food down for kitty?" He scratched the cat's chin. "No way. She's on the run, but it's nothing she planned."

Combs's phone rang. Uncle Stan again, he thought, and pulled it out of his pocket. He'd remind him about Simba. The old cat's arthritis needed watching and Mom had babied her—hell, they'd taken care of each other. Mom would have a fit if her cat was forgotten. When he didn't recognize the number, he almost didn't answer. "Combs here."

"Jeff Combs? Officer Jeff Combs?"

"Yes. Who's this?"

"We met this morning at my house when you saw smoke. You left me your card."

He waved at Gonzales. "September? Where are you?"

Gonzales gnawed his mustache. "You have to be shitting me."

Combs struggled to stay collected. "September, a lot of people are worried about you."

"Did you find Pam? At Gentry Park. Is she okay?" Somebody else, a man, spoke in the background, but Combs couldn't make out the words. "I...uh, you need to check out Star Mall. I've got to go."

"No. Wait!" So many things to ask, he needed to keep her on the line. "Pam, is that your friend with the dog at the park?"

"Is she okay? Please tell me she's going to be okay."

"What's at Star Mall?" Moving to the refrigerator, Combs jotted notes for Gonzales to read, and the man nodded and dialed his own phone.

"Tell me about Pam."

"Her dog's with Animal Control. You called them, right?" The cat mewed, and jumped back onto the fridge and began to wash. "What's your cat's name? Big brown and white fellow. He's a hungry cuss."

"You're in my house? Is Macy okay?" She sounded angry. And scared.

"Tell her Pam's dead," Gonzales prompted. "Tell her more people will die if she doesn't come in." He paused, spoke into his own phone. "Combs has September on his cell phone, and we've got the number." He read it from Combs's scribbled note on the fridge.

"September, listen to me." Combs paced. He had to get her to come in. "The police know you're in trouble. We found a body at April's house. Were you there when it happened?" If she knew the victim was his mother, she'd hang up. "We're looking for you, looking for your sister and her son. Whoever shot that woman might be after you. Are you safe? Are April and Steven with you?"

"Oh, no. . ." She whispered the words, defeated.

"We know you were at Childress's place, too. There's another body there." At Gonzales' pointed expression, he added, "Your friend Pam's dead, that's three—"

"Pam? Oh God, what have I done?"

"Stay with me, September. I can help you. Just come in, we'll sort things out."

"You're wrong. Nobody can help me. And it's not three. Go to Star Mall." Heavy breaths. "I'll make them pay." She hung up.

Chapter 27

September's eyes burned, her feet throbbed, and she smelled—no, scratch that. She stank. Amazing how pungent a person could get, even in icy weather.

Teddy's worn sofa soothed her sore muscles but did little to ease her guilt. So many dead or at risk, all because of Pottinger's damned flash drive. Now she'd involved Teddy, another innocent bystander.

She should have left him at the mall, but that would have been like kicking a puppy. It would have been better to drop him off at his house and leave, before he got hurt, too. But once here, he'd insisted on calling the police. She'd managed to beat him to the landline before the storm took out the phone, but he'd overheard about Pam and Gentry Park. She'd put him off for now. That was good, because otherwise he'd have insisted they kill themselves driving to the nearest police station, hospital or fire department.

In the nearby kitchen, Teddy dished cold cuts from a baggy onto a battered pie pan while Shadow watched and drooled. The pup must think he'd gone to heaven. She used slivers of cold cuts for training rewards.

Shadow's butt hit the floor, the puppy-polite request she'd taught him. Once the pan touched down, he scooted it halfway across the kitchen to lick it clean.

Lovely to be a clueless dog delighted by simple things like treats from a kind stranger, not haunted with visions of brains splashed against walls, or the fear she'd doomed April and Steven to a similar fate just by coming here. She'd gotten people killed. Cops inside her house meant Mom and Dad gave them keys. But she'd be damned if she'd drag more family into the mess.

September held the flash drive in one hand, and felt the outline of the phone in her pocket. She could end it now. Ring up Lizzie. She could reach her through April's phone, arrange to trade the flash drive for April and Steven and get them back safe. If she could do that, maybe it would assuage some of the guilt over Pam, Freda, and Wilma. She had beaten the 24-hour deadline when she found the flash drive, but that didn't count until the ransom exchange. Steven was still lost. So was April.

"You want coffee? I've got decaf or the real stuff. My doctor doesn't like me having caffeine, but I keep some gourmet around for guests." Teddy chuckled, a nervous unhappy sound. "Or, there's some diet Coke, or Dr. Pepper."

"I need to be fully caffeinated, so coffee would be great. Thanks." She'd never finished the mug from this morning. No wonder she'd zombied her way through the last several hours.

Teddy set a chipped ceramic bowl of water on the floor. Shadow's toenails ticked on the linoleum. He slurped.

"Hungry? I could scramble some eggs." Teddy pulled a cast iron fry pan off a wall hook. "When was the last time you ate?"

September realized she'd not eaten all day. "Been just a tad busy." Maybe the lightheadedness wasn't just from dodging bullets. "I'll grab a burrito later." She didn't want Teddy to waste any more time. Coffee would have to do. The sooner she got away from him, the safer he'd be.

"You need to eat." He stood in the doorway, pan in one hand and three eggs cradled in the other.

"Not hungry. Just the coffee will do me fine. High octane, the stronger the better." Decaf was a waste of beverage.

Shadow trotted to her, his ears flat. He shoved his wet muzzle into her arms to dry himself. He'd had a rough day, too. He offered a sly grin as he climbed onto the sofa beside her. "Shadow, off." She corrected him out of reflex. April didn't allow dogs on her furniture.

He flattened himself against the cushions, squirmed and wagged, doing his best to look pitiful.

"Let him be. More dogs have been on that sofa than people. Fur's part of the fabric by now." Teddy pulled a chair close. "Don't you ever let him on your furniture? On your bed? That's one of the joys of a dog, I always thought." He smiled. "Me and my wife had an old shepherd named Max.

He'd start out all polite at the foot of the bed and by morning he was my pillow, shoving me half off the mattress." He showed stained teeth. "German shepherds are the best."

Like Dakota. He'd been more than a dog. Losing him and Chris at the same time nearly killed her. September considered Shadow, and her lips tightened. No dog would ever replace Dakota. The pup was sweet but he was no Dakota. "Shadow isn't my dog. I'm training him for Steven." She glanced at her watch, surprised it was closing in on eleven. "How soon will coffee be ready?"

"It's brewing. Steven doesn't live with you? Is this a custody fight?"

Her hands sought Shadow's black fur and rubbed his ears. "Not a custody battle. It's hard to explain." She stared at the dog so she didn't have to look at the old man. "It's dangerous. I don't want you involved."

"I'm already involved." He huffed. "I get that it's dangerous. Freda got killed. I would've got shot, too, if he'd seen me. I'd like to know why."

No you don't, she wanted to say. You really don't want to know.

"You owe me an explanation." Teddy took off his glasses and polished them on his sweater, and replaced them. "That friend you told the cops about, Pam, she got hurt, too. I heard. I might be old, but my ears still work." He pointed an accusing finger. "And now those goons have your son. Is it ransom? Where's your husband in all of this?"

She winced. Lord, what would Chris do? She missed him so much. . . Abruptly she stood up. "Can I use your bathroom?" She could make the call to Lizzie in the privacy of the toilet. Get out of here before Henchman #12 showed up. Lizzie could have dozens of bad guys on call. She had to get away before the phone lines were fixed and Teddy got fed up and called the cops on his own. That would get Steven and April killed. And him, too.

Shadow whined at the tension. He yawned and turned away.

Teddy didn't answer for a long moment. "Down the hall, to the right. I'll get you towels. And I've got some sweats that might fit you, once you get out of those wet things."

She struggled to walk but her balance was off. She grudgingly accepted Teddy's hand. Shadow hopped off the sofa and leaned against her as if afraid to lose contact.

"Coffee will turn on the brain cells. Everything feels like mush." She tried to smile and failed. "Don't trouble yourself over the clothes, I'm okay."

"You'll change clothes." He shrugged to soften the harsh tone. "Clean clothes will make you feel human again." He'd changed out of his stained yellow sweater and jacket as soon as they'd arrived. Teddy led the way and motioned at the open bathroom door.

Metallic owl wallpaper aimed dozens of creepy bird eyes at September. She shuddered, and Teddy smiled. "The owls came with the house. You get used to them." He pointed. "There's a new toothbrush, even some deodorant in the cabinet. I'll scramble eggs and pour coffee." He raised a hand to cut off more protests. "Later we'll discuss." He glowered at her. "No excuses." He hurried to a nearby bedroom, and metal coat hangers jangled when he rummaged for the promised clothes.

Shadow pressed into the tiny room with her, and September didn't have the heart to kick him out. She closed the door and waited until he'd settled, and then she sat on the floor beside him to pull out her cell phone. She leaned back against the wall and silently rehearsed what to say. It was time she called Lizzie.

Chapter 28

Claire gazed out the bus window at the Kansas countryside. Flat, a white desert as far as the eye could see, only stubbled fingers of vegetation poked through. Even the drift fences offered little contrast to the barren landscape.

The serene view calmed Claire and mirrored her expectations. Though dormant now, spring would reveal fields lush with crops, just as her hopes for Tracy would bear fruit.

They'd acquired another seven children and their parents in Kansas City, and had planned to spend the night on the south side of town. Tracy slept on the seat beside her, exhausted from the earlier tantrum. The trip ratcheted up stress in parents, but for children, the cross country trek was torture. The kids didn't know or care that the discomfort was for their own good. Thank goodness most had nodded off, or sat in a sedated stupor. Parents just sought to get them through this last awfulness before a hoped-for better future became a reality.

Elaine lurched down the aisle and stopped to chat here and there with any parent who was still awake. Her mouse brown hair matched her watery eyes.

She'd yet to shed the frayed overcoat from her turn at the wheel. The driver's window wouldn't shut completely, and it sucked out the warmth the heaters struggled to maintain. But parents grateful for the ride bundled their children in extra layers and kept complaints to themselves.

When she tried to smile at Claire, deep lines cut canyons from each side of Elaine's nose making her look ten years older than her 38 years. They'd been friends even before Tracy was diagnosed with Autism Spectrum Disorder at twenty months old.

"Doing okay?" Elaine grabbed the back of the seat ahead of Claire to steady herself when the bus swooped through another intersection.

Claire flinched and returned a tight smile. "Tracy finally conked out." She whispered so she wouldn't rouse the little girl. "She got so wound up I'm amazed she can sleep at all." Claire loved to watch her daughter sleep. Tracy looked normal when she was asleep, a beautiful child no different than any other five-year-old. Only when she was awake did Tracy's differentness become obvious.

"Lenny's wired, too. I gave him his Rubik's cube. That should keep him focused for another hour. I hope." Elaine sighed and sank into a seat. "This is our last chance. He's fifteen, will turn sixteen next month."

"Oh, that's right. The program says children must be under sixteen." Claire hadn't thought much about the requirement since Tracy was so much younger.

"If Tracy missed this go-round, she'd have another chance at the next Gathering." Elaine swiveled to inventory the vehicle. "Most of the children are seven or eight. Only Lenny and Ricky Smith are older." She stifled a yawn. None of the adults had done more than doze.

Tracy was the youngest, and one of only four girls. "We can't afford to wait." Claire spoke with grim resolve. "We had to scrape together the deposit. But it's worth it. Did you see that before and after video on the website?"

Elaine nodded and sighed. "A miracle. That's what sold us on the treatment." She finger combed her messy hair but it didn't help. "Everything just fell into place: the timing, the location. My father-in-law lives nearby and wanted to help out, but he's near retirement and not made of money. He was thrilled when Dwayne called about the Legacy Center's offer to waive fees. Another miracle." Her face grew soft and she became almost pretty. "Of course, Lenny's his grandson, and his namesake. Dwayne insisted."

"How's Dwayne? He must be exhausted, too." Claire turned to see the lanky pastor. "I didn't know he could drive a bus."

"Better than me. He grew up on a ranch, and says this old bus reminds him of the tractor he drove as a kid." Elaine swayed when the bus picked up speed around a gentle curve. She grabbed the seat back again to steady herself. "Dwayne says driving a bus compares to preaching a sermon. You dodge potholes and ice along the way and pray you don't slide off the road getting home."

Claire laughed and stifled the sound with her hand. But Tracy didn't move. Most of the kids slept, exhausted both physically and emotionally. She noticed several adults were also nodding off at the back of the bus. At least three of the parents had more than one affected child.

"We're behind schedule. Two other parents offered to swap out driver duty." Elaine stretched and her back popped.

Her muscles always got tight from driving, too. "We're not stopping?"

"I cancelled the hotel. We've got to drive straight through." Elaine yawned again. "With good weather it's another eight hours. But in this snow we'll be lucky to get there in twice that time."

Claire adjusted the coat over Tracy's drowsy figure. "We can sleep after we get to the Legacy Center. I won't feel like resting 'til then anyway." Hell, she hadn't had a good night's sleep in four or five years. Why start now?

Elaine looked like she might cry. "It's got to work. I mean the treatment, it's got to work." She pulled a Chap Stick out of her pocket. "Our congregation raised funds for gas to get us there, did you know that?" She pressed her lips together to spread the balm. "Nice to have people care that much. They'll hold a prayer vigil for us Sunday, too. All of us, not just Lenny."

Claire's eyes glimmered with tears. "That means a lot. I can help with the gas." She reached for her purse.

Elaine stopped her hands. "They wanted to help. They love Lenny. He's a gentle soul like his dad, and sort of the church project." She propped her chin in her hand. "Other parents feel guilty, are relieved it's not them. I don't blame them. I wish it was someone else and not Lenny." She shrugged at the whispered admission. "Not very Christian of me, is it?"

"Lucky he's gentle." Lenny was built like a linebacker and could easily clear a room. Claire touched her own crooked nose, the result of one of Tracy's fits and her own inability to duck in time.

Autism Spectrum Disorders affected children in different ways, but those on the bus had the most severe problems. Claire, Elaine and the other parents had tried everything to help their kids, from behavioral therapy and nutrition changes to a variety of off-label drugs.

Most people knew nothing about off-label treatments. Food and Drug Administration clearance required years of hoop-jumping plus boatloads of money that prevented many promising drugs from ever reaching the market. Other times, unexpected benefits were exploited by savvy drug companies, such as when sildenafil citrate, initially marketed for hypertension, knocked it out of the park as Viagra.

Drugs just couldn't be advertised for a particular benefit unless they had government clearance. But they could be prescribed off-label by in-the-know doctors. Since there were no FDA-approved autism drugs, all treatments for the condition were off-label.

Claire pinned all her hope on this latest buzz-worthy treatment—an FDA-approved drug for Alzheimer's that had shown unexpected benefits in autistic children. She'd do anything to help Tracy, sign a waiver release and mortgage her soul for the opportunity. So would the other parents. No snowstorm dared stand in their way.

Chapter 29

September closed the lid on the toilet, gingerly sat down, and turned on the water in the sink to keep Teddy from hearing. No more delays. She locked the door and dialed April's cell. It rang once.

"Yes?" The Ghost Man. Her hand shook at the memory of his weird eyes so close to hers. September reminded herself he couldn't reach her, squeezing the flash drive in her other hand like a talisman to bolster her courage. She held the cards this time.

"I have what you want." Her voice wavered, despite her attempt at bravado. "Let me speak to April." Better. She needed to sound in control.

She heard him tell somebody, "It's the sister," and then Lizzie came on the line.

"April's in the other room." Lizzie was all business. "Describe the merchandise. Exactly what do you have?" The grandmotherly façade was gone.

September stared at the one-by-three-inch object in her palm. "A flash drive. Shiny, black, strung on a silver chain lanyard."

"Everyone has those. You get them at the grocery store. Tell me the truth, September. You wouldn't try to fob off a fake?"

The idea jarred her. Lizzie was right. Steven could've collared Shadow with the lanyard days ago. She couldn't prove it was the right flash drive unless she looked at the contents.

"Besides, I've grown quite attached to April, and now Steven has joined the party, so it's all in the family. Your sister's busy with her laptop in the room down the hall, removing all traces of Pottinger's information she accidentally-on-purpose emailed to herself. You remember the laptop, don't you? The one you nearly killed Gerald over?" The words were a slap.

September flinched. She'd never wanted to kill anyone, but if she'd hit Gerald-the-Ghost harder Pam might still be alive.

"April understands the stakes. Do you understand consequences, September?" She acted the part of fond schoolmarm teaching a hard but necessary lesson. "Steven isn't the only sick child, and you've endangered the lives, the hopes and dreams of hundreds of other children. If I have to sacrifice one little boy to save a hundred, what should I do, September? What would you do?"

Focus on April and Steven. That's what mattered here. "You want Pottinger's information, right? I swear to you, I have the flash drive. I can give it to you." She had to convince Lizzie. She looked closer, and found a logo pressed into the case. "There's a logo on the side of the flash drive case, a bird on fire." A Phoenix? "Just let them go, please don't hurt them." September ached with the effort to persuade Lizzie without alerting Teddy. Water from the tap gushed and gurgled in its race down the drain, rushing as fast as the hands on her watch.

September whispered more urgently into the phone. "I found Pottinger's information. That's what you wanted, and I did it. Steven looped the chain around Shadow's neck. I'll give it to you, but I have to know my sister and Steven are both okay." Her pulse thrummed. "I won't give it to you 'til I know, so let me talk to my sister."

"You're in no position to make demands. So Steven hid it on the dog. The treatment unlocks hidden talents. It worked for my Gerald, after all." She sounded delighted. "We could have resolved this amicably, but I can't forgive you for nearly killing my boy."

September licked her suddenly dry lips. "He's your son?"

"Gerald is brilliant. You should thank him for Steven's cure." Lizzie's pride blossomed with the opportunity to sing her son's praises. "Gerald couldn't speak, either. He had violent rages. He was locked inside his own head for years. Then a happy accident created the miracle we are now able to share with the world. I didn't even recognize it; Gerald figured it out for himself."

"Happy accident? What are you talking about?" Shadow woofed and pressed against her thigh. She welcomed the contact and her nerves steadied in response. September wondered if the pup recognized Lizzie's voice over the phone. Probably.

"That's right, September. Gerald took some of my dad's prescription medicine by accident." Her breath quickened. "He started talking. After twenty-five years of silence, he started talking. Are you listening to me? You need to understand what's at stake, September. Are you paying attention?"

"Yes. I hear you. He started talking, it was a miracle." She couldn't stop shivering. She wanted to speak to April but was afraid to interrupt Lizzie's grandstanding.

"That's right. Gerald told me what he'd done. Taken Daddy's medicine. We told the doctors and they refused to believe us, and they wouldn't give us more when we ran out." Her voice turned grim. "Can you imagine that? They spit on the miracle! And it nearly cost Gerald his life. I won't tell you what we had to go through to keep him well . . . never mind that. But we knew right away we had to share this joy. Gerald finished school in three years. Only three years and he's a doctor, a Ph.D. Can you imagine?"

September closed her eyes and nodded.

"I didn't hear you."

"Yes, I can imagine. Gerald's brilliant, like you said."

"That's right. My boy's a genius. He met Dr. Pottinger in school, and together they've brought Gerald's legacy to other poor children who can benefit from this miracle." Her voice hardened. "That flash drive has information that you don't need, that only parents of these special children would understand. April understands. You haven't looked at it, have you? Don't lie to me, I'll know. You must give it back. Don't make me spell out the consequences." She paused. "You didn't answer me, September. Do you understand consequences?"

"Yes. Yes, I understand." September stiffened her back. "But if you want the information, let me talk to April." She didn't bother to modulate her tone.

"For the love of . . . Oh all right, I'll go get her. Just wait a minute, but you must make it quick."

September waited several impatient moments.

"September?" The voice, though soft and hoarse, was April. "They found Steven. He's safe here with me. We're fine. Everything's fine." She paused, as though choosing her words with care. "Lizzie says you found Dr. Pottinger's flash drive information."

"April, are you okay?" September choked back tears. She was alive, Steven was alive. "Yes, I found it. Where are you? I'm ready to make the exchange."

"Of course I'm fine. We're both fine. We're at Lizzie's getting ready to drive to the Legacy Center." April said. "See? Everything worked out." She paused. "September, you must return that flash drive. You don't need it anyway, and I already know what's important. That information doesn't belong to us, it's proprietary. I signed papers. Once you give it back, Steven will keep getting his medicine, and he won't have those nasty side effects, and he'll be cured." She paused. "What exchange?"

"The ransom. They want me to trade Pottinger's information for your safety."

"Ransom? Don't be ridiculous. Just give back the flash drive, and you can go back to your life and we can go back to ours. Like I said, all debts wiped clean—"

Lizzie came back on the phone. "Satisfied? They're fine."

In the background September heard April's questions become angry and siren into a shriek that was silenced mid-scream.

"What's happening?" Shadow barked back at September's anguished words.

A breathless Lizzie came back on the line. "Everything's fine. Your sister's fine. Steven's fine. I promise. Trust me." She hesitated. "I'll call you back."

September stared at the dead phone. Do killers keep promises?

Teddy rattled the locked handle and pounded on the door. "Why are you yelling? Open up, right now." He banged again. "I'll pick the lock, break the door. Open it. You're scaring an old man." He juggled the door, and it finally opened. He stared. "What happened?"

"I don't know." She was numb.

He shut off the water that threatened to overflow the sink, and looked at the phone in her limp hand. "Who were you talking to? I thought your phone was dead."

She didn't answer. The phone dropped, and the flash drive followed, the chain snaking to the floor. She didn't care.

Shadow pushed himself into her lap, and September wished the doggy weight was Dakota. Her arms hugged his big, warm body. Cold, she was so damn cold. "I think I just killed my sister."

Chapter 30

Lizzie struggled to contain her anger and consciously smoothed her expression. She had cultivated the mild mannered persona for just such occasions. She dismissed April's body prostrate on the floor, and focused on keeping Gerald calm. Control, she had to keep control. Thank heavens Steven was locked in the bedroom. A child shouldn't see his mother get killed. "Give me the gun." Her tone brooked no argument.

"We don't need her now we've got Steven." But Gerald offered the pistol without protest. "She was a loose end."

"She didn't matter. She's a mom; she'd do anything to protect her child. Besides, we could hold Pottinger over her head 'til the cows come home. She was no threat." She sighed, and straightened her hair. "Spilt milk now, and no cleaning it up." She set the pistol on a nearby table. "You already lost one gun. At least they can't trace it back to you." She'd taken Daddy's old surplus .45 pistols away from him when his Alzheimer's got too bad. Funny how his disease had saved Gerald and hundreds of children.

She knelt beside April. "She's not breathing." Her mind raced. Yesterday, everything was under control, with lots of lost souls to save. Too bad Pottinger became smitten with Little Miss Perfect and her son, Steven, or he'd still be alive and they wouldn't be in this mess.

Gerald stood tall. No concern clouded his pale, handsome face. He looked like his father, and sounded like him, too. "We have two hundred clients scheduled to arrive at Legacy Center in less than twelve hours. That's the largest Rebirth Gathering yet. We can't risk that payday, Mother, not when we're poised to go global. April knew the consequences. And you didn't tell me not to shoot her." Gerald moved to a chair and sat.

"We've talked about this. You can't take everything so literally." She covered her exasperation. A consequence of his disability, she reminded herself, and his genius. "You didn't have to shoot that woman at the park."

"You weren't there. She sicced that dog on me. I couldn't shoot the dog. He reminded me of Neptune."

"Neptune's a Pomeranian. Dammit, don't distract me."

He tsked. "Bad word, lazy English."

She ignored him. "Murder is lazy."

"You shot someone."

"She tried to play the God card; you know how I feel about that." God hadn't saved Gerald, scientific medicine made him well, just as it would cure the children. "I won't have the true miracle devalued by some mumbo-jumbo-spouting bible-thumper. And besides, if she was right then God would have stopped the bullet, don't you think?" She waited for his nod of agreement. "We save lives, Gerald, we don't shoot people. Or dogs," she added grudgingly. "Your research saves other children. That's all that matters. Nothing else can get in the way."

Gerald rubbed his temple where a goose-egg purpled the skin. "My head hurts. I might have a concussion." He straightened and looked at his fingers as if he expected to see blood. "She deserved to die. Dr. Pottinger died because of her."

Lizzie frowned. Pottinger had been Gerald's PhD advisor, and they'd worked together—with her, of course—to make Legacy Center a reality. The treatment helped so many kids. But there was no way it would pass FDA screening, not with the occasional aberrant side effects. They couldn't afford to go public and have folks scared away, and prevent children from gaining the benefits. If a few children had adverse reactions because parents couldn't follow the rules, that shouldn't doom the thousands who could be cured.

Now that the FDA had released new off-label guidelines to the industry, it was even more vital that Legacy Center enlist parents to vote with their funds at Rebirth Gathering. Gerald had a point. April was a potential liability, but her sister was even more dangerous.

They couldn't allow Pottinger's flash drive to end the dream. "If April's dead, September won't cooperate." She couldn't stop the worry. The children depended on her.

"She doesn't have to know. We've still got Steven."

She nodded. They could hold the child over September's head to get Pottinger's flash drive. Until it was found, she'd never feel that Legacy Center was safe. Damn the woman and damn Pottinger. The information could derail twenty years of work, and sentence all those children to a lifetime of disability and pain.

Gerald was right. April broke the contract and she knew the consequences. They were better off without her. Once they got the flash drive back, she could refocus her attention on the program where it belonged.

But the spilt milk wasn't Steven's fault. He shouldn't be penalized. Steven deserved his miracle.

"What do we do with her?" Gerald nudged April with his foot.

Lizzie smiled. "Doug Childress killed her. After all, it was his gun that shot Pottinger." Yes, that could work. That wove all the threads together. "They fought over Steven's treatment and April's fitness as a mother when she let him get lost in the storm." She turned on the persuasion. "You took care of Pottinger's body so well—"

"Once he was garbage I dumped him like you said. But now my head hurts. Get someone else." He looked toward the bedroom where Steven was confined. "That fellow who collected Steven for us, get him to do it. He's connected. He can pull strings so she's never found, making sure the police connect the pistol to Childress." He smirked, and Lizzie admired the expression. It had taken Gerald years to learn to smile like that and fake normal emotions. "Who doesn't notice when guns go missing?" said Gerald. "Such stupidity deserves an appropriate reward."

Lizzie considered the option. The man had lots to gain by delivering Steven to them unharmed, but he might get a conscience with April dead. "No, you'll have to do it. You shot her. Clean up your own mess and put April on ice, out of sight. You understand?"

He nodded. "On ice."

She smiled again. What a good son.

Chapter 31

Several police cars, an ambulance, and a fire truck swarmed near the entrance to the Star Mall. Combs had needed a breather but now rejoined Gonzales in the food court. The little man didn't seem fazed by the lateness of the hour, and stood with his cell phone glued to one ear. They'd called Doty from the road and beat her to the scene. The victim was already dead, so they'd secured the area and waited. So far, she'd ignored him either by accident or design. That worked just fine.

"Damn. We're hamsters running wheelies today." Doty stared at the mix of blood, ketchup and fries swirled with mud, and whistled through the gap in her front teeth. "What's the latest on body count—I can't keep up?" She aimed the sarcasm at Gonzales, as if he should have anticipated and prevented the bloodbath.

"You know more than I do." Gonzales ignored her tone as he disconnected the call. "Same shooter for all of them?"

"God, I hope not. But too early to know details. Ballistic tests take forever, but you can see the caliber from the shell casings, so it's at least two different guns. Maybe three." Doty gave a nod, acknowledging Combs. "We found shell casings under a table at April's, .45 caliber consistent with a semi-automatic. Our prelim says the FBI's GRC database suggests it's from a Remington Rand."

Gonzales scratched his head. "That's a World War Two surplus pistol. Lots of them floating around."

Doty grunted. "Either the same one or similar shot the vic at the park. Shell casings look like a match. Want you to take a look, though, and do your gun voodoo, Gonzales. The lab takes forever." She watched impassively as the EMTs zippered the dead woman into a bag.

"This one's different. Looks more like a .380." Gonzales sounded surprised.

Combs couldn't stop himself. "That's two guns. Makes no sense it would be the same shooter."

"Actually, it's three guns. Number three is a bullet we dug out of the ceiling at April's. Don't think it had anything to do with your mom, but it does cloud the situation." Doty spoke directly to Combs for the first time. "Type of old bullet hasn't been made in years, a .32 caliber S&W short. Hell, the bullet's so old, it's oxidized."

"Yes they do. Still make the bullets, that is." Gonzales explained when Combs raised his eyebrows. "Guns are my passion. I grew up in my dad's gun shop, spent more time at gun shows over the years than my wife cares to remember. I can tell you anything about make, model, and ballistics." Gonzales smoothed his tie. "Comes in handy when ballistics is delayed."

Doty popped her gum. "He's been right, ten for ten. So far," she added as if the compliment pained her. "Lots of bets in the department riding on him getting something wrong. Including mine."

"Childress collects antique guns." The man hadn't been forthcoming about that little tidbit, and that bothered Combs. A lot.

"But thousands of those pocket guns were made from 1880 to the 1930s." Gonzales smoothed his mustache. "Still, there's a distinctive shaved slice on the bullet, characteristic of wear on the bolt action. Makes it freakin' easy to match to the gun. If we ever find it."

Doty took a breath and offered a bit of what-the-hell speculation. "My guess is the same antique gun killed the guy we found in the car over at Childress's place. One of the bullets was a through-and-through, and fell out of the carpet when they unwrapped the carpet around his body. Gonzales says it's a match to the ceiling bullet at April's house."

Gonzales continued the argument. "Too much of a coincidence for unrelated shooters to use the same kind of antique gun and hard-to-find bullet. I don't believe in coincidence. And if Pottinger was killed at April's, it ties all four together. But what was he doing there?"

Doty unwrapped another stick of gum and stuffed it in her mouth, talking past the wad. "Maybe your mom walked in on something she shouldn't have, and Pottinger shot her, so April shot him with that funny gun."

"Nothing came up when we checked gun registry in April's name." Gonzales clapped Combs on the shoulder. "Unless she's carrying unlicensed. Not unheard of in Texas, but surprising since she's got the kid."

"Childress left it behind when he got divorced?" Combs guessed.

Gonzales made a note on his ever present pad. "My wife was into guns when we first got married. All that went away when we had the first kid. My guns stay locked up now in a padlocked room, and as soon as I hit the door my service weapon goes nighty-night out of kid reach. And Mercedes hasn't been at the shooting range in six years."

Combs agreed. His wife—ex-wife, he silently corrected—felt the same about guns around kids. Hell, so did anyone with half a brain. His phone vibrated. Uncle Stanley again. He let voicemail take the call. He couldn't deal with family right now. Not until he knew more and had answers.

"Lots of old guns aren't in the system. If April had to defend herself, and there's at least one more shooter out there, that'd be reason enough to run." Doty consulted her own notepad.

"Best explanation we've got so far. September protects her sister, and they both run from whoever shot Pottinger. They must have split up." Combs rubbed his eyes. "September went to Gentry Park with her dog tracking friend to look for Steven. Meanwhile the shooter must have followed September, and maybe the dog lady got in the way?"

"Your mom. Pottinger. Dog lady. And now a bus driver at Star Mall. Four murders in less than ten hours." Doty began pacing, her frustration clear, as she watched EMTs trudge to the ambulance with the latest victim. "Who is she anyway? Do we know if there's a connection, or is this just our day for bodies?"

"HART-Line bus driver." Gonzales read from his notes. "The bus is parked outside, and that little VW belonged to the victim. Dispatcher said they shut down HART-Line service because of weather right after her shift ended."

"September called and pointed us here. There's a definite connection." Combs waited for Doty to connect the dots.

She whistled tunelessly through the gap in her teeth and then motioned Combs closer. "Your mom was killed at April's house. Childress says his ex-wife and September are close, and she came there to find April. We found Pottinger at Childress's place right after September was there. And her supposed friend, the dog lady, met her at Gentry Park and got shot. Then she calls you and directs us here, where we find yet another body. Maybe it's not some mysterious stranger chasing after the sisters. Maybe we already know who's shooting up the city." Doty's eyes narrowed. "You took the call. What's your gut on this?"

Combs considered the question with suspicion. Doty kept score. Whatever he said would be remembered to use against him later. He shrugged.

"Talk to me, Officer Combs. Sure, I told you to stay out of this, but you're up to your holsters in it, clearly against policy, and I'm not taking the blame for you messing with my show." Combs heard her teeth grinding. "In case you haven't noticed, I've run out of hands. And clove gum. That chaps my hide." She glared. "This weather has traffic snarled; we've got multiple crime scenes, Dallas PD cain't git here from there." Her broadened accent mocked his rural upbringing compared to her own big-city credentials. "We've more than enough work to go around, and I'll try to look the other way as long as you play fair with me. So spit it out."

"Part of the team?" He ignored Gonzales's smothered smile. Combs wanted in, but the info-sharing had to flow in both directions.

"No way, this stays unofficial. You're still poison, Combs. I won't burn my own butt so's you can play. It's still my sandbox." She paused, held up a hand when he would've argued. "Since September pulled you into the investigation, it's my duty to debrief you." Her expression remained deadpan, reminding Combs of how well she'd always covered her ass while cutting corners. He both admired and despised the talent. "Play ball, Combs. And maybe we'll talk to you." The hint of a promise in her tone was real. "Has September gone serial killer on us?"

He snorted. "Hardly. She's calling us, reaching out for help. Sure, September's involved, no question, but only indirectly. Probably covering for her sister." He looked around the chaos. "If she was in control, I think she'd come in. I get the feeling she's being coerced about something. Maybe threatened?"

"April's motivated to protect her son. That has to involve Childress." Gonzales spoke with conviction. "You think Childress holds something over April's head?"

"Wouldn't put it past him," Combs said. "April and Steven are in some kind of trouble, maybe on the run from Childress. I don't like the guy. I think September tried to dig them out of a hole, and fell in over her head. That's my gut." He stifled a yawn, and wished he had a drink. Hell, he needed a drink. But coffee would have to suffice.

Doty's nose scrunched up like a rabbit after carrots. "We got problems at April's. Need more than the antique bullets to prove Pottinger died there."

Gonzales pulled out his phone. "I'll call the coroner again; get them to check for GSR. If Pottinger's a shooter there'll be trace on his hands or clothes. He wasn't wearing gloves. Means he must have been inside the house where it was warm before any gunplay." He shook his head. "We need the connection between April and this Dr. Pottinger. Who is this guy? That should answer lots of questions."

Doty's glare raked the big room. "How'd September know to come to Star Mall? It's not Black Friday for two weeks." She considered the food court floor, and glowered. "Can't tell the blood from the ketchup."

Combs looked closer at the mess. There were distinct tracks of three or more individuals in the debris. And a dog. A good size dog by the paw prints. "Fish from the radio played the recording of April's call. She was hysterical about her missing son, and she mentioned a dog." He pointed at a paw print.

Gonzales sniffed. "September knew about the bus driver, so she was here. That's why she called you." He yawned, clearly feeling the same fatigue they were all fighting. "But I don't buy that she shot the bus driver. What reason would she have?"

"Isn't it obvious?" Doty painted a possible version. "September managed to track down her nephew and the dog to the mall, and shot the bus driver when she got in the way."

"No. Steven's not with her. You can't fake that kind of panic. September's still running solo." Or maybe not. Combs recalled that soft male voice in the background when she'd called. "I count two...no, three cups. There's one under the table." He pointed. "So that's the bus driver, the boy and September. Or somebody else."

Gonzales crouched to examine the shoe and boot prints at each of the chairs. "Remember those prints outside Pottinger's car, the ones we figured for September's? None of these match. Whoever was here sat long enough for the mud to dry. See, there's a kid's tennis shoe, and this is the bus driver's print. That third set, it's a man's size. Dry, too, so he was with them." He stood, and followed the prints back toward the entry until they disappeared.

Combs pointed at another. "Could be September's. But it's over top of the kid's print." He rubbed his jaw. "So she came after they'd been here a while. Or even after they'd left."

Gonzales tiptoed around the telltale prints. "Here's another man's shoe print, that's got to be a size fourteen at least. That's a big guy. Dress shoes, slick soles. In ice?" His phone buzzed and he listened and quickly ended the call. "That was Pike."

Doty looked up sharply. "Fast work. What's he got?"

"I thought Pike went home." Combs yawned again.

She shrugged. "Everyone's on duty until further notice. Pike lives near a witness—that kid manager of the coffee shop at the mall—so he handled the call." She frowned at Gonzales. "What's the kid say?"

"He served a boy, an old man, and the woman bus driver before he closed shop and left. The dog was with them."

"Any names?" Doty's nostrils flared when Gonzales shrugged.

"Pike says the manager didn't recognize them. But they mentioned the kid's father was on his way to collect him."

"Really." Doty popped her gum. "Mr. Childress just put his foot in it, literally. That asshole has more questions to answer."

Chapter 32

Water thundered in the small room until Shadow's ears hurt. Wet clouds billowed, and the hot air was hard to breathe. It tickled his nose. He blinked to clear away the steam.

Shadow paw-stirred the pile of clothes September had shed before stepping under the indoor-rain behind the curtain. He alternated deep sniffs with muzzle-clearing snorts, and read the clothes like a cryptic Post-It: fear-stink, and normal sweat, pee, perfumed lotion.

He sneezed, withdrew his muzzle, and whined. Why did she just stand there and let water gush all over her? He'd never do that. Rain made his fur itch.

Humans didn't have fur. They covered themselves with cloth, and shed it onto the floor before they washed. Maybe that's why she didn't mind so much. He wondered how it would feel to be tummy-naked all over.

His nostrils flared. Shadow stuck his muzzle past the curtain to squint against the water. He licked and discovered hot rain had no flavor. When she moved close, he nosed the back of September's bare thigh.

"Oh!"

Shadow jerked his head out of the shower, shaking off the wet that clung to his head.

"You okay?" Teddy stuck his head partway in the door.

The water stopped. "Shadow cold-nosed me." She peeked from the wet place, and hair dripped down her form. "Take him out of here, will you, Teddy? While I get dressed."

"Sure." Teddy opened the door wider, one hand beckoned. "C'mon, boy. Leave September alone."

Shadow whined. September was upset. And a good-dog's job was to make his humans happy. He'd like to make her happy.

Teddy spoke again. "You come with me." He paused, and his tone coaxed. "I have a cookie with your name on it."

Shadow's ears twitched at the "cookie" word, but he didn't move. He stared at September until she looked at him. She smiled with her mouth, but it wasn't a true happy face—he could tell the difference. He sighed.

"Go with Teddy. Be a good dog."

Shadow wagged in acceptance. He'd do what she asked. But he didn't have to like it.

"His stuffed bear is in the back seat of the car. He's more toy-oriented than treats, especially after a meal." She grabbed a heavy cloth from the wall and retreated once more behind the curtain. "His toy will keep him occupied."

Shadow reluctantly followed Teddy. The stolen sniff from September's leg was enough, anyway. At the thought, his tail wagged and his wrinkled brow smoothed. Indoor-rain washed away the fear-stink. Nobody wanted to wear fear-stink. That invited trouble. September stood under the rain to wash off scary smells, so she could smell happy again.

Happy smells made him feel better, too. That's why he rolled in happy smells like dead birds or cow stuff. Shadow wished Teddy had a dead bird around the house somewhere.

People didn't smell stuff the way dogs did, though. Steven's mom didn't like dead-bird-smell. Shadow was sad humans couldn't appreciate such things. Why, smells colored everything. It must be dreary to be scent-blind in such a scent-rich world. Instead, people liked odd bottle-smells they rubbed on hands, faces, and even underarms to cover up self-scent. He didn't know why. No dog would do that. A dog disappeared without self-scent.

Shadow liked people self-scent, liked to poke his nose at underarms and crotches to get to know them. People didn't like that, either. How odd. He wondered how people recognized each other, scent-blind to each other's most noteworthy spots. He shook himself hard, in a doggy shrug.

"Shadow, come. We'll get your teddy bear." The old man hurried down the hall.

He knew what "come" meant of course, but it was the prospect of his bear that hurried his paws. Happy words like "teddy bear" and "good-dog" were nearly as good as rolling on a dead bird.

He skidded to a stop once they reached the front room. Shadow sniffed and stared but didn't see his toy anywhere. His ears drooped. Sometimes people promises didn't happen. People sure were hard to understand. To figure them out made his head hurt.

"Wait here, pup. I'll be right back." The old man pulled on a heavy coat, still wet from outside.

Shadow danced around Teddy's legs, and pushed nearer. People used that "wait" word when dogs got left behind. He didn't want to be alone.

"Shadow. Sit. Stay."

Teddy's strong hand gripped the fur on his neck to hold him back as he opened the door and slipped out, shutting it against Shadow's nose. Yelping, he pawed the door and backed away, hurrying to the nearby window where he pushed aside the curtain to see into the darkness. Wet smears frosted the surface as Shadow listened to Teddy's feet crunch outside, followed by the slam of a car door. Shadow whined with anticipation, and woofed as the crunchy footstep sounds returned. When the door opened, he dashed outside in a rush to take-a-break.

Teddy gasped but smiled and waited until Shadow finished his squat and sniffed the spot. "Good dog, Shadow. See, I wasn't gone for long" Teddy urged Shadow inside and carefully latched the door. "Look what I've got. Is this your bear? Whew, it stinks."

Shadow cocked his head, and stared at the soft black object in Teddy's hand. His tail thumped until he couldn't maintain the polite pose any longer. He leaped, grabbed Bear by its head. He shook Bear hard and harder still, and shook it once more until his neck was loose and the tension drained from his body.

"You like that, do you, boy? Like your bear?" The man made happy laugh-noises.

Shadow killed the toy again and pranced about the room. He launched into a joyful doggy canter around the room, leaped from floor-to-sofa-to-floor with Bear clutched in his jaws. Laughter was good. Butt high and head low, Shadow sneeze-laughed. He held his teddy with both paws—claiming ownership—and gawked at the old man, daring a game of keep-away. Oh, it was good to play. A fun game always made everything better.

But the man turned his back, shrugged off his coat and tossed it over a chair. "Have fun, Shadow. Play with your bear, and I'll fire up the search engines." He hurried back down the hallway and passed the little room where September had showered. Steam was still escaping from beneath the door.

Shadow stared after. Then he grabbed the toy and padded after the man, stopping in the open door at the end of the hall. Shadow shook Bear a final time and dropped the toy in the doorway. Would Teddy take the dare, and grab for it? Play keep-away?

Teddy ignored the invitation. He limped to a desk and pulled out the chair.

A small bed occupied half the space in the room. He wondered if good-dogs could sleep there. Shadow hurried to nudge the man's arm. He nudged again, and leaned against him, moaning when Teddy's hand rubbed the hard to reach place at the base of his ear.

"Go on, that's enough." Teddy patted him and then pushed him away. "Let me do some work. Go talk to your bear. Bear is lonely."

Shadow grabbed Bear by the head, and sprang onto the comforter. A poof of dust rose, nearly invisible but implication clear. Nobody slept here. Too bad for such a soft spot not to have an owner. Maybe he could claim it. Shadow waited for the man to tell him to get off.

Teddy smiled. He shuffled stacks of paper on the desk. "Enjoy the bed for now, pup. When September comes in, she'll have the final say."

Shadow panted happily, turned three times, and sank with a groan against a pillow. He pretzeled himself to chew an itch, and tasted salt where September had wiped tears against his fur. He sniffed the spot, worried. It wasn't a good-salty taste; it had an acrid tang of fear. He grabbed Bear's head, and sucked until his own jangled nerves fell quiet.

The man fiddled with the boxy objects on top of the desk. Lights flickered; buzzes and whirring noises twitched Shadow's ears. Teddy's fingers made clack noises. Shadow's eyes drooped.

"Teddy?"

Shadow wagged his tail when September appeared in the doorway. His jaw tightened on Bear.

September was wearing different clothes, clean, baggy ones that flapped over her hands and bare feet. The fear-smell was still there, but not as strong. Her hair didn't drip but it smelled wet. Shadow wondered why she didn't shake off the water. Instead she rubbed her head with a cloth.

Did she want him off the soft bed? He pulled his ears flat to his head. Shadow rolled to show his tummy, Bear in his jaws. He wagged and the comforter bunched beneath his tail. He'd been a good-dog, couldn't he stay on the bed this once?

"S'okay, pup. No rules today." She sat on the edge of the bed beside him.

He dropped Bear, rolled upright, and pushed himself into her lap, licking her face and eyes. Her breath smelled stale, though, and he didn't argue when after a brief hug, she pushed him away. Shadow lay with his hip snugged against September's—needed the contact—and grabbed his toy once more. She stroked his brow. He shut his eyes. Bliss.

"Why does he do that? The bear's head is lopsided and it stinks."

The clack stopped when the man spoke, but Shadow didn't move. He had Bear, a soft bed, and September's touch. Nothing could be better. Except maybe bacon.

"I don't know. Why do kids suck their thumbs? Comfort, I suppose. Pam told me his dam did it, and all his littermates, too. He'd just about do backflips for his teddy. Gets real possessive."

"Backflips?" He chuckled.

"Figure of speech. Here, let me show you." She shifted on the bed, and Shadow pulled back when she tugged the toy. "Shadow, drop it. Wait."

He whined, but released the toy and sat up, watching with interest as she held his teddy. Now what?

She turned to the man. "His recall isn't solid, but he does a pretty good wait. Especially if he knows there's a cool reward for the job. Like Bear." September made eye contact with Shadow, crossed the room, and held up his toy. "Come."

He leaped off the bed and bounded to her. The closed-fist signal meant to plant his tail on the floor. He sat. When she pointed to the ground, he dropped into a down. His focus never left Bear.

"Good-dog." She tossed Bear, and Shadow deftly caught the toy, turned and hopped back onto the bed.

"Neat. Can I try?"

September nodded. "Drop it." She waited for Shadow to comply, and tossed Bear to the man.

No—she gave Bear to the stranger? Shadow cocked his head. Was it a game of keep-away after all? With a frustrated yelp, he hopped off the bed, loped to the old man, and leaped against Teddy's chest to grab his toy.

The old man rocked backwards into the desk. Bear fell from his hands—success!—and before it could hit the floor, Shadow scooped it up. He pranced to the other side of the room, tail wagging high and fast. He hoped Teddy would chase and try to grab Bear again. He loved that game.

"Shadow, settle. That's enough."

Shadow's tail fell at September's disapproval, signaling dejection.

"Teddy, are you okay? My fault, I didn't tell him to wait first." She moved to help him up.

Teddy seized her arm and staggered upright. "We're not thinking straight. Small wonder, with what we've both gone through."

He didn't know what all the words meant; only that Teddy sounded sad. Shadow slunk to the other side of the bed to keep a safe distance from grabby Bear-thief hands. He didn't like one-sided games. He settled with the head firmly in his jaws. His breath slowed. September's presence made it safe to rest.

She sat on the bed. "Thanks for the fresh clothes. The shower helped clear my head." She paused. "You could do me a huge favor, and keep Shadow for me. I'm on a deadline."

Hearing his name, he moved closer to September.

"I'm thinking more clearly, too, and did some research." Teddy turned back to the plastic box and clacked the keyboard. "You're famous."

September's hand tightened in his fur, rousing Shadow. She smelled scared again, and suddenly started sobbing and dropped her head into her hands. Shadow pawed September's hands, nudging them with his muzzle. He didn't like this. Loud words hurt, and weepy eyes made his tummy flip-flop.

Then Shadow froze. Noise from the box on the desk, one voice in particular, raised his hackles. He knew that voice. A low growl bubbled deep in his chest.

September jerked away. Teddy staggered backwards in fear.

Shadow glared, eyes hard, searching for the voice that was inside the box. He sniffed but detected no scent, despite that despised voice. Shadow's bubbled growls exploded into angry barks. His tail wagged with fury. He raged, wanted to punish, to make right what had gone wrong. But there was nothing to bite. No way to reach the hated voice of the boy-thief.

Chapter 33

Combs sat in his car in front of the brick ranch house. He'd put it off as long as he could. It was time to talk with Uncle Stanley and Aunt Ethel. He plugged his cell phone into the charger since he'd be in and out within ten minutes, just long enough to make an appearance and support the family. Doty and Gonzales didn't want him at the press conference anyway. He sighed heavily and left the car.

Before he could ring the bell the door opened. Light spilled into the morning gloom and haloed the tiny woman in the doorway. Combs gingerly embraced Aunt Ethel, careful her tears didn't breach the wall he'd erected around his own emotions. She offered a sad smile as she stepped back and motioned him into the hallway. He stifled a hiccupped breath despite his best intentions, so he turned away to latch the door and regain his composure.

"Aw, honey, I'm so sorry." Aunt Ethel again hugged him tight. Her close cropped dark head barely reached his shoulder. She wore a favorite green Baylor sweatshirt, jeans, and moccasins, and her high cheekbones and dark eyes needed no makeup. She smelled like sunshine, safety, family. Like Mom.

His first sob surprised him.

"Let it out, sweetie." Her arms tightened. "I've got you, you're safe. Let it out."

Oh God, it hurt. He couldn't catch his breath. Cops don't cry. But sons do. The dam broke, and he shook in her arms for endless moments.

He broke the embrace. Without a word, Ethel handed him a hand towel. He mopped his face and cleared his throat. "I can't stay." He handed back the towel, and straightened his shoulders. Didn't look at her. He had to be a cop again.

"I know. You're on the job. So go see your uncle. He's in the kitchen." Her hands fluttered a tattered tissue. "He's biting nails to be involved. You know Stan. They made him take retirement, or he'd still run things."

True. Uncle Stan always knew what should be done and he'd tell you in no uncertain terms. Other folks often fell short of what was expected. He'd failed in his uncle's eyes. Again.

"I appreciate you coming, I know you're busy. But tell Stan something, calm him down." She hesitated. "The rest of the family left hours ago. I sent them away. They just got each other more and more riled." She wadded the tissue and stuffed it in her jeans pocket. "All but Naomi. She's upstairs, asleep I hope. I gave her one of my magic pills."

Thank God Naomi was asleep. He hadn't the courage to meet his sister and uncle together. "Don't think I'm the best person to calm Uncle Stanley." His smile softened the understatement.

She raised her brows. "You mean all that business with your job? Never mind that. Stan's a hard man, a proud man. The stuff they said about you hurt him because he knew they were lies." She smiled but her lips trembled. "Your mom was so proud of you, and Stan worshipped her."

The scandal not only killed his career and marriage, it drove a wedge through his family, and by default tainted Stan's reputation in the police force. Combs didn't even know the informant's real name. He'd never seen "Spider" without the black-on-white makeup or spiked black hair, until that day in the morgue when he'd learned she was a lawyer's kid, a lawyer with juice. Hell, Combs didn't blame the parents, he'd have stroked out if he lost one of his kids. But after Spider's diary surfaced, Doty used it to point fault at Combs and away from her own culpability, and Uncle Stanley stayed silent when Combs lost his detective's badge.

"He could have done more to defend me." The old hurt was hard to ignore, but he shrugged an apology. Aunt Ethel always defended and believed in him, even after Cassie lost faith and left with their kids. And of course, Mom's support never wavered. "Old news doesn't matter. Today it's all about Mom."

"Yes, it's about Wilma."

"Somebody has to take her cat." He forced a smile. "She'd kick my butt if I didn't mention that."

"Never mind the cat, your sister has that covered. Simba is upstairs sleeping with Naomi. They'll be good for each other. No more foot dragging. You go to Stan before he has another coronary." She grabbed his arm, a grip surprisingly firm for such a birdlike woman. "It's okay to show you're hurt, too. You are more like Stan than either of you wants to admit." When he would have argued, she interrupted. "Honey, help your uncle by helping your mom. She's what held us together, and with her gone . . ." Her chin rose, and her blue eyes glinted with more than tears. "There's been enough hurt in this family, don't you think?"

"Who's there, Ethel? Any news?" Stan called out.

"Keep your voice down, you'll wake Naomi." She searched Combs's expression for something, and smiled as if she'd found it. "Jeff's home." She squeezed his arm and whispered. "Give him what he needs, what you both need." She pushed him down the dark hallway toward the bright kitchen. "It's what Wilma would want."

He braced himself and strode into the light. Uncle Stan towered above the sink, coffee pot in one hand and empty cup in the other. His barrel chest, covered by the trademark leather vest, belied the heart condition that forced him into early retirement. Iron gray hair held a permanent wave from years of wearing a cowboy hat. His trimmed and waxed mustache hid humorless lips. Uncle Stan was a taller, broader version of Yosemite Sam.

"About damn time. Sit. You'll be here a while." Uncle Stan always spoke in foregone conclusions, and had no patience with what he called weenie hedges. He poured thick, black liquid into his mug before a sip and grimace. "It bites. Want some? This is the fourth pot, I think. Not bad with enough sugar."

Combs sat at the pine table in silent assent. He accepted the cup, warming his hands with it, and braced himself.

"Tell me." Stan returned the pot to the coffee warmer. He remained by the sink, braced against the counter as his knuckles turned white on the handle of his mug.

Combs had practiced before he arrived. "Single shot to the forehead." He coughed to cover the quaver in his voice on the last word.

Stan's mustache twitched. "So it was quick." He breathed in and out, his jaw working. "What else?"

"We're looking for April Childress and her son. Been in touch with the sister, September Day, who's considered a person of interest." Combs stared at the mug in his hand. An oily film floated atop the liquid. He tasted the coffee. Vile. Just what he needed. He took another slug.

"You attended school with them." Again, not a question. Stan pulled out a chair, flipped it around, and straddled it. The posture strained the seams of his pressed and starched jeans. "Miz January already called to offer condolences. Their whole family is tore up something fierce, waiting for word."

Combs unzipped his heavy coat. Ethel kept the furnace cranked to shirtsleeve temperatures. After Dad died, he and Naomi spent lots of time at Uncle Stan's house with their friends, including some of the January kids. He wasn't surprised they'd been in touch.

Stan peered toward the kitchen doorway, checking for his wife before he spoke so she couldn't hear. "Who chatted up the ex-husband? Miz January ain't a fan, some disagreement about the grandson's medication or something." He cleared his throat. "Divorce can be a messy beast, so I'd take it with a grain of salt, but wanted to pass it on."

"Gonzales visited the parents. I was there for the initial talk with April's ex." Combs rose and carried his mug to the counter. Messy, indeed. He didn't get to see his kids like he should. It made a man do and say things, changed a man into less than his best.

"I remember Gonzales. Dapper little guy, straight shooter from what I hear. He's like a rat terrier but you don't want to mess with them either, especially not if you're a rat. Partnered with Doty after you . . ." He stopped. Reached for his hat, and smoothed his hair when it wasn't there. Stared into his coffee.

Combs stiffened but didn't rise to the bait. He found the sugar bowl—the fake sweetener stuff Aunt Ethel preferred—and stirred a spoonful into his coffee. He tasted the coffee, added more sweetener, and stirred.

"Hey, bring the pot over, will you?"

Combs returned to the table, his mug in one hand and the carafe in the other, and reheated Uncle Stanley's cup. "Naomi make this?" He smacked his lips. Sweetener didn't help.

"Yep. Nasty, ain't it?"

Combs sat down again. It'd been ten months since he'd had a decent conversation with his uncle. He'd missed this. Hell of a situation when Mom's murder brought them back to the table—literally.

"Argument between the divorced parents over the little boy makes for interesting dynamics, and motives."

"Tell me about it." Combs slugged down half his mug, and set it aside. Now it was too sweet. "Steven's autistic. He's got a dog that September trained that's supposed to help."

"Autistic. So they disagree about the dog as part of the treatment?"

Combs paused. "I don't know. Good question."

"At least he's with his mom." Gonzales looked surprised at Combs's expression. "No? The boy's on his own?"

"Gone lost in the snowstorm with his dog. We think he took off before Mom was killed." Combs recited the facts dispassionately. "That's why April called September. We don't know if they were present for the shoot, only that both are on the run, probably from the killer."

"Or on the run *with* the killer?"

He considered, and then shook his head. "Not September. Maybe April, though, and that would put the sisters in conflict instead of cahoots. We're flying blind until we figure out what they're running from—or with—and why." Combs rubbed his eyes. "Mom was just at the wrong place at the wrong time."

"I cain't see either sister putting the boy at risk." Stan reached to adjust his missing hat again, and scowled. "It's April's house, so she's the bull's eye, and everything else revolves around her."

Combs agreed. "Or her son. She's a mom, so anything that affects Steven motivates April."

Stan fingered his handlebar mustache the way Ethel played with her rosary. "Something she has, something she knows, that's what this is about. April won't give it up, so he shoots Wilma to raise the stakes, and takes April hostage to arm-twist September to deliver the goods. The bastard."

Combs cracked his knuckles. That made an awful, chilling sense. He stared at his coffee as if the black reflection held answers. "Even if April partnered with the bad guys, the timing and body count doesn't compute with a single shooter."

"Body count? Wilma's not the only one?" Stan's hand slapped the table, and the cup sloshed. "Ethel? Turn the damned police scanner back on," he yelled. "I'm missing too much. Dang woman thinks she's protecting me."

"You should monitor the radio show, too. I'm sure that Fish character milked all the gory details to hell and gone." He carried the empty carafe back to the sink. "We found some doctor's body, and another shooting happened at Gentry Park, a friend of September's. And I just came from Star Mall after September directed us to a dead bus driver. Bloody paw prints and a kid's sneaker tracks all over the floor. But no dog, no kid, no witnesses. Except for the coffee shop guy that Pike interviewed, but he didn't really know anything. I think the killer kidnapped Steven."

"September called that in? Shit, I didn't buy her as the shooter."

"Nope, she came late to that party. We think Steven got on the bus with his dog, and got off at the mall. But he didn't drive himself away. Somebody took him. The bus driver objected and got herself shot."

"I'll buy that." Stan slurped his coffee.

Combs rinsed out the pot and left it in the sink. "That extra leverage—the kid—keeps September on task. She can't come in to the police, or her sister and Steven get hurt."

"So pressure's on September to produce—whatever it is." He wiped coffee from his mustache. "She didn't give you any hint?"

Combs's shrug sent a sharp twinge down his spine. Tension always settled in his back. "You'd think she'd know better. Her husband was a cop." He flexed and twisted but it didn't help. Only finding Mom's killer would relieve the unrelenting ache.

"A cop?" Stan frowned. "Not around here. What's her story, anyway?"

"You don't remember?" Combs leaned against the counter. "Lot of gossip at the time. She was a musical prodigy, ended up on a concert tour sponsored by her school. Must have jumped the tracks when she fell in love, ditched school to marry, and gave up her scholarship." Yep, love could derail even the best laid plans. "Childress was pissed that September had some little sister crises over a supposed stalker late in April's pregnancy. She flew to the rescue, and Steven was born in Chicago during the trip."

"He didn't get to see his kid being born? I'd be pissed, too."

"More than that. Steven was a premie, hospitalized for a month before he came home, and Childress says that caused the autism. Blames September." Combs shrugged. "Anyway, September married the cop, threw away her music career and ended up with dogs."

"Makes no sense. Music to cop hubby to dogs? That's screwy. How'd they meet? Was he security for a concert?"

"Nope. SVU in Chicago."

"Special victims? Huh." Stan's tone suggested you had to be nuts to prefer the big city. "What's she do here? Heartland's a sleepy 'burb compared to Chicago."

"You do avoid the gossip, don't you?" Combs smiled at his uncle. If it didn't happen in church or on the scanner, it didn't matter. "She and her husband moved from Chicago to South Bend."

"Fighting Irish?"

"Yeah, Notre Dame land. They won the lottery, and then he got himself killed. Scuttlebutt says the stalker followed September from Chicago and nailed her husband. But nobody got arrested for the crime. Anyway, between the winnings and his insurance, September's financially set for life so she moved back home and bought the old Ulrich place. She's got it tricked out with more security than Fort Knox. Locks, bars, you name it. Her folks think she's still antsy over the stalker, but they don't seem to take it seriously. I'm just surprised she doesn't have a guard dog."

She looked younger than twenty-eight, and he'd been charmed by her quick wit. She didn't remember turning him down for a date all those years ago, and he hadn't reminded her. "She's smart. She worked SAR with the police, but both her husband and the dog died in some hinky convenience store shooting."

"That explains the security overkill, I suppose." He paused. "Married to a cop. Worked tracking duty with cops. Why didn't she go to the cops?" Stan's ferocious look still had the power to castrate.

"If these bastards have her sister, and now Steven, she's not taking chances. She's a victim, too. They pull the strings and she dances."

"It's all these damn cop shows. Has the whole world believing they can solve crimes all by their lonesome." His brow wrinkled. "Wait a minute. Did you mention a doctor? One of the victims is a doctor? What sort of doc?"

"Yeah, we found Dr. Pottinger's body outside of Childress's place." He tugged at his collar. The fabric, wet from the snow, had begun to chafe. "Pottinger's a researcher. Probably studies cockroach races or how many nose hairs the average teenager grows. Not really any connection other than proximity to Childress. But we found an antique bullet in the ceiling at April's house that the in-house ballistics guru says may be a match to the bullet that killed Pottinger."

Stan slapped the table again. "That's it!" He dismounted the chair, crossed to Combs, and gave him a bear hug. "Pottinger's the connection. That's the name Miz January mentioned, the doc who helped with the kid." His mustache quivered like a hyperventilating squirrel. "Pottinger—sounds like that Peter Rabbit storybook writer I used to read to you kids. Beatrix Pottinger, that's how I remembered."

"That's Beatrix *Potter*. Shit." Combs reached for his cell phone and then remembered he'd left it to charge in the car. He checked his watch. "Doty's holding a press conference in about two minutes. I need to get over there."

"Take me." Stan drew himself up to his full 6'2" height. "Don't shut me out."

Zippering his coat, Combs headed for the door. "You know what the brass would say. And since when did you become a rule bender?" The cold words sounded more abrupt than he intended. Stan didn't deserve that.

"Please."

Combs stopped at the door, his hand on the knob, and turned back. He knew Stan's request took enormous effort. The man granted favors, not the reverse. And from his own experience, Combs knew a view from the outside, stripped of power, took an enormous toll. Might as well lie down in a coffin and wait for the first shovel of dirt.

"I can't. You wouldn't in my position." The words cut Combs to the core. They'd finally reconnected, found each other again, only to have this happen.

"Don't suppose you can make exceptions." Stan hitched up his jeans. "You always did follow the rules, more or less. You were always a good cop, and a great detective. I think I knew that all along." His mustache twitched. "Wouldn't Wilma just blow a raspberry if this got you back into the fold again?"

Yep, Mom would be tickled but that didn't change reality. "I can't take you with me, but I can by-damn keep you informed." Combs held out his hand. "I don't want either of us to ever get lost in the shuffle again."

Stan grabbed his hand, squeezed hard. Blinked back tears that Combs knew were reflected in his own eyes. Aunt Ethel was right, they were very much alike. No need for further words.

Combs opened the door and hurried back into the cold before he embarrassed them both.

Chapter 34

September stood and backed away from the agitated dog. They'd waited for hours for Lizzie to take the next step. Worrying about April had her nerves on fire, so much so that she'd nearly come out of her skin when Shadow tried to attack the computer. The dog's attention never wavered from the computer monitor. He'd stopped barking, but his growls shook the bed.

"Turn up the volume. Shadow, good boy. Hush."

"What the hell's wrong with him?" Teddy gingerly reached for the audio. "I didn't think dogs could see TV." He fooled with the keyboard again as the video clip finished, and the image returned to the live feed. A heavy cop moved away from the podium and joined two detectives. "That's the courthouse."

September leaned closer to the monitor. "The video they played showed Henry Pottinger, Steven's doctor. Shadow must have recognized him."

Doug Childress seized the podium. "I just want my son back." He leaned into the microphone, and a picture of Steven filled one half of the split screen. "He's seven years old, and has been missing since noon yesterday." His voice caught. "He may be with his mother, or aunt. But Steven needs to come home. To me. To his father."

Shadow continued to growl, but September's hand on his ruff calmed him. He licked his lips, yawned, and lay down, but his focus remained glued to the computer.

"You sure the dog recognized this guy? How do you know him?"

"I don't. But the doctor is the thread that ties everything together. Shadow couldn't have met anyone else in that video, so that must be what got him riled." Her mind flashed to the bundle of bloody workout clothes. Did the blood belong to Pottinger? That would explain why April wouldn't call the police when Steven got lost. "There's so damn many people involved, I don't know who to trust."

"Would the dog recognize people on the screen?"

"Doubtful. Flat faced breeds like bulldogs or cats more easily react to TV, especially the latest high definition ones. Something about their eye placement and retinal differences compared to longer-nosed dogs. Shadow must have heard Dr. Pottinger before." Maybe yesterday morning. That was the only thing that made sense.

On the computer screen, the spiky-haired detective moved Childress aside, and pulled the microphone close. "September Day remains a person of interest." A picture of September with a cello, and without the white skunk streak in her hair, filled the screen.

The detective came back on screen. "We're also looking for April Childress and her son Steven." April's glamorous picture appeared side by side with a somber photo of Steven. "We believe the little boy caught a ride on the HART-Line bus and got off at Star Mall. The child could be in the company of a large, black German shepherd, a service dog. The police welcome any additional information the public may have about the whereabouts of these individuals."

Somebody from the press shouted. "Detective Doty, what about the other shootings? One at Star Mall and another at Gentry Park. Are they connected? Is this drug related?"

Doty held up one hand for silence. "I have no further comment on other pending cases. The deceased have not yet been identified pending notification of next of kin."

"How are they related?" Several reporters called out the same question at once.

"We're not prepared to say at this time," said the detective. "We welcome information, and you can call the number on the screen."

Teddy reached for the desk phone. "My turn."

"What are you doing?" September lurched to grab for the receiver. "Please, you can't call the police." She might not be hero material, but she was Steven's only chance. "Give me half an hour head start—"

"I'm dialing." He punched numbers, and then paused. "Unless you want to clue me in. It's time."

He was right. She didn't know if April was alive or dead. She'd already failed her sister, and the only way she knew to redeem herself was to save Steven. Lizzie would call, and she'd obediently hand over the computer drive, and be left with empty prayers they'd keep their word and release Steven.

"Tell me." He hung up the phone. "I want to help."

Reaching for the dog, she sat on the bed. Shadow wagged his tail, licking her hand as she stroked his soft, black fur. September felt her stress slowly ebb to barely below the scream-threshold. "Okay, what do you want to know?" She checked her watch for the millionth time. Six hours until the deadline.

"From the beginning. Give me the digest version, because the way you check your watch, time's short."

"You don't know the half of it." She struggled to gather her thoughts. She took a big breath and spoke quickly. "Some bad people kidnapped my sister and her son."

"Dr. Pottinger?"

"No. Lizzie Baumgarten and about a million henchmen. There's a pale man who looks like a ghost. That's her son, Gerald." She reached into the top of her borrowed sweatshirt and pulled out the flash drive. "They want this. It belonged to Pottinger."

His glasses twitched. "That's why Freda was killed?" He reached for it. "Why didn't you just give it to them, for Christ's sake?"

She slipped it back under her shirt. "I just got it. Shadow was wearing it."

He scratched his head. "The dog had the flash drive? Wait, don't tell me." He wrinkled his brow. "Steven, right?"

September nodded. "April said Pottinger was at the house yesterday morning, so I think that's why Shadow reacted just now." She hugged herself, and spoke her fears aloud. "That detective said Pottinger was murdered, probably at April's house."

Teddy gulped. "Your sister killed him?"

"No. I don't know. Maybe." September forced herself to finish the story despite the bad taste it left behind. "April was frantic when Steven disappeared in the snowstorm. I think Steven got scared when Pottinger was killed, and ran away." She braced herself against a chair back, gripping the upholstery so hard her fingers turned white. "Lizzie shot the babysitter, and threatened to kill my sister unless I returned the flash drive." The room reeled and then steadied again, a side effect of unburdening herself. Or maybe she just needed more caffeine. "She gave me twenty-four hours. That's two o'clock. April doesn't know about the babysitter. She just wants to help her son."

"That's how you got beat up?"

"You should see the other guy." The joke fell flat. Sure, she smacked Gerald, but in retaliation Pam was killed. "They've been ahead of me every step of the way." Her hand covered the flash drive. "This is first break I've had, the only hope to save Steven and April."

Shadow whined and pawed her until she shushed him, and he leaned hard against her. She avoided Teddy's eyes. Lizzie may have already killed April. If Teddy called the police, Steven could die, too.

He picked up a glass paperweight and immediately appeared calmer as he massaged its smooth surface. "I can see why you don't want to call the authorities. But do you think these jerks will return Steven? You can identify them, right?"

"I've got no choice."

"You always have a choice." He turned back to the computer. "First things first. Let's see exactly who we're dealing with." Teddy gently kissed the paperweight and set it down. "Channeling my wife, she was always the brains in the family. That was a fiftieth anniversary gift from her." He smiled, touched the glass again, and then his fingers clacked on the keyboard. "The phone's dead anyway. So until I can call the cops, might as well do some research."

September breathed again. "What are you doing?"

"Find out about this Pottinger character."

"Hold that thought." She hurried from the office to the living room, rummaged in her coat for her notes from the conversation with Fish. Gerald's pistol came out first. The greenish parkerized finish looked dull even in bright light. She'd never liked guns but she respected them, and Chris had taught her how to use them. September stuck the pistol into a pocket of the borrowed sweatpants. She wanted it within reach. She returned to the office bedroom. "My friend at the radio station found Pottinger on the internet. He works for NeuroRealm."

"Why didn't you say so?" Teddy typed the company name into the search engine, and soon had the website on the screen. "Here we go—all sorts of research. Hmm."

"How does this help?" Her toe stuttered in rhythm with the silent tick-tock in her head. Lizzie could call any minute. She had to be ready.

"Interesting." Teddy clicked on the media button, found the list of press releases, and opened the most recent. "Looky there." He backed away to give her room to see.

She scanned the press release. "Rebirth Gathering. April mentioned that." She read further. "It's a retreat for parents with autistic kids, and hints at some breakthrough treatment that cures the condition, extensively quoting Dr. Pottinger." She devoured the information. "Holy shit, it also quotes Dr. Gerald Baumgarten" She read further. "Sounds too good to be true. And it is. There's the contact person—Lizbeth Baumgarten, RVT."

"RVT, what is that? Some kind of nurse?"

"Registered veterinary technician." September's gorge rose. They must be using veterinary drugs on kids. "Look at that fee. You've got to qualify for placement, Rebirth Gathering won't accept everyone."

"Oldest sales trick in the book." Teddy snorted. "Make it exclusive, so folks want to be part of the elite."

"Doug refused to pay for the treatment, so April came to me."

Teddy whistled. "You didn't blink at the price?"

September shrugged. "I've got the funds, I'm comfortable."

"But it costs twenty-five grand just to get in the door, and they limit it to the first two hundred who register. Enough reason to kill." He shuddered. "Wonder how much the cost goes up once the children qualify for the full treatment? The bastards."

September read further, and gasped. "The full treatment goes up to seventy-five thousand." When did April plan to hit her up for that amount? Chris left her okay financially, but not if Steven's treatment fees hemorrhaged her funds. "April said Steven improved tremendously on the new therapy. Snake oil? Maybe. But placebo can be a powerful persuader. Parents grasp at straws, and will try any crazy cure for their kids, even unproven stuff."

"I didn't know you could experiment on kids." Disgust filled his voice.

"FDA studies mostly use adults, true. To run the same trials with kids would increase the cost even more, so they extrapolate doses and go off-label with drugs approved for other things." She shrugged. "Happens all the time. I think parents just sign a consent form acknowledging they know the treatment hasn't been FDA-approved. Of course the insurance won't pay for experimental treatments, but desperate folks accept the risk." She re-read the press release. "My God, Rebirth Gathering starts this afternoon! That must be the reason for the deadline. Whatever's on the flash drive must be explosive."

"So let's see what's so important." He held out his hand.

September's fist closed protectively over the drive, and she walked away. April got herself into the situation, but Pam was already on her conscience. She didn't need to add more to her guilt. Once she ransomed Steven she'd retreat to her reinforced rabbit hole, bolt the doors, and never come out again.

"Do you think these yahoos will let you off the hook? Grow up." He shoved his glasses up the bridge of his nose. "It's not just about Steven anymore. People have died."

"Who made you the savior of the world?" She whirled to confront him, and chewed words through a clenched jaw. "Don't you dare play the guilt card with me. I didn't ask for this. I owed April. Steven belongs to her now, he never belonged to me. I never even wanted kids; don't even like them, how long can she hold that over my head?" She clamped her hands over her mouth. Shame heated her face.

Teddy made a face. "Yes, I can tell you're an evil person only out for yourself. You hate kids. Probably beat that dog." He waved at Shadow and the dog wagged his tail. "So do you want Lizzie to kill more kids with her treatment? Do you let Lizzie get away with murder?"

She looked away. He didn't know. Only God knew who she really was, and what she'd done, and there was a very good reason God didn't hear her prayers anymore. So be it. She slapped the flash drive into his palm. "It's your funeral. If you get killed, I'm not going to cry."

"I have no plans to die. But they murdered my friend. Freda only wanted to help."

"Don't you think I know that? I know it's my fault." The flush left her cheeks, and September grabbed the wall to steady herself. She needed an IV bolus of caffeine or she'd never be able to finish this race.

Teddy plugged the drive into his computer. "Information is power. That's the shovel we use to bury them. We not only look at what's on this thing, we make a copy as insurance."

Pottinger's information might offer leverage, but she wondered what other horrors it might reveal. September mentally shook herself. Save them first, and save worrying for later. Teddy was right. She needed every advantage possible to come out of the storm. "Go ahead and copy it, Teddy. But hurry." She touched her watch. "When they call for the exchange I've got to be ready."

Teddy tapped keys.

"They'll come after your computer if they find out."

"They won't find it on this machine." Teddy boasted, still hitting keys. "I have an online storage site, password protected. In fact, Pottinger password-protected the file." He bared tobacco-stained teeth in a wolfish expression. "They don't know who they're messing with. I am the original badass hacker. And I flat love a challenge."

She smiled despite herself. "How much time do you need?"

His fingers flew. "Half an hour, give or take, when it's an amateur job. Professional encryption takes longer." He typed some more. "This is amateur hour. Piece of cake. I can save the file."

September returned to the bed but didn't sit down. She stroked Shadow, needing the contact to calm down. "They have to keep them alive at least until I return the flash drive. I have to believe that." The circumstances of his birth weren't Steven's fault. She had to stop blaming him. And herself.

Shadow nudged her hand. What the hell. She always thought better, worked out problems best around dogs. She'd learned that during the dark time eight years ago, when even her beloved music had forsaken her. She'd been lost until Dakota found her and brought her back to life. Dogs have a way of connecting and healing the broken pieces of one's soul that people can't always reach, although it was Chris who brought Dakota into her world.

September picked up the glass paperweight. Fifty years married. Something she'd never know. Chris wanted kids. Desperately. He shouldn't have counted on her for that most basic dream. Chalk up another failure.

Stop it. Picked sores don't heal. And she no longer had the luxury of feeling sorry for herself. She couldn't hide this time. Locked doors wouldn't protect her from this horror.

Shadow waited on the bed and watched her every move. He was tuned in to her, even more than Dakota. She tamped down that disloyal thought.

Holding the paperweight in her right hand, she picked up his bear in the other. "Watch," she said. She held the glass paperweight high, out of the dog's reach. "This is glass." She held up the bear. "This is Bear." She lowered both hands within reach of the dog. "Show me glass."

Without hesitation, Shadow reached forward and poked the glass globe.

September "clicked" her tongue, and tossed Bear to him. He caught it and dropped the toy and watched for what she'd do next. His tail slowly waved. He loved games, loved learning. Shadow was a trainer's dream.

Pulling a tissue from the box on the bedside table, September repeated the drill. She held the requested item in the opposite hand this time. "This is paper. This is glass. Show me paper."

Shadow lunged forward, poked the balled tissue, and received the tongue-click. "Good boy. What a smart dog."

His wags grew more exuberant. He woofed and play-bowed.

September searched for another pair, and bumped into the bed when she turned. Her pocket thunked against the footboard. She paused. Couldn't hurt. She pulled out the pistol, and checked the safety was on, and held it aloft. "This is gun."

"What the hell are you doing?" Teddy paused from his keyboard dance. "Is that thing loaded? Put it away."

"The safety's on." She glared.

"Do you have a permit? Where'd you get that thing?"

"It's Texas, y'all. I've got a license, but this isn't mine. Gerald dropped it and I accepted his donation." Turning to Shadow, she began again. "This is gun. This is—"

"Good God, put it away, September! What are you doing, anyway?"

"Vocabulary." She set the pistol on the desk. "It's a mental stimulation game. Some words he already knows, like paper, but he's not yet generalized."

"Generalized?"

"'Generalized': a generic word to a family of similar objects. He's generalized "bear" to include any stuffed toy. With paper, there are so many kinds I wouldn't want to confuse him by making him pick." She considered other objects, grabbed two, and turned back to Shadow. "This is candle. This is book. Show me candle."

Shadow poked, she clicked, and Teddy stared.

Teddy turned back to the computer. "It's a trick. No dog learns something that fast." He typed even faster.

"Hard to believe, isn't it?" She replaced the book on the shelf, and the candle on his desk. "I watched a horse demo at a behavior conference once. This mare could even tell what group an object belonged to—if it was a food or a tool." She rubbed the dog's head, and enjoyed the silkiness of the clean fur under her hand. "Had to try with Shadow, since he already knows so many action commands. Once he learned "show me," teaching him object names was a breeze."

Shadow woofed again. He pedaled his front paws from side to side, anxious for the game to continue.

"Nice parlor trick. But what good is it?" Teddy turned back to screen. "Nearly got it."

She shrugged but he didn't see. "Good for lots of things, especially for a service dog. It's most important that he gets a kick out of learning. Naming objects and behaviors teaches language. Just like the commands "kiss" or "sit" have meaning once the action is named. You've got to have a common language to communicate with people, computers, and even animals."

"Like new software, or a different language, huh?" Teddy bobbed his head. "Okay, that makes sense, I guess." He poked the gun. "With the trouble we're in, you ought to teach him something helpful. When's a dog ever going to shoot a gun? Teach him something we can all use, like "sic-'em.'"

His words punched a fist-size hole in the conversation. For a moment the dog play had pushed horror aside, but the upbeat mood evaporated quicker than fog on a sunny day. "He's already protective, Teddy. He's a German Shepherd."

"Can't you, I don't know, get him to go after the bad guys? Get him close enough, he could do some damage? He nailed that guy at the mall."

She smiled, but shook her head. "The man took Steven. Of course Shadow would go after him. But Shadow's a service dog, and he's been taught restraint. It takes more than a few drills to turn a dog into Schutzhund material." It had taken years to train with Dakota, herself more than him. They'd nearly read each other's minds, but it required time to develop that kind of rapport. "TV has you think it takes thirty minutes to bully a dog to behave any way they want. A lot of that's creative editing, and the rest is the dog with the pee scared out of him."

Teddy scowled. "Well, you know dogs. I know computers. Let's stick with what we know in the time we've got left."

Time. That defined her world. She could teach Shadow anything if she had time. He worked for praise, he was easy. Dakota wanted to be paid with his ball. Macy demanded treats. Even people worked best for pay. If she could figure out what payday would float Lizzie's boat and used it against her, she just might survive the deadline.

"Got it. By damn, I got the sonofabitch's password cracked." Teddy swiveled in his chair. "'Paddlefoot,' the name of Pottinger's dog when he was a kid. Go figure, he'd be a fan of Clutch Cargo."

"What? Never mind." It didn't matter how he'd cracked the code. "Let me see." She shoved Teddy away from the desktop to stare at the screen. Time to find out what was worth so many lives.

Chapter 35

April regained consciousness when an ambient droning sound stopped. It could have been hours, or minutes, but now she was back.

Glittery light refracted through translucent crystals piled inches deep over her face and body. Florescent lights flickered overhead through countless prisms. She was buried in ice cubes. She tried to move. Nothing. Maybe she was dead. But no. The ice anesthetized everything.

Her mind was mush. Dr. Pottinger's threats, his death, hiding his body, Steven lost—the nightmare kaleidoscope couldn't be real. Steven found, safe in her arms, letting her hold and hug him. . .

It was hard to breathe. *I'm dying. Who will take care of Steven when I'm dead? Who will give him his medicine, work with him, help him—love him?* She gritted her teeth. Not September. She didn't want him. And not Doug. He'd given up on Steven.

April tried to move again, and the ice shifted. Had the ice been shaved, or any smaller than cube size, she'd have suffocated. Nuggets melted slightly by her breath fused and created a small cave-like shell about her head. That had taken some time.

Ice had numbed everything. April moved her jaw, explored lips, cheeks and teeth with her tongue. She tasted salt, how odd, and then understood. It was blood. The gag-making flavor primed her memory of September's phone call telling her the flash drive was found, and of Gerald pointing the gun.

She'd been shot. Each breath rattled deep in her lungs. April coughed, choked, and warmth dribbled down her chin.

A sound. Somebody outside. Voices, at least two people. April couldn't make out the words. But a woman's high pitched complaint argued with a man's rumbled answer.

Move. Get up. Shake off the ice, climb out. But her body refused to obey the silent drill sergeant commands in her brain. She could manage only a few finger twitches. Her ring clacked against the side of the container, but ice hog-tied the rest of her body.

She moaned. The numbing properties of the cold didn't extend to the stabbing pain of internal organs. Despite temptation to drift away, April gathered herself to yell over the anticipated hurt.

"Help! Help me." The cry rasped her throat like a file on metal.

Footsteps. Shoes scuffing carpet. The sound of the argument drew near.

"Help. Me. Please." With each breath she inhaled glass. She had to tell someone. Get help. Not for her. For Steven. He needed his treatment. The cost was beyond money. September had the means. Doug never understood.

Lizzie was an angel. Saving children meant everything to her, so getting shot had to be an accident. What did the movies call it? She was collateral damage. Just like Pottinger was collateral damage, an unintended consequence. Lizzie cared about the kids, cared about Steven; she didn't really care about the money. What price could you put on a miracle? The children would be the biggest losers if Legacy Center shut down. People without special kids wouldn't understand. Legacy Center must survive—even if she didn't—to ensure Steven's cure.

The strangers came closer. "I don't care what your momma wants," the woman said. "She's never liked me anyhow. I'd rather stay here in the hotel, or just bundle up at home 'til the electric comes back on. Pete, I refuse to spend the night at her house. She'll make it like she's doing us this huge favor. I don't want to owe her nothing."

So she was in a hotel. That made no sense. Lizzie hadn't wanted her to go home to an empty house where Pottinger had died, but all the hotels were full. So April had accepted Lizzie's considerate invitation to stay with her until Steven was found. Lizzie's down-home kindness was nothing like Mom's insistence on perfection.

"Aw, Julie, we don't have to talk about that now." Pete's exasperated tone matched Julie's volume. "Momma tries to be helpful. She's got that big hide-a-bed and gas heat, leastwise unless the gas line freezes."

"She stares at me." The pouty tone could have been a teenager's complaint. "Gives me the willies. Always judging me, she is, like she thinks she's the queen of the world." They drew closer. "And don't you dare suggest we go to that woman's place for Thanksgiving this year. Never again. Nobody makes fun of my rhubarb pie."

Black spots told April another blackout was imminent. So much easier to let go. But when she closed her eyes, Steven's face filled her world. She tried again. Whispered a silent prayer they'd come one step closer. Her ring clanked again on the metal wall of the ice bin.

"I got the pay-per-view ready to go. Work's cancelled for the next couple of days. Might as well make a holiday of it. So just get the Dr. Pepper, will you? I'll get ice, and we'll raid the mini-bar and have us a party. At least the hotel's got heat."

"Oh, honey, I've got enough heat for the both of us." Shoes clopped onto the tile of the vending room. Smacking sounds, mumbling, and a giggle.

Something tore inside when April struggled to expand her lungs. Fresh blood filled her mouth, and she spat out the foul wet. She heard the rattle-thud of a soda machine relinquishing a can. Ice over her body shifted as Pete scooped.

April's fingers fluttered; her ruby ring a metal flail against the confinement. Her hand broke free and thrust above the ice.

"DAMN!" Pete fell backwards. Julie screamed.

Big rough hands scooped away ice. Pete grabbed the plastic ice bucket, filled and dumped it on the floor. April wanted to thank him, but it required every bit of will just to fill her lungs.

"Is she okay? Why's she in there? Liked to give me a coronary." The blousy woman with lavender lipstick leaned close. "Pete, is that blood? God almighty! I'm calling nine-one-one." Julie jabbed at a cell phone she'd pulled from tight jeans.

"She's bleeding, sweet Jesus, she's bleeding. Hurry up, Julie, make the friggin' call!" Pete turned back to April. "Don't talk, you can talk later. How the hell you get in the ice dispenser?" He lifted one of her numb arms and looped it over his neck. He grasped her shoulders and cradled beneath her knees to lift her free of the box. Ice clung to April's clothes, reluctant to let her go.

Her vision turned dark but her mind cleared. Everything made awful sense now. She knew what to do. To save Steven. Her son. "Listen to me." Pete's expression morphed from fear to pity and horror. "I need to tell you—" April coughed. Red spattered his face.

"Shit." He recoiled, and nearly dropped her, but then gently lowered April to the tile floor. He swiped his cheek with his sweatshirt sleeve. "Julie, move your butt, girl, tell them to hurry. And go get us some towels or a blanket or something before the lady freezes." He grasped April's hand, leaning close with a forced smile. "Hang on. Let's get you fixed up first. There'll be time to tell what happened later." He swiped at his cheek again, and grabbed the phone away from his wife.

April coughed again, and tasted blood. "A drink? Some water? Please, can I . . ." She was so thirsty. Warmth spread over the surface of her chest but coldness filled her insides.

"Honey, what happened" Julie knelt beside her.

"Tell them." April gasped. "Protect my son. Tell them who did this to me." Julie leaned close, and April strained to whisper until she couldn't make her voice work. But it was enough. April relaxed, and fell into blackness with a bloody smile on her lips. She'd kept her promise.

Chapter 36

September leaned close to the computer screen. She found the mouse and clicked to enlarge the text. "Damn, there's dozens of pages, all in ten-point, single spaced type. And it's in medicalese." She wrinkled her nose. "Do you understand this stuff?"

Teddy stood back, hands on hips. He removed his glasses and leaned closer. "It describes some test protocol." He pointed to the pertinent sentence.

She dipped her head. "The first page is an abstract. There's the medication—Damenia, and the dose. That fits. Same drug listed on Steven's empty pill bottles." She read farther down the page, but shrugged away from Teddy's old man breath.

"Damenia. That sounds familiar. I think Molly takes that." He shrugged at her raised eyebrows. "Molly is my wife."

She stopped. "I thought she was dead."

He adjusted his glasses. "Molly's got Alzheimer's. I take the bus every day to the mall, and on her good days she comes and we visit. Today wasn't a good day." His sarcasm cut deep.

A buzzer from the distant kitchen startled them both. Shadow woofed under his breath and hopped off the bed. "He thinks it's something for him." September smiled and then felt guilty. Had to be hundred years since she'd smiled. She shrugged an apology.

Teddy laughed. "Sometimes life's so shitty you got to laugh in the devil's face." He stood as the buzzer grew more intense. "The rolls will burn, I better get them. You want cream in your coffee or black?"

"Coffee, any way you have it is fine. Maybe that'll help clear the cobwebs."

"Be right back." He hurried from the room.

September puzzled out the text on the computer. The document listed no authors or co-authors. She paged down and discovered the document included Pottinger's own notes and conclusions. It appeared that Dr. Pottinger had simply cut-and-pasted from some larger document to include the initial abstract that detailed the study structure, subjects, expected outcome, and what had transpired.

The paper detailed research compiled from seven groups located in Dallas, Houston, Kansas City, Oklahoma City, Chicago, Indianapolis and Detroit, each composed of between nine to fifteen subjects. A mix of males and a handful of females aged five to fifteen, diagnosed with mild to severe autism made up each group. The children were not identified other than by group code, sex, and age.

In all, the measure of eye contact, verbal communication, and one-on-one interaction increased by at least three-fold within the first six weeks on the trial drug. Objectionable stereotypic behaviors—repetitive self-stimulating actions or "stimming," such as spinning, hand flapping, rocking—and tantrums decreased by twenty-five percent within the same period, and these symptoms were eliminated in fifty percent of cases by the end of the first phase study. A small percentage of children started to talk virtually overnight. No wonder April was excited by the new treatment.

Nothing on the flash drive seemed worth Lizzie's efforts to recover the information, though. Sure, the drug composition and test results were proprietary. But all the parents signed an informed consent to enroll their children. April would have been told of any possible adverse effects of the drug, and must have deemed the risks to be minimal compared to the potential for improvement. Hell, any parent would willingly risk a bit of diarrhea to have a normal relationship with their child.

The old guilt stabbed anew. Chris had been sure he could change her mind about kids. "But I'm a freak," she said. Chris saved her, and she couldn't bring herself to give him what he wanted. Then he was dead..

She shrugged off the pain. None of that mattered in this moment. She returned to the tedious copy. The conclusion with Pottinger's annotations began on page 29 and continued for five pages. September reached the last few paragraphs and stiffened. She re-read them.

September opened an email and attached the document. She addressed it to herself, her parents, and siblings and hit send. Whatever happened in the hours ahead, the whole family would know. They needed to understand, and protect themselves, especially when Steven came home.

If he came home. Because the consequences of missing the 24-hour deadline went beyond returning the flash drive. For Steven and the people around him, missing the deadline could be fatal.

Teddy hurried back into the room balancing a tray with two coffee mugs, a saucer of steaming biscuits, a tub of margarine and a beaker of honey. "Help yourself." He settled the tray on the desk. "So what did you find out?"

Shadow sniff-tested the air, and wagged a polite request for a taste.

September closed the file. Did she want him to know? "They've found a cure for autism. At least, that's what they say."

He looked so relieved she thought he'd dance a jig. "But that's marvelous!" Her expression tempered his joy. "Isn't it?"

"It's awesome for about seventy percent of the kids. But the others . . ." She stopped. Dear God, Steven had taken the drug for weeks. She forced herself to continue. "They can't stop the medication. Not ever. They price it low to get parents to sign kids into the program, and once they're hooked, they raise the maintenance fee at the Rebirth Gathering to stay on the drug. Without the drug the children revert to their original state."

"Like a diabetic needs lifelong insulin therapy. That means millions of dollars are at stake." He licked his lips. "People do awful things for money."

"It gets worse." She couldn't stop thinking about what this meant for Steven. "Withdrawal causes side effects. Bad ones. They develop severe— um, anger issues." She couldn't tell him. It was hard to believe something that cured autism also caused psychosis.

A little girl told to eat her vegetables stabbed her mother repeatedly with a salad fork. Another child set the family cat on fire. One boy Steven's age beat and drowned his four-year-old sister in the toilet. The document listed dozens of examples of explosive violence along with video evidence, but she couldn't bring herself to watch.

Pottinger brought the evidence to convince April, a drugstore blackmail to pay the extortion or risk Steven's sanity. And her sister must have gone ballistic and killed Pottinger when she didn't have the funds, and knew what would happen to Steven without the treatment. April was a victim, but she also must be a party to Lizzie's cover-up. God only knew how many other children were on the treatment, maybe hundreds of children with ticking time bombs inside their heads. Getting cut off from the drug would turn them into an army of psychotic youngsters. September shuddered.

Teddy plucked at the long sleeves of his sweater. "There are always side effects. Parents wouldn't mind risking a few problems for the chance of a cure."

"Even violence?" She didn't buy it. "Either the researchers didn't know about the problems, or the parents weren't told until it was too late."

"Don't autistic children sometimes have tantrums? That's not beyond the realm of normal." Teddy buttered a biscuit. "I know parents can be extra sensitive." He took a bite, glanced at Shadow's drooling face, and tossed him a piece. The dog snapped the treat out of the air and wagged for more.

"Parents didn't complain. The researchers documented it. Don't you see? That's why Pottinger visited April, to hold this over her head so she'd pay. It's all in his notes."

April would have held out for the promise of a cure. Steven was her world, and she'd do anything to protect his chance for normalcy. "Read it for yourself."

Teddy moved to the desk when she stood up. He adjusted his glasses.

"Worldwide distribution of the drug's already begun." September paced in the small room. "They've got plans for before and after interviews with miracle children slated for an international market push. Forget millions, that's billions of dollars and thousands of kids." She sat on the bed, patted the comforter for Shadow to jump up beside her. Smoothing his fur helped calm her nervous energy that had to go somewhere or explode. "I remember what you said about backups, so I emailed a copy of the document to myself."

Teddy picked up his mug of coffee, started to sip, and stopped as he read. "Oh, God." He set down the mug, sloshing some of the liquid onto the tray.

"I know it's horrible. Desperate people risk everything for a maybe cure. They don't know they could kill their kids or push them to hurt someone else. We can't let that happen." She glanced at the tray of food, but had lost her appetite, perhaps permanently. Still, she needed to eat or would crash, probably when she least expected. "I sent my email public to de-fang the snake. Doctors won't prescribe it, parents will sue, and the recalls would bury NeuroRealm." She picked up a biscuit, chewed fiercely and swallowed half before she washed it down with a mouthful of scalding coffee. She fed the rest of the biscuit to Shadow.

Teddy sat quietly and stared at the screen.

"They call it a cure. Meanwhile, the drug creates an army of children ready to go postal while their parents celebrate a miracle." She shuddered. "The liability is unbelievable."

He nodded, his face white. "Worth killing for."

Chapter 37

Humphrey Fish's voice blared from the speakers when Combs started the car. He'd left the radio on when he'd stopped to visit Uncle Stan. He reached to turn it off.

"Keep those tips coming, listeners. We're your up-to-the-minute, ear-on-the-air, reporting as the manhunt unfolds. Joining us is Carl Dorfman, with his eyewitness account of the shocking murder at Star Mall. He barely escaped with his life."

Combs's hand jerked away from the dial. "Sonofabitch." He over-corrected but managed to keep the car on the highway.

"Uh, yeah. I served them some drinks and f-fries." The kid's slight stutter rose from excitement. He had no reason to be afraid. "The cops asked me all about it. I could have been killed, you know."

Carl Dorfman must be the manager who served food to the victim, the kid Pike interviewed. "What the hell is he doing?" Combs turned up the sound.

"Must have been terrifying," said Fish. "How'd you get away?"

Combs seethed. Dorfman had been long gone before any shooting.

"That Freda lady got shot. She's a regular customer. And the old guy Mr. Williams shows up with his wife most afternoons. She's got that old-timers memory thing, you know?" Dorfman clearly enjoyed the celebrity. "I never seen that kid before that was feeding fries to his dog."

"Must have been the missing child, right?" Fish was joyful. "How did you get away from the killer?" He wheedled like a kid begging for candy.

"You never saw him." Combs slapped the wheel, disgusted. The Dorfman kid withheld information from Pike. The little shit knew Freda and the old man. They could have tracked this Williams fellow down by now. How had Pike missed that?

Combs found his phone, thumbed the number and cut off the connection when Doty's phone again went to voicemail. She must have turned it off for the press conference.

"Teddy and Freda was waiting on someone. The kid's dad, I heard them say. If I hadn't shut down early, I'd be dead, too."

Fish gasped. "Steven's father killed all those people? Listeners, are you getting all this?"

Old news, Combs knew. Gonzales already followed up with Childress. Steven's father hadn't been out of police sight, or his lawyer's presence, during the period in question.

Combs turned down the volume and increased the speed of the car. Doty needed to know that Pike missed the boat on his interview. He wondered why. He checked his watch. If he didn't slalom into a ditch before he got there, he should arrive about the time they finished the press conference.

His phone trilled. Doty maybe? "Combs." Combs lifted his foot off the gas and coasted.

"Jeffrey, I've waited for you to call. The children are beside themselves. Was Mom really shot?" Cassie's accusatory tone made it his fault. Again.

He couldn't remember the last time his ex-wife hadn't sounded pissed. This time she had every reason to be. "I'm on the job. Call Uncle Stan, and he'll fill you in."

"Is she dead? What the hell happened? Your own mother, Jeff, for God's sake." She breathed heavily. "I had to hear about it on the radio."

Shit. Didn't anybody have anything better to do than listen to Humphrey Fish flap his gums? That wasn't Cassie's style at all. "Sorry I didn't call. Yes, Mom's dead." He rubbed his face with one gloved hand, before quickly returning it to the steering wheel. The road straightened and his foot pressed the gas. Another three minutes and he'd be head-to-head with Doty.

"Jeff, we've had our differences, but couldn't you for once do the right thing for your kids? They've lost their grandma."

"And I lost my mother." He winced, wishing he could take back the words. Her quiet gasp told him he'd hurt her. Again. "I should have called, you're right." Too little too late, though. "I can swing by in an hour. Talk to the kids."

"They'd appreciate it. I didn't call for me, you know. Richard is here, and I'll get through this with his support." The subtext underlined that she'd moved on. "Whatever happened between us, you're still their father. They need you. Especially at a time like this. They love—loved their grandma. So did I."

Rick the prick. A damn CPA number cruncher, probably got off on the soap-opera style Humphrey Fish show. Cassie worked with him, and Combs couldn't help suspect the pair had plans long before his career-suicide tipped his marriage balance sheet into the negative column. "I'll be there soon as I can. Meanwhile, call Uncle Stan. Oh, and Cassie?" His voice turned hard. "Turn off the damn radio."

He pulled up to the courthouse. Media vehicles jammed all available parking spots. Combs slid into a disabled spot. Folks with mobility issues wouldn't risk this weather anyway. On the radio, Fish continued to take histrionic calls. Switching off the car brought blessed silence.

Combs hurried to the building and nearly wiped out on the steps. Nobody had shoveled or spread salt, and even the metal handrail shimmered with ice. One time, years ago before the kids, he and Cassie spent a memorable weekend in Salt Lake City at a ski lodge. Thirty minutes on skis convinced him snow was best experienced through a window, preferably accompanied by a roaring fire and an alcoholic beverage. This much snow all at once in North Texas was just wrong.

Pike came out of the building as Combs opened the courthouse door. "Watch out for Doty, she's in a mood." He started to brush past, ear flaps bouncing in the wind. He grabbed the rail and winced, stepping carefully.

He caught Pike's shoulder. "That Dorfman kid you interviewed from Star Mall blew smoke up your ass. He was on the radio just now, boasting he knew the vic and the old guy, Teddy somebody."

"Go figure." Pike shrugged off his hand. "I'll squeeze him for the address. Kids these days, too damn glib. They lie to your face and sound like choirboys. You're right; Steven might be with the old guy."

He noticed Pike's mincing gait. "What happened to you?"

The older man grabbed the handrail and took a careful duckstep downward. "Crap shoes on ice." Combs glanced down at the man's size twelve boats. "Doty's in such a rush, I didn't have time to change, and took a ride down some steps on my ass." He forced a rueful grin. "But can't let that stop this old warhorse. The kiddo is counting on me."

Combs stared after the limping man, frowning. Pike's kids were grown, but having a disabled grandson must make this case strike close to home. Maybe that distraction made him miss Dorfman's lies.

He stamped ice from his boots before entering the old building. Government offices closed due to the storm, but the press conference staged at one end of the great hallway drew a small crowd like flies to road kill. Doty was wrapping up.

"That's all for now." She stalked away from the podium with a phone to her ear.

"Doty." Combs called out, trying to stop her.

She held up a hand in a "one moment" gesture and turned away. He didn't see Gonzales, but Doug Childress stood to one side, his eyes downcast, cornered by a redheaded reporter.

"Have you received a ransom demand?" The reporter's buck-toothed smile pulled tight like a rat's. He shoved a digital recorder near Childress's mouth.

"Sly, why don't you crawl back under your rock?" Combs intentionally bumped into the man's beer belly. Sylvester Sanger had a reputation for creating bullshit to fill the holes in his less than meticulous research. He wrote for a tiny tabloid published in the next town.

"I've got a right to ask." Sanger pouted.

"Leave the man alone." Combs glowered. They'd gone to school together, and hadn't been friends then, either. "You just make shit up anyway." He'd been at the wrong end of Sanger's yellow journalism before.

Sanger sulked, turned away, and caught sight of Doty. He hurried in her direction, muttering into his hand-held recorder as he glanced behind him to be sure Combs wasn't on his tail.

"Thanks." Childress buttoned his top coat. He turned to leave, and pulled soft black leather gloves out of one pocket.

Combs stopped him. "A moment, please. What do you know about a Dr. Henry Pottinger?"

Childress dropped a glove. He stooped to retrieve it. "You can direct any questions to my attorney."

Combs scratched the stubble on his cheek. He needed a shave. "Mrs. January mentioned him. Said he's Steven's doctor?"

"Oh. Well, that could be true. April takes Steven to a slew of them." He pulled on one glove and flexed his hands. "April discussed that with her mother more than me, so I suppose she'd know." He tugged on the second glove and turned toward the door.

Combs blocked him again. "The body found behind your condo was Pottinger."

Childress sucked in a breath. "Steven's doctor is dead? My God, that's awful." He paused. "Can it have something to do with all this?" He waved one gloved hand to encompass the previous hours.

Combs waited. He wasn't disappointed.

Childress glanced toward the redheaded reporter held at bay by Doty. "Your detectives already questioned me. I have an alibi for when Steven was taken and that woman was killed."

Combs winced. Mom deserved better than "that woman."

"What reason under heaven would I have to kill Steven's doctor?"

"Yes, what reason?" Combs repeated. "I understand you and your ex-wife were not in agreement about Steven's treatment."

"I want the best for my son." His gloved hands clenched at his sides. "I will do anything to make sure he gets the best care." His visage glowed dusky red under the harsh fluorescents. "Right now, Officer Combs, I have more important issues at hand. If you were a father you'd understand that." He rushed toward the door, and this time Combs let him go.

Doty shut off her cell phone and strode toward Combs. "Good timing, Officer Combs." She leaned on the title, a perpetual dig she couldn't resist. She turned to the reporter. "Back off, Sly, or I'll run your butt in for obstruction."

The reporter saluted, but stood his ground. "Just doing my job."

She whipped around, glaring at Combs. "Walk with me."

He fell into step, pushed to keep up with her long strides. Something had happened. The information about Pottinger would keep at least until he knew the latest. All the reporters but Sly had dispersed, eager to file stories about something other than the blizzard.

At the door, Doty offered a death's head grimace. "We found April Childress."

Chapter 38

September's phone rang. She didn't recognize the number.

Teddy stared at her when it rang again. "Going to answer it?"

"Hello?" September held her breath.

"Deadline time."

Her throat constricted when she recognized Lizzie's voice. "You said twenty-four hours. There's still almost three hours left." She hadn't had time to set up her strategy, had wanted to run it by Teddy first. She waved at him, put her finger to her lips and switched the cell phone to speaker so he could hear.

"Change in plans." Lizzie's words crackled with authority. "You've got the merchandise early—hurray for you—so there's no reason to delay. You are not the only item on my to-do list, you know." She sounded surprisingly loud from the phone.

Shadow growled. His hackles rose.

"Wait. No, I can't. I need more time." September jumped up, leaving the phone on the bed. She had to call Fish and get him on task. He'd go for the plan. He wouldn't be able to resist.

"You've got until noon. Deliver by deadline or you can buy double funeral plots. Meet us at—"

"No." September's hands flew to her mouth as if to take back the words.

Shadow crept near the phone. Stretched his neck forward. Touched it with his nose, and growled louder.

September's heart stuttered before it returned to a steady rhythm. She stared at the phone. It sat on the bed six feet away. Maybe Lizzie hadn't heard what she'd said?

"No? Did you tell me 'no?'" Lizzie was incredulous. "You want them dead?"

She'd heard. "I mean . . ." September swallowed hard, and stared at Teddy with a silent plea for help. He held up his palms signaling he had nothing to offer.

What if her plan wasn't workable? She'd counted on brainstorming with Teddy for him to pick it apart first. September pantomimed a pencil and pad. Teddy juggled items on the desk and silently handed them to her. She scribbled quickly, and handed it back to him and turned back to the phone. No do-over. "I want to talk to April. Prove to me April's still alive. Or there's no flash drive."

"Is this déjà vu? We've already traveled this road, and you got April so upset she's indisposed."

Shadow snarled, and began to bark at the phone. He jumped at it, pawed and batted until September snatched it out of reach. "Are you still there?" She checked to be sure Shadow hadn't disconnected the phone.

"September, September, I thought we had an understanding. You're nearly at the finish line. It would be such a disappointment to have you renege at the eleventh hour, so to speak. If you insist on proof, Gerald could make April scream. Again. Or maybe you'd rather hear from Steven this time."

Her stomach flip-flopped. "Don't hurt him. He's just a little boy." September turned to the dog. "Shadow, shut up!" They were still alive, they had to be. But April couldn't protect Steven, and Steven hadn't asked for this, he was the real victim here. "I'll give you what you want." She looked over at Teddy, who frowned at her chicken scratch notes and scrawled a couple lines of his own.

"Of course you will. I never doubted that for a minute." Lizzie paused, and then spoke with deadly intent. "You understand that I. Do. Not. Bluff."

"I understand. I really do understand." She took the notepad from Teddy, read it, and nodded. He gave her a thumb's up and a grin. September crossed the fingers of both hands, and couldn't contain the quaver in her voice. "Lizzie, you're in control. Whatever you want, tell me and I'll do it." She inhaled sharply before she dove off the virtual cliff. She had one chance to make this work. Teddy said it was a go. Fish surely would help. But the plan would only work if Lizzie agreed to the location. "I name the place."

There was dead silence for a long moment before Lizzie laughed, a claws-on-chalkboard sound.

"Listen, you've got the power. You control everything else, haven't you proven that?" September bulldozed on. She had to convince the woman to agree, that it was in Lizzie's best interest. "It won't do either of us any good if I kill myself on icy roads on my way to reach you. You named the time. You say how the exchange goes down. But I'm new in town, I could get lost, miss the deadline and then Steven loses. Neither one of us wants that, do we?" Dead silence. One more try. "I only want to name the place so I don't accidentally break your rules. Help me help Steven."

She prayed she hadn't just killed them, but she bet everything that Lizzie wanted the flash drive so much she'd concede the minor point in the game.

Lizzie blew out her breath. "Very well. But the cops show up, and everyone loses."

September smiled at Teddy. "Meet me at two-oh-five Rabbit Run Road. There's no other house within half a mile. Plenty of time for you to get away, watch for the police, whatever you want." She gave a thumb's up back to Teddy. "I don't care about the information; I just want my sister and Steven safe."

"I know you do, dear. Your sister told me why. She explained what happened in Chicago with you and Steven." She laughed. "Play by the rules, and maybe your debt to that little boy will finally be paid."

Chapter 39

Combs's car skated into the hotel lot. The EMT vehicle had already arrived, but only one squad car. The Heartland PD was stretched thin despite officers and detectives who were pulling double shifts. He recognized the ME's car snuggled into the narrow area beneath the covered entrance. The cars overflowing the lot made it looked like a damn convention. Doty and Gonzalez's unmarked car also crowded beneath the awning.

The nearest empty spot was next door at the Sonic, a football-field distance away. His feet protested at the thought. Like his partner, Pike, he'd not been home to pick up appropriate foot gear. "Screw it." Combs double-parked beside the ME's hail-dimpled Toyota and hurried inside.

Detective Gonzales met him before Combs could reach the desk. "Back in Doty's good graces?" Gonzales sipped from a Starbucks cup.

"Seems like. As much as anybody can be. For now we're working on the same side." Combs stomped his feet to increase circulation. He noticed the man's drink, and his stomach gurgled, a reminder he'd not eaten since late yesterday. His nerves already jangled with buckets of caffeine from Uncle Stan's. He didn't need more.

"Doty beat you by three minutes." Gonzales nodded.

Combs followed his gaze. At the front desk, the detective loomed over the clerk.

"Nobody knows much." Gonzales sipped his coffee. "The couple that found April is in the manager's office."

Combs waved a hand toward the parking lot. "I figured we'd have folks trampling all over. The hotel's packed."

"Yeah, it's the weather." Gonzales indicated his soaked topcoat. "Ice and snow knocked out transformers and power lines in three counties. Hotels booked within hours, and there's a run on generators. Most of the guests want to stay snuggled up in their rooms, thank God. Be a rash of babies next summer."

His stomach growled again, and Combs winced, unzipping his coat. They had the heat cranked to a tropical climate. "Maybe September's in a hotel. You got somebody to check?"

Gonzales frowned. "We gave up. Too many people sneak under the radar, more than you'd think with dogs. We don't have the manpower to follow all those leads." He pointed at the clerk. "Fella says there's a four-guest limit per room. But he's turned a blind eye a few times and doesn't want his boss to know. I'd bet more'n half are over the limit with six or even eight to a room, and can't afford to pay extra if they get caught."

"Yeah, this sure isn't a holiday destination accommodation." Combs braced himself when Doty finally noticed him and briskly approached.

"What have you got?" She directed the question to Gonzales but included Combs in a tight smile. Doty held her pad and pencil at the ready.

"EMTs are still with her. She's barely alive, unconscious and not talking. Touch and go if she'll make it." Gonzales waved toward the stairs and pointed at the elevators. "I've got uniforms on all entrances and exits. I had the front desk call all the guests and threaten them with arrest if they poked their heads out the door."

"Yeah, we'll want to interview some of them. No sense having rumors ruin any real leads." Doty jotted a note. "Let's be especially thorough with the guests near the vending machines." She closed the pad and slapped her thigh with it in rhythm. "CSIs found blood in the men's bathroom where someone washed up."

Combs stifled a yawn. Maybe another infusion of caffeine would help after all. He felt for the January family. He'd had to deliver the bad news too often, but when you knew the victim, it made things personal. "April's blood?"

Doty gnawed her pencil. "Probably, but could be the perp's." Glancing briefly at Combs, she turned away, reluctant to admit anything. "We need extra hands. But you're still not officially here. Don't make me sorry I cut you some slack, Combs, or it'll be my ass in a sling."

"Understood." Combs felt grateful he wasn't at home, shut out from information. Like Uncle Stan.

"It's damn frustrating." Doty showed her teeth in a snarl. "I flashed pictures, and the desk guy doesn't remember anyone who resembled September. He doesn't recognize Steven, either. Or a dog. But Steven must have been here based on what April told the couple who found her."

"She spoke to them? Identified her kidnappers?" Combs's stomach clenched. Damn, he needed to eat or he'd pass out. "What'd she say? Where'd they find her? Did they get a look at the perps?"

"On ice. Literally. Witnesses came for sodas and found her."

"Vending?" This case got screwier by the minute.

"She got buried in the ice case." Not a flicker of emotion revealed Doty's thoughts. "The killer used this freaky weather as inspiration. In public, no less, but the ice bit him in the butt on this one." She smiled. "The ice saved her life. She can't talk yet, but once she can—if she can—April will identify the bastards."

"That's a shitty in-your-face, all right. But why would they dump her here if they checked in? There's a camera in the lobby." He shook his head. "Makes more sense they'd dump her far from bad-guy-central. Maybe wanted to send September a message and have her found quick. Can't escalate much more." He pulled off his gloves and mopped his brow with them.

Doty had also opened her coat, and Combs knew they all felt the heat, in more ways than one. News sources had already dubbed them the "Blizzard Murders." His mother's name would be inextricably linked with the worst spree killer in North Texas history.

Combs turned to Gonzales and surreptitiously massaged his stomach to stem the complaints. "So? Crime scene first, or witnesses?"

Before the man could respond, the desk clerk waved them over with a telephone receiver. Doty took the call, listened and handed it back to the clerk. "EMTs moving her out and we can take a look at the scene." She started toward the elevator. "The witnesses who found her aren't going anywhere."

The elevator smelled of urine. Combs's head throbbed. Despite exhaustion, sleep held no allure. He'd gone sleepless for longer when his wife had left. This was different. He didn't want to sleep, not until Mom's killer was found.

They waited as a gurney flanked by medics rolled down the hall, emerging from an alcove already beribboned with yellow crime scene tape. The ME stopped and stared. "We have to stop meeting like this." He shrugged. "First time I ever got called for a live one."

"Not much room, is there?" Doty picked her way with care, and Gonzales and Combs followed suit. Foot traffic of guests, EMTs and responding officers mucked up any helpful evidence, but better to limit the potential for contamination.

"What's the scoop?" Doty didn't enter the alcove, just leaned over the crime scene tape. Combs, slightly taller than Doty's imposing height, could see just fine and almost wished he didn't have such a great view.

"She nearly bled out. Gunshot again." The ME grunted. "Not as much blood as you'd think, because there's no exit wound. She could have drowned on her own blood, and survival isn't a given. Bullet's still inside." He motioned a tech forward to share digital images of the victim in situ.

"What type of gun?" Doty glared at the pictures as if she had X-ray vision and could find the bullet if she tried hard enough.

"Entry looked consistent with .45, that's the gun of the day, seems like. But no shell casings so you'll have to wait for autopsy to recover the bullet."

"Same caliber as . . . ah, the first victim." As Mom, he'd almost said. Now Steven might lose his mother, too. He hoped the little boy hadn't seen it happen.

The photos showed April's body sprawled on the scabrous linoleum, muddy footprints mixed with crimson where spilled ice had melted and been tracked by a parade of shoes. Her glorious blond curls were matted and her makeup had run.

The ME asked, "She our missing person?"

Combs nodded. "One of them." September and Steven were both still out there. But if Steven was with his mother's killer, Combs doubted he'd last much longer.

"Hell of a way to go, but she got lucky. The weight and temperature of the ice packed around her body slowed the bleed."

"The Good Samaritans fished her out and watched her bleed?"

"That's the bottom line. Then they tracked blood and water to hell and gone, so the CSIs have to sift through that soup to find any trace the killers might have left. Found a bloody hand towel over there." He pointed down the hall. "Witnesses said they used it to try and stop bleeding and gave CPR." He shrugged. "Kept her going until the EMTs arrived. They were already here for somebody else. Like I said, it was her lucky day."

Gonzales pointed out the several prints on the cracked linoleum. "Lots of different feet, but only two are clear. A woman's sock prints and a man's tennis shoe, both consistent with the couple who found her."

"Wait, you said killers? Plural?" Combs homed in on that comment. "How many?" They'd found one size 12 men's dress shoe print at April's house that probably matched the shoes Pottinger wore. The shooter at the mall had been more careful, maybe more of a pro able to cover his tracks. They did have blood evidence near the exit, though, that couldn't have come from the bus driver. Combs figured the dog had nailed the sonofabitch. He'd be hurting pretty bad, if the dog latched on with any force. Once they located the dog, they could match dentals to the suspect when they caught the guy. And they would.

"Did Pike get back to you about that Dorfman kid from the Mall?" Combs got blank stares. "The kid was on the radio spouting off to Fish, said he knew the bus driver and an old man with Steven. The boy might be with the old man."

"Pike must not have followed up yet. He'll check in with anything new." Doty made a note.

Gonzales grunted. "Shoe prints here aren't even close to the ones found at the other crime scenes. You don't need CSIs to confirm that." His bloodshot eyes flicked away—he wasn't getting much sleep either. Combs knew the man had avoided mention of his mother.

"They'll have to get her stabilized before they can dig out the slug," said the ME."Maybe we'll get another match." Doty caught Combs's look. "Wishful thinking. Reeks of amateur hour." She turned and stalked back to the elevator.

"It all stinks." Combs turned to follow her. "A professional hit team gets in and out quick, bing-bang-boom. They have a plan. It's done before anyone knows about the game. They cover their tracks, like at the mall." He waved at the vending area, his gesture encompassing the whole situation. "These guys don't have a plan. They're improvising."

Gonzales's grim smile agreed. "That's why we'll catch them. I just hope we get lucky before these assholes kill the little boy." He couldn't hide his anger. "Every time the phone rings, it's about another body." The smaller man took it personally.

Hell, they all took it personally. And something didn't fit. Lots of trace left at April's, at Gentry Park, and here at the hotel. But nothing at the mall. Two different teams?

"Combs, what about September? Any more calls from her?"

"I left a message we found April. Tried again on the way here and the mailbox was full." But he pulled out his phone to try the number again.

"Hey, Detective Doty." The ME waved them back. "The victim's phone is ringing, you want to take that?"

Combs dashed back and caught up the phone before Gonzales or Doty could react. He took the phone with gloved hands and peered with surprise at the caller ID. It was September.

Chapter 40

September waited as April's phone rang a third time. Teddy stared at her, unasked questions palpable. Lizzie had called on a different phone. There was a chance a call to April's cell would actually reach her sister.

"Hello, September?"

Confused, September nearly hung up when the man's voice answered. But it wasn't Gerald the Ghost. "Who is this? I want to speak to April. Is she all right?"

"It's Officer Combs. Jeff Combs. We've talked before. I've left you phone messages and I've been trying to reach you." He paused, and she could hear voices in the background but not the words. "Where are you? Are you all right? Do you have Steven?"

"Why do you have April's phone?" She ran a hand through her hair, pacing. Shadow tried to follow and nearly tripped her.

"April's been shot."

The words were a stomach punch. She suddenly found herself sitting on the floor, the big dog licking her face while Teddy patted her shoulder. September pushed the dog away. "Shot? Is she okay?"

"You need to come in. It's time." His calm voice sounded so reasonable. "April's been taken to the hospital. Steven wasn't with her. Is he with you?"

If they took her to the hospital, she was alive. "Is she going to be okay?" She shrugged off Teddy's comforting hand.

"Where's Steven?"

September closed her eyes. Lizzie had lied. Big surprise. "Shadow bit the big guy who took Steven, but he couldn't stop them." She struggled to regain her feet, fear for her sister quickly changing to angry demands. "Is my sister going to be all right?"

Combs didn't answer for a beat, and she knew it was serious. "You need to come in now, September. Let the police handle things."

"How? How will you handle things?" She turned away from Teddy's fearful expression. The time for fear was over. "You don't know where Steven is, either. How will my coming in help? Will it save my sister's life?"

"Come on, September, tell us what you know and let us take it from there. I can send someone to get you. We know you're trying to help April and Steven. But you're in over your head. What can you do? You're only one person."

She looked at Teddy, and placed a firm hand on Shadow's shoulders. "I'm not alone." She punched off the phone connection.

***

Fur bristling, Shadow raced after September. The fear-stink so recently washed away rose in waves, and September's wide eyes, quick breath and charging heart shouted louder than words. The excitement was contagious. He wagged with a short, high-held semaphore that punctuated his excitement.

Teddy followed, and watched as September reached for her wet shoes. Shadow sniffed her foot. Shoes meant going somewhere. He whined and licked September's hands as she tied the laces. He could hear her pulse sprinting fast and hard, even through the layers of borrowed clothes that smelled like a stranger.

Teddy paced. "Why didn't you tell the cop our plan?" Shadow cocked his head and watched.

She shook her head, bright spots coloring her cheeks. September pulled on the other shoe, stood, shrugged on her coat, and patted the pockets for the car keys. They jingled.

Keys meant a car ride. Too often humans neglected to include the dog. Shadow's fur smoothed, and he waved his tail and yelped, frustrated but determined. He danced his "take-me-with-you" request with whirls, twirls and whines. She needed him. And he needed to be with her. She acted frightened, and that made his tummy tighten, too. But she didn't have teeth, and he did—teeth that could protect them both. That's what good-dogs did, they protected their humans. He whirled again and yelped.

"Settle, Shadow." September held out her hand, and he stopped to push against it.

He'd always wanted to be a good-dog, not just for Steven. September said being a good-dog for Steven was the most important job in the world. But his boy wasn't here. Steven didn't even like Shadow, he could tell. And Shadow liked September, a lot more than he liked Steven. Good dogs do what they're told. But it felt wrong this time.

Shadow yawned, but it didn't help. He licked his nose, and slurped September's hand. He didn't know what to do.

Except watch her face. Smell her body. Listen for the special words that explained everything. The joyful "click" noises September made for good-dog behavior. Only September made the special click noises. Only her "good-dog" made his heart leap. Only September made his world right.

He would not leave her.

Teddy retrieved and pulled on his own coat.

Shadow's brow furrowed. Maybe they'd all go for a car ride together. He'd like that. Shadow pranced and twirled between September and the old man.

September grabbed Teddy's arm. "I won't get you killed, too." She guided him back to the sofa. She swallowed in a loud gulp even a human could hear. "Stay here with Shadow."

He didn't like that "stay" word. With a whine, Shadow stared from face to face and checked hands for hidden balls, anxious for the game to begin. He loved games. He didn't want to stay.

Teddy sat down so hard the sofa squeaked in protest. "They'll kill you."

September's jaw tightened. "They'll try. But I'm not running this time, not hiding anymore." She headed for the door.

Shadow woofed, and raced her to the entry. No game after all. Instead she wanted to leave. Not without him! He pushed between September and the wall. His tail hammered the door.

"Baby-dog." September's gentle words gave him hope. He pressed his head against her side, reveled in her touch. "You can't go, Shadow. Be a good-dog, and stay."

He yelped. The "stay" word hurt worse than a fist. He had to change her mind. Shadow leaped to reach September's face. He had to tell her, show her. His place was with her, how could she not understand?

She knelt on the wet tile, opened her arms. Shadow whimpered and washed the salt from her eyes. "I know, baby-dog, but you can't. You just can't."

He didn't understand the words, but her tone told him everything he needed to know. Shadow's hopes deflated.

Teddy struggled to stand. He held the gun.

September gasped. Her arms tightened around Shadow.

His hackles lifted at the renewed fear-stink that filled the room. Something had changed between the two people. He cocked his head, trying to puzzle it out.

Chapter 41

Combs stared at April's phone. September had disconnected before he could convince her to come in.

Doty shrugged. "At least the stupid woman's still alive."

Combs flinched, but covered it with a cough. Typical Doty, going for shock value. "She's gone to ground, but she's not stupid. She'll come up for air when she's ready."

Gonzalez and Doty stared at him, clearly doubting his grasp on reality, but he didn't care, and knew he was right. She had something planned. He just hoped she could stay alive long enough to make it work. "Let's find out what the witnesses have to say."

The herky-jerky ride back down the elevator made Combs's stomach leapfrog. He breathed with relief when the doors opened. The burn in his gut was an old friend, an ulcer born during the last months of his marriage. It faded once the divorce was final, but the gnawing flames announced its resurrection.

At the desk, the manager straightened when they approached. "They're still in my office. They wanted to leave, and I told them they couldn't until you said it was okay." His aggrieved tone implied great effort on his part.

"You did good." Combs tossed the fellow an atta-boy before following Gonzales and Doty to the employee entrance. He hesitated. Something smelled wonderful. His mouth watered and he swallowed hard.

The manager reached beneath the counter to the hidden oven. "Warm chocolate chip cookies. Specialty of the hotel. Guests get a couple when they check in, but I suppose we could spare some for Heartland's finest." He held out a small paper bag. Slow steam rose from the open end.

What the hell. Combs stuffed one in his mouth, chewed and swallowed before biting into a second and pocketing a third as he rushed after the two detectives.

"It's about time." The male witness wore a threadbare robe, and his sharp knees could cut fabric.

Doty waved the man to a chair. "We appreciate your patience, Mr. and Mrs.—" she checked her notes. "Pete and Julie Green. Can we get you some coffee? Cookies?" She smirked at Combs and pantomimed a napkin.

He flicked crumbs away.

"Don't have much of an appetite." Pete was oblivious. "Honey, you want something?" He leaned down and brushed a kiss against his wife's temple.

Julie ducked her head and refused to look at anyone, keeping her bare feet pulled under her overlarge Dallas Cowboy's sleep shirt. Her long, straight hair fell in pigtails past her collar. She chewed on one, her expression unfocussed.

Trauma witnesses suffered shock, too. She'd tracked through the gore and the CSIs collected her socks. Pete's CPR attempts left him stained with blood. Hence, the borrowed robe.

"We've been here forever. I want to get my wife back to the room to rest." He stood behind his doll-size wife and gripped her shoulders. "We can't go home until the storm quits. And now this happens." His eyes scoured the room like a trapped animal seeking a bolt hole. "The management won't give us a new room, either. Tried to be a good guy, and what d'ya get? This sucks."

"Mr. Green, Mrs. Green, Heartland PD appreciates your cooperation." Doty's conciliatory tone didn't hide the sarcasm. "A woman nearly died. That trumps your inconvenience. I ask the questions, you answer them. We'll get you out of here when we're through. Are we clear?"

Julie patted her husband's hand. She sniffed, and glared at Doty with distrust, but offered a quick smile to Combs. "She told us what happened."

"Good. That's real good, Mrs. Green." Gonzales scribbled on his note pad. "Did she describe her attacker?"

She shivered. "I've never liked them. Told Pete over and over they are dangerous. Was a dark one with pointed ears gave me this when I was only three." She pointed to her lower lip, and Combs saw a faint scar stitched on the flesh.

"Ma'am, I think you're confused—" Gonzales tried to interrupt, but she pushed on, growing more and more animated.

"Pete wanted us to get a baby and raise it up." Her gaze darted about the room. "But they turn into killers. You just can't trust them. I put my foot down. And I saw folks sneak the dirty things into the hotel. I did." Her husband started to speak, but she shrilled over top of him. "No more arguments Pete, we're never ever getting one. Look what happened to that poor lady. And to her kid, too. She had to climb into the ice to get away."

"I don't think that's what happened, honey." Pete's calm countered her strident tone.

Doty's brow creased with puzzlement, but she encouraged the woman to continue. "She mentioned a kid? What'd she say?"

"She did. She wouldn't have said it if she didn't mean it. You didn't hear." The tiny woman turned from haranguing Pete to confront Combs. "She grabbed my hand, pulled me down to whisper in my ear. I even got blood on my face when she . . ." She gulped, calmed herself with several deep breaths. "That poor lady was clear as glass, even if she was all tore up and hurt awful."

"So what happened?" Combs tried to soothe. "What did she say?"

"She said the dogs did it." Julie hugged herself.

"What?" Doty rocked back on her heels. Her exasperation startled both witnesses.

Combs couldn't hide his incredulity. Mrs. Green had, after all, experienced a shock. "What exactly—and I mean *exactly*—did she say? Not what you think she meant, but the actual words. It's important." He held out a hand in a placating gesture. "It's easy to misunderstand in moments of stress, but even if it makes no sense, we want to know the exact words she used. Okay?"

Julie stared up at him before squeezing her eyes shut, maybe to clarify the memory or to shut it out. "She said the dog did it. That it was the dog's fault." Her chin jutted at their collective expression of disbelief. "I swear that's what she said."

Chapter 42

Teddy's hand trembled unsteadily with the weight of the Remington .45 pistol.

September wanted to cry. Maybe it was time to give up. April was probably going to die; Combs had as good as said it. She couldn't win, not when even Teddy was one of Lizzie's henchmen. She leaned into Shadow's ruff. His breath warmed her cheek. His tension screamed beneath her hands, a coiled spring aching for release. With sudden clarity, she knew exactly what to do.

"You almost forgot this. I hate these things. Maybe you'll need it—"

"Shadow, show me…gun!"

Shadow sprang. He muzzle-popped the target. The pistol spun away.

Teddy cried out and grabbed his bruised hand. He staggered. Fell. The sofa softened his landing. "Why the hell did you do that?"

"Oh crap, sorry, Teddy. Are you okay? Sorry, I just reacted. Yes, Shadow, good-dog." Shadow leaped around, tail flailing with excitement.

September scrambled to retrieve the gun—the safety was still on—and stuck it back into her pocket. She dried her palms on the carpet. "I thought you'd gone to the dark side, Teddy. Are you okay?"

He rubbed his face, grumbling. "Guess that was good practice for the dog, huh? Glad he doesn't know 'sic 'em' after all."

Shadow wagged and wiggled. She crooned, "Good-dog, what a good boy, Shadow, good-dog." She pushed him away and waited for her pulse to slow. Now that the adrenalin rush had passed, all aches flooded back.

It took seconds to lever herself upright, and she steadied herself with one hand on Shadow's solid-as-a-rock back. She zipped up her parka. Her knees creaked. Growing old wasn't for weenies. Shadow stayed glued to her side, watching. September fumbled for words, repeating, "I'm sorry. Did he hurt you?" The gun in her pocket weighed a thousand pounds. It could have gone off. He could have shot her, or it could have shot him.

Teddy smiled, and the expression brought a sad beauty to his weathered skin. "Most excitement I've had in years. And I don't begrudge you or your sister's passion for helping Steven. I sort of know what April's going through. Molly doesn't know me half the time. But other days, she's bright as a penny, with the same sparkle when we first met back in grade school. If some drug could bring that back, keep me from losing her, well guess I'd do just about anything." He fumbled the buttons on his damp coat.

"What're you doing?" Her suspicious tone made Shadow's ears flick forward, and he yawned, nerves still strung tight. "Where are you going?"

"With you." Teddy pulled on his gloves. His stoic expression sanctioned no argument.

She turned to go. "I don't have time to argue."

"Then I suppose you'll have to hold a gun on me." Teddy headed to the door.

Shadow leaped at the handle with yelps of anticipation. His tail swatted the floor. He sat as taught, offering a polite "wait" to ask for the door to be opened.

September sighed. She hadn't planned to take him along. She might not have chosen Shadow, but he'd chosen her.

"Okay, Shadow, let's go." She'd leave him in the car once she got to the house so he'd be safe. Steven would need a service dog more than ever once this horror ended.

Lizzie and Gerald had forced her out of her rose garden fortress, threatened her family, and killed friends. Time to turn the tables, and flush out the rats with the flash drive as cheese. She'd run home to Texas to hide but it was time to cowboy up, before Lizzie called again. "You really want to help?"

"Of course. Steven's counting on us."

"Then c'mon." She opened the door, and dodged Shadow when he dashed ahead toward the car. "Do you have your phone?"

He patted his pocket in affirmation.

"Good. Make sure it's charged." September held open the rear door. "Shadow, kennel-up." She shut him inside one of Pam's dog crates. At least he'd be safe. She saw Teddy slide into the passenger side, and hurried to shoehorn herself behind the wheel. She started the car, and made one more call before pulling out of Teddy's driveway.

"Anita, it's September."

"Lady, you've got everyone worried sick. Phones here at the station have rung off the hook."

"Connect me with Humphrey." September turned the key in the ignition and it started on the first try. Maybe her luck had changed.

"Are you okay, honey?" Anita didn't wait for an answer. "Fish is still on-air, and you're still the star. I'll switch you—"

"No, let me talk to him off-air." She shoved the car into gear and did a doughnut out of the driveway.

"He won't like that. He's drooling over what this will do for his career."

"It's important, Anita. Life or death important. He'll want to take this call, I'm not woofin' you." September eased off the gas until the tires caught. "Just tell him . . . tell him I'm keeping my promise."

Chapter 43

Combs leaned his forehead against the glass in the hotel foyer door. The icy surface was a relief after the hothouse warmth of the manager's office. The several cookies he'd eaten to quiet his stomach instead turned to cement in his gut, and he hoped they wouldn't end up splattered on his shoes.

Doty and Gonzales finished with the Greens, and quizzed other guests, but nobody knew anything. They found a few illegal dogs, as Mrs. Green had said. A Chihuahua in one room, three Toy Poodles in another, a wirehaired mutt, two cats and a Greyhound in a third—all clearly killer dogs. What a colossal waste of time.

A tapping on the glass startled Combs. Gonzales hooked a finger, and Combs straightened and felt his back crack as he hurried back inside. "What?"

"A few more lap mutts, but that's all." Gonzales yawned. "Sorry."

Combs yawned back. Everyone was exhausted. "This weather, folks want to hunker down under the covers and blast some no-brainer TV show. It's only cops and killers out in this mess." Combs debated another cup of coffee to wash the old shoe taste from his mouth. His stomach gurgled. He dismissed the notion.

Doty strode toward them, buttoning her long coat. She growled into her phone around a fresh wad of gum, spearmint this time since she couldn't find clove. "You get this message, call me back ASAP. Screw weather excuses, I need answers now. Don't make me call you again." She disconnected, still scowling. "Thoughts?"

"Lots of 'em," Combs said. "All profane."

"Talk and walk." Gonzales moved off, and Doty and Combs followed. The little man couldn't stand still. Pacing helped Combs work out problems, too, but he was so tired he resented the request.

"Five casualties. What's the commonality?" Doty started the conversation. "Your mom, dog lady, bus driver, doc-in-the-box by the dumpster. Now April on ice." Recited facts stripped the victims of any humanity. Statistics, numbers, faceless puzzle pieces to manipulate and solve the riddle.

Combs used the same technique. It forced you to maintain distance. Emotion clouded judgment. But shit, he didn't want distance, not with Mom. He used that pain to razor through the fog.

"Commonality?" Gonzales held up his palms. "Steven. He's the connection to Combs's mom, the body at the mall, and April."

"Okay, but what about the dog lady at the park? And the doctor?" Doty asked, popping her gum.

"September called the dog trainer to track Steven, so it's still Steven. It all comes down to the boy, or something to do with the boy."

"Duh." Doty's sarcasm was born more of frustration than anger. "The perps kidnapped the kid. Let's come up with something we don't already know."

"But that wasn't why Mom was killed. April called the radio station because the boy went missing. That was before the first shooting, before April got snatched." Combs congratulated himself on taking a page from Doty's playbook and keeping his tone even.

"If September took Steven, she'd be out of town by now. The roads didn't close until a couple hours after he supposedly got lost." Gonzales increased his pace, reached the end of the hallway and turned. "No, I think September has something the killers want, and they kept April to make September comply."

That was the same general thought he'd discussed with Uncle Stan. "Meanwhile, Steven and his dog boarded HART-land bus to Star Mall with the bus driver, and she was killed when Steven was taken."

"Why was the kid taken? Killers already had April." Doty's yawn exposed an impressive cud.

"April wasn't cooperating? September didn't produce results fast enough?" Gonzales smoothed his mustache and loosened his tie. "Upping the ante."

"Then shoot April? They meant to kill her." Combs didn't buy it. "That's knowledge not in evidence. Unless this is personal and the bad guys have insider info, they'd figure September would risk everything to save her sister, and even more with a nephew at stake." He thought for a minute. "September refused to work for them, and went looking for Steven instead. So they got to him first to arm-twist September."

"Makes sense." Gonzales headed back to the lobby.

Doty kept stride. "Sure, that scans. And once they had the kid, they didn't need April, especially if she foot dragged, too. Easier to haul and hide a kid than a grown woman. Wonder if they threatened to kill April?" She buttoned her coat. "Bet that's why she called her sister's phone, checking to see if April answered." Doty turned to Combs. "Still no answer on her cell?"

"She's either ignoring my calls, turned off the phone, or ran out of juice. At least she cleared her messages. Now it goes to voicemail every time." He made a note to call Pike and see what he'd found out about the Dorfman kid. It bothered him that his partner hadn't checked in.

Doty pulled on gloves and Gonzales did the same. "City's turned into a friggin' morgue. Nobody's in office, I can't get any answers. The PD might as well be shut down." She sucked her teeth. "Still need details about Pottinger. Can't see how he's connected to this mess other than he landed on Childress's back porch." She turned to Combs. "You missed most of the press conference. Turns out he's some sort of researcher, but nobody offered any details. Maybe he was a Frankenstein that needed killing." She gave an exaggerated shiver, mocking the words.

Combs stopped dead and stared hard at the two detectives. "But he is connected. I didn't get the chance to tell you. Pottinger was Steven's doctor. So it still points back to the kid."

Chapter 44

Shadow braced himself against the side of the wire crate at the back of the vehicle. He hadn't protested when September asked him to kennel-up, although he'd rather ride loose on the back seat. The cage reminded him of his bed-crate at home. Only this one smelled of a strange dog. Adult. Male. Potent.

He rarely understood why humans acted as they did. But he trusted September. She and Teddy spoke from the front of the car. Going for a ride. He liked the "ride" word. Shadow trusted that when the car stopped, they'd be in the right place. Maybe home? He'd like that.

Hanging his head out a window was more fun than sitting in another dog's crate, though. Maybe September would let him do that soon.

Shadow sighed, and sank to the floor. The motion of the vehicle and warm air made him sleepy. The excitement at Teddy's house wore him out, and traces of the other dogs, more than one, comforted Shadow.

He nosed wisps of tawny fur left behind. No scent of nerves or fear, but the freshest footpad smells shouted with arousal. What had excited the other dog? Maybe a ball? The other dog smells exuded confidence. Would that other dog growl at him and show his teeth if they met? Shadow whined. He wouldn't want another dog in his bed.

Another crate, empty, sat nearby. Shadow stretched his muzzle and tasted the air. Another dog, female, spent time in the space. His ears flattened, and he withdrew. She had a sharp special scent, one that prompted caution, but he didn't know why. Shadow would give her a wide berth should they meet.

He stood up to get a better view of September, and braced himself when the car skidded around a corner. He whined and yelped. Shadow wanted her connection, if only just a glance.

September answered with a toothy smile humans used. But it didn't fool him. The lines in her brow, the quick movement of her eyes and lip licking told a different story. Worry. Stress. Fear. He whined again.

September turned away. Her gloved hand fiddled with something at the front of the car and a man's deep voice began to talk.

Teddy didn't say anything, but Shadow could see him shiver. The back of the seat blocked Shadow's view, so he couldn't read Teddy's face. Teddy's teeth chattered, despite the blister-hot air blast that ruffled a good-dog's fur.

Shadow was sorry for humans who didn't have the advantage of warm fur. The cloth that covered the old man smelled wet and sour. No wonder he was shivering.

The big car slowed, turned and pulled to the side of the road. Shadow rose onto his toes to peer out the windows. He could see a two-story brick house across the field on the left despite the sheltering arms of snow covered trees. It looked different than the last time he'd visited September's house, but he'd recognized the route even before they'd stopped. He pawed at the crate to rattle the door, but September and Teddy paid no attention. The latch flopped back and forth. He nosed it, moving it slightly.

"Wait for my signal." September unlatched the door.

Shadow yawned and pawed at the door. Snow blew inside and leeched warmth from the car as she examined the gun, fiddled with it, and stuffed it back into her pocket. She handed Teddy a piece of paper. She turned to Shadow. "If something happens to me, get Shadow to my parents. He's such a good boy." Her voice broke.

Shadow wagged and slicked his ears when she said his name, and wagged harder at the "good boy." He whined and yelped with excitement when September stepped out of the car and shut the door. He waited for her to open the big door in the back of the car to let him out. He danced with excitement.

Shoes squeaked on the cold white stuff. Shadow cocked his head. Listened. But the steps drew away.

He howled, clawed and battered the kennel door. September had left him behind.

Chapter 45

September stumbled from the car and plodded through snow drifts. Her feet clomped like dead blocks of ice. If she fell, she might not be able to get up.

Shadow's hysterical yelps followed her. She worried his noise might give away her location, but wished she could bring him along. He gave her confidence the same way Dakota had kept nightmares at bay.

Screw post-traumatic stress. She'd been lost without Chris or Dakota, but had to do this without them; forget about fear, find Steven, and call the debt paid. She fortified her resolve and trudged on.

At the property edge, September scooted beneath loose strands of barbed wire supported by century-old bois d'arc fence posts. The open fields surrounded her house with a mix of short-cut winter rye and brambles, so she hugged the fence line for extra cover. Cedar elm, burr oak, hackberry and mountain ash carried mounds of white in skeletal arms. In the knee high grass, prickle vines hidden under the snow clutched her ankles and clawed her pants until her thighs and calves cramped before she'd slogged halfway home.

She slipped, grabbing a nearby tree branch for purchase, and spines of the honey locust speared through her glove. September barely noticed. Hurray for Reynaud's numbness after all. Too many injuries, along with the combination of cold and adrenaline, anesthetized everything, but her brain revved into crystal clear focus. She gripped the enormous thorn with her teeth, yanked, and spat into the snow. September flexed her hand. It still worked well enough. Time to move. Find Steven. Stop the drug. Save the children.

September plowed another dozen steps before she peeked from the cover of the trees. Light spilled from her office windows. In her rush from the house yesterday she'd left on lights, although she had remembered to triple lock the front door. The place looked empty. Not even the police visit had disturbed more than tracks on the drive.

The drive circled the house in a dog-leg turn to reach the garage, and she couldn't see inside. That created a blind spot where Lizzie's cohorts could wait. Danger hid in unexpected places, even places you thought were safe, as she knew from experience. Her breathing quickened, and she almost gave in to the temptation to hide in the bushes outside and call the police when Lizzie arrived.

Suck it up, sweetheart. The old fears wouldn't rule this day, not again. She'd lost herself for eight long years. She couldn't let the killers get away. The lives of countless children, not just Steven's, hinged on her decision.

She looked over her shoulder and satisfied herself that Pam's dark vehicle wouldn't be visible from the house. September sprinted in an awkward crab-shuffle to the side of the house and the kitchen side door, spending several nerve-wracking seconds unlocking deadbolts until she could hip-bump it open. The door was such a bitch to latch. For the first time in recent memory, she slammed the door closed but left it unlocked.

The floor was wet. Snow had drifted through the laundry room's transom before someone—the police?—shut the window. The acrid stink from the dryer still clung to the walls. The 78-degree thermostat setting turned the room into a steam chamber.

"Mrrring." Macy loped from across the room and wound around her ankles.

"Hey kitty, good to see you, too." September smiled despite herself when he dropped Mickey on her shoe. But she couldn't have him underfoot. She needed to stash him someplace safe.

September scooped up and tossed the toy onto the counter and gave the "jump-up" hand signal. The cat obliged. She pulled off her gloves, and spent ten precious seconds nuzzling the cat, thinking it might be their last time together. "We get through the next hour, I'll buy you a plate of shrimp," she whispered. "But right now you need to stay out of the way."

His carrier was somewhere in the garage—where possible bad guys lurked—and would take too long to retrieve. The bathroom wouldn't work. He could open the door. The rest of the unfinished house wouldn't contain him, not when he could leap eight feet or more from a standing start.

"Macy, come." He did, but dragged Mickey with him. She collected the toy. "Macy, jump." She tapped the top of the refrigerator.

Macy merrowed and vaulted to his favorite perch. He watched September fill his bowl, top it off with several smelly salmon treats out of the canister, and set it beside him. His purr rumbled. He patted her head and settled down to crunch kibble. She prayed he'd stay with the food.

September unzipped her jacket, and moved to the stained glass table. The Number One Bitch mug was still half-filled with cold coffee next to the saucer from yesterday's breakfast muffin. She emptied her pockets, and stuffed Macy's mouse toy inside out of sight. Otherwise, once Macy ate he'd demand a game of Mickey-fetch.

Her phone needed juice. September pushed aside the treat canister and coffee maker and plugged it into the outlet to charge. The flash drive was bait, but the phone would spring the trap and, if she was lucky, it would save her life. And Steven's. She switched the phone to speaker mode, dialed, and hid it from view before anyone answered.

"WZPP, you've reached ZAP105 FM Radio, giving you the best easy-listening 24/7, how may I direct your call?"

Macy mewed. His ears twitched.

"Anita, it's September. Put me through—"

"He's expecting you, hon." Fish's broadcast came on the line.

". . . So for the latest on the Blizzard Murders, keep it tuned to ZAP105 FM Radio. I'm Humphrey Fish servin' it up fresh." He paused before saying, "Caller, you're on the air."

"Fish, it's time. Can you hear me okay?" She moved away from the counter, testing the range.

The stairwell door squeaked open behind her. Footsteps clumped on the landing. "I hear you just fine."

Chapter 46

Combs stared at Doty. "Pottinger was Steven's doctor." Combs repeated it for emphasis.

Doty's words were curt. "Perfect timing, Officer. When did you plan to enlighten us?" She did sarcasm well.

"Uncle Stan heard from September's folks. I came directly to the press conference from Stan's, and before I could say anything, you got word about April." Combs knew he sounded defensive but Doty always had that effect. He made an effort to smooth his tone. "Since then we've been busy." He could do sarcasm, too.

"So all the deaths are connected." Gonzales stuck his hands deep in his pockets. "Kid has some seriously bad karma."

"It's not like Steven pulled the trigger. But yeah, there's something rotten. Childress denied knowing Pottinger, and claimed April picked all the doctors."

Gonzales smoothed his mustache as if that would help him think. "You believe him?"

"They fought over Steven's treatment." Saying it out loud made Combs more convinced the man was involved.

"Hey, I'd fight for my kids to the death." Gonzales looked at Doty. "So would you, if you had kids."

So would he. So far he and Cassie had kept it civil, but all bets would be off if she tried to take his kids. "Crime of passion, you knock off the ex-wife. But all these other people? It's got to be something more. Something about reputation. Or money."

Doty's phone buzzed. "About time. Tell me you've got answers." She listened intently, and whistled through her teeth with exasperation. "So you don't know yet, but can tell me when? Thirty minutes? Ten? Bite me, we don't have the time. I need answers yesterday. And while you sit on your ass for some bureaucrat to answer his pager, add this to your to-do list. Do you hear me?" The angry pulse-beat in her temple thrummed faster. "Write it down. I want you to find any connection—anything—between Dr. Henry Pottinger and Doug Childress."

Combs muttered a curse. "That's it. That's what April tried to say." He pulled on his own gloves. "Gonzales, is anyone watching Childress? Do we know where he is?"

Doty spoke through gritted teeth, her patience at an end. "He's the father of a kidnap victim, so yeah; I've got a uniform with him. You know, in case there's a ransom call."

Ignoring her acerbity, Combs mentally connected the dots. "Check to make sure we've got eyes on him. I don't know how, or exactly why, but Childress is involved." Combs watched Gonzales make a call.

"How'd you come up with that?" Doty's tone softened into a devil's advocate role. "He's a victim here. Maybe an asshole for a father and husband, but that doesn't mean he's a killer."

Gonzales hung up the phone. "They lost him."

"What?" Doty's temple pulse quickened.

"They can't find Childress. They got separated after the press conference, figured they'd hook up back at his place. Pike's gone after him." Gonzales was disgusted.

"Damn it to hell. But why? He kidnapped his own kid? That's crazy." Doty headed for the door. "Gonzales, keep a watch on the guy's apartment, he still might show up. It's not like we know where else to go." She slammed through the door.

Combs dodged its rebound and followed. Gonzales hurried to catch up.

"I'm still not convinced. Childress wasn't anywhere near this place. Ex-husband goes after the wife to get custody of the kid. Why would he hurt the kid?" Her phone rang. "Talk to me." She listened, and then told the men, "They found two guns in Childress's car. One's a Remington Rand Model 1911A1, a .45 semi-automatic, shoots the same caliber that killed the dog park victim and your mom. What do you want to bet the other gun will match the wounds of the vic from Star Mall."

"Sloppy as hell, but that confirms it's him." Their breath fogged the air. Doty stopped and turned on Combs's next words. "April pointed him out with her dying breath. And I bet Steven's not his kid."

"Our witness never said…" Doty's brow furrowed. "What d'ya mean, not his kid?"

"My God, you're right." Gonzales slapped his forehead. "April didn't mean the dog. She wasn't talking about dogs at all."

Doty looked perplexed. Gonzales and Combs spoke at the same time, mimicking Doty's flat Midwestern accent. "April said it was *Doug's fault*."

Chapter 47

The stairwell door squeaked and thunked closed behind September. "Who are you talking to?"

She whirled and then hiccupped a relieved exhalation. "You scared the pee out of me." She wiped sudden wet from her brow with a shaky hand. Her nerves were fried. "Did Teddy already call? It's too soon." He'd spoil everything.

Officer Leonard Pike peered past her into the kitchen proper, and scanned right and left. "Been waiting for you. Where's Teddy?"

She stiffened. Nobody but Teddy knew she'd come home. Her breath quickened.

Pike examined the room. "I heard somebody else."

"You did." September spoke loudly in the small room. For once, please let Fish keep his big mouth shut. "The radio, it's a call-in show. Trying to steady my nerves, you know? But never mind, I'll turn it off." She chattered on the way to the countertop, and pretended to mess with the radio. "There, it's off, Officer Pike. No more noisy interruptions, we won't hear a peep out of the radio from this point on." That should be clear enough to Fish to go silent, just as they'd planned.

He limped further into the room. "I parked in the garage, but it's too cold to wait out there so I came inside." He smiled. "I told you the locks sucked."

"You can't be here, Officer. If they see the police, they said they'll kill Steven." She hesitated, her stomach an angry fist.

He rubbed his nose with a gloved hand. "Safer to let the police take it from here. You'll just get yourself killed, too." He limped toward her, his hand outstretched. "Give me the flash drive."

She backed toward the breakfast nook, avoiding his reach. Pike wasn't a detective. He was a beat cop, partnered with Combs. "Did Combs send you?" They could guess about a ransom. How did he know about the flash drive?

"Combs? He's clueless. He still thinks you killed his mom."

"What the hell are you talking about?" She sidled closer to the hidden phone, needing Fish's audience to hear anything that transpired.

"The babysitter. That was Comb's mom. But I can fix that, fix everything. You're in over your head." He took a step toward her. "When Dorfman, the kid from the mall, told me about Theodore Williams being a regular coffee customer, I figured you two hooked up, so I stayed mum and didn't tell nobody else. Nobody else needed to know if you'd just stayed put. I could have come to you, collected the merchandise, no muss, no fuss." He sighed. "That would have saved everyone lots of heartache."

She couldn't breathe. Wilma was Combs's mother, and his partner Pike worked with Lizzie. She'd been out-flanked again. She eyeballed the kitchen table where Gerald's gun sat next to the bitch mug in plain view.

"I'm all you got." He tilted his head sideways, his tone persuasive. "You've done enough, September. There's still time to get out clean. Give me the flash drive." He held out his hand again.

Shit. "But you're a cop."

He stopped any attempt at pretense. "Steven's safe. I delivered him to Lizzie myself." He sounded so sane, so normal. "I can save you, too. Just hand it over."

"You killed Freda at the Mall? Sonofabitch. How much did they pay? Murderer!" She screamed and picked up a ten-inch wooden pepper grinder, knowing Teddy would hear and call the cops as they'd planned. But it would take time for them to get here. September lobbed it at him. God, she was stupid, dumb to think Lizzie didn't have someone on the inside when so much money was at stake.

He easily dodged the grinder. "I didn't set out to hurt nobody. Didn't take no money. Didn't even shoot the damn dog when it bit me." He held out both palms to her—cards on the table. "I'm a good guy, never did nothing sideways before. But I got a grandson. He's like Steven, autistic, ya know? This is for him, for his future. Okay?" He advanced on her. "Amateurs get involved and it all turns to shit, and I won't risk my grandson. You've got thirty seconds to hand over the flash drive and get the hell out of here. I got no way to protect you once Lizzie's crew shows up."

September was incredulous. "You turned your grandson over to those killers? You trust them to keep him safe? Do you even know what's on the flash drive?" She hefted the matching salt cellar, and threw it at him. "Steven's my responsibility. I won't turn my back on him again. Do you think they'll even let you out of here alive?"

He stopped short. Pike hadn't considered that notion. "I can take care of myself."

She fumbled open a cupboard, grabbed a crockery teapot and brandished it. "You sent those psychos after me, after my sister—after Steven." She hurled it at him.

He batted it away. It crashed on the floor. "Dammit! I didn't send nobody after you! I just protected Steven and got him back where he belonged, with his mom. Nobody was supposed to die. It's about saving lives." His face turned red. "We couldn't afford the treatment. But your precious putz of a sister opened the door when she killed Pottinger."

The words slammed the air. "That's not true." She took a half step toward the table. He hadn't pulled out his own gun. Yet.

"Don't make this any harder than it already is, September. Don't make me hurt you. Give me the damn flash drive." He lunged.

She dashed to the table. Snatched up the gun. Fumbled the grip when her numb fingers wouldn't work.

Pike pounded after her. His wet shoes slid on the slate floor. But he reached her in four strides, gripping her hand and twisting her wrist.

September screamed. He wrenched her arm behind her back. The gun fell. Her cry rose to a shriek.

She ground her boot into his instep. He snarled, and loosened his grasp.

Once she started, September couldn't stop the screams that burned her throat raw until she gasped for breath. She twisted, shimmied, and left Pike with the empty sleeves of her coat, and stumbled away.

He parachuted the coat at her.

It smothered her head in a damp snare. Stumbling, she fell against a chair and blindly shoved it toward where he'd been.

"Oof." He grunted and fell.

She whipped the coat away from her face. It settled across the stained glass table.

His hand caught her ankle.

September yelled, kicked, kicked again, but was pulled on top of him. She rolled off. Pike came up with the pistol.

She scrabbled for something, anything, to pelt him. One hand found the plush toy in the coat's pocket. She cocked and threw. Wished Mickey was a brick when it hit Pike on one ear, and rebounded harmlessly onto the table.

He didn't pause. Struggling to rise, he lost his balance—one leg was injured, from the dog bite perhaps—he limped forward and pointed the gun at her.

September clambered to her feet. She threw the muffin saucer and dumped another chair in Pike's path. Sobbing, she hop-scotched to the door, thankful she'd left it unlocked. She had to get away, stay out of reach, and keep the flash drive until Lizzie arrived so she could trade it for Steven. She was his only hope.

To catch Pike wasn't enough. She needed Lizzie's broadcast to the world. Needed that for April, for Pam, for Teddy's friend Freda. And for Steven. And for herself, by damn. She'd lost too much to let those bastards get away with murder. Pike wouldn't risk shooting her as long as he believed she had the flash drive. September spun the last chair at him, and dashed to escape.

The door swung open. She skidded to a stop.

"Hello. How nice to see you again." Gerald smiled, and seized her throat.

Chapter 48

Combs banged the dashboard with frustration. Ice covered the front and back windows, and his defroster didn't work for shit. He drove hunched over blinking through the dinner-plate-size hole scraped with a credit card, and prayed nobody else was stupid enough to be on the roads.

Gonzales had headed to Childress's apartment, while Doty drove downtown to chew techie ass and update brass. He suspected his name would be conspicuously absent from her report. He finally could visit with his kids. Cassie would be pleased. He'd rather do nearly anything but tell them how their Grandma died.

He jumped when the phone rang, not recognizing the number, and answered cautiously. "Officer Combs." Combs pulled the phone away at the sound of ear-piercing barks. "Hello? I can't hear you. Is this a joke?"

"Hello, hello, hello, please help us please. Hello? Is anyone there?" He turned away from the receiver. "My God, shut up. I can't hear anything." He sobbed.

"Calm down, who is this?" The yelps and howls spelled the canine version of frantic. "Who are you? How'd you get this number?"

"I'm Teddy Williams. September told me to call. The nine-one-one people won't answer." Teddy wailed.

"Sonofa—Okay, quiet. Take a breath, Teddy. Where are you?"

"I don't remember the address. They're going to kill her, and I didn't get the damn address!" He blubbered. The dog howled. "Shadow, shut up!"

That was the dog's name, Steven's service dog. This must be the stranger from the mall. "Calm down, sir. Where are you right now?"

"In the car. A brown Jeep, she said it belonged to Pam." He stopped as whines sounded. "Guess you can hear, she left me with the dog." He paused. "Oh, God. Oh, God. Somebody else just passed on the road, they pulled into the drive. It's the killers, I know it is, oh, God, oh God . . ." The dog continued to yodel.

"Teddy, listen to me. Stay with me." Combs stopped his car in the middle of the road, and punched on the hazard lights. "Who just came? Can you see them? Describe the car—do they see you?"

The old man's voice was hard to hear over the crazed dog's yelps. "They drove right past me up to the house. I can't see their car anymore. But it didn't show up at the other end, so it must be at her house with Pike."

Combs sat up straighter. "Pike? Officer Pike, the policeman? You saw him?"

"No. I heard him. On the radio." Teddy cleared his throat. "September set up a phone line to a radio show. I can hear her over the car radio. That's why the dog's going nuts. She's screaming at somebody named Pike. He was waiting for her when she got home."

"Wait a minute. She's at her own house?"

"Yes." Teddy wailed again. "I'm sorry I don't know the address."

Combs stomped the accelerator. He left the hazard lights on.

Chapter 49

Shadow howled frantic harmony to September's cries. He didn't know how he could hear her in the car. She wasn't here. And she couldn't hear him, though he barked loud and long.

His fur stood at furious attention. He showed his teeth, snapped and snarled, eager to defend. She was his person. A good-dog protected his people. He had to find her. Shadow keened and paw-punched the cage.

"Stop it." In the front seat Teddy clapped his hands over his ears. "Shut up. Be a good-dog."

A good-dog obeyed people. Shadow paused and flattened his ears. He licked the wire of the crate and whimpered. September screamed, and Shadow threw himself against the wire again. The latch jiggled. So he did it again. And again.

"Quiet, no, no, no, no. Bad dog."

Shadow ignored Teddy's growls. He didn't care. He'd be a bad-dog on purpose. How could he ignore September's screams?

"Shadow, please stop. You'll hurt yourself." Teddy turned around in the seat and his brow wrinkled. His eyes rained wet.

Shadow paused. He whined. Maybe Teddy did understand. His tail wagged the hopeful question, and he tap-danced in place. He willed Teddy to understand.

"I called the police. They're on the way." The old man made no move to open the door. He just sat there, and ducked his head each time September screamed. "We just got to wait."

Yelping in frustration, Shadow bit the wire mesh of the door, growled, and snarled. Tugged—like with Bear-toy. His gums split on the sharp wire. Salt-copper tang raised his arousal. His tail churned the air and battered the cage, a drumbeat counterpoint to the tug-contest.

The old man's scent chemicals choked the stale air, and cried "uncle" louder than puppy pee. Teddy had given up.

Shadow grabbed the wire and shook it. Bloody drool spattered the floor of the crate.

Teddy covered his ears. He surged forward, fiddled with something, and September was silenced.

Shadow cocked his head. He licked his lips, shuddered at the copper taste, and stared at Teddy. Shadow woofed, yawned and whined, the most persuasive tone he could. He pawed the door. Two claws had torn loose, and added to the blood on the floor. He couldn't make it any clearer. He needed out.

The old man waggled his head.

That meant no. Shadow furrowed his brow, cocked his head. But he was right. He knew it. To protect Steven, he'd learned to think for himself, to make right choices, no matter what. It was a good-dog's job to know when to disobey. That time was *now*.

Shadow laced back his ears, lowered his head. He hurled himself against the front of the crate. Backed up and did it again. He'd force the door open. Get out. Go to September. Because he belonged with her. Because they belonged together. Because he *must*.

His body battered the cage like a furry mallet, and jiggled the clasp open increments at a time. The fastener worked like his kennel at home. He'd get out. He didn't need Teddy. Shadow wasted no further breath on howls.

"Please stop. I can't let you out. Be a good-dog, shush, just calm down."

Shadow knew the man was staring at him, but didn't pause. Each grunted impact moved the hasp closer to opening.

Teddy swiveled, flung open the door, and lurched out of the car.

Shadow redoubled his efforts. He pawed the hasp. It moved in his favor. Another claw caught, and he yanked it free with a yelp. But the latch almost opened. He uttered frustrated whines, and he switched paws to continue the onslaught.

Teddy rushed to the back of the car and opened the tailgate. "Damn dog." He reached to secure the fastener. "Hell, it's nearly open."

Shadow roared.

The old man flinched and yelled, "Back off!"

Teddy's sudden command stopped Shadow dead. He watched, suspicious but hopeful. The man stared at him.

"You convinced me, dog. It's your choice. And your grave." His voice caught. "So okay, you crazy sonofabitch, you want out?" He reached for the crate door.

Out, yes! Shadow didn't wait for Teddy. A final body-slam rocketed open the latch. The metal grate whipped into the man's glasses and sliced open his cheek. Teddy toppled backwards into the snow.

Shadow vaulted from the car, and cleared the sprawled figure with one joyous leap. He found September's scent, and hop-scotched and bulldozed through snow so deep it scraped his belly. But the bloody paw prints left in his wake spelled a message of fear, hope, and determination only good-dogs could read.

Chapter 50

September clawed the gloved hand at her throat. She stared into Gerald's pale visage—nobody home—and staggered backwards into the laundry room. Squeaky shoes on snow announced Lizzie before she was framed by the open door.

"Did you miss me?" Gerald squeezed harder.

"Careful, Gerald." Lizzie caught his arm. "She has the flash drive."

Dark sparkles floated before September's eyes. She struggled to draw breath, but no air moved in or out. She forced herself to go limp before she passed out. And when Gerald juggled to balance her sudden shift in weight, she stabbed her clenched knuckles into his windpipe.

He gagged, thrust her away and clutched the injury.

"Gerald. Honey-pie, are you okay?" Lizzie bustled into the room.

September wheezed. She fell hard against the clothes dryer, and her palm slammed against the "start" button. The stink of scorched fabric sparked a smile-worthy idea. She swallowed, and then swallowed again to soothe the ache. Her mouth was West Texas in August, drier than stubbled field corn. "Where's Steven?" She barely croaked the question.

"Locked in the car with his father." Lizzie turned as Pike limped into view. "Good job delivering Childress. Did he give you any trouble?"

Pike shook his head. "He just wanted to see his son, was grateful for my help." Pike glowered at September. "Not like some people." He adjusted his glasses. "Don't worry, Childress won't wake up for a while. That headlock restraint puts 'em lullaby every time."

Lizzie straightened, and she nodded at September. "Bring her back inside." She shivered elaborately. "And shut the door, Gerald, you're letting out the heat."

Gerald bared his teeth, but the smile didn't reach his faded eyes. "I will enjoy this." He swung the door shut but didn't notice that it caught in the jamb and didn't latch. "Show time, my dear." He gripped her arm.

Her stomach was knotted with butterflies. She was outnumbered, but her plan was still in play. Show time, indeed.

Gerald shoved her, and she crashed into the kitchen table, skinning her palms on the mosaic glass surface. He stood sentry behind her so she couldn't retreat. Lizzie blocked the stairway, and Pike stood before the gate to her office. She was trapped.

"Where is it?" Lizzie leaned toward her, the table between them. She noticed Steven's pill bottles, and pocketed them with a smile. "Time's up. Where is it?" Her whispers were more threatening than shouted demands.

September looked toward the hidden phone and away. Lizzie's soft words might not be picked up by the phone. She had to get them to incriminate themselves, put it all out there for Fish's audience to hear. Lizzie would clam up if she suspected anyone could hear beyond this intimate group. "Your cop lapdog, Leonard Pike, mugged me around so much, I can't hear so well. Say again?" She spoke with exaggerated volume.

Pike scowled. "She's up to something." He aimed the pistol. "Only the kids matter. So give Lizzie the damn flash drive."

September took a breath, ready to play the game. Keep them off balance. Keep them guessing. "Show me Steven. Or there's no deal." It wouldn't work if she gave in too quickly. Besides, she had to give the police time to arrive.

Lizzie dimpled a smile at Gerald. "Perhaps your special persuasive skills will do the trick."

"As you wish." Murderous intent shined in his expression.

"Wait." Her voice jumped an octave. "I'll tell you." This was it, no more delay. "I hid it. There, in the canister." She pointed and was gratified when Lizzie strutted to the counter, well within range of the hidden cell phone. "I never would have believed Steven's therapist would sell him out. You're a bitch, Lizbeth Baumgarten, and your son Gerald is a damn killer." She let the vitriol pour forth, unedited. "And you, Officer Pike, selling out for some pie-in-the-sky dream-cure. Don't you dare justify it helps kids." Fish damn-well better hear.

Gerald strode forward and grabbed her hair. He heaved her into the table, and she landed across the cat's tattered toy and barely caught the #1-Bitch coffee mug before it crashed to the floor. September grabbed and hugged Mickey like a magical shield. They'd kill her now. But she'd named them for all the radio-world to hear. She smiled; satisfied that Steven and the other kids would be safe.

Lizzie's double chins jiggled with rage. "Help her up, Gerald. I taught you better manners." She dumped flour over the counter, and finger-sifted for the hidden flash drive.

September grasped one of the toppled chairs and pulled herself upright. She didn't want Gerald to touch her.

Pike looked with contempt at the remodeled kitchen. "You have any idea what a cop salary is? Don't judge me."

Lizzie looked up. "You can't put a price on a miracle, the chance for normalcy. A real life." Pride added inches to her height. "Gerald was the first. And now he's a doctor, spreads the cure to other children." Joy lit her face. "Rebirth Gathering will give hope to two hundred children and their parents."

The woman believed her own sales pitch. "Psycho kids aren't my idea of a miracle." September deliberately picked at Lizzie's weak spot. "If he was the first, you should have stopped while you were behind."

Gerald shrugged. "No reason to second-guess a miracle over a few bad reactions."

Pike was worse than the others, selling out his own honor and his grandson's health for empty promises. "Did they tell you about the risk of your grandson going psycho?"

Pike turned away. He crossed his arms and leaned against the refrigerator.

Lizzie glowered. "You don't understand, being childless and all." She returned to the counter, combed through the last of the white powder. The drive wasn't there. "Which canister, September?" She dumped the next and hand-stirred the sugar. Nothing. Lizzie picked up the cat treat jar and shattered it on the tile. She mixed the morsels with her foot.

September thought she heard a bark. Wishful thinking.

Pike stepped forward, but his injured leg wobbled. "Can't you see, she don't got it? She lied the whole time, just to get the boy back. Hell, it's what I'd do." He braced himself against the refrigerator, and held the gun steady.

Macy roused from his perch atop the appliance. The cat yawned and stretched. Sniffed, and gave a silent hiss at the smoke gathering high in the ceiling space.

"But even if she don't have the flash drive, she'll tell. And that will spoil everything for my grandson, Lenny. For all the other kids."

September saw the cat's focus as Macy stared down at Pike. His ears turned sideways, furry airplane wings of disapproval. The cat's coffee-strudel tail twitched.

The spark of an idea flared. "I understand about your grandson, Lenny, is it? Here, I've got it, you can have it. It's here." Her shaky left hand pulled out the lanyard chain from beneath her collar. "Don't shoot. Here, take it." She held her other hand palm outward toward Pike, but the signal was meant for the cat perched above him.

He smiled with sadness, his voice gruff with what needed to be done. "That won't stop a bullet."

September's palm signal steadied and didn't waver. The cat's attention left Pike and followed the hand with intensity. She closed her outstretched hand into a deliberate fist around the drive.

Macy sat.

September hid her elation. She thanked heaven for all the foolish tricks she'd practiced with the cat. Maybe God answered prayers after all.

Green cat eyes monitored the lanyard's pendulum swing, tail twitched in a syncopated rhythm. Macy waited, forward pointed ears and whiskers eager with interest. Macy wanted the game to begin.

Chapter 51

Combs skidded through the intersection, and shouted into his phone. "They're broadcasting now. From September's house."

"How'd Fish manage that?" Doty laughed, but there was begrudging admiration in the sound. "That opportunistic jackass would sell his mother for a story."

Combs agreed. "September set it up. The secretary at the radio station said it's all via speaker phone." He approached an overpass and held his breath the tires wouldn't skid. "September got them to confess with radio listeners as witnesses. Including Pike."

"Save Pike for me." She and Gonzales were ten minutes behind him.

He didn't answer. He should have told someone else his suspicions. Pike doted on his grandson, it was the one soft spot he showed the world. Pike was a career cop, though, and you don't destroy a career over a suspicion, not like his own had been.

"Okay, Gonzales dialed up the radio show. We'll monitor the creeps as we go. Aw, shit." A thump and yelp from Doty followed.

Combs waited. "You okay? Hey Doty?"

"Sonofabitch. We're okay. But a mailbox is DOA." She snorted. "Can't see anything, and it's slicker than snot out here."

Combs removed his foot from the gas and waited until the tires regained purchase. He could hear the radio broadcast over Doty's phone, and dialed his own down to avoid the echo. "Fish is keeping his mic muted so they don't hear him over September's phone." The self-imposed muzzle must kill him.

"Ought to run Fish in for obstruction. The little shit should have called us, not waited until Teddy-come-lately decided to clue us in." By the garbled sound of things, she was up to four or five sticks of gum. "Gonzales has the old guy on the line trying to keep him calm 'til we arrive. Teddy's dictating a visual for us, but there's not much to see." She paused. "He's bent out of shape over the dog running away. What do I care about a stupid hound when we've got murdering scumbags to corral?"

Combs pressed the gas. This straight stretch of road, devoid of traffic or sudden curves, begged for speed. So did the situation. "We need backup. Pike is a crack shot." His teeth ached, and he forced himself to relax his jaw. "No sirens, Doty. They don't expect us, and our best chance is surprise." Besides, he wanted first crack at whichever asshole murdered Mom.

"We're pedaling fast as we can." Doty's tone, accompanied by more gum-popping, revealed her own frustration. Combs could hear a man in the background before she spoke again. "Gonzales is asking about the kid. Any word? Here, Gonzales, you take the phone."

Combs's grip tightened on the steering wheel. He couldn't help but think of his own kids. "Steven's onsite. Supposed to be locked in a car in the garage, with Childress."

"Hey Combs." The detective sounded as frazzled as Combs. "The garage is on the backside of the house, right? That's where they got Steven?"

Combs nodded, before realizing the man couldn't see him. "You saw the same thing I did. Old carriage house, big double door that opens out. We can't go in that way. Childress is with his kid. He's a part of this. He'd alert the goons in the house."

"There's a workshop door on the far side. Doty agrees we should target that entry."

She took back the phone. "Combs, you're what, about five or ten minutes head of us? Find this Teddy character, and wait." She paused, and must have removed her gum because the next words came direct and clear. "Wait for us. Do not—I repeat, do not go alone. We'll stage from Teddy's car and coordinate backup from there."

"Uh, say again? You're breaking up." Combs disconnected before Doty could argue. He wouldn't wait. There'd already been too much wheel-spinning. They owed him first crack. For Mom. Besides, Doty made it clear he wasn't on their team. With his career already down the toilet, he had nothing to lose. More than that, September and Steven were out of time.

He turned up the radio in time to hear September's contemptuous tone. "If Gerald was the first, you should have stopped while you were behind."

Combs sucked in his breath. "Don't do it, girl. Don't bait them." She wanted them on the record and so did he. But September was dancing a fine line. Just because she'd set up the sting with Fish didn't mean help would arrive in time.

"Toss it." The man's command lacked inflection. Must be one of the shooters.

"Tell me first. What does it hurt? Soon as I give you the computer drive, you've won. And Steven loses." September's voice caught on the child's name. "Your investment stands to make millions. And I'm dead. So humor me. Just who the hell are you people?"

September had courage, he'd give her that. "Hold on, I'm almost there." Combs growled at the radio, willing her to survive.

Chapter 52

September's hand remained steady as Macy's attention fixed on her closed fist. The cat's pupils dilated with sudden arousal. Pike stood in front of the cat's refrigerator perch, in perfect position. Then he moved. Damn.

"He said toss it." Lizzie's attention locked onto the lanyard. She made an imperative give-it-to-me gesture.

September stood in the center of a triangle with Gerald, Lizzie and Pike positioned at each point. As soon as the flash drive left her possession, she'd be killed. But she hadn't any choice. Fish had better be recording everything. It'd suck if she got killed and didn't nail the bastards. No. It'd suck no matter what. She held her breath, and tossed the flash drive to Lizzie.

Lizzie snatched it from the air. "It's a shame September kidnapped Steven, and Childress butchered all those innocent people." She pocketed the flash drive. "Not our fault she wouldn't give up Steven without a fight, and just lucky that Officer Pike was able to save the little boy. Too bad the dad died in the battle."

September gasped. "Doug's dead?"

"No. Childress is fine, just unconscious in the car with Steven." Pike raised his eyebrows.

Lizzie stared at him. "Work with me here. You said you'd do anything for your grandson."

"Childress doesn't have a clue. He just went through hell to get his kid back." Pike's sympathy was clearly with the father.

"Give me the gun. I'll do it." Gerald sniffed. "You smell something?" September stifled a smile.

"Burning. That's smoke." Gerald returned to his point of the triangle near the laundry doorway.

Pike coughed. "It's the damn dryer again. Shut it off."

Gerald glared at the smoke that thickened near the ceiling. "Leave it alone." He turned to Lizzie. "Let's burn the place. September dies in the fire trying to save Steven from his father. Pike gets the boy out just in time. That'll take care of any unanswered questions and destroy any evidence to the contrary. These old houses are such fire traps." He turned to Lizzie. "Don't you just love it when a plan comes together?"

A cold gust shivered September's skin. The unlatched door had blown open. All heads swiveled at the same moment.

Shadow stood in the doorway. His hackles bristled from fang to staccato tail.

Pike pivoted and shot.

The tip of Shadow's left ear exploded. He shrieked. He shook his head and crimson flowers bloomed against the wall. But he stood his ground.

"Shadow. Look at me." He blinked through the pain and met September's gaze. It was enough.

September hurled the Mickey toy at Pike's head.

He caught the toy with one hand.

Shadow followed the arc of the toy. Her voice a whip-crack, September shouted, "Shadow, get Bear."

The dog sprang. His 80-pound weight slammed Pike square in the chest.

The cop's gun spat. Shadow howled.

Pike's head hit the wall and the floor in a hollow ripe-melon double thud. The pistol spun away. The stuffed toy skidded.

Officer Pike didn't get up. Neither did Shadow.

September scrambled to reach her dog.

"Get her, stop her!" Lizzie's command was a verbal slap.

Gerald's hand wrenched her shoulder, his other hand aimed Pike's recovered gun. He twirled her like a dance partner. And September let him.

She whirled to increase the velocity of her spin. Her outside hand played crack-the-whip with the hefty #1-Bitch coffee mug. The crockery hammered Gerald's temple. He dropped like an egg from a tall chicken.

September's knees gave way. She caught herself against the table, and stepped around Gerald's body to reach Shadow.

Shadow lay atop the unconscious Pike. He stared up at her, woofed and wagged his tail. "Good-dog, Shadow." She felt dizzy with relief. Despite his bloody ear, the dog seemed without further injury. Shadow sniffed the man. Satisfied, he directed a solemn stare at Lizzie.

September marveled at the pup's composure. That mangled ear must hurt like a bastard. Her own body throbbed in places she didn't know could hurt.

"You killed my boy, you bitch, oh my poor Gerald." Lizzie reached toward her fallen son, but Shadow blocked her way. The woman shuffled side to side, looking for escape.

"It's over." September choked on thickening smoke. She noticed Pike's fallen gun and lunged for it in the same moment Lizzie dove for it.

The older woman won the race and came up with the handgun. September rolled, and backed away. "You won't stop the miracle." She turned, aiming the gun at September's forehead.

September realized Lizzie was in the perfect position. "Macy, kill it!"

The eighteen-pound Maine Coon sprang from the refrigerator onto Lizzie, and hugged her head.

Lizzie screamed, and dropped the pistol.

Pike gathered himself, levering himself to his feet. He staggered to regain balance.

Lizzie yanked double fists of cat hair.

Macy yowled and the play attack became real. Cat claws thumbtacked Lizzie's face. Rear feet dug bloody furrows through fabric into flesh. Teeth sank deep and met in the middle and the woman's screams ratcheted to window-shattering proportions.

September scrambled and retrieved the dropped gun. "You're on the air, being broadcast to the world. You're through. The police are on the way."

Panic filling his face, Pike loped from the kitchen and pounded to the front exit.

She had to let him go. He was no danger to Steven. September heard Pike struggling with the multiple locks and flinging the door open.

Lizzie wrenched Macy off and hurled the cat across the room.

The cat's brain shifted into panic mode, and Macy pin-balled around the kitchen for a way out. He careened into Shadow, hissed and slapped a paw, and the dog flinched backwards with a confused expression. With a mighty leap, Macy levitated onto the counter, clawed open a cupboard door and disappeared inside.

Screams whooped from Lizzie as blood guttered from her cheeks.

Shadow tucked his tail. He slunk as far from the crazed Lizzie as he could get. September didn't blame him. Her own ears hurt. The dog's sensitive ears must be aching.

September crouched on the floor on the opposite side of the kitchen. She trained Pike's gun on the woman, surprised her hands didn't shake, and waited for Lizzie to shut up. Waited for Fish to send the cavalry. Waited to believe she was still alive.

The screams trailed off to intermittent gasps. Lizzie flushed tomato bright, and she braced against the counter directly in front of the hidden cell phone.

"Fish, are you getting all this?" September cocked her head. More shouts, this time from the front of the house, and sounds of a brawl. She grinned when Pike stumbled back into view, hands behind his back, escorted by Combs.

A gunshot stopped Lizzie's sobs. The woman gripped her arm. Wet soaked through the fabric.

September stared at her gun, confused. Had she pulled the trigger and didn't know it? Her eyes met Combs's, but he looked equally puzzled. A cold wind blew snow into the room. They'd never shut the door. She pushed to her knees, swiveling to see.

Gerald was gone. A car revved in the sudden silence, and the engine's grumble faded into the distance.

None of that mattered when September saw the revolver. Shiny. Kid-size. Pointed at Lizzie.

"Loud. No loud. Loud hurts Steven's ears." He fired again.

Chapter 53

Shadow whined and pressed against the wall. The gunshots hurt a good-dog's ears. So did the woman's screams. The men at the kitchen doorway yelled, adding to the confusion, even though the boy-thief from the Mall had his wrists bound. So much noise it made his fur stand up and his teeth ache to bite.

But Steven was here. He focused on his boy. They could be together again. It was a good-dog's job to take care of his boy. He should be happy.

But Steven wasn't happy. Steven was—what? Steven wasn't Steven. How could that be?

He tuned out the woman's screams. Ignored the men's yells. Tried to center himself. Shadow watched. Sniffed. The air prickled his fur. Beneath the smoke-filled air, his boy smelled different. Moved different. Not like his boy at all. And he had the gun. Like before.

His torn ear throbbed, a hot and hurty reminder of what guns could do. His muzzle burned from the angry cat's claws. Broken toenails screamed with each step. He should go to his boy. But that boy wasn't Steven, wasn't his boy at all. Shadow whined and pressed harder against the wall.

Shadow looked to September for direction. She called him good-dog. That made up for the hurts. But he was confused, uncertain. Tired.

"Steven. Drop the gun, honey."

September wasn't scared. She sounded in charge. He liked that. Human pups like Steven would, too.

Shadow paced a hopeful step closer to September, her confidence adding to his own. He watched Steven. He jumped and yelped when his boy made the gun pop again.

The gun reached out somehow, the way guns do, and bit the bloody-faced woman in the tummy. Her mouth opened in a silent disappointed "oh" shape as if somebody had stolen her favorite toy. She fell against the counter and slowly slid to the floor. She screamed again. "Steven, please, Steven. No."

"No-no-no, no-no-no." Steven parroted the words. His boy still pointed the gun at the lady.

Shadow yelped. A question—what do I do? His hackles bristled. He barked a high-pitched warning at his boy. But he kept his ears and tail low, respectful. He didn't want that gun to bite him again.

"Shadow, shush." September was quiet but forceful. "Combs, get Pike the hell out of here. Everyone, be quiet."

Shadow stood, his tail waving fiercely, as the two men backed away from the doorway.

"He shot me. I can't believe he shot me."

"I should let him shoot you again, Lizzie." September stood, held out her hand, palm down toward the boy. "Steven, drop the gun. And we'll make everything quiet, okay?"

But Lizzie kept yelling. "Shot me! How could he shoot me? After all I did for him and his bitch mother, how could he shoot me?"

Shadow wanted to bark back, but September's finger-to-lips signal stopped him. Instead, his front paws tap-danced his frustrated indecision. He felt lost. Should he go to Steven? Run to September? Flee out the door? The bristled hackles caused an itch that could only be scratched with action. But good-dogs follow the rules.

"No-no-no-no." Steven's free hand covered one ear, the other still pointed the gun. He flushed, and a sudden, sun-bright rage burned the fog from his expression. "Stop the bitch-noise stop the dammit hurty noise Steven says stop-stop-stop-STOP!" He ranted, the words repeated over and over again.

Shadow stood tall, his tail high. He moved toward Steven, woofed under his breath, and backed up and repeated the action. He stared at September. Steven's tantrums weren't new. But this wasn't a tantrum. He waited for September's signal for what to do.

September gulped. Even the shot woman fell silent at Steven's rant. The boy sidled forward and pointed the gun at the woman's bloody forehead.

September's eyes cast about the room. Shadow woofed again—pleading 'look at me.' When she did, he wagged and willed her to understand. He was ready.

And then she was ready, too. He saw her chest expand with a subtle breath. His head cocked, intrigued, when she scooped up the toy at her feet. He was ready for whatever she asked.

"Shadow, this is Bear." September held up the toy.

He stared at her, focused, ready.

September held out her other hand. "And this is gun. Show me gun." She pointed at Steven's revolver with the final command, and held her breath.

Shadow's ears came forward. He launched himself. His nose-punch spun Steven's gun across the room. And then, because it just seemed the right thing to do, Shadow pinned his boy to the floor and dodged screams and flailed limbs until within seconds, Steven calmed down.

"Good-dog, Shadow." September hurried to the tangled pair and knelt beside them. "What a smart dog, good boy." She reached to touch Steven, hesitated, and stroked Shadow's brow instead. "Good boy, such a good boy."

Shadow thumped his tail, licked her hand. She tasted of tears and pain, blood and joy. Nothing else mattered, not his ball, not his bear, not even his boy. Nothing mattered, only this. Approval in her voice. Her touch. Her scent.

Sudden sunlight spilled through the bars of the stained glass windows and bathed the room in a warm peacock glow. The storm had ended.

Shadow's hurts didn't matter, not anymore. Home wasn't a place. Home was a person. And Shadow was home.

Chapter 54

Claire O'Dell awoke with a start. It took a moment to realize where they were, but the bus had long since stopped moving. She sat up, swinging her legs off the side of the bed, and checked Tracy on the other side of the mattress where she'd nested in the purple comforter.

Yawning, Claire consulted her watch, and started. She had to hurry. Orientation began in less than ten minutes.

They'd arrived at the Legacy Center a little after 10:30 that morning, only an hour and a half late for the official check in time. The complex looked more like a refurbished motel than a medical facility, but was clean and felt luxurious after so many hours bumping on the drafty bus. She'd lain down beside Tracy for only a moment to settle her, and drifted off.

Quickly she stood, donned the lanyard with her registration number and name tag, and jostled the bed to rouse her daughter. "It's time, sweetie. Let's go see the other kids, okay? Grooby is awake and ready to go. Shall I take Grooby and you'll come later?" Claire held out the green and purple stuffed toy just out of reach. Tracy rubbed her eyes and strained to grab the now-shapeless dinosaur. "Ready to go? Need the potty?" Claire smiled when Tracy rolled out of bed, snatching the toy to her chest and ignoring the potty offer as she followed Claire to the door. Claire grabbed the folder with her daughter's medical records and clutched it to her chest.

Several other parents and children filled the hall, all moving in the same direction. The adults offered tight-lipped nods of acknowledgement, identical hopeful expressions stamped on their faces even as often beautiful youngsters registered very little. Each kept a respectful distance from one another and spoke in whispers, if at all; cognizant their children were in a strange, and therefore stressful, environment.

The tide swelled as it spilled into the lobby area, and began to flow into an adjacent meeting space that held classroom-style seating. Claire urged Tracy to a nearby spot where the little girl began play with one of the pens, rolling it back and forth, back and forth. Two enormous screens hung at the front of the room, with a slide of the Rebirth Gathering logo centered on each display.

Claire saw Elaine enter with Dwayne and Lenny. She waved and stood to catch their attention, not wanting to cry out and break the taut atmosphere. Her heart thumped as they hurried to join her at the table. She and Elaine silently embraced, and Dwayne wiped his eyes and grinned. She guessed every parent in the room felt the same excited anticipation.

The lights flickered, and the soft murmurs fell silent as everyone took their seats when the room grew dark. Her stomach flip-flopped, and Claire saw Dwayne hug his wife with excitement. She wished Mike could be here, holding her hand and sharing this special time as a family. Tracy rolled the pen back and forth, finally picked it up and began drawing circles within circles within circles, cloning the window art from the bus. Claire wondered if Tracy's fascination with circles would stay with her, after the successful treatment.

An hour later, Claire felt dazed but happy. She watched the clinic personnel escort Tracy and Lenny along with four other children out of the meeting area to a nearby examination room. The treatment sounded so simple: twice daily medication for six weeks, dosed specifically to each child's age, weight and metabolism, monitored by home-care visits every two weeks to adjust the dosage based on individual improvement. Claire eagerly signed the authorization for the off-label protocol, and handed over Tracy's medical records to the nurse. Not a single parent balked at the opportunity.

Claire had counted 178 children in the room. She figured the storm had prevented some of the 200 from keeping their appointment. Her heart ached for the absent parents and their missed opportunity.

The children were processed in shifts by last name. Tracy and Lenny had to wait until they reached "O" and "P" to be examined and cleared for the treatment by staff physicians. Claire felt comforted that the doctors were so careful.

"So far, none of the children have been turned away." Elaine spoke aloud what the other parents also worried about. Claire wouldn't be able to breathe, either, until Tracy returned and had received her first dose.

The treated children were returned to their parents in the large meeting hall, and served a light meal. The orientation explained that the medication should be taken with food to prevent upset tummies.

"Mac and cheese. Tracy loves that, thank goodness. Does Lenny like it?"

"It looks like they've got two or three options." Elaine pointed to a distant table where the children were offered hot dogs or chicken nuggets. "Lenny likes chicken, so we're okay." She hesitated. "Did they mention the side effects? I mean, just so we could watch for them, just in case?" The presentation emphasized the importance of sticking to a strict regimen, and that side effects could occur if doses were missed or given too close together.

"No. I didn't hear any details about side effects." She wouldn't have cared if the consequence was growing a tail, though. Side effects would never touch Tracy. Once she got on the medicine, Claire was determined to follow the directions to the letter, and give her child the best chance for success.

"Randolph, Ronald, Rudd, Rudd, please proceed to the exam room. After them, please have Salk, Salk, Schultz, Simmons and Sultani take your turn. We will take the Ts in three groups of three each, and then the Ws. Thanks for your patience."

The PA system announced the children's names as Tracy, Lenny and the other two kids were escorted back into the room. Tracy clutched Grooby, and it was all Claire could do to keep from hugging her daughter. Instead, she urged her back to the nearby table, requested the mac and cheese, and watched with a happy smile as Tracy ate. She knew not to expect any change for two or three days—the reason for staying at Legacy Center for that period—but couldn't help thinking that Tracy already seemed calmer and more focused. Claire couldn't wait to call Mike. Once again, she wished he was here. Lenny eagerly munched chicken nuggets while Pastor Dwayne hugged Elaine as she sobbed happy tears.

The lights in the room flickered, and general conversation died when the screens at the front of the room lit up once again. Claire frowned. Why would the presentation begin before all the children received their first treatment and were back in the room?

"What's going on?" Elaine voiced her concern as murmurs from other parents grew louder. "That's not part of the presentation. That's some sort of broadcast with Skype."

A broadcast of not particularly good quality flickered on the twin screens, and a pale face pulled back from a laptop video-cam. One of the assistants herding children in and out of the examination room stuck his head out the door, glanced at the screen and his mouth dropped open. "That's Dr. Baumgarten. What's going on?" He rushed to the side of the room and checked the AV connections, tapped keys on a keyboard, and suddenly the figure on the screen could be heard.

" . . .unexpected events beyond our control, this session of the Rebirth Gathering has been suspended."

"What?" Claire felt heat rush to her cheeks. "What's he talking about?" Her words joined the cries of denial from other parents. "We've already paid for the treatment. They can't take it away from us, not now!"

"Shush, be quiet. Let's hear what he's saying." Dwayne's pastoral voice boomed over the assembly, immediately silencing the discord.

Claire noticed the attendants had gathered in a knot, heads close together, urgent hushed discussion too quiet for any of the parents to hear.

"Again, my name is Dr. Gerald Baumgarten, and I developed the treatment that will give your children their rebirth. But as I speak, forces are at work to stop this miracle. Those who don't understand seek to stop me, and will go to any lengths—even fabricating lies about me—to discredit this medical marvel." He paused, his face an icy mask. "I know that it works because I myself suffered from autism the same as your children. The treatment gave me a rebirth, and it will for your children, too." He held up a vial of bright pills. "I have instructed the attendants to dispense the medication immediately. You must be responsible for dosing your children appropriately. I cannot caution you strongly enough to follow your dosage instructions."

Elaine covered her mouth with her hand, her eyes wide. She looked as shocked as Claire felt. Tracy continued to stir circles into her mac and cheese, oblivious to the growing tension.

Dr. Baumgarten continued. "My apologies that the full three-day Gathering and training isn't possible, but we—you—must work quickly if you want your children to receive their legacy and their right to a healthy future." He paused, and the parents in the room once more began to murmur. "I will not let you down. Never fear, I will find you, help your children to recover from their affliction. Have faith, they will be healed. And don't let anyone's lies persuade you to betray your child's future. I am their only hope—and I won't let them down! Tell the authorities nothing about me. Protecting me protects your chil—" The connection was broken.

Immediately the room erupted. Parents called to their children, attendants rushed out with trays laden with medication vials. The PA system spat to life. "In an orderly fashion, please line up according to alpha-list and wait for your name to be called. Stay calm. Your children's medication will be dispensed per Dr. Baumgarten's orders. You must show your identification number, to ensure each child receives the proper dosage."

Despite the called-for order, tempers flared, and shouts and shoves grew more frequent. "Stay with Lenny." Elaine barked the order to Dwayne, and moved to the line forming at the mouth of the exam room.

"Please watch Tracy, too." Claire rushed after her friend. The ten minutes they waited seemed like hours, but finally they each claimed a precious vial of pills—enough for six weeks—for Tracy and Lenny. The two women hurried back to Dwayne. Claire felt like she'd run a marathon.

Dwayne's face was gray. "What? Is Lenny okay?" Elaine immediately turned to her son, but the boy sat quietly having finished the last chicken nugget.

"It's Dad." Dwayne swallowed, and gestured with his cell phone. "I just got a call from the hospital."

"Oh, no. Was he shot?" Elaine held Lenny's pills in her fist like a talisman that could wipe out all horror. "I've always worried he'd end up shot. Is he okay?" She turned to Claire. "Dwayne's dad is a cop."

"He wasn't shot." Dwayne rubbed his eyes, and pulled out a chair and collapsed. "He was bitten by a dog."

"A dog?" Claire almost smiled at the outlandishness of the situation. It sounded like the punch line to some weird joke, but Dwayne wasn't laughing.

"He's in the hospital and under arrest. For kidnapping."

"What?!" Elaine gasped.

A police car, siren blaring, pulled up outside the Legacy Center. Claire carefully tucked Tracy's precious vial of pills into her bra. Parents all around her secreted their own vials and fell silent, arms crossed and lips tight. None would risk betraying their children's miracle.

Chapter 55

April opened her eyes, and licked her desert dry lips. She looked around the darkened room, taking in the plain walls and metal railings on the bed. In the dim light an IV drip beside the bed and beeping monitor offered the only motion in the room.

She tried to turn, and gasped as fire laced through her side. She'd been shot. This was a hospital. It hadn't been a dream. The nightmare was real.

"Steven? Steven!"

A figure roused from a nearby chair.

"Where's my son?" She grabbed the railings and tried to pull herself erect. But the stabbing throb of her injury sapped strength from her arms. "Please. Tell me about Steven, where's my boy?"

"Steven's in the hospital, too." Childress levered himself from the chair and stepped closer to the bed. "The doctors are taking care of him. Relax, April, you need to rest." His face was drawn and gray as the putty-colored walls. "You were in surgery for hours. I thought I'd lost you." His voice shook and then steadied, and he carefully clasped her hand as though it might break.

She fell back against the pillow and took several shallow breaths. It hurt, God it hurt. Were they at the Legacy Center? Lizzie's state-of-the-art medical team was the best, but how had she gotten here? "Where is Steven? I want to see him."

"April, you were shot and the ambulance brought you here, to Heartland General. Steven's here, too. He's in . . . in another ward, they had to sedate him. He's under observation."

"But he's okay? Steven's fine?"

Childress hesitated and then nodded. His hand tightened on April's.

As she relaxed on the bed she squeezed his hand back. "Good. Then he's safe." Her eyes fluttered. She felt so tired.

"He's going to need help, April. He's been through a lot. God, I love him so much." Childress's voice broke.

She levered her eyes open, surprised. "But Steven's cured, Doug. I found a miracle for him. You wouldn't listen to me, but I found a way to make it happen." She sighed. "I don't want to fight with you anymore. What's done is done."

He stared at her, lips tight, then nodded. "You're right, April. What's done is done. You rest now. When you feel better we'll talk about next steps." He smiled. "We'll get through this together, for Steven. Whatever he needs, April, we're a family."

"My son . . ." Her eyes drifted closed.

"OUR son." He squeezed her hand again, and to April it felt like she'd finally come home.

Chapter 56

Two Weeks Later, Thanksgiving Day
September poured coffee, added a slug of flavored cream, and pulled out a chair at the stained glass table. The new clothes dryer hummed in the next room with a load of clean towels. The door stayed closed with the laundry room window open, though. Two weeks' worth of odor neutralizers eliminated most of the stench, but she'd rather keep it confined to one room. September didn't mind. She considered it a badge of honor. The roasting turkey had already masked any lingering smell in the rest of the house.

Memories took longer to erase.

The scrabble tap-tap against the stained glass window brought her halfway to her feet. Coffee sloshed, hot on her thigh, and she yelped. The tap-tap came again—the Belinda's Rose danced in the 68-degree breeze. It sported three bright pink blossoms as if to celebrate the unseasonable Thanksgiving weather in proper style.

"Crap. Get a grip." September grabbed a towel and dabbed the stain as Macy stared from the top of the refrigerator. He yawned, shifted his weight, and burbled annoyance. He always had to have the last word. "Sorry I disturbed your nap, your highness." She jumped again when the wall phone rang.

September ignored the phone. The machine on her desk would pick up.

The first week after the Blizzard Murders the phone hadn't stopped ringing with demands from reporters. The second week, parents of autistic children took turns praising her heroism and cursing her for dooming their kids. The parents and their 178 children found at the Legacy Center, though, stayed strangely silent.

The doorbell made her stomach drop. Nobody was due to arrive for another hour. She had set the new dining table with five places. Side dishes remained to finish, and she'd fix whipped cream later for the warm gingerbread dessert. September checked out the wine bottles on the counter, debating the benefits of an early beverage. Instead, she sighed and hurried to answer the door.

Macy leaped to the floor and dashed ahead. The pet gate had come down after the contractors finished in record time. Everyone in town wanted an excuse to rubber-neck the house, inside and out.

September peeked through the glass, relieved it wasn't reporters, but still on guard. She sighed, unlocked the deadbolts and cracked the door. "What are you doing here?"

Combs stood on the lowest step. He shifted his weight and fiddled with a brown paper grocery bag. He looked more relaxed out of uniform in the gray windbreaker and jeans. "Wanted to check in." The lines on his forehead looked deeper, but September guessed she'd gained some crow's feet, too. He looked around. "Doty pulled off the surveillance?"

"Yeah. I asked." September blocked Macy with one foot, frowning with exasperation. "Come in before the cat gets out." She scooped Macy into her arms and draped him like a tawny mane around her shoulders. "Guess you don't have good news." She waited until he stepped inside, and then shot the bolts and jiggle-tested the door.

"No sign of Dr. Gerald Baumgarten. Alert's still up, but he could be out of the country by now. He transferred Legacy Center funds to an offshore account within an hour of his disappearance."

Lizzie's son had melted away with the blizzard. "He won't come after me. No percentage in it." September sighed, stroking the cat and relishing the purr that relaxed her shoulders better than a masseuse.

One eyebrow went up, questioning. "If you believed that, you wouldn't be peeking through windows before answering your door."

"Just because you're paranoid doesn't mean they aren't out to get you." She smiled to show she was joking. "But I am getting better about that." Hiding from the maybes and what-ifs just meant you'd be trapped when they found you. Better to keep watch and have your boots ready for the storm clouds.

Macy's tail stroked her mouth, and she spat out hair before gently moving him to the floor. He raced away up the entry stairs, and she heard the thunder of him clawing a favorite scratch post outside her bedroom door. Now that the pet gates were gone, she needed to add more cat trees to keep him happy throughout the house.

"The offer of a gun still stands." The paper bag crinkled in his rough hands.

She shuddered, and wondered if a gun was inside the package. "No thanks. I've had enough of guns to last me nine lives. And enough funerals." She walked back to the kitchen to retrieve her coffee cup, and he hesitated before he followed. She didn't offer him any, didn't think he'd accept it. Maybe he'd go away.

She'd be polite because Combs had been supportive, but his presence made her uncomfortable and wary. "I'm sorry I missed your mom's funeral." She was, but the words sounded stiff. Hell, she'd not been welcome at Pam's memorial service. Eugene tried to be cordial, but couldn't help blaming her for his wife's death. After all, she blamed herself.

"You would have been welcome. Aunt Ethel asked about you." His smile took ten years off his face. He looked sincere.

She was grateful for the kind gesture, and wanted to believe him. It was more than her family had offered. She'd tried to visit April in the hospital and been turned away.

"None of this was your fault. You've got to stop blaming yourself." He set the paper bag on the table, and cracked his knuckles. "I thought you'd want to know. Lizzie came out of the coma."

Tears pricked. "Thank you." She had no love lost for the woman, and cared not a whit if she'd ever see her again. She'd scrubbed the spot on the slate floor until she'd erased the blood reminder, but a death in her home would have left a stain she couldn't have lived with. She sat down and motioned him to a chair. "What about Pike? He'll stand trial with Lizzie?"

"Eventually. I think they'll want to try them together." Combs pulled out a chair on the other side of the glass table. "The court wants bad guys fully recovered before they sentence them to death. You got to love the Texas judicial system." He snorted. "The lawyers will have a field day. Both sides want you to testify. NeuroRealm, of course, denies any connection."

She wasn't surprised. "It was extra-label use and April signed a waiver. So did the others. Suing NeuroRealm makes as much sense as you taking aspirin to cure cancer and yelling foul when it didn't work."

He glowered. "Give me a break. Pottinger worked for them, they had to know." He sucked in a big breath and blew it out to calm himself, and forced a tight smile. "Preaching to the choir, right? But they say the drug is FDA-approved for Alzheimer's patients."

"Yes, Teddy said the drug sounded familiar. His wife Molly took Damenia for a while."

"Well, NeuroRealm won't pull Damenia from the market just because Lizzie went bat-shit crazy and gave it to kids and made them nuts." He looked stricken. "Sorry. How is Steven?"

"Stabilized, I think. I hope. I'm really out of the loop on Steven." September propped her chin in one hand and stared into the cold coffee. "His father has custody, of course, until April's situation is resolved. Steven's in a mental treatment facility."

"Poor kid. He's the big loser in all this."

"Yes, but the doctors say there's hope. They're weaning Steven off the drug little by little to try and avoid the side effects of cold turkey withdrawal." She rubbed her face. "Steven won't be prosecuted for shooting Lizzie. He's just a child, and he was under the influence of medication. Besides, they've got enough real bad guys to prosecute without the bad PR of targeting a child that's more a victim than anyone."

"I keep thinking about my own kids." Combs looked haunted for a moment and then shook it off. "Parents will do anything for their kids."

September agreed. "The drug does work wonders in some cases. With all the publicity, parents are clamoring for clinical trials. More research might eliminate the side effects." She prayed that would be the case. But it would be years before they'd figure all that out, and in the meantime some parents would continue to jump off the ledge without further tests. At least it would be more difficult with all the extra scrutiny. "It could be a long time before anyone knows what damage Steven has suffered, or if it's reversible."

"But you think kids might benefit down the road from this craziness?" He looked incredulous. "Sounds like wishful thinking. But Mom would like that. Crises bring families together."

"Maybe it does in your family." She snorted. "Doug Childress wants nothing to do with any of us, and especially me. April will have to stand trial for Pottinger's death. She insists Steven had nothing to do with it. I want to believe her. We'll probably never know, unless Steven someday is able to tell us." She really didn't want to know. She sipped coffee. "Actually, you're right in a way. This did bring April and her ex back together."

Combs looked surprised.

"Yep. Childress splits his time between Steven in the psych wing and April in ICU. Mom says they're talking again. Instead of fighting over him, they're determined to get Steven help and plan for his future."

"That's got to be a relief."

She glared at him. "What the hell is that supposed to mean?" But it *was* a relief that Steven was taken care of. And that he was no longer her responsibility. And that made her feel guilty as hell.

Combs spoke softly. "I know what happened in Chicago."

Deep breath. She didn't want his sympathy, didn't need this, let the past stay buried. "Lizzie's a liar." She looked away. April should never have told anyone. They'd had a pact.

"Lizzie didn't need to say anything. Nobody believes her rants anyway. But cops talk." He leaned forward over the table. "When you were on the run, questions were asked. Uncle Stan has connections all over the country, even the Chicago Special Victims Unit."

She inhaled sharply. "Jeff, that's private." She glanced at her watch. "I've still got mashed potatoes and creamed corn to fix." She pushed away from the table and stood."What happened in Chicago wasn't your fault, either." Combs leaned back in the chair, not going anywhere until he'd had his say. "You were a kid when you got pregnant. April helped you out of a tight spot."

"Let it go, Jeff." She felt heat flood her cheeks.

"It should have been a happy ending."

"Well, it wasn't." She strode to the stained glass window, and put her hands against the cool surface to stop their trembling. The sun played hide and seek with clouds and created dark hideaways beneath scraggly overgrowth. The garden needed an overhaul. Maybe a flame thrower. "This is none of your business." She crossed her arms to cut short the conversation. "Maybe I do need that gun to keep out obnoxious visitors."

"September, look at me." When she did, he smiled and held up his hands in a *what can you do?* gesture. "Doesn't take a rocket scientist. I'm just saying others might notice and ask questions. April and Doug both have blue eyes. Steven's eyes are green. Like yours." He cocked his head sideways. "That's a hell of a secret to keep."

She stared at him. "Are you quoting your high school science to make a point? Check your genetics, Jeff. That eye color stuff doesn't prove anything."

"No. But April's medical history does. She had never been pregnant. But you already know that."

She crossed her arms. "Everyone has secrets. I hear tell you've got some doozies." She felt satisfaction when he flinched.

"Yes, I know what it feels like to be a target." He took another calming breath. "I know it's not my business. But I like you. You shouldn't blame yourself. Most rape victims that get pregnant—"

"I don't want to hear this."

"It wasn't your fault."

"Children of rape are reminders of the worst moments of your life—and that's not fair to the kid. Not fair to anyone. It wasn't Steven's fault, either," she cried. "Look, I know I'm a terrible person. Because I can't love him. And April could. Damn you!" She rounded on him and flung the words like stones. "You can't say anything. Doug can't know. When April is indicted for Pottinger's death, Doug Childress is all Steven will have left." She shuddered. "His biological father is still out there somewhere. I lost myself for a lot of years hiding away from that scumbag. But Steven doesn't need to know that. God knows what Doug would do if he knew."

"You saved your son. You're not a terrible person. But I won't tell anyone. It's not my secret to tell."

She relaxed just a little. "That's it? That's why you're here?"

He stared at his hands. "I'm here because you caught Mom's killer. I never said thank you, and today's the day for it." Combs cleared his throat. "I'm here because Doty pulled surveillance. I'm here because I like you and don't want you to hurt anymore—that includes beating yourself up." He hesitated and poked the paper bag on the table. "And I'm here because I got nowhere else to be."

Despite herself she was touched and a little sad. "What about your family?"

He shrugged. "Kids are with my wife. I'm still suspended until further notice, and honestly, not sure I want to go back. Anyway, I'll go over to Uncle Stan's tonight for dessert. I don't feel too much like celebrating this year. Nobody does." He cracked his knuckles again. "You understand. We don't have to explain anything to each other. Right?"

She nodded. "True, that."

He sniffed the air with appreciation and his stomach growled. "But you've got guests coming, so I'll get out of your hair." He stood.

She laughed ruefully. "Mom finally agreed to let me host Thanksgiving this year, but nobody feels like gathering. Too many unanswered questions, too much suspicion and blame. It'll take a long time to sort out all the crappiocca, if ever." She shrugged. "But I already had the turkey, and it was a shame to let it go to waste." Galloping thumps sounded overhead, and September pointed at the ceiling. "Besides, Macy loves turkey. He once stole a frozen bird out of the fridge and I had to serve a lame bird after he amputated a drumstick."

"No way." Combs chuckled.

"Way." She smiled back. "Don't get between Macy and dinner. Anyhow, it's too much for one person. I invited Humphrey and Anita from the radio station, and Teddy and maybe his wife if she's having a good day. There's plenty. I could set another place. " She hugged herself and said softly, "Sometimes you have to find your own family." Something banged into the kitchen door. "There's the rest of my family now."

Combs wrinkled his brow in puzzlement, and watched when she hurried to the door and grabbed the handle without reaching for the deadbolt. "You don't have it locked?"

September grinned. "Like I said, I'm getting better about that. But I've got extra security now." The door banged again, and she timed the next bump with the doorknob twist.

Shadow burst into the room.

The dog stopped short in the doorway and stared at Combs. The missing tip of his left ear lent him a rakish expression. His hackles began to rise until

September stroked his brow and spoke with soft authority. "Shadow, settle. It's okay." He looked into her face with adoration. His tail waved.

"Steven's service dog, right?" Combs stood still when Shadow came close to politely sniff-inspect his pants. He backed away, wagging his approval.

September pushed the door closed and hip-bumped it to latch. She didn't bother with the lock since the back garden had been securely fenced. The *'beware of dog'* signs kept strangers at bay, especially when they saw Shadow's size. His recent experience made him more cautious, but he was far from a guard dog. But nobody had to know that.

"I guess Steven will need him now more than ever."

She shook her head. "Doug doesn't want him around. It's his decision. He's Steven's father." Her hard look brooked no argument, and she smiled. "I'll just have to put up with the goofy baby dog, won't I?" She rubbed Shadow's undamaged ear, and shrugged. "Sometimes your family chooses you."

As if on cue, Macy thundered down the kitchen stairs. He spun around the landing with his Mickey clutched firmly in his jaws. But when he saw Shadow, the cat dropped the toy, hissed, and sprang atop the table.

Shadow woofed, tail waving, and grabbed up the toy. He pranced around the room, daring the cat to play keep-away with the stolen Mickey.

"Shadow, enough. Macy is the boss of you." September's voice was stern. She traded the Mickey for a dog chew, and tucked the toy inside Macy's favorite cupboard hideaway. She couldn't help being tickled at Shadow's antics. And the pup knew it. Shadow grinned, and began to gnaw his rawhide treat.

"He's big." Combs eyed the dog with a dubious expression. "I dunno about the cat being the boss."

"Believe me; Macy puts him in his place." Curiosity finally got the better of her. She nodded at Combs's paper bag. "What is that?"

He looked sheepish. "In case I got invited to dinner. Can't blame a guy for hoping. It's a house warming gift. Don't worry, it's nothing pricy. Just a joke replacement for that rude coffee mug you liked so much."

"Really?" She looked at him with wary suspicion. Nothing could come close to replacing the #1-Bitch mug from Chris.

"I couldn't find a duplicate." He suddenly acted nervous. "The fancy wrapping was pretty dang pricy, too." He handed her the grocery sack.

She gingerly looked inside, and pulled out the thermos-size mug. September read the printed legend out loud. "Son-Of-A-Peach."

Jeff Combs was a wise-ass. She liked that in a person.

EPILOGUE

The camera loved her. Haunted green eyes, sweet uncertain frown, tumbles of dark silken hair...and a ripe, unwilling body. His tongue slicked across wet lips, gazing with hunger at September's visage on the television news. The memory of her taste, her smell, her touch haunted him. Oh, how he'd missed her.

The fear still lived on within her. He could tell. Good! His breath quickened.

She'd shown unexpected courage when she ran. And surprised him when she married that cop—the sonofabitch got what he deserved. She'd disappeared before he could collect her, and hidden herself away for months and months. But now, nothing stood in the way of his desire, of his revenge. He wasn't sure which mattered to him more.

His plans would quickly come together. He'd prepared for this ever since that night she betrayed him. He already had new name to go with his changed, buffed appearance. Nobody outside of Chicago ever heard of *Vince Grady*, the actor. He stroked his bald head, and flexed his abs. Even September would be hard pressed to recognize him now. Perfect.

This time, he'd make her *earn* his trust. His eyes narrowed and he licked his lips again. He'd been played, lied to, and publicly humiliated. But still, he forgave her. He'd choose a new name for her, and change her appearance in case anyone objected to her sudden disappearance. Nothing would stand between them, ever again.

He'd teach September, oh how he'd teach her a new symphony of sensations. And she'd welcome his music this time, for each command performance. She'd never leave him again. He could hardly wait.

ACKNOWLEDGEMENTS

After 24 award-winning nonfiction books I thought I had "acknowledgements" down pat. But fiction writing is a whole different animal. I'll do my best to be concise.

I must first thank Cool Gus Publishing, Bob Mayer and Jennifer Talty for the opportunity, and my parents Phil and Mary Monteith who always believed I had a novel in me. I've been part of the incredible Cuchara writers group for more than twenty years, and these savvy writers continue to inspire and support my crazy notions and helped birth this book. Special thanks to my editor and friend Jessie Stephens, and first readers Kristi Brashier, Carol Shenold and Frank Steele for your eagle eyes, spot-on comments and unflagging encouragement and support.

I am incredibly indebted to International Thriller Writers and the Debut Authors Program. The people who make up this organization are some of the most generous and supportive folks I have ever met, and my novel journey and LOST AND FOUND would never have become a reality without this organization.

A vast number of veterinarians, behaviorists, consultants, trainers and pet-centric writers and rescue organizations have helped me help pets over the years, in particular members of the IAABC, APDT, DWAA and CWA. The Kayce Cover SATS seminar presented some years ago at an IAABC conference inspired the dog training vocabulary game described in the book, which my own dog loves to play. Much of the story is based on science, including behavior and learning theory, the current use of "off label" drugs in children and the benefits of service dog partnerships. Since this is a work of fiction, however, be aware that liberties have been taken to further the plot.

I am delighted that Gillian Salling, a tracking dog expert and owner of Fernheim German Shepherds, graciously allowed her gorgeous and talented Uschi Von Fernheim, TD to serve as the LOST AND FOUND cover dog.

I am also grateful to my readers for embracing "Name That Dog" and "Name That Cat" contests to help me find the perfect choices for some of the furry characters in the book. More than 85 terrific names were suggested with close to 800 votes resulting.

Caren Gittleman suggested the winning dog name Dakota because it means "trusted friend" and is also the name of her lovely Sheltie (who helps her co-write Dakota's Den Blog). Raelyn Barclay offered several dog name suggestions including Bruno, which won the second hero dog spot. Patricia suggested the winning cat name Macy, garnering more than a hundred votes from readers, wow! Macy is the name of Patricia's seven-year-old yellow tabby, and named after a character in the *Bold and the Beautiful* television show. Karyl Cunningham has been one of my most faithful blog followers and her suggested name Simba is the second cat name winner. Simba is the name of Karyl's slightly chubby, arthritic senior citizen kitty, a perfect choice for this character. The four winners received advance copies of the book, their pets' namesakes serving heroic roles in the book, and my eternal gratitude.

Finally, I'm grateful to all the cats and dogs I've met over the years who have shared my heart and sometimes my pillow. These days, Magical-Dawg and Seren-Kitty are my furry inspiration for all-things-pets. And of course, deepest thanks to my husband Mahmoud, who continues to support my writing passion even when he doesn't completely understand it.

I love hearing from you. Please drop me a line at my Bling, Bitches & Blood blog AmyShojai.com or find more pet-centric books at www.Shojai.com where you can watch for the latest *Thrillers With Bite*!

SEPTEMBER'S STORY CONTINUES in HIDE AND SEEK...

*A mysterious contagion will shatter countless lives unless a service dog
and his trainer find a missing cat . . . in 24 hours.*

A STALKER hides in plain sight.
A VICTIM faces her worst fear.
AND A DOG seeks the missing—and finds hope.

"...a creepy must read mystery for animal lovers...Shojai knows her stuff."
–J.T. Ellison, New York Times Bestselling Author

KEEP READING for a sample of HIDE AND SEEK!

HIDE AND SEEK: Prologue

Tommy Dietz grabbed the car door handle with one bloody fist, and braced his other hand against the roof, worried the carcasses in the back would buck out of the truck's bed. Despite the precaution, his head thumped the muddy window. He glared at the driver who rode the truck like a bronco, but BeeBo Benson's full moon face sported the same toothless grin he'd worn for the past two weeks. Even BeeBo's double chins smiled—including the rolls at the nape of his freckled neck.

The ferret thin guy in the middle snarled each time his Katy Railroad belt buckle chinked against the stick shift he straddled. Scraggly hair straggled from under his hat and brushed his shoulders. He had to slouch or risked punching his head through the rust eaten roof. Randy Felch's snaky eyes gave Dietz the shivers even more than the freezing temperatures spitting through windows that refused to seal

Three across the cramped seat would be a lark for high school buddies out on the town, but the men were decades beyond graduation. Dietz was in charge so Felch could either ride the hump or share the open truck bed with two carcasses, and the new Production Assistant.

Dietz stifled a laugh. Not so high-and-mighty now, was he? The man must really want the job. Grady had turned green when told to climb into the back of the truck. Just wait till he got a load of the dump. Dietz remembered his first visit three years ago when scouting locations. He wondered how the spit-and-polish Grady would react.

He'd hired locals for the rest of the crew. They needed the work, and didn't blink at the SAG ultra-low pay scale, the shitty weather, or the stink. In this business, you took anything available when pickings were so slim. Then the show got picked up and union fees grabbed him by the short hairs. Amateur talent screwing around and missing call times cost even more money, so he needed a Production Assistant—PA in the lingo—with more polish and bigger balls to keep the wheels greased. A go-to guy able to think on his feet, get the job done. No matter what.

If Grady wanted the PA job, he'd have to be willing to get his hands dirty, and stand up to BeeBo and his ilk. Riding in the open truck bed was illegal as hell, though here in North Texas even the cops turned a blind eye unless it was kids. This was an audition, and Grady knew it.

He had to give Grady props—he'd not blinked, but clenched his jaw and climbed right in when they collected him at his hotel. He'd been less enthusiastic after following the hunters most of the morning, tramping to hell and gone through rough country until his eyes threatened to freeze shut. Something drove the man, something more than a PA credit for piss-poor pay and worse conditions. Hell, something drove them all to work in this unforgiving business. Dietz didn't care about anyone else's demons as long as they stayed out of his way.

Dietz craned to peer out the back to be sure the man hadn't been tossed out the tailgate. Grady gave Dietz a thumbs up. *Probably wants to point a different finger,* Dietz thought. Grady wore the official Hog Hell blue work gloves and ski mask—dark blue background and Day-Glo red star on the face—or he'd be picking his frostbit nose off the floor.

Prime time in the back woods. Dietz's quick smile faded. Nothing about this trip was prime, not even the butchered Bambi in the back. Deer season ran November through early January and it was always open season on hogs, so they were legal for any follow up film footage. The two deer hadn't looked good even before BeeBo dropped them, but that's what viewers wanted. Crocodile wrestlers, duck dynasties, and gold rush grabbers with crusty appeal and redder necks

Nobody wanted actors anymore. Casting directors looked for "real people." So he'd caught a clue, jumped off the thespian hamster wheel, moved to New York and reinvented himself as Tommy Dietz, Producer. He'd found his calling with a development company relatively quickly.

A movie star face didn't hurt. Everyone these days had a little nip-and-tuck, it was part of the biz. He'd been selling his version of reality for years anyway, and always came out on top.

He hit it out of the park on his third project, HOG HELL, with Felch, BeeBo and their ilk. HOG HELL kicked off the next step a Texas-size leap.

He'd show them all, those who laughed at his dreams, called him a loser. And he'd make them sorry.

The shabby pickup lurched down and back up again, and its engine growled and complained. Dietz was surprised the seat hadn't fallen through the floor. The overgrown road the hunters called a pig path consisted of frozen ruts formed from previous tire treads. They damn well better not get stuck out here.

"Don't worry, she'll make it." BeeBo talked around the stub of his unlit cigar. "This old warhorse made the trip so often, she could drive herself. Ain't that right, Felch?" BeeBo reached to downshift and Felch winced as the other man's ham-size fist grabbed and jerked the stick between his knees.

Dietz sighed. Out the window, skeletal trees clawed the pregnant sky. Weird flocks of blackbirds moved in undulating clouds, exploding from one naked tree after another to clothe the next with feathered leaves. Spooky.

Thank God the icy cold weather stayed dry. Heartland, Texas had dug out of a record-breaking snowfall, and the locals hadn't quite recovered. It put a kink in HOG HELL filming and they'd barely met the deadlines. Delay turned his balance book bloody with red ink.

Back home in Chicago they'd been hit with the same blizzard and so had NYC. But big cities knew how to manage winter weather. Apparently North Texas rolled up the sidewalks with even the hint of flurries. He wondered if BeeBo and Felch knew what to do in the snow, and didn't want to find out. The thought of hunkering down overnight in the truck with these men turned his stomach.

Dietz adjusted his own ski mask. He'd folded it up off his face so the blue cap hugged his head while the DayGlo red painted a bull's-eye on his forehead. He wore the official coat, too, dark blue with the bright hunter-safe star on the front and back, with the Hog Hell logo. The Gore-Tex fabric crackled with newness, and his blistered feet whimpered inside wet, dirt-caked boots. No way would he wear his new $300 Cabela's purchased for photo ops at the upcoming watch party. He had a gun, too. In Texas nobody blinked if you carried

BeeBo's preferred weapon, an ancient short barreled shotgun loaded with deer slugs, contrasted sharply with Felch's custom double gun he'd had specially made last season. Felch shot 44 Magnums, and the cut down double barrel rifle boasted enough fire power to take out an elephant, or a charging feral boar hog. They sleeved the guns in canvas cases stowed in the back of the truck, but the hunters cared far less about their own attire.

BeeBo and Felch would wear official HOG HELL gear at the watch party in six weeks, and not before. Dietz didn't want them stinking up the outfits. Today they wore wash-faded coveralls, heavy work coats, earflap hats, clunky boots with thorn-tangled laces, and frayed gloves with fingertips cut out. A bit of peeling DayGlo tape formed an "X" on the back and front of each coat after Dietz insisted on the nod to safety, even though he knew the two hunters paid little mind to official start and end hunting season dates.

That was the point of the original reality program, *Cutting Corners* that focused on people forced to skirt the rules to make ends meet. The unlikely stars of a single episode, though, turned Felch and BeeBo into overnight sensations and birthed the new show after *Cutting Corners* tanked. The two hunters were experts at skirting rules. Dietz was no slouch, either.

In the truck bed, Grady swayed back and forth. He'd pushed up the HOG HELL ski mask enough to expose his mouth. White breath puffed out in a jerky tempo, and Dietz wondered if the man would pass out. If Grady took a header off the truck bed, the liability would kill the show. "Find a spot to stop, BeeBo. I think our new team member has had enough."

Felch grunted. "No place to stop till we get there. Unless you want us to get stuck." He grinned, but the expression never reached his eyes. "You don't want us lugging that shit back to your hotel. The stink ain't something you want close by."

BeeBo guffawed. "Got that right. With all the hunters unloading, it's what y'all might call a renewable resource." He twisted the wheel, and the truck bucked, jittering the decades old pine-shaped deodorizer suspended from the rear view mirror. "The critters take care of the stink pretty quick, though." His hairless wide-eyed face was a ringer for the Gerber baby. "It's around that next bend. You might even catch a whiff of Jiff by now."

Dietz wrinkled his nose. The pungent aroma wasn't assuaged by the out of dated air freshener that probably came with the vehicle. He shielded his head from another thump, and squinted ahead through the crusty windshield. The wiper blades had torn loose on the passenger's side, and smeared the detritus rather than clearing the view. It didn't bother BeeBo

The trio remained silent during the final bump-and-grind through the trees. They pulled halfway into the clearing, and Dietz waited impatiently until BeeBo cranked the steering wheel, turned, and backed beneath a massive tree with pendulous clusters hanging from the branches. Grady ducked, or would have been beaned and scraped off by low limbs.

Several similar trees bordered the clearing, and another smaller truck squatted beneath one at the far end of the area with an elderly couple nearby. The man stood in the truck bed and flailed tree branches with a long pole, while the woman dodged and weaved beneath to gather the resulting shower in a bucket.

"What's that?" Grady wasted no time to jump off the truck bed. He gagged when the wind shifted.

"Nuts." Felch unfolded himself from the cramped middle seat. "Pecan trees. They're gleaning the nuts."

Dietz's stomach clenched. He pulled the ski mask over his lips and breathed through his mouth, imagining he could taste odor that closed his throat. Neither Felch nor BeeBo seemed to notice the stench.

Grady wipe his watery eyes. The breeze paused and he gulped a less contaminated breath. "Pecans? To eat?"

The truck squeaked, rocked and grew two inches when BeeBo stepped out. "Back in town they'll pay $8-$10 by the pound, once shelled. I got my daddy's old commercial sheller, held together with baling twine and spit, but works okay. I only charge fifty-cents a pound to shell." He shrugged. "Every little bit helps. It's too early for most of the big-name commercial farms but for the gleaners, if you wait too long the squirrels get 'em off the trees, or the pigs root 'em off the ground. Pigs eat lots of the same stuff the deer and wild turkey eat, acorns and suchlike. But they get ground-nesting bird eggs, too. Pigs'll root up and eat damn near anything." He jerked his chins at Felch. "Gimme a hand." He lumbered toward the truck bed, and waited at the tail lights.

Felch vaulted in the back of the vehicle, and adjusted his gloves. He pointed. "Smorgasbord, y'all. Hey Slick, you might want to get video of this. Bet your big-city cronies never seen the like." His yellow teeth gleamed. He bent low, and grunted as he pushed and tugged the black plastic bag to the rear of the truck bed, hopped down and joined BeeBo. Together they slung the truck's cargo into the pit. Yipping and growls erupted from below. Dietz stayed back, he'd seen it before. This stuff he wouldn't put on the air. This'd be too much even for the hard core viewers without the added value of aroma.

Grady covered his mouth and nose in the crook of his elbow. He edged closer to the deep trough, a natural ditch-like runoff that sat dry three quarters of the year. Piles of gnawed and scattered bones mixed with carcasses in various stages of decomposition. A family of coyotes tried to claim BeeBo's tossed deer remains, but was bluffed away by a feral boar.

Grady ripped off his ski mask, puked, wiped his mouth, and grabbed his camera with a shaking hand. He spit on the frozen ground and jutted his chin at Dietz. "So?"

Dietz smiled. "You got the gig."

***

The damn ski mask dragged against his hair so much, the normally clear adhesive had turned chalky against his scalp. He'd removed the wig after dissolving glue with a citrus-scented spray, a much more pleasant olfactory experience than the afternoon's HOG HELL visit to the dump. A shower rinsed away lingering miasma, but he gladly put up with the stink, the rednecks, and the sneers. The payoff would be worth it.

Until then, he couldn't afford for anyone in Heartland to see him without the hairpiece, couldn't risk being recognized. For the price, nearly fifty bucks for a four ounce bottle of adhesive, it damn well better hold the wig in place for the promised six weeks. He rubbed his hands over his pale, bald head and grinned.

Even without the wig, she'd be hard pressed to recognize him. Muscles replaced the beer gut, Lasik surgery threw out glasses, teeth caps, chin implant, the works. It had taken eight years to track her down, eight years spent turning himself into a man she couldn't refuse.

He'd done it for her. Everything for her.

He dialed the phone. "I want to order flowers, Forget-Me-Nots, in a white box with a yellow ribbon. Got that? And deliver them December 18. It's our anniversary." He listened. "A card, what a good idea. Can you use red ink? Fine, I want you to write 'payback' in red ink. No signature, she'll know who they're from. Deliver the flowers to two-oh-five Rabbit Run Road, to September Day." He paused, and chuckled softly. "Yes, it will be a lovely holiday surprise."

(end of sample)

What happens next? To find out, get **HIDE AND SEEK**.

ESCAPE into the September Day series. Ask your favorite booksellers for your copies today! Stay tuned for the next installment and find out what happens next to September, Shadow and all their friends.

ABOUT THE AUTHOR

Amy Shojai is a certified animal behavior consultant, and the award-winning author of more than 30 bestselling pet books that cover furry babies to old fogies, first aid to natural healing, and behavior/training to Chicken Soupicity. She has been featured as an expert in hundreds of print venues including The New York times, Reader's Digest, and Family Circle, as well as television networks such as CNN, and Animal Planet's DOGS 101 and CATS 101. Amy brings her unique pet-centric viewpoint to public appearances. She is also a playwright and co-author of STRAYS, THE MUSICAL and the author of the critically acclaimed September Day pet-centric thriller series. Stay up to date with new books and appearances by subscribing to Amy's Pets Peeves newsletter at www.SHOJAI.com.

Made in the USA
Las Vegas, NV
05 July 2024

91928944R00154